# Exile's Redemption

by

Lee Dunning

This is a work of fiction. All of the characters, organizations and events portrayed in this novel are either products of the author's imagination or are used fictitiously.

Exile's Redemption

# To My Parents

Thank you for my life and all of the love and kindness you've shown me along the way. Thank you for instilling in me a love for the written word.

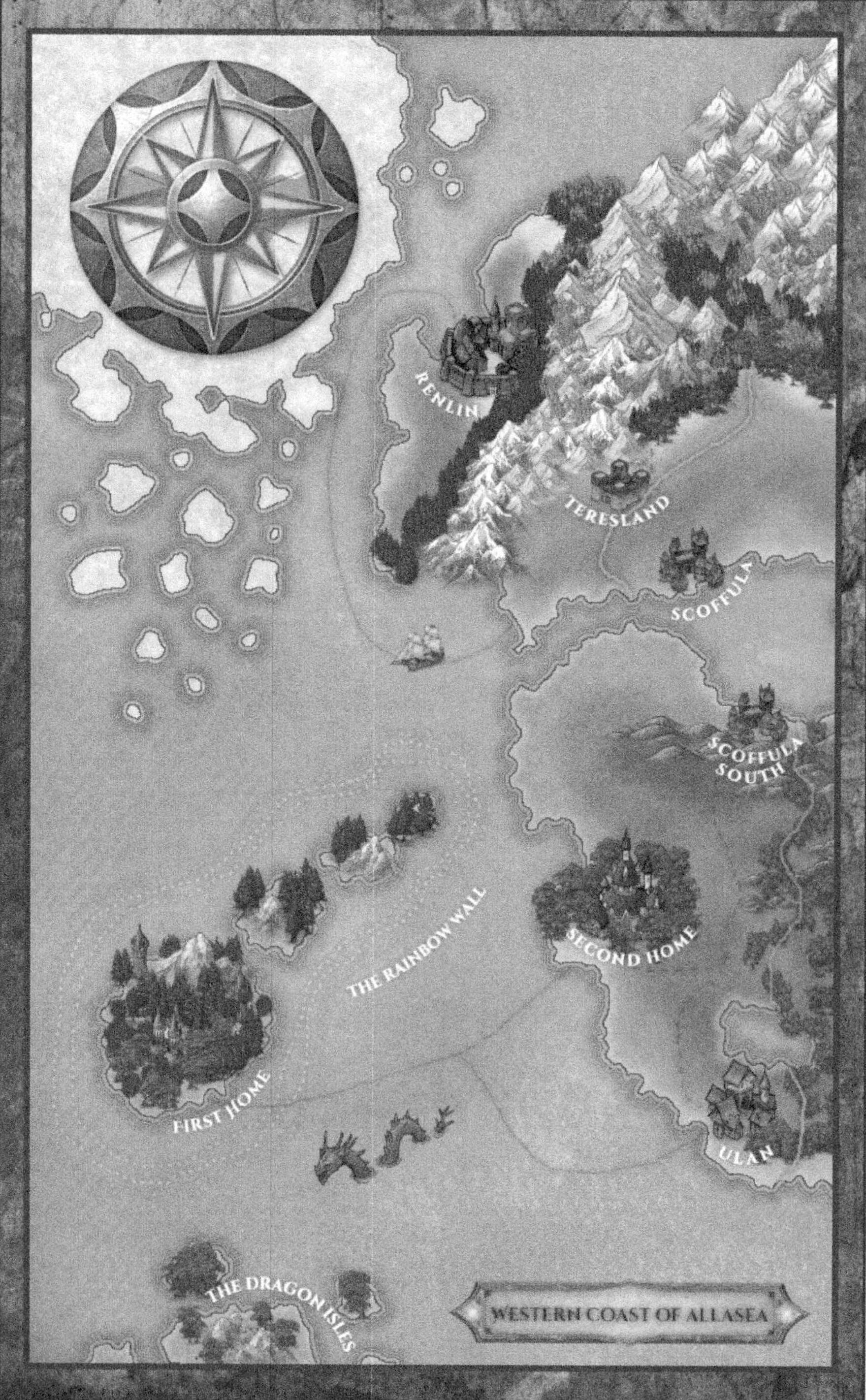
RENLIN
TERESLAND
SCOFFULA
SCOFFULA SOUTH
THE RAINBOW WALL
SECOND HOME
FIRST HOME
ULAN
THE DRAGON ISLES
WESTERN COAST OF ALLASEA

# PROLOGUE

When the doorway opened, Umbral knew. Not once during his imprisonment in the Abyss had the scent of life and growing things reached him. He couldn't call it a memory exactly, for even during the days of his youth, the world of Allasea had been little more than extremes of heat and cold. And enemies.

Oh, so many enemies.

Yet something about it called to him. Something more than freedom. Not that he scorned the idea of fleeing the dead wastes he'd called home for ten millennia. Curiosity, certainly, pulled at him as surely as a lodestone reached forever north. His people lay beyond the doorway somewhere.

The same people who'd exiled him to this realm of horrors.

Would they even know him if he strode among them? So much had changed over time. He'd changed. He'd grown stronger, strong enough to kill the demon lord who'd forced him to bend the knee. Yet, surely his kin had also expanded their powers.

The lure of Allasea drew Umbral toward the sooty light at the mouth of his cave. He trod over the remains of the unfortunate beast he'd most recently reduced to detritus. It had chosen poorly in seeking refuge within his rough sanctuary. He'd consumed it raw, cracking its bones for the marrow hidden within. Such a feast did not present itself often.

Umbral stepped outside the black of his primitive lair. He drew in a deep breath of the fetid miasma of the Abyss. From all around, and in the distance, the air reverberated with the claws-on-slate screech of unwholesome interest. He was not the only one who sensed the alien touch of another plane. Thousands upon thousands of the Abyss' twisted denizens slithered, lurched, flapped, and oozed toward it.

He must hurry. The demons would reduce Allasea and its denizens to the same sorry state as the creature spread about his cave floor. Umbral had no desire to rule over the dead.

No, that would not do at all.

# CHAPTER 1

Raven used the time to people watch while she waited for her escort. Though she'd been in Second Home for two weeks now, she still found the presence of so many races fascinating. In the down below where she'd grown up, she'd seldom seen anyone other than fellow Shadow Elves. Most others served as slaves for her former people.

The Exiles.

Raven straightened her shoulders and smiled at the passersby, hoping she looked like she belonged. Unlikely that, considering she hadn't noticed any other Shadow Elves since her arrival, not even those from the island nation to the west the surface elves called First Home. Wood Elves were a rare sight in the city as well. The arboreal elves mostly kept to themselves farther north in the great forest which pressed against the feet of a jagged ridge of mountains serving as a roof of sorts to the down below.

She'd spent the last three years with the Wood Elves, learning what she could of her new sun-bright home. But she was young and anxious to explore. The Wood Elves had few books and little interest in history. They lived from day-to-day hunting and struggling against the dangers of the northern wilds. They liked it just fine, but she wanted more.

Then word came Second Home had opened its gates to all who would like to expand their minds in the enormous library buried within its vast halls. Despite the many arguments against the trip set before her, she determined to explore Second Home and its wondrous library.

So, here she was gawking at the beautiful architecture and the people walking its halls as she had every day since her arrival. Through a massive release of magic, the elves had raised a city with soaring walls designed to look like trees. Tree trunks of pristine white marble reached toward the sky, topped by a stylized roof which mimicked a canopy of leaves. Sunlight streamed through the spaces between the stone leaves, giving the impression of a natural forest.

Raven dragged her attention from the lofty heights of the city to study its denizens once again. Willowy Sky Elves flitted through the dappled light like elegant ghosts. Soft halos of light emanated from them, adding to their otherworldly aura. The massive forms of the elves known as First Born didn't so much glide as stalk, most wearing the red armor of experienced soldiers or the green of new recruits. Among them a fascinating collection of exotic beings like gnomes, halflings, and humans went about their business dressed in a variety of styles and colors. Even a few dwarves moseyed along the hall, their deep voices as rumbly as a waterfall.

Her eyes lit on a young First Born soldier sporting green plate armor and a lopsided smile. He was a good deal older than her, but still hadn't reached one hundred years, so he hadn't taken on a family name yet. He went by his child name of Linden and stood as sturdy and tall as his namesake. She waved and tried not to conceal her excitement at seeing him. She failed utterly and his smile broke into a huge grin.

"You do realize," Linden said, "hopping up and down on your tiptoes completely ruins your reputation as a scary Exile, right?"

"I was just stretching my calves," she said. "You're so late, I started to cramp up."

"I *am* late, and I apologize," he said.

"I may have to report you to your superior officer," she said, crossing her arms and regarding him with mock disapproval.

"My superior officer is the reason for my tardiness," he said. He gave her a bow, much lower than etiquette required. "I beg your forgiveness, oh great and terrible mistress of the subterranean wilds."

"I suppose I can forgive you this one time," she replied with a derisive sniff.

When he rose back to his full height, he towered over her by a good two feet or more. He shook his head, obviously not intimidated or even remotely abashed in the slightest. "If you want anyone to take you seriously, you're going to have to wear something besides pink."

Raven straightened the hem of her short fuchsia kimono. She'd never owned such a pretty thing living among the Exiles. "I like pink."

"Our High Council's Shadow Elf representatives, Lord T'sane and Lady Reaper, always wear black. I'm told it helps them lurk in shadows."

"That does explain why I'm total rubbish at lurking."

Linden laughed and swung one of his long arms toward the doorway of the library. She fell in beside him and they headed into the cool, hushed spaces where Raven had spent most of her time during her visit. As usual, Linden either forgot or ignored the rules against loud chatter. "Okay, so you're not a lurker. But you must have some armor for when you go into battle."

"Battle?" She just barely caught herself and managed to whisper at the last minute. "I know Exiles have a reputation, but do I look like I could hold up in a fight, even with armor? About the only thing I ever carry around is a knife, and that's just for eating. I'd probably end up stabbing myself if I tried to fight with it."

"You're kidding?" Linden's robust voice echoed off the thirty-foot tall bookshelves. "How do you protect yourself?"

"With my dry wit," she grinned. She winced at the glares the librarians shot their way as they passed in search of a table with plenty of room to spread out. "Really, truly, I'm no warrior. You've been with me since I arrived. Have you seen me wield anything more dangerous than a quill? My only ambition is to be a scholar. It's my hope that if I ever need protecting, someone like you will be around who knows which end of the sword to hold."

Linden shook his head. "All you need me for is to haul piles of musty old books for you."

"Which you're exceptionally skilled at," she said. She pointed toward a table which by some miracle remained vacant. By the end of the day, she'd have piles of tomes and scrolls spread out for her research. She pulled out a chair but didn't sit, instead she leaned against it, elbows locked, frowning at the endless shelves full of enticing mysteries. Really, she only needed to solve one mystery though, and the sheer number of books, memory cubes, scrolls, loose sheaves of vellum and magically preserved wax tablets was staggering. She'd only intended to spend a couple of weeks searching for the answers she sought, and already she'd surpassed that. By the looks of things, she could spend another century in the library and still not find what she sought.

She sighed. "How am I ever going to find everything I need here?"

Linden brushed her words away with a wave. "It's only been a few days. You're young—you have plenty of time."

Raven made a face. "I hadn't planned on staying here long enough to find out if elves can die of old age."

"Maybe if you would let me in on the what you're researching, I could help. I admit, hacking things into bits is more where my skill set lies, but there are plenty of scholars here who can help narrow down your search. All the tomes you've been having me lug around have been history books—maybe we could start by focusing on something specific? What exactly are you studying?"

Raven hesitated. She'd been purposely vague up to this point, unsure of how her escort would react. After getting to know him better though, he seemed fairly open-minded. "I'm trying to find ancient texts that will shed some light on the events leading up to Umbral's attempt on the First's life and the civil war which followed."

"You don't need the resources of this place to study that," Linden said. "There isn't an elf here who hasn't had that drummed into their head. I can probably dig up a few old books I had to study—you're more than welcome to have them."

Something in her expression made him take a full step back.

"Sorry," she said and finally plopped into the chair with a frustrated huff. It wasn't his fault he didn't understand why she found his offer offensive. She pointed at the chair across from her. "Let me try to explain."

Once he was settled, she leaned toward him so she could keep her voice low. "I didn't come all the way here to read the history your government approved," she said, opting to be blunt.

Linden started to object, but Raven raised a slim black hand to forestall him. "It's the nature of the beast—the winners write down the history that shows them in the best light. I've read the propaganda your High Council doles out. And before you spurt blood out your ears, I've read the distorted histories the Exiles wrote as well. What I want to find is something... probably a diary, or maybe a collection of letters from that time. I want to read the actual thoughts of the people who lived through it all. It was a very different world back then. We didn't have beautiful cities and libraries stuffed with books. It's a mistake for us to place our values and world views on the people from the past. I want the truth—not what passes for the truth today."

Linden took obvious pains to calm himself. Like the fires which birthed his people, the First Born, he tended toward the more passionate end of the emotional spectrum. "So, you think everything I've been taught is a lie," he said. His voice was tight, angry.

"I didn't say that," Raven said, her voice rising to meet his. "I tend to believe there's more truth in your histories than what passes for fact in my birth city. Still, there are plenty of things which strike me as slanted in the writings of your historians."

The nearby tables full of more sedate visitors wrinkled their noses in displeasure. One gnome made a hushing motion, and Linden bobbed his head in apology. "What exactly? Can you give me an example?" he whispered.

Raven took the cue and dropped her voice as well. "I've gone through dozens of books and they can't seem to agree on much of anything, not even what Umbral looked like. Some say he was so physically distorted, with a twisted spine and severe limp, that it could be nothing but a reflection of his corrupt soul. Only the compassion of his father, the First, made it possible for him to survive."

"Okay..."

"Others say the First relied upon Umbral to gather information and to strike at the heart of the enemy through key assassinations." Raven spread her hands. "So, which is true? Was he an invalid protected by the grace of his father, or was he a deadly assassin integral to the war effort?"

"I see what you're saying," Linden said, "but does it really matter? Umbral tried to kill the First, failed, and got exiled to the Abyss. End of story. Who cares if he was deformed or not?"

Raven's scowl returned. "It's important because an entire segment of the Shadow Elves split off from the rest of the Elven Nation due to what happened. Somewhere along the line, my people changed from staunch supporters of Umbral, to a people who hate him so much they consider all males tainted. I want to understand what happened so I can fix it."

"Fix it? After all these years?" Linden managed to stop just short of laughing in disbelief, but his voice had once again risen above the accepted library whisper. A mixed group of humans, dwarves and halflings rose from their seats, muttering angrily, and headed deeper into the library, presumably to find some peace and quiet.

"Like you said, I'm young," Raven said. She'd never spoken of her dream out loud before. Now that it was out there, it seemed ludicrously implausible. Something a foolish child would dream up.

"Hey, I'm sorry," Linden said. "It's unlikely, but it's a worthy goal. And despite doing my best to avoid philosophical discussion most of my life, I admit I'm a little intrigued. So where were we?"

Raven knew he was just being nice, but she allowed his kind words to lure her back into the conversation. "Deadly assassin or pitiful wretch?"

"Hmm, I'm going to go with the *deadly assassin* scenario myself," Linden said. "That seems much more likely given the times."

"Which makes sense since he nearly succeeded in his bid to kill the First," Raven said. "But what was Umbral thinking by making the attempt? There have never been all that many Shadow Elves, so he couldn't have thought he could take over with just with their backing—there just weren't enough of them to win in a civil war. Regardless, patricide isn't usually all that well-received. I think there is more to the tale."

Linden mulled that over for a moment. "It happened after the fight with the frost giants, right? Maybe a giant managed to injure the First and Umbral thought he could kill him and place the blame on the enemy?" He'd finally managed to get his voice under control and spoke in little more than a whisper.

Raven wondered if it had finally occurred to him her snooping was bound to ruffle feathers. The nervous way he checked around them suggested as much. However, as best Raven could tell, no one, not even the grumpy gnome at two tables over, paid them a bit of attention. What few visitors remained nearby seemed engrossed in their own studies.

"You really think you'll find your answers here?" Linden asked when she remained silent.

Raven slumped a little. "I don't know. The information might have been destroyed, or it may never have existed in the first place. But if it does exist, I can't think of a better place to search."

"Maybe," Linden said. "Back on First Home they keep archives in the Tower of Mages. They're considered too sensitive to allow off the islands."

Raven's slump turned into a full sulk. "If that's the case, then I'm out of luck. The only Shadow Elves allowed on First Home are those born there."

"Not entirely accurate."

Raven twisted around in her seat to find a Sky Elf stood directly behind her. When had she snuck up? How much had she heard?

"Councilor Stormchaser!" Linden said, disturbing the peace of the library yet again. The councilor glared at him in exasperation. He closed his mouth, eyes wide.

Satisfied, the councilor turned her attention to Raven, and set down a small pile of leather-bound texts. "There is a provision in our laws allowing an Exile to gain citizenship if they provide a great service to the Elven Nation. Something heroic in nature."

"That should be easy," Linden said. "Lady Raven, sixty pounds soaking wet, slays the ancient red dragon with her dry wit."

"You really have no impulse control, do you, child?" the councilor said.

"No ma'am. I apologize." His abashed expression was spoiled by the smile which refused to leave his face.

Councilor Stormchaser pursed her lips but refrained from commenting further on Linden's shortcomings. "True heroes don't go searching for trouble, but when the need arises, they find within themselves a strength they never knew existed," the councilor said. She pushed the books over to Raven. They were thin, barely deserving to be called books. Despite their excellent condition, they looked to be terribly fragile. "Perhaps these will give you the answers you seek. They're journals from the very beginning."

Raven gaped at the elfess, but quickly turned her attention to the books. With the greatest care, she opened the top one and scanned through what looked to be a list of names on the inside cover. She could only read the last few as the writing of the earliest owners bore no resemblance to modern Elven. The three she could read all clearly had the family name of Stormchaser. "By the First!" Raven said. She looked back up at the Sky Elf. "How old are these?"

A flicker of sadness followed by resolve emanated from the councilor. "They've been in my family since Lady Uruviel Stormchaser first created our written language—some ten thousand years ago. I'm giving them to you now."

"What?" Raven said in a shout which made Linden seem demure by comparison. Every head around the room popped up in irritation. She ducked her head, blushing furiously. "That's ridiculous. You don't even know me. How could you simply hand over something like this?"

"You're an empath, are you not?" the Sky Elf asked.

"Yes...," was Raven's hesitant reply.

"And something more, no?"

Raven shrugged. "Sometimes I have dreams of things that are going to happen. They never make sense though, so I can't interpret what they're trying to tell me—pretty useless."

"What did you dream before you came here?"

Raven's embarrassment quadrupled. She snuck a peek toward Linden, who watched the conversation with blank confusion. "I dreamed of metamorphosis. I became someone I'm not. I met my one true love."

The elfess reached down and cupped Raven's cheek. "Oh, child, you don't become someone you're not. You become who you're meant to be. There are many changes coming to our people, and you will be a part of that." Her gaze moved to Linden, and Raven felt the councilor's sadness again.

"I don't understand," Raven said. The councilor wasn't making any more sense than her dreams.

Councilor Stormchaser turned to go. "Read the books. Keep them safe. Help unite our people."

"Wait! I can't do all that alone—help me."

The Sky Elf swallowed hard. Tears threatened to spill down her face. "I have scried the future and I am not in it. *You* are." Head bowed, she hurried toward the exit.

"Councilor!" Linden shouted, jumping to his feet. He ignored the exasperated glares he drew as he chased after her. He caught up to the Sky Elf and grabbed her arm only to release her immediately when she turned her wet face up to him.

"I'm so sorry," she said. The councilor twisted away, hurling herself toward the door just short of running.

Raven and Linden stared after her, as frozen as the marble trees of the main hall. She made the door just as a gout of flame blasted in from the hall. Lady Stormchaser made not a sound as it engulfed her; as if she'd rushed to greet it. Councilor Stormchaser simply ceased to exist, consumed by the inferno.

Linden reeled back toward the table with a cry. The library rocked. A tremendous explosion, more felt than heard, threw everyone to the floor. An ominous rumble rippled through the floor. Tile cracked. The enormous shelves began to sway.

The screaming began.

# CHAPTER 2

Thrown from her seat, Raven hit the floor, shrieking. She tumbled partway under the table, the councilor's books clutched tightly to her breast. An arm's reach away, Linden stared at the spot where Councilor Stormchaser had died. His mouth hung open in horror, plain for anyone to see, even a non-empath.

Another explosion tore through the room. The floor tilted. The room skewed. Flaming books rained down. The burning missiles smashed into tables and struck down those trying to regain their feet. Flames licked hungrily at all they touched. Smoke bloomed to choke and blind.

"Gods! What's happening?" Raven's voice came out high-pitched, frightened.

"I don't know," Linden said. He reached across the floor, grabbed Raven's arm and dragged her closer. "We can't stay here. We're both pretty resistant to the smoke and heat, but eventually those book cases will collapse and crush us."

Linden pulled Raven against his chest. The First Born began chanting, his brow furrowing. Once he completed his spell a glow encircled them. "Magic isn't really my strong point, but I can manage to shield us from falling debris," he said. "It should help keep the smoke back too."

The two struggled to their feet. Despite her terror, Raven retained enough presence of mind to protect the precious books the councilor had given her. Sliding them inside her kimono, she and Linden toward the exit.

"The attack came from out there," Raven said, her fear making every word an effort.

"I know, but I don't see any alternative," he said. "We'd never make it to a different exit. My powers aren't strong enough to keep us protected that long."

Raven nodded, though she doubted Linden noticed. She allowed him to guide her through the smoke while she tried to focus on the councilor's words. She'd said they had a future, so that had to mean they would survive this. Her dreams had indicated a great change would come into her life. She just had to keep her head and let Linden guide them. Her trembling lessened and her stride steadied.

❦❦❦❦❦

Linden blinked through the soot stinging his eyes. They had made progress, but the books, furniture and bodies littering the floor made it impossible to take a straight path to the exit. He worried that his magic would fail. No ordinary fire could have affected anything in the magic-built library. As it was, the protective bubble he'd summoned did nothing to improve visibility. The young elf willed his eyes to penetrate the smoke. Was that movement ahead?

With startling suddenness, a powerful wind swept away the smoke, and the phantom movement proved to be two chainmail-clad Sky Elves. Their helms made it difficult to see their eyes, but anger had set their mouths into a grim line, and fear had turned their normally blue-tinged skin pure white. They worked their magic in unison, clearing the lingering smoke from the front of the library. Rain, much weaker than Linden would have expected, drizzled down, hissing and sputtering as it hit the flames.

More elves poured into the library, nearly trampling Linden and Raven. At least three dozen elves split into units of four and started to work their way through the inner portion of the library. Survivors, many of them injured, stumbled past them toward the exit. People clung to one another, struggling forward in desperation.

Another Sky Elf shouldered her way in. Dressed in the black and red plate of a blood mage, she belonged to an elite sect of casters who used the blood and bones of the elves' enemies to heal and protect their people. She scanned the devastation, an awful array of fury and hopelessness playing across her pristine features. She gestured with her scythe, and others swarmed in to tend to the wounded. "Save as many as you can," she ordered. "Only do what's necessary to get people mobile. Make sure they know we're evacuating to the Eastern Glade. I don't want anyone thinking they can hole up here and hide from what's coming. That's not going to happen."

As if on cue the ground rippled like water, tearing up tiles and spilling people to the floor. Linden and Raven staggered painfully into a wall. Screams echoed throughout the cavernous structure. Terrified people cried out to their various gods. Cries and curses in a dozen different languages added to the chaos. "What in the hells in going on?" Linden said, adding his own voice to the din.

The plate wearing Sky Elf swung around and spied Linden and Raven. "You two," she said, "you're not hurt?"

"No ma'am," Linden replied immediately. "I'm part of Sergeant Bloodmane's company. I should regroup with him."

"He'll have to manage without you, soldier. I need you to lead the folk still able to walk to the Eastern Glade."

Linden started to protest, but another explosion drowned out his words. Green flames streaked down the causeway outside the library. People tumbled by, shrieking, burning and fighting off unseen horrors.

"Commander!" one of the chain-clad casters called out. "The defense in the Western Glade is failing. We're out of time."

"Shit!" the commander snarled. She dug into a pouch at her waist and pulled out a triangular-shaped tooth the size of her hand. She raced to the doorway, fast and sure for someone in plate. She threw the tooth into the causeway, chanting all the while. As the tooth hit the ground she made a sharp, cutting motion with her scythe. Black smoke writhed up from the tooth and an infernal roar rose up, shaking the walls. From out of the smoke uncoiled an immense skeletal nightmare.

"Dracolich!" Linden gasped, as he and Raven caught up to the commander.

"Not anymore," the commander said. "Now he's just an undead servant. He won't hold for long, but long enough for you to make your escape. Now go!"

Linden, Raven, and a dozen or so others fled and headed toward the east. The skeletal dragon filled most of the area and they had to press against the north wall to slither past it. It bellowed a challenge to the host of death approaching from the west. As one they turned to see what terrible foe bore down on them. Raven cried out.

Demons.

Linden had never seen one, but he knew without a doubt they were demons. Nothing from this plane could have spawned such grotesque abominations. Some flew, some crawled or slithered. Some even scuttled along the walls. Yet others leapt from spot to spot, savaging anyone or anything they landed upon. Many possessed no stable shape, using undulating tendrils of flesh to pull themselves along.

They drove before them the remnants of the soldiers sent to keep them from spilling into the rest of the city. The soldiers had done little more than slow down the horde. Even now, the elves fired spells into the demonic host, but it was just too little against so great and numerous an enemy.

Confused by the poor showing of the soldiers, Linden tried to call upon more of his own elemental power and felt it sputter, weak and nearly useless. He had never excelled at magic, but something clearly interfered with what power he did have. A hollow pit opened up inside him as the answer came to him. The thick walls and floor kept him and the other First Born from reaching Father Earth. The enclosed ceiling kept the Sky Elves from the sun and the wind. Gods! No wonder none of the soldiers had earth or air elementals assisting them. Their beautiful new city cut them off from the bulk of their power. *We've killed ourselves.*

Two magi exited the library to take up defense next to the undead dragon. Finding Raven and Linden wedged between the wall and the dragon, gaping at the oncoming demons, one of the mages leveled an angry glare at them. "What in the hells are you still doing here?"

Linden and Raven looked around and found themselves alone. The others from the library had fled the instant they'd seen the demons. The Sky Elf shook his head. "Idiots. Is that sword of yours even magic, soldier?"

"No," Linden said. His stomach churned. The commander had given him one simple order, escort people to safety. Already he'd failed.

On the far side of the dragon, people began to stumble past, civilians and those too wounded to fight. A few clusters of evacuees with a caster and a heavy fighter in the red plate of a seasoned soldier, moved by at a more orderly pace.

A human woman staggered nearby, clawing at the remnants of her clothing, and boil-covered flesh. Her liquified insides oozed out, clinging to her legs. She collapsed with a squelch. Squirming creatures erupted from the boils. The Sky Elf pulled a wand from his belt and sent a searing bolt of magic toward them. White and blue flames engulfed the newborn monsters.

"Gods!" Raven cried. She clamped a hand over her mouth in an effort to keep from vomiting.

"Oh, you're one of those," the Sky Elf said, rolling his eyes. "You'd best get over that quick. If you're expecting some great and powerful being to blast these bastards back to the Abyss, you'll die faster than the rest of us. Here, take this."

The mage waggled the wand in Raven's faced. She swallowed hard, and removed her hand from her mouth so she could gingerly accept it without having to relinquish her grip on Linden. The Sky Elf expelled an exasperated puff of air. He started to trace glowing symbols in the air over Linden's sword. "It has only nineteen charges left, so use them wisely." To Linden he said, "The magic I cast on the sword should last until tomorrow. If you're not gone from here by then it won't matter. Now get going!"

The mage gave the two young elves a shove sending them squirming past the rest of the skeletal dragon. They joined the other panicked people fleeing the demons. Overhead, the sound of wings made the hair on Linden's neck rise. A shadow dropped out of the sky and snatched up a hapless gnome. His shrill cry disappeared into the dark.

*Dark? When had night fallen?* Linden risked a glance up and saw a boiling mass of clouds where before beams of light had made their way through the canopy of sculpted leaves. Black streaked with green and ochre, the mass covered the sky, shutting out the sun. Flying demons, only discernible through their movement, streaked about the folk racing east.

Ahead, more soldiers appeared. Armed with bows, they shot at the flying monsters. Glowing streaks of light soared skyward. Wails of pain attested to the archer's success. Heavy bodies spilled out the air, creating a new hazard.

Linden pulled Raven closer to the buildings lining the road to gain some cover. Bodies tumbled down squashing anyone not quick enough to escape. Limbs of the unfortunate stuck out from under the demon carcasses. The air stank like a mass grave. Linden's insides roiled. He forced himself to greater speed, pulling Raven along, desperate to get her away from the terrible scene.

More soldiers ran past, heading west. Among them traveled two Shadow Elves, one a female in plate, wielding two short swords, the other a male clawing at a metal collar around his neck. Raven's eyes grew wide as she sensed the power residing in the male. He couldn't access it, though. Something kept it trapped inside him. His panic was palpable. "Get it off! Get it off!" he panted as they raced past. Blood ran down his neck where he'd raked at his skin in his desperate attempts to remove the collar.

They flashed by, disappearing in the murk, but Raven continued to try watching them over her shoulder as she ran. She stumbled but Linden's strong arm steadied her. "You okay?" he asked.

"Yes," she replied. "Did you see those two Shadow Elves?"

Linden had fallen silent since they'd escaped the area where the archers took aim at the flying demons. When he finally spoke he sounded hoarse as if all the moisture had left his throat. "They're the Shadow Elf representatives from the High Council."

Raven had to force herself not to look over her shoulder again. "What was wrong with the male?"

Linden's unease washed over her. When he answered his words came out reluctantly. "He's collared," he said. "It suppresses his powers. He can't do much of anything unless two other council members remove the collar. All of the Shadow Elf males wear collars to suppress their psionic powers."

"Oh," she said, not trusting herself to say more. She'd assumed those Shadow Elves who continued to support the First and the Elven Nation were trusted like any other elf born on First Home.

"I know—not exactly the idealistic vision you probably had about life on First Home. I'm sorry."

An explosion ripped through the thick stone floor directly in front of them cutting off Raven's reply. Raven and Linden reeled back. Deadly shrapnel pinged against Linden's conjured shielding. A ghastly worm burst through the stone. The creature swelled. Gasses spurt out of fissures along its putrescent body. The gas enveloped a group of terrified evacuees. They melted into pools of gore.

Linden's arm tensed within Raven's grip as he prepared to launch himself at the worm. She stepped in his way and blasted the creature with her wand. It blazed with white and blue flames. Its silent scream ripped into their minds and they cried out, falling to their knees, clutching their heads. Just as suddenly, the pain left them as the fiendish worm fled back underground, leaving them panting and shaken. As their minds cleared they stumbled to their feet. “Come on, now’s our chance,” Linden said.

They began their trek to the east once again, shaky at first but more surefooted as they shook off the last of the worm’s mental howls. All around, things leapt from the shadows and scuttled alongside, herding them. Twisted things, with too many joints, twitched and lurched toward them. Others lurked at the edge of Raven’s peripheral vision, disappearing into the gloom when she tried to focus on them.

The elves’ fear gave them new energy and they ran as swift as deer. Nightmares reared in front of them only to be cut down by Linden’s ensorcelled sword. Raven greeted those who fell upon them from above with a blast of blue fire from her wand. They left behind them a wake of dead and dying demons. The sounds of chewing and thrashing floated after them. The fiends had paused to feast upon their own.

“We’re almost there,” Linden panted.

Stress and exertion wittled away at Raven’s reserves. She tripped more and more as she struggled to match the longer stride of the tall First Born. Finally, even Linden slowed. She thought he’d grown too spent to keep up the furious pace. Only then did she notice the fog creeping across the ground ahead of them.

“What now?” Linden muttered, his voice heavy with dread.

At his side, Raven sagged. The empathic ability she so relied on when dealing with others, worked against her now. The fear and despair of those in the dark around them beat at her like an ocean wave. Exhausted, keeping their feelings at bay grew increasingly difficult to manage. A barrage of emotions hit her, buckling her knees.

Linden scooped her up and supported her. “Just hang in there a little longer,” he said. “I promise we’re almost there. We just have to get past this fog.”

“Sorry,” Raven said. She clamped down on the fear and tried to force it out of her mind. She’d never had any training on the use her powers. She fought for control. Gradually she felt a little of herself return.

She focused her attention on her companion. She sensed his struggle to project a confidence he did not feel. He was as out of his element as she. She fished inside herself, searching for the confidence she’d felt earlier. It endured, but had scuttled into a corner of her psyche, overwhelmed by the flood of outside emotions. *It's foretold that we* will *survive. Just focus on that.*

"All right," she said at last. "I'm okay." She flashed a smile at Linden she hoped looked genuine.

Linden nodded. "Let's go."

Umbral, hated son of the First, stood breathing in the air of a world denied him for some ten thousand years. He barely registered the horrors going on around him, overwhelmed by the sensations touching him. Even with the charnel smell of demons permeating the air, the scent of plants and all things wild came to him.

Beside him, a demon reached out, caught up a halfling and stuffed it into its maw. As the beast chewed, blood spurted, spraying Umbral, disrupting his reverie. The elf's crimson eyes flared, and a psychic blast vaporized the demon before it could register its mistake.

Umbral stepped away from the magical gateway bridging the Abyss to this place of life and light. Determined he would never again pass through that doorway, he bent his will toward it. The magic which had opened it was unbelievably powerful. Most likely the work of many casters working in concert, it resisted his psionics. With a snarl, he invoked words of power and pitted both against the portal. All at once, the magic collapsed and the doorway winked out. The front half of a demon flopped onto the ground, cut off from the rest of its body.

A cacophony, full of monstrous dismay, erupted from an endless array of throats, thoraces and bubbling oozes as the demons found themselves cut off from the world to which they were attuned. A wave of weakness flowed through Umbral. *I've been gone too long. My body thinks of the Abyss as home.*

To his right, a mass of shimmering red scales rippled with demonic amusement. "So, little lord, you've cut us off from home—the better to seek revenge against your kin," it rumbled. "Can you hear their screams? Do you delight in their pain? Have no fear. I hold no anger toward you for marooning us. Come, I would enjoy your company as we lay claim to this place and tread across the backs of the suffering and dying. Just like old times."

*Old times?* Umbral tried to place the demon, but could not. A more intelligent specimen like this one could easily wear different forms. If he had worked for Ruaz'Daem, as had Umbral, it was likely he'd spent most of his time in the guise of a less repulsive being. Ruaz had enjoyed acting the part of a genteel, sophisticated lord, and had forced his minions to adopt his mannerisms and mode of speech. He'd insisted on proper etiquette at all times. Failure to conform resulted in painful, often fatal punishment.

Ruaz died by Umbral's hand, and this fellow had probably lost status and power with the fall of his lord. Demons could not to be trusted at the best of times. Those who nursed a grudge would merely wait until you dropped your guard before striking.

"You do realize that by coming through the portal to this plane, rather than being summoned as a spirit to serve a mage, you can truly die here? You won't wake up whole in the Abyss. You risk more than just an injured ego now," Umbral said, sounding bored.

More amusement shook the demon's bloated form. "Even so, we tread like gods among these pathetic creatures. I know the risks, and I dismiss them. Your concern, little lord, is... touching, but unnecessary." "Not at all," Umbral replied. "I merely wished to make certain you fully appreciated the situation. For you see, you grotesque cretin, I do intend to wreak vengeance, and I'm starting with you."

The eruption of power from Umbral took the demon by surprise, ripping it into hundreds of tiny pieces. The wave of power continued on, spreading out in an expanding circle, tearing apart every demon still within the Western Glade.

Umbral staggered from the exertion. Fortunately, no enemies still breathed to witness his sudden weakness. Departing the Abyss had left him even more fatigued than he'd realized. He would have to take care not to overextend himself. He straightened his shoulders, trying to appear more robust than he felt, and made his way through the torrential downpour of severed limbs, internal organs and blood of various hues. He used just the slightest amount of power to create a protective bubble around himself to keep the deluge from covering him in a shroud of gore.

Umbral entered the city proper, but ignored the majesty of the place. Built and sculpted with magic, it was as if an enormous forest had sprung from the white marble, but he focused his attention on the endless span of corpses stretching to the east. More demons swarmed here, busily eating and savaging the dying. The air reeked of despair and the monsters wallowed in it like hellish swine.

A lone female Sky Elf struggled in vain to drag herself from the carnage. Already the demonic parasites consuming her from within had begun to burst from her flesh. With a final scream of agony, the newborn monsters tore her apart, swarming the remains in a feeding frenzy.

Umbral tore his eyes away from the tableau and found himself looking into the terrified eyes of a female Shadow Elf. Enormous claws had ripped through her plate armor as if she wore cloth. She sat on the ground clutching her entrails to her gaping torso. Worse, she too had been implanted and Umbral could see the squirming parasites inside the translucent boils covering her body. They'd kill her in the same horrific manner as the Sky Elf long before she could regenerate from the evisceration.

"I'm sorry, child," Umbral said.

She stared at him in confusion and said something back that Umbral did not understand. With a start he realized his native tongue had altered into something else entirely since his exile. She spoke again and gestured with her chin to a spot behind her. Umbral's eyebrows rose as he spied a male Shadow Elf sprawled nearby. He sidestepped the dying female and stooped to examine the male.

The first thing he noticed was the fellow's grey skin. The female had the same condition, but he'd blamed that on blood loss. The male appeared to have died from demonic poison, or some other subtle death, as the gashes along his neck, where he'd clawed at a collar, seemed his only wounds. Umbral sensed the powerful magic within the collar and his lips curled in disgust.

With a thought, he caused the collar to spring open and he scooped it up. He returned to the female. Tears poured down her face, either in sorrow over her companion's demise, or because she'd realized her body's regenerative powers could not save her.

Umbral waved the collar in front of her face. Her ruby eyes grew wide with surprise. "Tell me about this," he said.

The female shook her head and babbled incomprehensibly. Blood poured out of her mouth and she choked and coughed. *This won't do.* Umbral touched her in the middle of the forehead, more as a warning about his intentions, than any need for physical contact. She flinched, but her weakened condition prevented her from doing more. Umbral bore into her mind and immersed himself in what turned out to be a surprisingly short life.

"Lass," he said, his thoughts clear to her, though his words had not been. "Lass, I have much to learn and I need to know all you know. I need your language, your culture—everything."

Her mental wail of anguish filled his being. "Please, save me," she pleaded.

"I cannot. Once infected with the young of a Kal'gorath you are doomed. All I can offer you is a quick death, far preferable to the agony you'll experience when the parasites hatch from your flesh.

"I'm so afraid," her mind wailed. "Have I been forgiven? Will the First accept me?"

At the mention of his hated father, Umbral mentally recoiled. "What could you have possibly done that would warrant forgiveness by *him*, child?"

"I'm tainted. We're *all* tainted. We bear the sins of the Traitor. I've worked all my life praying for redemption, but..."

Aghast, Umbral refused to listen to her further. What had happened to his people? This whining, pathetic creature bore no resemblance to the proud race he'd known before his exile. Unable to solve that mystery, he instead turned himself to the task of acquiring the knowledge he needed.

His mind burned like a firestorm as it tore through the dying warrior's brain. He absorbed her language, came to understand the political structure of the Elven Nation, the fate of those who had sided with him all those years ago, and bits of trivia concerning the elves. He wished he had time to absorb more, but the basics would have to do.

When at last he pulled free he saw his intrusion had greatly added to her agony, and made her aware of whom she faced, but his fury was so great, he cared little. He nearly walked away then, leaving her to the parasites. Instead he snarled into her face, "You're the descendants of those who stayed loyal to the First. You have no need to seek redemption in his eyes. But *I* will not forgive you."

He held the collar up before her pain filled eyes. "This stops now."

The last thing she beheld was his look of contempt as he reached forth and plucked the last bit of life from her and sent her spirit spiraling into the ether. She went limp and the parasites, deprived of her life force, shrieked and died. Umbral turned his back on her corpse and continued on into the city.

Umbral passed through a dying city. All around the dead lay in piles and pieces. The elves had killed thousands of demons, but the invaders grossly outnumbered the elves, and even magic had its limitations. Umbral thought of the male Shadow Elf. Even dead, Umbral had sensed the power lying trapped within him. Free of the collar, he could have cleared the glade as Umbral had. He couldn't have won the day, but he could have easily given the elves a chance to retreat without such heavy losses. *Instead, you fools let a crime several millennia past kill you. Kill him.*

His mind churned, awash in pain and anger. He thought he'd stopped caring about his people long ago. Apparently, he'd merely deceived himself. Worse, he had to shoulder some of the responsibility for the current state of the elves.

His youth and stupidity had brought them to this point. If only he had known patience. Used subtlety. Planned. But no, his arrogance and temper had controlled him that day, made him reckless. Oh, he didn't regret trying to kill his father. He regretted failing the attempt. He hated that his people hadn't had enough faith in him to fully support him. Those who had sided with him had become exiles themselves, and had warped into a people so vicious, they were no better than the demons running rampant through the city street he now walked. And those who had stayed true to the First? Their descendants had grown sickly, practically crippled with self-loathing.

The shrieks of a female Sky Elf interrupted his mental turmoil. Clearly out of her mind, she staggered along the road, waving at unseen horrors. Her screams served to make the demons stalking her giggle like errant children. She spun around, but seemed incapable of recognizing the real threat just a foot away from her. Her eyes rolled and she nearly fell. She spun around again, arms pin-wheeling, her shrieks turning into hysterical hiccups.

Umbral took stock of his energy levels. He definitely wasn't at his best, and in truth he wasn't in the mood to take mercy upon anyone. But as he gazed upon her, a twinge of something stirred in his breast. Guilt? Or just a distant memory of the one person who had shown a foolish child kindness? Despite her mania she did bear a strong resemblance to *Uverial Stormchaser*.

Uverial Stormchaser: The first civilized elf, as he liked to call her. She had created the first written version of the Elven language. She had invented poetry, and written songs which the elves could enjoy for their beauty, and not just as a battle hymns. She had done and been many things, and Umbral owed her much.

"Very well," Umbral said to her memory. "However, if I die doing this, I shall be quite cross with you, Uverial."

Umbral breathed in deeply and opened his mind. He focused his power and allowed it to spill forth as he scythed his arm through the air. In an instant the gibbering elfess stood within a circle of eviscerated corpses. Her hiccups turned to a series of hyena laughs and giggles. She waved in childish delight at the rain of demon blood splattering down on her.

Umbral marched up to the female, and without ceremony, reached into her mind. A powerful psychic attack had left her in this pitiable state. Umbral ignored the nightmares charging at him. He had lived with the real thing for too great a time for phantoms to hold any fear for him. He sorted her thoughts, arranged her shattered psyche back to its normal state, and erased the images the attacker had planted. Then, satisfied, he retreated back to his now trembling body. Killing was easy. Healing was exhausting.

⁂

Lady Kiara Swiftbrook stared down at the diminutive Shadow Elf before her. She'd never seen a being so wild and savage looking. It didn't appear that he'd ever washed or combed his white hair. Thick and matted, it hung down his back, trailing along the ground behind him like some great serpent. His only clothing was a leather kilt, studded with bone, and pieced together from the skins of numerous creatures. And boots. Boots that smoked as if they would burst into flames at any second. Ancestors! The stench!

"Madam?" he said.

The incongruity of his deep, cultured voice and his barbaric appearance left her speechless for a moment. Lady Swiftbrook realized she was recoiling from him. Embarrassed, she straightened and tried to take a dignified step back. Breathing through her mouth, she tried to lessen the effects of his odor. She had the sudden suspicion his kilt had been made from something thoroughly unwholesome and improperly cured.

Lady Swiftbrook's attempts to regain her composure faltered as the tableau of demonic corpses around her caught her attention. With a start, her circumstances came back to her and she cried out, reaching for a sword she'd lost at some point in the battle.

"Madam," he said again, and moved up, ignoring her disgust. He took her by the elbow. "We are the only survivors in this part of the city. We must move on."

Her shoulders slumped at the news. Her keen gaze traveled down the roadway, into the distance, taking in the destroyed skeletal dragon and just beyond it the razed library. She moaned when she recognized the black and red plate of the commander who had died fighting at the side of her soldiers. *I should have been with them. Why am I still alive?*

She turned back to the strange Shadow Elf. Despite his calm manner, an inferno of rage burned in his eyes. In his hand he held a sprung psychic containment collar. He noticed her gaze and lifted it for her to see. "You lost two council members, and hundreds of others, because the male could not access to his powers."

She turned her head in shame. "I hate those things," she said.

"It pleases me to hear that, Lady..."

"Swiftbrook. But you know that already." He inclined his head in acknowledgement, and an involuntary shudder rippled through her. She could still feel his intrusion into her head. She appreciated that he'd saved her, but understood now why others feared psions. He knew things about her. Things she shared with no one other than her lover. Some things, even he didn't know. "You have me at a disadvantage, sir," she said, pleased her voice didn't quaver.

"Of course—how very rude of me. You may call me... Wrath," he said, the faintest of smirks settling onto his features.

"W'rath?" she mused, putting an Elven accent to the word. "It suits you."

"And now, madam, if you don't mind?"

"Of course," she said, and started to trudge to the east on shaky legs. She stopped when she realized her new companion had fallen behind. She peered over her shoulder to see him cocking his head, surprise plain on his face.

"What?"

"Quickly!" he hissed, rushing to her, his great mass of hair slithering along behind him. "I sense another Shadow Elf. A female. Her powers are immense!"

"That's impossible," Lady Swiftbrook protested. "Everyone knows females have minimal psychic ability."

Umbral, now W'rath, took her arm and grinned a feral grin. "Then prepare to meet the impossible, madam," he said and teleported them away.

One moment Raven and Linden crept through the murk and fog, their footfalls echoing as if they moved through a vast, subterranean cavern, the next, dozens of grinning, leering creatures materialized out of the surrounding black. The two elves lurched to a stop. That they had nearly reached their goal made the acid burning Raven's throat all the more bitter.

"Where is everyone?" Linden whispered. "Surely, the others will come to our aid."

*Unless everyone else is dead.* Raven hated to think that way, but they had not seen another soul for the last several minutes. And something about this new mob of fiends struck her as different. Her eyes grew wide. Unlike everything else they'd faced thus far, these weren't demons from the Abyss, but devils from the Nine Hells. "Gods," she moaned, despair returning in a flood. "These are beyond us. Your sword, my wand... they'll do nothing to these."

Linden didn't respond. Raven suspected he didn't know a demon from a devil, but surely he could sense these creatures were vastly more powerful than anything they'd encountered previously. "Why don't they attack?" she whispered.

"If I had to guess, I'd say they're enjoying our fear."

One of the devils gave off a hyena laugh. He stroked himself obscenely, giving them a preview of the fate awaiting them. "It can't end this way," she whispered. "The councilor said we have a future."

"No, she didn't," Linden corrected, his voice tinged with sadness. "She said *you* have a future. For me she had only tears."

"Don't say that!" Raven shook her head, refusing to accept his words.

Linden squeezed her close to his side. "I'm sorry we didn't get to know each other longer," he said.

"Please ... don't."

Linden ignored her plea. "When you get to First Home, tell my mother I didn't shame her."

Raven tried to cling to him, but she couldn't match even a fraction of Linden's strength. He gently pushed her aside and swung around to face his foes. He bellowed a challenge at the wall of fiends and charged them. Raven cried out and emptied the last of her wand's charges into the foremost devils. As she'd feared, the blasts had almost no affect. And then Linden rushed in among them, his sword, his strength, and the power of the molten earth of his ancestry, taking his foes by surprise.

Raven gasped as one went down, its head severed. The others, shocked, fell back as two more fell to Linden's savage assault. They continued to retreat and Raven's heart surged with hope. He could defeat them. They could both escape this nightmare!

Then a massive being appeared out of nothingness, filling the void left by the fleeing devils. It grinned at Raven before turning its attention back to Linden. It had toyed with its prey, allowing them to think they stood a chance. That some of its minions had been sacrificed for the sake of the ruse mattered not.

Watching, keeping itself invisible, the monstrosity dropped its invisibility at just the right time so it might crush every last vestige of hope. It flicked a finger as long as Linden was tall, sending him sprawling. Instantly, a dozen giggling, slavering, oozing horrors swarmed him. His soul's scream reverberated through Raven's psyche as the devils tore the life from him, and her heart burst with her anguish. Her mind erupted with fire. She howled in fury at the slayers of her friend.

Then the world exploded into shards of light and death.

ЖЖЖЖЖ

W'rath and Lady Swiftbrook teleported to the top of a cornice overlooking a terrible scene. He spied the psion he'd sensed, a tiny, stick-limbed Shadow Elf girl. With no armor or weapons, she stood helpless as creatures, more vile than even W'rath was accustomed to, prepared to savage and destroy her.

Next to him, the Sky Elf gasped as the broken body of a First Born male tumbled to a stop at the girl's feet. Even at such a distance they could hear the howl of anguish and fury that erupted from the girl's throat. "Oh, ancestors," Lady Swiftbrook whispered, "she's just a baby. Can you teleport her out of there?"

W'rath barely heard, so consumed by the brilliant psychic power washing over him. The girl was a prodigy. Completely untrained and currently consumed by her emotions, but still more powerful than any other Shadow Elf he had ever seen.

The devils felt it too. Having dispatched her protector, they should have leapt upon her in savage glee, but instead they shifted uncomfortably. Not even their terrible leader dared close on the child.

The girl crouched down and tugged at the sword still clutched in the First Born's lifeless grasp. Her tiny hands fumbled with the hilt, inept and unfamiliar with such a massive weapon. She slowly straightened, staggering in her struggle to lift the blade. The tip rasped against the stone of the roadway.

Lady Swiftbrook grabbed W'rath's arm shook him. "She can't fight them. Help her!"

"Not just yet," was his only reply.

Lady Swiftbrook spun away, with a furious hiss. She raised her arms and started to call upon her powers. Her fingers danced, making the passes needed to call upon the elements. Sparks of electricity danced around her, but they were weak, useless. She cast an anguished gaze toward the false canopy of leaves enclosing the city.

"Your beautiful city cuts you off from the natural world, madam," W'rath said. "For now you must stand down."

The child, weighed down by a sword she could not use, raised her head. A howl, not of fear nor even of sorrow, ripped from her throat. Pure rage radiated from her. Where her eyes should have been twin suns blazed.

The spell forgotten, the crackle of power dissipated from Lady Swiftbrook's hands, leaving only the smell of ozone. "By the First."

A concussive force rolled outward from the girl, and the front ranks of devils disintegrated into mist, coating those behind in a film of blood. The survivors panicked and fought their way through their fellows. A few took to the sky and fled, not paying the least bit attention to the two elves perched on the cornice.

For his part, W'rath allowed the glorious super nova of the girl's power to wash over him. His soul vibrated with the terrible force of her vengeance. Her purity burned him and yet drew him closer.

The girl's psychic blast swept through rank upon rank of devils, destroying them utterly. W'rath moaned. Beside him, Lady Swiftbrook cast a concerned glance his way only to quickly avert her eyes. He caught a sense of her unease at the look of pure ecstasy he knew suffused his face.

Below, only the monstrous devil survived. Presumably the leader, the fear twisting its face pulled a chuckle from W'rath. Seemingly unable to flee, it quaked as the tiny Shadow Elf slowly strode toward it. The only sign she remained aware of the world around her was the careful way she stepped around the fallen First Born. Still dragged along, the sword's razor edge etched the ground.

W'rath pulled himself out of the girl's mind, gasping. She was losing herself, burning up from the inside out. "She's lost control, and I can't bring her out of it," he said. "She keeps calling upon more and more of her mind."

Lady Swiftbrook shot him a glance. "Can you do anything? Maybe take that *thing* out?"

"That thing is a duke of the Third Hell. And yes, I can kill it, but that won't keep her from self destructing. She has a better chance of surviving if she channels the power building in her out and into him. She's had absolutely no training, though. Indeed, until now, I doubt anyone knew she had so much potential. It's lain dormant in her until an emotional break stirred her brain."

"What do you mean? You can't help her? You won't help her?"

"What I'm saying, madam, is she needs to work it out for herself. At this moment she's more powerful than any elf I've ever met, and much too out of control for me to guide her."

ЖЖЖЖЖ

Raven stalked the bloated fiend. Her mind burned with ice and fire. For a brief time, another had shared her mind, but he'd left when she'd ignored his attempts to reign in her power. She was killing herself, she realized that, but right now the power burning her from within seemed the only way to purge the guilt she felt.

Too small. Too weak. Not even capable of defending herself. A young elf, who barely knew her, had given his life to save her and she couldn't even help—until it was too late. Where had this power been before he'd landed dead at her feet? To the Hells with visions and dreams. She would go up in a ball of psychic power and take this squirming, loathsome creature with her.

She drew closer, keeping the thing bound to the spot. She didn't allow it to speak. It could cast no spells. It quivered, helpless for probably the first time in thousands of years. It's terror tasted like hopelessness.

She stopped short. A hand had appeared, pressing the flesh out from the devil's abdomen. Then a tortured face joined it, the devil's skin distending. More joined in and soon Raven saw a mass of frightened, pained people silently screaming at the horror of finding themselves trapped within the flesh of a nightmare.

A trick. It had to be. Raven tentatively reached out with her mind and recoiled as the anguish of fifty or more beings nearly dropped her to her knees. Swallowed whole, they now found themselves slowly merging with the devil's body. It could take decades before the monster completely absorbed them, and they'd stay fully aware the entire time.

Gods! If she detonated herself she'd destroy them along with the monster. The devil leered, sensing her faltering conviction. Raven screamed in frustration. She was too far gone. She didn't know how to stop herself now. She needed a new direction for her power. Too late, she regretted rebuffing the entity who had tried to help her.

The devil's mass rippled, shaking with silent laughter. It understood her quandary. She glared at it. This never would have happened if she were a hero instead of a victim. She suddenly hated the skinny arms, and the slim hands clutching Linden's sword. She snarled at the fiend's grinning face and locked her eyes with his. His smile faltered as he saw the sneer of triumph slide onto Raven's face.

She began her deliberate pace toward the devil. All the power that had been radiating out from her began to swirl and coalesce around her, drawing in at an increasing rate. The hiss of tearing silk whispered through the hall. Three slim books fell to the ground. The scrape of blade across stone stopped.

ЖЖЖЖЖ

"What is she doing?" Lady Swiftbrook said.

W'rath blinked, stunned. The girl had seemed determined to work herself into an explosive end. All that remained was to see how large of a crater she'd leave in the city. But now she'd begun to draw her power back in, forcing it into her body, into her limbs. His eyes grew wide. *Remarkable! What an extraordinary child!*

Lady Swiftbrook's mouth fell open. "That's not possible," she breathed.

"Indeed. And yet, here we stand witnessing it. Still, we have one problem," W'rath said.

"What?"

"She's drawing all of her power inward. Any second now her playmate will realize she can no longer constrain him."

As if he'd overheard W'rath's words, the devil's face lit up in evil glee. It knew. Its tail whipped around in a deadly sweep toward the girl and the swirling power enveloping her. The tail never made contact.

The devil screamed in fury, twisting about in search of its new tormenter. Lady Swiftbrook shuddered as its fell gaze found them on their perch. It bellowed something and the force of its voice staggered the Sky Elf. Beside her, W'rath waved at the devil. "Sorry about that, old boy," he called.

With a roar of frustration, the devil swung back to face his doom.

Raven had transformed into a being of pain and light, blind to all but the power she drew into herself. Every vessel in her body altered, metamorphosing to her will. Her control over the devil vanished and her power continued to turn inward. She paid no heed, as she knew with certainty the being who had briefly shared her consciousness would take over that task with ease.

Raven propelled herself forward. The final, furious remnants of her power shot her skyward. She flew, soaring above the devil's twisted face. Reaching her apex, she screamed as everything she had been, and everything she would become, pulled into a singularity where they compressed into one being. Motes of crimson light announced her rebirth.

Below her, her victim recoiled in terror. Yes, *her* victim. She'd no longer suffer at the hands of the evil and the cruel. She smiled. Gripping the sword, she felt the responsiveness of her new muscles, and plummeted like an avenging angel.

Something delicate fluttered against Lady Swiftbrook's arm. She cracked open her eyes, hoping to find she'd awoken from a terrible dream, and in reality lay safely in her bed. A storm of scarlet wings swirled about her, and throughout the vastness of the city. One of the creatures landed on her hand. A butterfly. She stared at it, confused, disoriented.

With a start it all came back to her, the searing light, the Shadow Elf girl, naked and greatly transformed, falling from the sky, sword raised above her head. The devil had wailed as the blade struck its forehead. The blade had continued on down the length of its body. So much blood. Hundreds of feet of entrails. And people. *Ancestors!* So many people.

"Are you back with us, madam?"

Lady Swiftbrook blinked up at W'rath and realized she'd collapsed. Had she fainted? "There's butterflies," she said, only vaguely aware of how addled she must sound.

"Heralds."

"Heralds?"

W'rath offered her a hand and helped her rise. He made a sweeping gesture, taking in the field of carnage sprawled out below them. In the midst of it stood a lonely figure, white hair falling to her bare calves. Around her, dozens of gore-covered elves staggered, some fallen in supplication before her. The crimson butterflies spun in a frenzy, alighting in her hair and dancing along her skin. "They're heralding a new heroine."

"Her power?"

"Gone. She burned herself out remaking herself."

Lady Swiftbrook clapped a hand over her mouth, but the tears came anyway. "Don't mourn her, lady," W'rath said. "She only did what she needed to do. She saved not just the devil's victims, but herself as well. Her power was like a dragon's breath upon a candle. She would have destroyed herself if she hadn't redirected its fury. In the end, she chose to live, and for that you should be grateful."

The Sky Elf wiped her face and W'rath nodded his approval. "Good," he said. "Now it's about time we introduce ourselves and get these people out of here."

Without further warning, the Shadow Elf grabbed Lady Swiftbrook's arm and teleported them into the midst of the massacre, among the many sobbing, wounded elves, and one stunned, nude warrior standing amid the carnage.

# CHAPTER 3

The young Shadow Elf didn't flinch when W'rath and Lady Swiftbrook teleported to her side. Slowly she focused on W'rath. He allowed her to see the flames of pain and anger burning there so that she would recognize the soul who had briefly shared her consciousness. "You," she said, her voice raw from her ordeal.

"Me," he agreed.

In that one word he acknowledged far more than the obvious, but the girl, Raven, was in no condition to make the connection. Instead, she took a step back, her eyes going wide as she realized something. She stared down at him. Her gaze switched to Lady Swiftbrook and then back to him. *Ah, she's noticed she's much taller than me, and nearly as tall as a Sky Elf.*

Raven dropped the sword and stared at her hands. Then the arms that bore them. Then everything else. "What have I done to myself?"

Neither W'rath nor Lady Swiftbrook answered. W'rath cocked his head in the direction of the wounded and Lady Swiftbrook nodded and slipped off to assist them as best she could. Smoothly, W'rath bent to retrieve the dropped sword and presented it hilt first to Raven.

"This belongs to you now, Lady," he said.

Raven grimaced and dropped her head in shame. "No," she said quietly, "I'm not worthy of that. My friend..."

Deliberately she turned to where Linden lay. Horror replaced shame as her eyes fell upon his green armor. She rushed to him and knelt by his side, heedless of the blood and organs covering the ground. Her hands fluttered over him as agitated as the butterflies that continued to swarm the air.

"Gods! What happened to him?!"

W'rath joined her. Little of the First Born remained. Hardly more than a skeleton lay within the armor. "The mass needed for your transformation had to come from somewhere," he said.

"*I* did this?" Raven gasped.

"Better you absorb a fallen elf than draw in the essence of a devil," W'rath reasoned.

Raven's barely suppressed sobs made it clear his practical view of the situation brought her no comfort. W'rath scowled and prepared to try again. Sensitivity was definitely not one of his strong suits.

Raven wrung her hands. "This is the very thing Exile females do to gain power," Raven continued. "I'm no better than my mother! I destroyed him."

W'rath spared a glance back at Lady Swiftbrook. While she seemed like a level-headed sort, he wasn't sure he wanted her privy to Raven's words. Fortunately, she appeared absorbed in arranging for the less injured to assist those who couldn't walk on their own, allowing the two Shadow Elves to sort things out for themselves. Good enough. That just left the task of trying to calm down his young heroine.

He tried to quickly sort through the information he'd picked up when he'd resided in her mind. The Exiles did indeed have some vile practices, their "ritual" nothing more than a corruption of an ability Shadow Elf females had used since they first walked the world. While the means by which Raven had accessed the ability had been unusual, it had certainly resulted in a state much closer to its original intent. The girl just didn't understand what had happened. Therein lay his chance to remedy the situation.

He knelt next to her and placed the sword between them. "Lass," he said, and reached up to take hold of her shoulders, forcing her to face him instead of Linden's desiccated corpse. "Your mother, and those like her, seek out demons for the sole purpose of absorbing their essence so they can gain access to magic that doesn't come to our kind naturally. You did *not* do that. You had a need—an unselfish one. You were driven by the desire to aid others, and your friend's soul responded to that. You took nothing by force and you did not destroy your friend. If you look within yourself—truly search—you'll see that you and he have melded into one being.

"You didn't destroy his soul. You gave him a second chance at life. The Exiles perverted it, but when used as originally intended, it is a gift. Our ancestors called those like you *twin-souled.*"

Skepticism suffused Raven's face. He could see her wrestling with the ideas he'd presented to her. She plainly wished to believe, but could not help but doubt his words. Then a look of awe replaced the distress on her face. Her friend had made his fire-touched presence known, filling her heart. "You *are* there," she said in wonder.

W'rath released her shoulders and lifted the sword to her once again. Her face now alight with a quiet joy, Raven accepted it. The crimson butterflies lit in her hair like a crown of rubies.

W'rath didn't realize he was staring until a feminine hand slapped him on the back of the head. "Lecher," Lady Swiftbrook scolded, wiping her hand on her blood soaked tabard as if it were somehow cleaner than his head. "You should offer her a cloak instead of salivating as if you haven't seen a female in a hundred years."

*Try ten thousand.* He rose, offering a hand to Raven and a wink to Lady Swiftbrook. "I appear to have misplaced my cloak, madam."

"How very convenient." The Sky Elf sniffed in mock disgust.

The sobbing of one of the rescued elves sobered them instantly. "The portal these fiends came through most likely endures," W'rath said, gesturing at the fallen devils.

"My unit was attempting to fight its way to the gateway in the Western Glade when..." Lady Swiftbrook's voice trailed off.

"You managed to close it," W'rath said. Enough gaps lingered in the Sky Elf's memory that he could easily lead her to believe her people had succeeded in closing the gate before the demons overwhelmed them. He thought it prudent she stay ignorant of the full extent of his powers. No doubt many questions concerning his origins would arise. No need to provide even more mysteries for clever elven minds to ponder.

"But these are devils," Raven said. "They're not from the Abyss. He's right, another portal exists."

"Oh Ancestors!" Lady Swiftbrook said. As one they turned to the East.

ЖЖЖЖЖ

Getting everyone moving toward the Eastern Glade proved more problematic than W'rath anticipated. A great many of the elves Raven had rescued were reluctant to even stand. Several seemed intent on curling into a fetal position, and simply waiting for a great host of saviors to come spirit them away to safety. While they had endured a terrible ordeal, this complete lack of fighting spirit appalled him.

"Have patience," Lady Swiftbrook said. "They're civilians not trained soldiers."

"Insanity," he hissed, exasperated. "The very idea that a few live to protect the many puts all of you at risk. No wonder these monsters ran amok slaughtering you. Every single elf should have the skills to fight back. This lying about, expecting others to give their all while they do nothing, is shameful."

"I agree," Raven said, her shoulders drooping as if W'rath's words had been directed at her.

"But not everyone possesses that kind of spirit," the Sky Elf said. "Some are sculptors, or tailors or musicians. Our nation needs more than warriors. We need art and beauty too."

"If you can't fight to protect those things, then it doesn't matter. Your enemies will drive you to extinction and fill the world with statues of *their* heroes."

"We live long enough there's no reason we cannot excel at both," Raven said.

Raven's words jarred W'rath. Uverial had often said very similar things. She had waded into battle, fearsome, wielding both spell and sword with ease. Yet she put word to vellum and urged others to follow suit. How his father had scoffed at her, calling her soft, even as she regarded him from the mountain of enemy corpses at her feet. *I always thought of you as a gentle soul, Uverial. Whatever would you think of these pathetic creatures?*

Lady Swiftbrook sighed. "We can debate this until the next wave of demons or devils falls upon us, or we can figure out how to get everyone to the Eastern Glade."

*Slit their throats and be done with it. Probably not a popular option. Very well then—so much for keeping a low profile.* "I can teleport the whole lot to the Eastern Glade," W'rath said.

"You can *do* that?" the two females asked in unison.

"Certainly," he said. "I sense quite a few elves there already, engaged with the enemy. Mind you, if I teleport us there, these *civilians* will find themselves close to the fighting. I'm just warning you—I shouldn't wish for you to regard me as ... insensitive."

"Would you kindly stay out of my head," Lady Swiftbrook growled.

"Simply reading your face, not your mind, madam."

"I don't think we have much choice," Raven said. "We can't leave them behind, and we have to help the others fight off the demons long enough to get the portal closed."

"Devils," W'rath corrected. "However, you have the right of it. Madam? I believe I can place us close, yet not directly within the fire fight."

"Do it," the Sky Elf said. "Better that than wait here hoping it's elves and not more hell spawn who find us."

"Very well," W'rath said. He clapped his hands to get the attention of the civilians. "Listen up, lads and lassies. If you will stop mewling for a moment, I need for you to all link hands."

Raven and Lady Swiftbrook moved forward and assisted in getting people organized. W'rath tried not to grind his teeth at the slowness of the proceedings. When at last the civilians had gathered together hand in hand, he waved to his two companions to join in.

As he started forward to form the final link to the circle, the glow of magic, emanating from the gore-covered ground, brought him up short. Stooping, he pulled forth what turned out to be three books. As he lifted them, the blood coating spilled off, leaving them pristine. Powerful magic indeed, if it protected against hell spawn blood. Intrigued, he placed them in a pouch he had built into his kilt. When he returned his attention to the people before him, Raven gaped, wide-eyed in his direction. *Ah, well, the mystery of where they came from is solved.* "I'll just keep them safe for you, lass," he said.

He stepped forward, fighting to keep from grinning at Lady Swiftbrook's scowl, and grasped her and Raven's hands. He willed them from that terrible place, and the next moment they popped into existence elsewhere. As promised, W'rath had brought them close, but not directly, into the fray.

Perhaps a fifty feet away gaped a bloody-looking wound, the doorway connecting the elven city to the Nine Hells. Before it raged a battle that stirred memories within W'rath of a time long ago when he'd been young, and the world so brutal, the only music to be heard came from the roars of the triumphant and the screams of the dying.

Some twenty First Born, knee-deep in the corpses of their brethren and devils alike, battled furiously against a like number of ash grey devils. Unlike the unruly demons, the devils carried fine weapons. Purple flames danced along the blades of their swords. Some used barbed whips to bind up the sword arms of the elves. For their part, the elves had more discipline. Working as a cohesive unit, they cut their allies free from the whips and created a wall of tower shields that thwarted the devils' attempts to push their way from the portal.

A second group of elves, their slighter frames and furious spell casting marking them as Sky Elves, focused their attacks on flying devils. A couple of them, wearing the black and red armor of the Blood Magi, concentrated on drawing the life force from the enemy to use it as fuel for healing their comrades.

Despite all this, the elves could not hope to win. Their numbers were finite while there seemed no end to the number of devils. Every time one fell to the sword of a First Born, another stepped through the portal to take its place.

Lady Swiftbrook prodded the mossy ground with her boot and sighed in relief at the sight of open sky above them. "At least we have more access to our elemental-based powers here, but there's not enough time to summon our companions. We're on our own, and the casters need relief so they can turn their efforts to undoing the gateway," Lady Swiftbrook said.

"My pleasure, madam," W'rath said. He drew in an impossibly deep breath, threw out his chest and let forth a blast of sound and thought. The shock wave hit the flying devils obliterating them. The Sky Elves turned to stare at W'rath in wonder. Lady Swiftbrook gaped as well. With some effort, she snapped her mouth shut and ran to her people to lead them in the destruction of the portal.

As such she didn't see W'rath topple over in exhaustion. Raven caught him just before he hit the ground. "I think you're done for the day," she said.

W'rath shook his head. "They'll never get that portal closed with magic alone. They'll need my help. I just need to catch my breath."

Raven pursed her lips, dubious, but nodded. "Okay, you rest and we'll make sure nothing disturbs you."

"We?"

Raven placed a hand over her heart. "We," she affirmed.

"You won't stand alone, lady," came a voice. The two Shadow Elves lifted their heads to see one of the rescued standing nearby, gripping a scavenged sword. Behind him others clutched bows, knives and staves. About half of those rescued had found the courage to take up weapons.

"You saved us, lady," he said. "It's time we do our part."

W'rath saw a flash of panic cross Raven's face. She wore the body of an adult, but inside a child still dwelled. Precocious, no doubt, but lacking in experience. She hadn't been raised from birth as a weapon, expected to lead others into life and death battles.

Though exhausted, it still took little effort for him to send a tendril of thought to Raven. *Give them this, lass. They can stand here looking fierce for a few minutes while I recuperate. Let them feel like they matter.*

Raven swallowed and nodded, but remained unconvinced. W'rath made a shooing motion with his hand. "Go! Lead them, and leave me in peace, child."

W'rath's ploy worked, and Raven rose unflinchingly to face the expectant gazes of her tiny group of would-be heroes. Her posture stiffened to that of a soldier and W'rath suspected the soul of her friend had come to her aid, stepping in, influencing her, giving her the benefit of his training and the discipline needed to lead others. "Those of you with bows stand back there and shoot at anything that flies this way. The rest form a perimeter here with me. Nothing gets through us. Our job is to allow this bedraggled lump to rest long enough so he can do something about the portal."

W'rath ignored the assaults upon his dignity and concentrated on entering into a meditative trance. Despite his skill, it took every drop of discipline he possessed to manage it. Relying upon others to watch over him while he lay vulnerable did not come natural to him. In the end, though, there really wasn't much choice in the matter. Cut off from the Abyss, his stamina had dropped to a pitiful level. It could take another lifetime for his body and mind to readapt to this plane.

Once he finally shut out the chaos around him, and began the task of recovering, his mind worked to put itself in order. He'd been living from moment to moment since he'd escaped the Abyss. Now that he had some time for reflection, he could analyze what he'd learned, and determine his next move.

Until now, returning to his childhood home had seemed such an impossibility, he'd never done more than dream of vengeance against his father. Actually reuniting with his people, perhaps even reestablishing himself as a leader among them, had never seemed realistic. Now the opportunity lay within reach. The question was ... did he want it?

Deep inside persisted a remnant of the furious boy who had lashed out at the First. That child wanted nothing more than to teleport away and leave the elves to their fate. He listened to the boy rant for a time and then dismissed him, exiling him to the part of his mind reserved for his many regrets.

Perhaps he would rue his actions this day as well. The effort required of him to close this second portal could kill him. Was the risk worth it? If it meant being instrumental in remaking the elves into a proud people once again—a people molded by his will and not his father's—then certainly. *That* was worth any risk.

Of course, he couldn't contemplate such things without considering the fate of the First. His brief time in Reaper's mind had turned up no sign of his father other than as some vague deity-like being she hoped to appease. Nor had he found any memories of the other elves from his past, making any immediate confrontations unlikely. But eventually he could find himself facing someone from his past, perhaps even his father. While disconcerting, only a fool would ignore the possibility existed. Could he defeat the warlord this time? Certainly not in his current condition. But would it even be necessary? He had learned much during his years in exile. He had patience now. He had learned subtle manipulation, and even bent demons to his will. He had an entire nation to sway now. A challenge to say the least, but then anything worthwhile usually was.

Yes, if he had the loyalty of the entire Elven Nation, it wouldn't matter if the First returned. He could defeat his father without spilling a drop of elven blood. And oh, wouldn't that be the sweetest revenge of all?

When Raven came to break him from his reverie she found him smiling.

Raven helped W'rath up. Despite the smug smile, he didn't look much recovered to her. She could tell he had more pride than ten elves, so when he accepted a steadying arm, her worry deepened.

"Make way," she said and the elves who had stood guard while he rested reluctantly parted. Once they'd made up their minds to help, they'd fought fiercely, determined to prove themselves. Fortunately, the only threat they'd faced had been a small devil with a broken back, attempting to drag itself to safety. They'd fallen upon it with the savagery of wolverines. Only a blood stain persisted to show it had ever existed.

Thanks to W'rath's earlier psionic attack, not much else lived to cause them trouble. The Sky Elf, Lady Swiftbrook, had taken charge of the casters, and they had turned their attention to the pulsing sore of a portal, which continued to spew out devils, even as others of their ilk fell to the weapons of the First Born.

The Sky Elves and several First Born had begun to tap their magical talent, engulfing the portal in a kaleidoscope of power. Like any pureblood Shadow Elf, Raven had never had any affinity for magic. Now that Linden was a part of her she felt its pull. It suddenly felt natural and made sense to her.

She noticed W'rath scrutinizing her. "I think I can cast magic," she whispered to him.

"And you're thinking you should help them," he finished for her.

"Every little bit..."

W'rath shook his head. "Believe me when I tell you this: No matter your good intentions, the minute the others notice you casting, they'll see you as an enemy, no better than these devils."

"Because of Umbral," she sighed.

W'rath chuckled. "Don't despair, lass. You can still put your new gift to work—we'll just have to be circumspect. Help me so I can stand with the casters. I'm going to augment their power in order to overload that gateway. Without your assistance what I plan to do will most likely kill me."

W'rath smiled at Raven's look of alarm. "Don't worry, you're strong, and with your power we'll get through this. You can already feel the tug of the magic. Don't resist it. However, once you start to see it flow from you, impose your will upon it. Most casters do this through chants and rituals, but in truth you can apply what you know of psionics to the same end. The magic doesn't care about the method used. It just needs direction."

Raven's eyes narrowed. "You seem to know an awful lot about such things."

W'rath gave a weak shrug. "Many of our people make a study of magic despite our inability to use it. We often have to fight against it, and it helps to understand its workings and its limits."

"I didn't know it had any limits."

"So you do know more than you let on, clever child. You are so very right. The limits lie with the individual using it. Most people find that channeling power in a certain manner suits them. Your friend..."

"Linden."

"My pardon. Linden, as a First Born, most likely had an easier time with fire magic, or perhaps earth magic. It's all the same magic, it's just how it manifests for that person. Lady Swiftbrook likes lightning."

"So does that mean I'll have an affinity for fire like Linden?"

"Possibly, but I doubt it. He's opened the door for you, but yours is the dominant personality in your relationship. The magic shall most likely manifest more in line with your personality. This spot will do nicely."

*So what now?* Raven mused. All around them raw energy made the air itself vibrate. It felt alive to her, far more real than it ever had. The elves around her staggered, their clothing soaked in sweat, their hair clinging to them in dank tendrils. They couldn't continue slinging magic much longer. They'd start collapsing from exhaustion and then the First Born would find themselves on their own, trying to fight back the horde attempting to breach the doorway.

"What do I need to do?"

"Why, my dear, whatever comes natural to you."

"That's not any help!"

W'rath winked at her. "I have the utmost faith in you. When the time comes, you'll know exactly what to do."

With that he went from sagging, nearly limp invalid, to a great, bristling pillar of energy. She almost lost her grip on him, so shocking his transformation. His eyes flared into blinding spheres of light and his mouth twisted into a rictus of determination. *Gods! Did I look like that?*

The other elves fell back, some nearly losing their concentration, but the group magic held and then strengthened as the searing energy of the small Shadow Elf male melded with it. A roar of excitement went up from the First Born as the portal shuddered. The devils went into a frenzy, but the First Born threw themselves into the fray with renewed vigor.

Raven felt W'rath's skin grow hot. She hissed as her hands blistered from the radiant heat. Surely that signaled it was time for her to do her part, but what exactly did that mean? Panic threatened to rise in her again. This day had been too much. Too much pain. Too much loss. Linden had given everything as had so many others. And now—this strange newcomer. When he'd entered her mind, she had felt darkness and anger and a terrible past. Yet he had entrusted his life to her, to use a power newly born to her.

He had said to simply allow it to flow, not resist its pull, and so, she willed herself to relinquish her reign on it. It proved easier than she'd expected, and it poured from her like life blood. But it spilled away without direction, wasted and she snarled in frustration. She had to guide it, mold it to her need. But how?

The others around her had practiced their craft for centuries. She had only sensed she could touch magic less than an hour ago. *Gods! Linden, how did you shape your magic?*

In response to her need, the magic pulled in, warmed her and took on the appearance of embers. She felt its structure, its ability to both protect and destroy. Of the two, protection most closely resembled what she wanted, but it wouldn't provide the healing she needed to channel. *I need life. Life is wild and growing.*

The embers shimmered and reformed into green leaves. The air around the two filled with the scent of moist earth and plants. *Yes!*

She wrapped her arms around the quickly-fading male. From deep in her chest, Raven pulled upon her will and directed it at the magic and her target. *Live!* A great rush like a river filled Raven's ears. The scent of evergreen grew impossibly strong.

With a triumphant roar, W'rath came alive in her arms and a massive surge of power erupted from him. Everyone, elves and devils alike, were thrown to the ground. The pulsating portal shattered into a million motes of light, the screams of those trapped on either side echoing through the air. Ears and noses bled, and consciousness was ripped from every soul in the glade.

# CHAPTER 4

Raven woke to the cry of seagulls. She'd only heard them once before, when she had traveled to the coast to watch elven ships leaving the mainland for the winter. How she'd ached to board one of those vessels. The seagull's cries had seemed to echo her need.

She opened her eyes and blinked back tears brought on by the intense sunlight. So bright.

"You don't do anything by half measures do you, lass?" came a now familiar voice.

Raven pushed herself up. She sat on the deck of a ship. Someone had found a cloak and draped it over her. She pulled it close, it's crimson fabric reminiscent of the butterflies that had swarmed about her... when? It felt like a lifetime ago. How had they even arrived on this ship? "What do you mean?" she said to W'rath.

"You pushed nearly your entire life force into me."

Raven leaned back against a crate and shut her eyes. She did feel weak. Her arms trembled from the little bit of effort she'd expended to sit up. "I panicked. You were dying and I had no idea what to do. You didn't exactly give me much in the way of instructions."

"I can teach you how to fight, how to sneak, how to slit throats or to target a kidney, but handling your *gift*," he said, eyeing those moving about the ship, choosing his words carefully, "is a personal affair. You own it now. You're a healer. A protector. You're the first paladin of our people."

Raven gave a bitter laugh. "Paladins represent a god. I think I'm the only elf who believes in gods."

W'rath made a face. "Gods. There are no gods. Mind you, I find this ancestor worship most elves embrace just as ridiculous."

Raven's eyes widened. She'd been scorned for her belief system before, but she'd never heard anyone so bluntly disparage the practice of venerating the first elves. Emulating the honorable manner in which the First conducted himself remained first among the tenants taught to young surface born elves. Even the Exiles spoke of the First and his contemporaries in hushed tones. Only Umbral did they dare curse openly. They blamed him for all of their woes. And the males of their people suffered for his sins. "How can you call me a paladin if you yourself don't believe in anything?"

"A paladin doesn't have to represent a god," W'rath said. "She can champion an ideal—help restore her people's pride." He pulled the collar he'd removed from the dead Shadow Elf male, from some hidden spot in his kilt, and placed it between them.

Tentatively, Raven touched the hated thing. She could sense the magic within it. It's malignancy conjured up the image of the male's panicked face as he'd raced to his doom. She turned her attention back to W'rath and tried to read his motives, but her empathic abilities were gone, burned out by her brief, fiery, psionic overload. She hadn't realized how much she relied on her talent to guide her when dealing with others, so it came as a surprise when she saw his inscrutable expression suddenly transform into one of true fear.

She peered over her shoulder where his gaze fell. Lady Swiftbrook stood there conversing with an enormous First Born clad in red and gold plate mail. He had turned to regard the two Shadow Elves. Raven didn't think she'd ever seen a face less likely to smile.

She turned back to W'rath. In the few seconds since she'd altered her attention, his mask had returned. He seemed completely at ease, but Raven knew she hadn't imagined the fear on his face. "Do you know him?" she asked.

"No," he replied, appearing for all the world as calm and confident as ever. "He simply... reminds me of someone. But that was a long time ago and this chap is actually much smaller."

"Smaller?" Raven asked, incredulous. The armored First Born had to be close to eight feet tall. She'd read the very earliest First Born had reached nearly ten feet in height, but she'd assumed the author had exaggerated in order to add to the ancient elves' mystique. Now she wasn't so sure. And just how old did that make W'rath?

W'rath's eyebrows arched, and even before she heard the creak of armor and the groan of the deck, she knew the First Born approached. "My Lady says she owes you her life," said a voice reminiscent of a newly awakened volcano. What should have been the lead-in to a statement of gratitude sounded full of suspicion and threat.

"It was my pleasure to be of *service*," W'rath replied, rising to his feet. Just the hint of a smile played across his lips. Raven thought she heard a snarl from the First Born. Now, even more, she missed her empathy. She had little experience with males beyond the pitiful creatures from her home city. Some sort of sparring match had ignited, and she couldn't follow it.

"Oh, by the First!" Lady Swiftbrook snapped, apparently more familiar with males than Raven. "K'hul, would you rather the demons had torn me apart? And you, little imp, don't think my gratitude extends so far I won't have you tossed overboard and dragged behind the ship. It might—just might—get some of that filth off of you. Ancestors know it won't get rid of your self-satisfied smirk."

Neither male responded, their gazes fixed upon one another, postures stiff with territorial challenge. Lady Swiftbrook threw her hands up in exasperation. "To the Nine Hells with the both of you. You can puff yourselves up and compare cock size all you want. I shall help Lady Raven find something more suitable than a cloak to wear."

That seemed to get W'rath's attention, and he offered Raven a hand up. She accepted, grateful for the strength of his grip as her legs refused to stop shaking, and not just from her exhaustion. K'hul was the family name of the First. She swayed and Lady Swiftbrook steadied her. "Slowly," she said, the heat gone from her words.

W'rath gave her a wink and released her hand, allowing the Sky Elf to turn Raven around so she faced the one Lady Swiftbrook had inadvertently identified as a descendant of the First. "Hmmph," he said. "The heroine who slew a devil lord. Tell me, what happened to your clothes, lady?"

"Lost in the fight," Raven said. The strength of her voice surprised her. From his deepening scowl, K'hul had expected to intimidate her. He had, but she wouldn't let him see that. *You can't compare to what I've already faced this day.*

He broke eye contact first, but disguised it as a stiff bow and a not so gracious side step to allow the two females passage. "Find her something to wear quickly," he muttered. "She's distracting the crew."

With the two females gone, K'hul drew himself up, attempting to appear even larger. He had to be young. No one of any maturity would behave so. W'rath smirked, only too happy to teach the lad a lesson or two. "I'll concede you are the more puffed up," he said. "However, I believe I have the second half of our competition wrapped up."

"Ridiculous."

"If you doubt me, we can call the ladies back and let them judge."

K'hul actually blushed and turned away. "I'll have you know I am a direct descendant of the First. I'm his grandson—tenth generation."

*Lovely. I have a half nephew. Let's have a family reunion.*

When W'rath didn't respond K'hul swung back around. "Since you're an ignorant savage, I'll explain to you what that means. It means I shall ascend to the High Council since my father perished today fighting hell spawn."

"Hmmm. Being an ignorant savage, I might have my facts wrong, but I thought council positions were awarded based on merit and not a hereditary right."

"Who more worthy than blood of the First?"

"Oh, I don't know..." W'rath began.

"I fought at the Eastern Glade as well," K'hul interrupted. "I rallied the warriors when my father and Councilor Scald perished. I *shall* be offered a seat."

*Unless, of course, you and that armor of yours topple overboard and sink like a stone.* "Then I suppose congratulations are in order," W'rath said, bowing gracefully. "On behalf of Councilor Raven and myself, allow me to welcome you to the High Council."

So startled by W'rath's graciousness, K'hul started to return the bow before the rest of the Shadow Elf's words sunk in. "Wha—what? What!"

"Ah, I'm sorry, I assumed you knew," W'rath said, all innocence. "Since Lady Swiftbrook was the only councilor present at Second Home to survive the attack, she exercised her right to appoint two worthy individuals to the posts left vacant by the untimely demise of the Shadow Elf councilors."

"That's impossible! You're Exiles—you're not even citizens of the Elven Nation!"

K'hul's shouts drew attention from the mostly Sky Elf crew. W'rath smiled at them apologetically. "For heroic actions in service to the Elven Nation, we have been granted that honor," he said, quietly, in his most maddeningly pleasant voice.

"A councilor can't grant that honor without the approval of others. It requires at least three witnesses."

"Try fifty."

K'hul glared at the Sky Elf approaching them. W'rath hadn't caught the fellow's name, but recognized him as one of those Raven had rescued.

He had rallied the others to stand with their savior. "We all swear to the heroism of Lady Raven and Lord W'rath," he said. "Without them, all of us, even you, Lord K'hul, would have perished."

Without another word, the Sky Elf walked purposely to the containment collar and picked it up from deck where it lay. He carried it to the side of the ship and hurled it as far as he could. It hit the ocean with a quiet splash and disappeared. A great cheer went up from the crew.

ЖЖЖЖЖ

Raven stirred, rousing herself. The heat from the bath made it difficult to stay awake. Lady Swiftbrook entered the room, a bundle of clothing in her arms. K'hul's angry, incredulous bellows echoed off the walls. "Well, the halfling is out of the bag," the Sky Elf said.

A few seconds later cheers replaced K'hul's tantrum. "What is going on?" Raven asked. The curious commotion had wakened her fully, and she strained to hear more clearly.

"If I had to guess, I'd say Lord W'rath *accidently* let slip that I named you and him to the High Council. I expected K'hul to react... loudly."

"Gods!" Raven gasped. "I don't know that I blame him. Isn't it rash to appoint two strange Exiles to such important positions?"

"Definitely," Lady Swiftbrook said. "I have no doubts concerning your honor and goodness, but I saw your transformation, so I know I've appointed a child to the council. As for W'rath... I don't want to imagine where he popped up from. No one would have allowed him through the gates of the city looking like something an owlbear coughed up. That means he had to have wandered in after the fighting started. He's a smartass and too clever by half. Indeed, I expect to regret ever having met him.

"However, as you will soon see, regardless of these concerns, you two are not only the best, but the *only* choices for filling the vacancies on the High Council."

"That's unsettling."

"You've no idea. Ancestors, *I* have no idea. It's been years since we've seen any Shadow Elves aside from T'sane or Reaper. The two wouldn't allow any of the other Shadow Elves to mingle with the rest of us. As much as I tried to work with T'sane and Reaper, I couldn't convince them they didn't carry the taint of the Traitor. They refused to fight for the rights of those they represented since they felt all of them bore the stain of Umbral's legacy.

"Despite your youth and W'rath's guile, I believe you two could be the best thing to happen to the Shadow Elves in quite some time. I can only hope you won't despise the rest of us when you see what your people have been reduced to."

"Do you lobotomize your males?" Raven said, her eyes haunted.

"Lo...? Ancestors! No, of course not! We have the suppression collars to control their powers. That's barbaric enough."

"Then you have nothing to fear. No matter how badly you think you treat the Shadow Elves, it's nothing compared to the cruelties the Exiles visit upon their own."

Raven captured the sponge floating near her and vigorously scrubbed herself. Lady Swiftbrook put down the clothing she had brought and sat down on a nearby storage chest. She had changed out her bloodstained and savaged armor for a blue gown. Her silver tresses shown in the light cast by some glow balls floating along the walls. "How long was I out?" Raven asked, trying to ignore the heaviness of her past.

"A few hours. W'rath's blast knocked us all out, but you must have taken the worst of it, being so close to him. Fortunately, nothing came along and finished us off."

Raven bit back her instinctive inclination to correct her. W'rath probably thought nothing of misleading people, but it felt unnatural to her. But he'd said she shouldn't allow others to find out about her new talent for magic. Sadly, he was probably right. "And the ship? How did we get here?"

"When we awoke, we activated the Eastern Glade portal and fled the city. One of our trade ships, *The First's Dream*, had just left port from the human city of Ulan, and made a detour to Second Home to retrieve us. So few of us survived the attack, we easily fit on board.

We *abandoned* our city. What have we become?" She turned her eyes toward the ceiling as she tried to maintain her composure. The tears spilled down her cheeks anyway, and she brushed them away with quick, angry sweeps of her elegant hands.

Raven looked away. She had asked much the same question as she watched the people of her city go about their tragic lives. That she'd escaped that place of horrors still seemed a miracle to her, made all the more amazing by her savior—her father.

Most denizens of her former home considered Raven's mother, Isil Eledhwen, lenient, even soft. She didn't lobotomize her males. Instead, she kept their heads encased in helmets that suppressed their powers. In that sense the helmets acted much in the say way the containment collars the elves of First Home used. However, the helmets had the added ability to administer punishment when desired. Raven cringed in her bath as the males' sobbing screams filled her memory.

Soft or no, Isil remained merciless in one area when dealing with her males. Those she took to her bed, who failed to give her the one thing she desired most, a female heir, did not survive. Dozens died because their seed resulted in yet another unwanted son. Once her fury cooled, Isil would regret the deaths, not because she felt anything for those who had died by her hand, but because the males' deaths meant money wasted. To regain some of her losses she sold the boy babies as breeder stock to other households. It wasn't until she acquired a male during a successful raid on a rival city, that her dream finally came true. While not particularly gifted in the psionic area, Raven's father managed to do what no other male had—provide his mistress with a daughter.

As a reward, and because Isil deemed him harmless, she freed him from his helmet and allowed him to wander about the household freely. Isis even provided him with a pair of gnome servants. Most considered him privileged to the point of being spoiled.

Of course, regardless of the small kindnesses, he was still no more than chattel. He had endured many indignities, but Raven thought the worst humiliation came from her mother loaning him out to friendly households for stud services. One family in particular, Raven recalled, had experimented with adding Shadow Elf hybrids to their numbers.

They had acquired female surface elves from somewhere and used them as broodmares in the hopes of breeding natural born Shadow Elves with a talent for magic. She had never seen any of the resulting offspring, but she'd heard they inherited their mother's greater strength and height. *Very much like my transformation.*

"You ready to come out of there? You're going to shrivel up." Lady Swiftbrook's had forced her earlier distress from the surface, and she seemed as elegant and gracious as someone who hadn't just lost thousands of her people to a senseless attack. She held up a towel for Raven to wrap herself in.

While Raven dried off, Lady Swiftbrook put out the clothing she'd brought in. "I'm afraid it's not going to fit well. You're built more like a First Born, but the ship's crew is made up of Sky Elves. It's going to be a tight fit.

Raven accepted the tunic and pulled it on. Indeed, it proved very tight in the shoulders and chest. Less than a day had passed when she had been as scrawny as a stick. Now she stood over two feet taller, and found herself endowed with both muscles and curves. Suddenly self conscious, she crossed her arms over her new breasts. Thank the gods she didn't have to face K'hul now. She doubted she could keep her voice steady. She sat down on a storage locker, certain her legs were about to betray her.

"I'm sorry," Lady Swiftbrook said, misreading her distress. "I didn't mean to dredge up so many terrible memories. Still, I admit, I'm curious how you managed to escape your city. For that matter, what made you realize you *could* leave?"

Raven gave a wan smile. As bad as her past had been, she welcomed the distraction. This new life she'd stumbled into filled her with so much uncertainty, she didn't want to focus on it. Better to deal with things she'd come to terms with years before.

"Believe it or not, my father helped me escape," she said. "My father played his role as the docile male perfectly, and tricked my mother into thinking him harmless. It turned out, while he wasn't much gifted in terms of psionics, he had other talents. Clever and patient, he insinuated himself into my life as much as possible. When my mother wasn't looking, he'd give me small gifts—lovely minerals, a jar of subterranean glow mist, a book about surface world insects—over the course of many years.

"On their eighteenth birthday every female in my city undergoes a ritual. Only about half survive, but those who do gain demonic power. They're forever tainted with the essence of the demon they... absorb, but for most the lure of power generally overcomes any qualms they might have.

"I was terrified. I wanted no part of the ritual. My mother must have realized I wasn't of the proper mindset as she went to great pains to deceive me about the ritual's nature. My father, of course, made sure I knew every gruesome detail. I begged him to help me. He said, despite the dangers, he could have me smuggled out of the city, and escorted to the surface world.

"I realize now he'd already made the arrangements—probably years in advance. I was too naïve at the time to understand, so when my father's people attacked my escort on the way to the ritual, I was just as surprised as those tasked with taking me to my doom. The attackers didn't make a single sound. They executed every single servant and guard. They knocked me unconscious and spirited me away. When I awoke they told me they implicated a rival of my mother's. Supposedly, the two families have fought ever since."

Lady Swiftbrook had sunk down onto another storage chest. Belatedly, she realized her mouth hung open and shut it with a sharp click of teeth. "That is one of the most incredible stories I've ever heard," she said. "Whatever happened to your father? He didn't suddenly gain incredible psionic ability?" The Sky Elf looked toward the upper deck.

"W'rath? Oh, gods no," Raven burst out laughing. "I've never seen him before today. I have no idea what to make of him. Even my father, who plotted to steal my mother's most cherished possession, always remained quiet and differential—even to me. I believe this one would tweak the nose of the Traitor himself.

"But my father? I don't know what happened to him. He wasn't there when I woke up. I asked, but all his people would tell me was that he still had a lot of work to do, and couldn't see me off. From what little I learned, he's only one of many who help Exiles escape so they can start new lives away from people like my mother. I think they hoped I would join them, but the lure of the surface world pulled at me, and I insisted they take me there.

"Once there, I made contact with some Wood Elves and they introduced me to others who had made their way to the surface to start over. I spent three years there and then made my way to Second Home to study. And now..." she shrugged, bemused.

"I'd like to tell you that your trials are over," Lady Swiftbrook said. Finally remembering the leggings she held, she passed them to the Shadow Elf. "But you'll have your work cut out for you once we reach First Home. Despite the passage of so many years, quite a number of the People, especially the First Born, don't easily trust Shadow Elves. Some ten generations have passed, yet most First Born act as if Umbral tried to assassinate the First just yesterday."

"I noticed. Lord K'hul seemed less than pleased to make my and W'rath's acquaintance."

"He takes his role as descendant of the First very seriously. His father was among those who perished at the Eastern Glade, and K'hul desires to step into the position of First Among Equals. While all members of the High Council receive a vote for all major decisions, the closest blood descendent of the First provides the deciding vote for any ties that occur."

Raven sighed. "That explains his hostility. How awful to lose his father like that. If only we had arrived sooner, we might have saved him."

"Don't start down that road. K'hul held no love for his father. He's wanted onto the council since before he turned a hundred. His father had no interest in stepping down from his position. Today's disaster not only removed Councilor K'hul as an obstacle, but gave his son a chance to shine as *War Leader*, and ensure no one will deny him the chance to fill the vacancy his father's death opened up."

Raven grimaced in disgust, but refrained from speaking out against K'hul. If Raven's mother dropped dead at her feet, she wouldn't shed a tear. She had no right to judge K'hul.

"K'hul is a difficult person to fathom. I won't claim you'll come to love or even like him, but I expect you'll come to know him as a worthy representative of the First Born. He and whomever we choose for the other vacancy."

"You lost both First Born representatives?"

Lady Swiftbrook nodded. "All told we lost five councilors today. In addition to both First Born and both Shadow Elf representatives, we lost Lady Stormchaser for the Sky Elves. If not for W'rath, I would have perished as well. Fortunately, neither the Wood Elf or Sea Elf councilors were present during the attack. Even so, we're faced with replacing half of the High Council."

"Who could have done this?"

"Determining that, Councilor Raven, shall be our first order of business when the council next convenes."

*So, who did you lot annoy*? W'rath tapped his chin and gazed out to sea. Despite the knowledge he'd picked up from the dying female Shadow Elf, terrible gaps in what he knew about the current state of the world left him frustrated and uncertain. When he'd last walked this plane, no glorious elven ships swept across the seas. The ocean had been deadly with volcanoes and undersea earthquakes. Boiling chemicals, more akin to acid than sea water, covered the planet. The politics had been simple. There were elves and then everyone else. The goblinoid races and their allies sat at the top of the hate list, but in truth any being competing for the limited resources of the savage world could expect to get smashed down by elven magic or weapons. He vaguely remembered humans. Pitiful and primitive, even compared to orcs, they had found themselves at a terrible disadvantage. The dragons had briefly taken the humans under their wing and begun to teach them. W'rath had personally ensured that alliance dissolved quickly. Dealt a terrible blow, the surviving humans had loped back to the caves and swamps to hide from the world. Even as his father had forced him through the gateway into the Abyss, W'rath had felt certain he'd ensured the extinction of the ape-like humans.

*Well, you called that one wrong, old boy.* As best he could tell, the humans had not only survived, but had become one of the most dominant races the world had ever seen. Their cities covered the lands. The elves even traded with some of the friendlier human countries. Countries! Yet another concept he didn't quite grasp.

A contingent of Sea Elves swam past the bow and W'rath watched as they continued down along the starboard side. They'd traveled with the ship since they'd left port, keeping alert for trouble for several miles around the ship. He'd yet to meet one, though he'd at least heard of them. The Wood Elves he'd heard the ship's crew members refer to, were completely new to him. He had a great deal to catch up on, but he'd have to take care to hide just how little he knew. Even a former Exile like Raven knew the basics of the world. If he didn't cover his ignorance well enough, people would notice. Curiosity would eventually lead to suspicions. Things would deteriorate from there.

He inhaled and nearly choked. So used to the ash laden filth that passed for air in the Abyss, his lungs rebelled against the invading sea air. Everything ached too, and his head felt ready to explode. *You're a mess. Don't you dare pass out with that golden-haired half-nephew of yours watching.*

From out of the corner of his eye he saw a group of young Sky Elves huddled together. One of them slouched and broke away from the pack, dragging his feet as he came across the deck toward W'rath. Even though he towered over W'rath, he twitched with nerves.

"You draw the short straw, lad?"

The youngster turned scarlet and glared over his shoulder at the others who watched expectantly. When W'rath switched his attention to them, they split up and started to fuss with jobs that didn't need doing.

"So, did Lady Swiftbrook order me thrown overboard after all, and you're the poor wretch who has to deliver the news?"

"Oh, no, Councilor—nothing like that!" the boy said, almost in a panic. He fidgeted and tugged at a silver lock of hair as he struggled to find the proper words. "It's just, um, sir... Well, no one is much fond of standing downwind of you."

"You Sky Elves have very delicate noses," W'rath said, sniffing at his shoulder. He grimaced. "All right, I do seem a bit ripe. Slogging through demon entrails can have that affect on a person. I assume you have a solution for this terrible state I find myself in?"

The sailor visibly brightened, W'rath's attitude taking him by surprise. "We've prepared a bath for you below decks," he said. "And we have someone who knows several handy cantrips. She thinks she can, um, *detangle* your hair."

"Or we could just shave the whole mess off and let you start from scratch," purred Lady Swiftbrook, joining them. Behind her a freshly scrubbed and dressed Raven fought to hide a smirk.

"I'll have you know, madam, I am rather vain. I merely misplaced my comb a few years back and have not had the opportunity to acquire a new one. If you don't mind, I shall forego the sheers, and enlist the aid of the young lady with her arsenal of cantrips."

Lady Swiftbrook gaped. "You actually have the gall to stand there and claim that solid mass has ever known the kiss of a comb?"

"It *was* a very trying few years."

Raven hid a smile behind her hand and Lady Swiftbrook rolled her eyes. She stepped aside, waving to the young sailor. "Please, sir, get him to his bath. And while he's soaking, do us all a favor and burn that thing he's wearing."

"I made this myself," W'rath said, for all the world sounding hurt.

"You're supposed to cure the leather before fashioning it into clothing. If you stand there much longer it shall simply rot off and we shall never manage to scrub that sight from our minds."

"Since that is your attitude, I suppose I'd best return these to their owner," W'rath said, digging about in what was turning out to be a kilt with some amazing storage capacity. He withdrew the three slim books he'd retrieved from the gore-covered ground of Second Home. He presented them to Raven.

Raven accepted them gratefully. "Thank you," she said. "With all that happened I forgot about them. Losing them would have been awful."

"Your smile is thanks enough, lady," W'rath replied. "Pity though..."

"What?"

"Ah, it just occurred to me I rather prefer your earlier state of dress over this one."

"But I didn't... Oh!"

W'rath deftly sidestepped Lady Swiftbrook's attempt to slap him, pausing just long enough to bow to the two flustered females before drawing himself up regally, and following after the young sailor to the promised bath.

ЖЖЖЖЖ

The water was so hot W'rath thought he had probably burned off a couple layers of skin. Even so, he found it the most wonderful of experiences. The heat of the rising steam eased his lungs, and the aches that had assailed him all but disappeared. His head continued to scream, and he suspected he had done quite a lot of damage to himself by overusing his psionics. Even so he couldn't recall ever feeling so content.

When the sailor had first brought him to the room, the young lady with the cantrips had waited by the door. She explained to him how she normally used her spells to straighten out nets, tangled rigging and rope, but saw no reason why she couldn't apply the same principles to hair. In the end, she'd had to cast her little spell eleven times, but her efforts paid off. W'rath sank beneath the surface of the water and let his freed tresses float about the top. Yes, this was very close to pure ecstasy.

When he surfaced, he found Lady Swiftbrook standing a few feet away, in the doorway, a wry smile on her face. "I thought for a minute you had simply dissolved," she said.

W'rath pushed his hair out of his face. "Merely enjoying the full experience."

"The full experience includes the use of soap and a sponge. If you can't manage, I'm sure I can find someone with too much free time to come ensure every nook and cranny gets scrubbed."

"You seem intent on playing mother, madam. You're more than welcome to scrub my back."

"Careful, or I'll ask Lord K'hul to come down here and bathe you. Somehow I don't think you'd much enjoy his attentions."

W'rath made a face. "A decidedly unpleasant character. It's tragic that a lady of your obvious intelligence would..."

"Do not finish that sentence. My personal life is of no concern to you. However, that does bring me to another subject—Lady Raven."

Lady Swiftbrook stepped into the small room, and made a show of placing the bundle of clothing she'd brought onto one of the benches lining the wall. When she turned back, W'rath had settled back against the tub, and dutifully scrubbed his arms and shoulders with the sponge. He cocked his head at her intently as if awaiting whatever wisdom she chose to bestow upon him. She placed her fists on her slim hips in irritation. "Is everything a game to you?"

"Not at all, madam. Thousands of dead elves... I take that very seriously."

W'rath's sudden switch to sincerity took her by surprise. He was as changeable as the sea and about as easy to control. Her annoyance flamed up a tad higher.

"But you wanted to discuss Lady Raven? She's a bright star of hope in this otherwise dismal situation. I fail to see why you approach the subject of her in such a dour manner."

Lady Swiftbrook's left eye twitched. "You're trying to keep me unbalanced and it's not going to work."

"It already has."

"Gah!" She squeezed her eyes shut for a moment and then grasped the edge of the tub, bending over so she could look W'rath directly in the eye. "Enough of the games. I've seen you leering at her."

"Admiring, not leering. She's an incredibly lovely lady," W'rath said.

"She's also, despite appearances, a young, inexperienced girl. You and I both saw her before she transformed, so don't pretend otherwise. Your smartass flirting is out of place, and if you have some fancy idea about bedding her, you'll have to go through me first."

W'rath politely refrained from commenting on the obvious interpretation one could take with her words, but she realized what she'd said and flushed. "You know what I mean," she muttered, her eyes darting to an empty corner.

W'rath continued to scrub himself and studied Lady Swiftbrook. If he narrowed his eyes, with the aid of the steam, he could almost imagine Uruviel Stormchaser stood before him. She too had often had an angry tirade sputter out due to a poor turn of phrase. A sad smile twitched at his lips. She had been his only friend in those dark days. He could certainly use one now as well. Alienating this proud, angry lady over this, especially when he agreed with her, would be foolish. He sighed. "I apologize, madam. I've lacked polite company for far too long. I swear to you I shall conduct myself in an honorable manner in regards to Lady Raven."

Lady Swiftbrook's gaze drifted back from the corner. "You won't lay a hand on her until she's at least a hundred?"

W'rath resisted the urge to ask what was so significant about turning a hundred, and instead raised his hands out of the water. "Not even a finger. And most certainly not without her permission."

The Sky Elf nodded her approval. "You're turning into a prune," she noted.

W'rath examined his puckered fingers in dismay. "I would get out, but I believe I've already scandalized you enough for one day."

"Try a year," she said. "There's clothing for you there. You'll find it's too big, but it will have to do until we make land."

With that she swept out. Just outside, a male First Born waited, brow furrowed. He had, no doubt, been posted there to make sure nothing improper went on while the lady visited the naked barbarian in the tub. W'rath pinched the bridge of his nose. All of this prudishness and stuffy decorum would take some getting used to. *If only you genteel folk knew how your beloved "The First" had actually behaved. What a rude awakening that would be.*

ЖЖЖЖЖ

When W'rath finally made his way back to the top deck he saw no sign of Lady Swiftbrook or his unpleasant half-nephew, but a crestfallen Raven had claimed a bit of shade for herself.

"I thought I would find you deeply engrossed in your books," he said.

She head shot up, startled, and stared at him as if he'd sprouted horns and a tail. "It's the clothes, isn't it?" he said, fussing with the too long sleeves. "It must appear as if the wretched stuff is consuming me."

"That's not it at all. I flat out didn't recognize you. You clean up well."

"Truly?" W'rath said, genuinely surprised.

She gave a shy smile in response and gestured for him to join her. "I'm not reading the books because I've discovered I can't. The writing looks vaguely Elvish, but I can't for the life of me decipher it. The lady who gave them to me said they'd been in her family for ten generations. I'm assuming they're so old our language has changed to the point where it might just as well be Orcish."

"I'm sure given time you will learn to read them," W'rath said.

"Sure—maybe in a year, with a good instructor, I can learn, but I want to read them now."

"Ah, the impatience of youth."

Raven gave him a sour look. "It's not just that... Councilor Stormchaser implied the contents were important for me to know. Important for us, to all the Shadow Elves."

"Did you say Stormchaser?"

"Did you know her?"

"No, but I do know the name, and you should too. The Stormchasers can trace their lineage all the way back to the beginning. Most likely, Uverial Stormchaser was the original owner of those books. She's responsible for creating the first written form of our language—or at least what passed for our language back then."

"Of course! I knew that. I don't know where my head has been that I didn't make the connection," Raven said, pulling the books back out to stare at them, her expression trapped somewhere between frustration and wonder. "I guess I'll have to consult the scholars on First Home, but honestly I'm not sure it's a good idea to share the contents too freely. I think these books may hold the full truth about Umbral and the First, and I'm not sure that will go over well with a lot of people."

"The truth? What a remarkable young lady you are."

"How so?"

"As you said, people won't welcome the information contained in those pages if it refutes their beliefs. People don't take it well when they find their heroes aren't as noble, nor their villains as utterly despicable, as they've been taught. It takes a great deal of courage to challenge such deeply held beliefs."

"Or stupidity. But it doesn't matter—I can't read them, and if they do hold anything truly controversial, someone will make sure they disappear."

"Or you could let me have a go at them," W'rath suggested.

"You can read ancient Elvish?" Raven breathed in deep, eyes going huge.

"I *am* more than just devilishly handsome."

"I don't recall phrasing it quite that way, but sure I'll give you that." Raven handed the books over and watched expectantly as he shuffled through them. W'rath settled on a red-bound volume and flipped it open to the first entry. He frowned. He turned a few more pages. His frown deepening. He squinted. He held his arms out from himself as far as he could.

"What's wrong?" Raven asked.

"Are there truly words on these pages?"

"Yes, they're plain as day. The books are ancient, but the ink looks like someone placed it there yesterday. It's crisp and clear and utterly indecipherable. Can't you see anything on the pages?"

"Just a blur. Someone must have imbued the pages with magic. Perhaps only the person gifted the books from the previous owner can read them."

"Or," Raven grinned, "you're incredibly near blind."

She took back the books, got up and moved several feet away. She opened one and aimed the open pages back toward W'rath. "What do you see now?"

"Fascinating," W'rath said. "I can see it now, just as you said. I've never heard of *near blind*."

Raven came back over. "And I've never met anyone ancient enough to *be* near blind." She laughed at his offended look. "*Near-* or *farblindedness* are about the only ways to tell if an elf is truly ancient—at least five thousand or more. Even though we don't age like other races, we do tend to adapt to whatever lifestyle we've lead. A scholar over time may develop very acute vision for reading at the expense of their distance vision. You sir, seem to have spent most of your life avoiding books. I suspected you were old, but now I have confirmation."

"Hmmm, that's inconvenient."

"It *will* raise questions in people's minds if that's what you're thinking."

"Indeed. Not to mention I'll find it annoying to have to read a book from across the room. I'll need my psionics to turn the pages."

Raven laughed again. "We can fix that particular problem easily enough. We have optics which will allow you to read up close. But someone will have to make them for you, and then the speculation will begin."

"And why exactly do you think that would concern me?"

Raven looked at him levelly. "Is W'rath your given name or your family name?"

"As far as K'hul is concerned it's my family name, and *Lord* should precede it at all times. On the other hand, you and Lady Swiftbrook may forego the honorific."

"In other words, it's something you made up."

W'rath chuckled. "And you're going to tell me Raven is your given name? It doesn't even have the sound of an Elven word."

"Ah, you're right, it's not. It's a northern human word for the first living thing I saw when I came to the surface world. It sounded exotic to me, and, well, I felt a new life deserved a new name."

"Precisely, a chance for a new beginning."

Raven gave him a crooked smile. "That's won't satisfy a lot of people. You practically bleed secrets. Your age is just one more thing which will pique their curiosity."

"If people wish to know where I came from, they should ask me. Not a single person, not even yourself, have questioned me about anything."

"Well, I just assumed that Lady Swiftbrook..."

"Exactly, you assumed." W'rath made a dismissive gesture. "Not to worry though, in the coming days, I expect First Home and its citizens will have much greater concerns than one mysterious Shadow Elf."

# CHAPTER 5

A cry of horror, followed by wracking sobs stirred Ryld from his stupor. He'd slipped into a torpor, staring into the black for... well, in truth he had no idea how long he'd been like that. Hours blurred into days in this hell he called home. He turned to his twin who half sat, half lay to Ryld's left. "Caeldan," he said. His voice broke from lack of use. He tried again. "Caeldan."

"Hmmm?" came the drowsy reply.

"Is that Seer?"

"What?"

"Don't you hear the crying?"

"Oh, I thought I was dreaming. I didn't know Seer could actually drum up that much emotion."

"She *is* stoic," Ryld agreed.

Caeldan snorted. "That's putting it nicely. Don't you get sick of hearing how we deserve to rot in this hole?"

"You know I do."

Caeldan groaned and struggled to his feet. Shaking with exertion, he swayed, bowed legs threatening to buckle. "What are you doing?" Ryld asked.

"You're the one who woke me because Seer's finally lost it. I'm damned well going to see what can bring that martyr to tears. Come on."

Ryld used the cave wall to help him stand. The world spun and he nearly went down again. How long since he'd eaten? Not that it really mattered. The subterranean fungus that made up the bulk of their diet couldn't possibly provide what their bodies needed to survive. *We'd be dead by now if we weren't elves.* But even Mother Magic could only do so much. If something didn't change soon, they'd wither away and simply cease to exist. Worse, it had become increasingly difficult to care.

"You coming? Or would you and the wall like to be alone?"

"Get stuffed," Ryld replied, but staggered after Caeldan, back into the underground castle built for them thousands of years past. More like an elegant, unkempt prison these days.

It was slow going. They both had to stop and catch their breath several times, but eventually they found Seer. She sat hunched on the floor, face buried in the woven mat covering the wood, hysterical sobs emanating from her huddled form. Three other members of their sickly community crouched around her. They reached out to her, but fear kept them from actually touching her. They peered up as the twins approached, their bulging eyes making them resemble terrified frogs.

"What's going on?" Ryld asked.

"Seer had a vision," the one called Seismis said. His voice shook and he seemed on the verge of wringing his spider-like hands.

Ryld and Caeldan exchanged looks and shrugged. They squatted down next to Seer. Caeldan took her by the shoulder, giving her a little shake to get her attention.

Seer continued to wail until Ryld grabbed her chin and forced her to look at him and Caeldan. She gaped at them through her sparse, tangled hair, her grey skin slick with tears. "Ryld... Caeldan," she said as if returning from a dream. Not surprising, her visions always had that affect on her. Being female, she wasn't collared, as most female Shadow

Elves had so little psychic power they weren't considered a threat. Seer had only one true psychic gift, but it was a powerful one; she saw visions of events as they happened, and physical distance in no way hampered her abilities.

"What did you see?" Ryld asked. A trickle of dread made its way down his spine. Something truly awful must have happened. Only something disastrous could reduce Seer to such a state.

Seer's face crumpled. "Second Home is no more," she managed. "Thousands perished. Less than two hundred survived."

"Traitor's balls!" Caeldan gasped. Face twisting, Seer began to sob again. The brothers released her and she collapsed, burying her face in her hands.

"How could this happen?" Ryld asked. He looked to the others, but only blank, frightened faces surrounded him. They had no more answers than he did.

"They failed!" Seer suddenly screeched out.

"What? Make sense. Who failed?"

"Lord T'sane and Lady Reaper," Seer howled. "They had their chance to redeem us, but they failed. They died and now we're alone and still unclean."

"That again," Caeldan snarled.

"Always the same story, Seer," Ryld sighed. "Why can't you get it through your head that what happened ten generations ago isn't our fault?"

"You're wrong," Seer said, pulling strength from her fanaticism to fix the twins with a deranged glare. She reached out with talon-like hands to clutch at their clothing. "We all carry Umbral's taint. Only in selfless service to the Elven Nation can we escape his legacy. Now our only hope for redemption is gone. None of us have enough strength to do more than die, cursed and unworthy of the First's forgiveness."

"Would you listen to that?" Ryld said, brushing away Seer's grasping hand with ill-concealed contempt. "Close to half the elven population gets wiped out and the only thing she cares about is T'sane and Reaper's failure to hold back a devastating attack."

He took stock of everyone. He knew Caeldan shared his views, but the others stared at him as if he babbled nonsense. "What will happen to us?" Seismis whispered, tears starting to fall from his eyes. His two companions joined him.

"All of you have gone mad," Caeldan hissed. "T'sane and Reaper ordered us to stay down here—they're the reason we've grown sick and weak, and yet you lot act as if they were benevolent guardians. They're why we're pathetic, sick and loathed. Traitor's balls! This is our chance to break free of their cycle of self-hatred." He tried to stand, but his legs failed him, and he had to settle for waving his hands in exasperation.

"That's the most I've heard you speak in ten years," Ryld said, impressed "Too bad it's wasted on the insane."

"Screw this! They're dead, they can't force me to sit here in the dark any longer. I'm marching up there and putting the two of us forward as candidates for the High Council." Caeldan tried to struggle to his feet again, sputtering in frustration.

"We only just turned fifty-two," Ryld said, dubious."

"So? Name one person down here who's over a hundred. There's no adults left, and you and I are the only ones who still have any self-esteem."

"They've already named new councilors," Seer said, her voice now so soft they almost didn't hear her.

"Who?" Ryld said, genuinely curious. As his brother had said, only a few of them still lived and not a one had reached adulthood.

"Two Exiles," Seer said. "Outsiders hold our fate in their hands now."

Ryld and Caeldan cocked identical eyebrows. "Fascinating," they said simultaneously.

"You thinking what I'm thinking?" Ryld asked.

"They must have killed half the enemy by themselves," Caeldan said.

"Yeah. To not only gain citizenship, but to be named to the High Council? That's unheard of," Ryld marveled.

Caeldan chewed on his lower lip, a sure sign he'd arrived at a decision. "I think we need to meet these two," he said.

"I don't want to wait for them to come down here and find us huddling in the dark."

"No, we should go to meet them on the surface," Caeldan agreed.

"Right. Seer, how long 'til they arrive at First Home?"

"Three days," she said. The emotion had drained from her as if her previous outbursts had exhausted her ability to feel. If anything, it was worse than her wailing.

Ryld frowned. "It's at least two miles to the surface."

"In our current state..." Caeldan began.

Ryld cut him off. "You three, stop your blubbering and go find the others. Tell them to meet us here, and to bring what food and water they can carry. If anyone has any of those blind cave fish, those would be best."

Seismis turned away, sullen. "What's the point?"

"Just do it, and then you can go back to feeling sorry for yourselves."

"They'll want to know why," one of the others piped up. Ryld couldn't quite remember his name. Riva? Rica? No, that wasn't it. Bugger all.

"Tell them Umbral called and he said to grow some spines. The Elven Nation needs us," Caeldan said with a grunt, finally finding his feet, and waving for the rest of them to follow his lead.

Ryld snickered.

"You're both mad," Seer said, her voice still flat.

The twins shared a look. "That's rich," Ryld said, and the two burst out laughing.

⁂

The trip had stretched into its third day. The novelty had faded and W'rath paced, anxious to reach their destination. At night, only a skeleton crew manned the ship, and the sound of sobs drifted up from below decks. Raven, who had gone down there in the hopes of getting some rest, gave up and returned to her spot from earlier in the day.

"I couldn't sleep with all that misery around me," she said, settling down near where W'rath prowled. She drew her knees up and wrapped her arms around them as if trying to comfort herself.

"Sleep," W'rath said, shaking his head. The concept of sleep struck him as foreign. He understood it no better than he did the elves hiding below decks, crippled by their grief. During his childhood, no enemy alive would have dared launch an attack, such as the one visited upon Second Home, against the elves. Of course, the elves of that time couldn't have conceived of a society where a thousand soldiers would be expected to protect many times that number of helpless sheep. Every elf would have carried a weapon, known how to use it, and fallen upon the enemy with untold ferocity. True, against such a foe, they'd have still suffered terrible losses, but, in the end, not a single demon or devil would have survived. Instead of slinking off in defeat, leaving the remains of their kin in the hands of the surviving fiends, the elves would be honoring their dead and restoring their city.

And this sleep thing? Lying unconscious for several hours provided a perfect opportunity for your enemies to take you unawares. Insanity.

"How can you pace around like that?" Raven wanted to know. "Aren't you exhausted."

"I meditated earlier. I need time for my brain to heal itself before I can use my psionics again, but aside from that, I'm fine."

"Everyone needs sleep." She raised an eyebrow, skeptical.

"Elves do not. I have no idea how such foolishness got started, but since we are the embodiment of magic we regenerate. Barring severe injury, we have no reason to fall unconscious for the sake of rest. Meditation takes care of our mental fatigue."

"So you really don't sleep?" Raven asked.

"Sleep gets you killed, lass," he replied.

The night passed, chased away by the sun. Despite all W'rath had said, Raven slumbered in her patch of shade. She'd scrounged up a satchel from somewhere, and was using it to store her precious journals. As she slept, she kept the satchel tucked under her head as an impromptu pillow.

W'rath shook sighed and searched for something to take away some of the monotony. His gaze settled on the crow's nest, the one place he had yet to explore. Sadly, his injury left him in no condition to teleport up there, so he would have to climb.

Climbing was as second nature to W'rath as walking. Survival in the Abyss meant treating even the most mundane act as a combat maneuver, practicing to the point where it required no thought or planning to accomplish. He'd perfected his skills at moving unseen. Even in daylight he could remain nearly undetectable. As such, the sharp-eyed sailor manning the crow's nest didn't notice the Shadow Elf's approach until W'rath nimbly climbed in with him. The sailor let out an involuntary squawk, nearly jumping out of the crow's nest when W'rath appeared next to him, seemingly out of thin air.

"Hope you don't mind, lad," W'rath said, pretending he hadn't noticed the sailor's brief bout with terror. "My first ship, and I'm trying to take it all in."

"No, of course not, Councilor," the sailor said, voice a few octaves higher than normal. He cursed and started to fumble for a thin tube of burning paper that had fallen from his lips when he'd panicked.

"What is that?" W'rath asked. The smoke slipped into his lungs and cleared away the ache put there by the fresh salt air.

"Sorry, sir, just a bad habit I picked up down south. That's why I get stuck with crow's nest duty. No one wants to smell the burning tobacco. It's why everyone calls me Stench."

"No need to apologize, lad. You needn't put out your burning stick either. After all, I'm the one invading your space. In fact, if you have another?"

Stench blinked. "None rolled, I'm afraid. At least not like this one. I have these others I rolled—there's cloves and other spices mixed in with the tobacco leaves. I thought I'd like them, but they just don't agree with me."

"Those will do," W'rath said, and the surprised sailor fished one out for W'rath, lighting it with the tip of the one he'd finally managed to retrieve from the floor of crow's nest. He handed it to W'rath.

“Takes some getting used to,” Stench said. “You pull the smoke down into your lungs. Don’t worry about the coughing, you’ll get used to it.”

He stopped talking when he realized the Shadow Elf had not succumbed to a coughing fit, and in fact, appeared as though he found the burning air he inhaled soothing.

W’rath blew clove scented smoke into the early afternoon air. “Lad, you are a life saver,” he said. “I refuse to call you Stench. What is your proper name?”

“Elaugh’den, Councilor.”

“So tell me, young Elaug’den, how does Councilor K’hul feel about this... smoking?”

“Loathes it, sir.”

“Ah, lad, you have just made my day.”

ЖЖЖЖЖ

The would-be welcoming party sank to the ground and sprawled on the hard stone path, panting. They’d managed to stagger just a few hundred feet toward the surface of First Home. Of the forty they had cajoled or bullied into making the journey, only thirty remained. Barely into their trek and already ten had given up, too exhausted to go further.

“How embarrassing,” Ryld gasped. “I knew we were in bad shape, but we’re pathetic. Why in the hells did we allow this to happen?”

Caeldan shrugged, still too winded to reply.

“I know we’re just kids, but we should have stood up for ourselves. Reaper and T’sane had no right to keep us down here, cut off from everyone.”

“Haven’t exactly seen any of the other elves coming down to help us,” Caeldan said, between gulps for air.

“When we lived topside our teachers treated us well. They never acted like we were tainted.”

“But they didn’t stand in the way when Reaper and T’sane decided to drag us back down here, did they?” Caeldan countered.

"True, though that would have meant defying members of the High Council," Ryld replied, thoughtful. "I wonder if they realized what awaited us down here?"

"We make it topside, you can ask them."

"We make it out of here, I'm going to want a lot of questions answered."

Caeldan grinned at his brother's newfound fire. "We'd better start moving then. At this rate it'll take us a week to get up there."

"Okay, folks, rest time's over. Let's get going."

Ryld's words elicited many a groan, and even a few curses, filling Caeldan with new hope. If they could manage enough energy to curse his brother, then maybe, sad as they were, they still had some spirit left to them.

⋈⋈⋈⋈⋈

Raven found herself surrounded by demons. They reached for her with dripping talons. She stood helpless as, once again, Linden died trying to protect her. This time, despite her inherent resistance to heat, she burned. The smoke filled her lungs and she struggled for air. With a gasp, she dragged herself from the nightmare.

"At last you rejoin us," W'rath said.

To her chagrin, Raven realized the smoke from her dream had followed her into the waking world. "Gods! You're on fire!" she choked.

"Ah, so dramatic. It's just this bit of rolled paper and leaves. This is the best I've breathed in three days."

Raven waved the smoke away. "You must be part fire elemental if that helps you breath."

A shadow fell over the two and they looked up to find Lady Swiftbrook, arms crossed, glowering at W'rath. "I didn't think it possible for you to make yourself more annoying, and yet here we are."

"I take pride in exceeding people's expectations."

"You *are* a glib one."

"I am at that."

A chuckle escaped Lady Swiftbrook's throat, spoiling her scowl. She shook her head and gave up trying to appear stern. "I actually came to find you because we're getting close to the veil separating us from First Home. Down here in the shade you two can't see where we're headed. If you come up to the quarterdeck, I think you'll find the view quite spectacular."

"Oh, I've heard of it, but never thought I'd get to see it," Raven said, scrambling to her feet, yanking W'rath up as if he weighed no more than her book satchel. "I've heard it makes the colors of the northern lights pale by comparison."

W'rath glared, shaking off her grip in an attempt to regain some dignity. The young female, oblivious, practically bounced with excitement, her eyes alight with the sights of this new world. Lady Swiftbrook felt a smile tugging at her lips. She couldn't remember a single moment with Lord T'sane and Lady Reaper when she'd had any cause to smile. Despite the risks of inviting two Exiles into her home, she believed she had done the right thing.

The three made their way up the stairs to the quarterdeck of the ship. Before them stretched a massive curtain, shimmering in the distance as if made up of molten gems of every hue. "Incredible," W'rath breathed.

"It surpasses all of the tales," Raven said. Her eyes glittered with the reflected light of the veil.

"As beautiful as it is," Lady Swiftbrook said, "it is first and foremost a wall. It prohibits any non-elf from crossing into the waters of First Home."

"What about Exiles?" W'rath fell back to the practical.

"They're elves, so it will allow them to pass."

W'rath sucked thoughtfully on his smoldering twig. "That doesn't strike you as an obvious flaw in your defenses? They could easily teleport an army into First Home and cause all sorts of havoc."

Lady Swiftbrook shook her head. "They'd have a real challenge ahead of them. Exiles live underground, sailing isn't something they excel at. They'd have to build several ships, or get someone to build them for them, and then hire a crew to sail them here. Then they'd have to hope no one, like say the Sea Elves, noticed them and put a stop to their little adventure. Even if they succeeded in getting here, they'd have to teleport blind and that's suicidal."

"Truly?" W'rath said, turning to Raven. "Are psions from your city so incompetent they can only teleport for short distances?"

"I've never heard of any able to go beyond line of sight. Not to mention, most male psions aren't allowed to use their powers much. They certainly don't get the opportunity to practice their craft and develop their skills." Raven winced with the utterance of each word, as if speaking burned her throat with acid. Her joy at the sight of the brilliant wall had withered with the reminder of her people's vile practices.

"Extraordinary," W'rath said. "I'll grant you it takes no small amount of skill to teleport blind, but after our time in Second Home you must realize an experienced psion can manage it quite nicely. I moved over fifty people, without incident, to a place I'd never been to before, with only Lady Swiftbrook's memories to guide me. I find the concept of a distance limitation ridiculous. A foot or a thousand miles matters not. Only those with small imaginations and weak spines allow themselves to suffer such limitations."

Lady Swiftbrook felt the blood drain from her face. "I hope none of them ever figure that out. Where did you learn such fine control?"

W'rath shrugged. "I'm self taught."

He scowled at the dubious glare she gave him. "Living on one's own requires a certain amount of experimentation, daring and quick thinking. As Lady Raven has kindly pointed out, the life a male has to look forward to in a typical Exile city is less than pleasant. If I hadn't taken extraordinary measures and risks, I wouldn't have survived."

"I can't argue with that," Raven said. Her grimace said more than any words could. "I have heard of a few cities where males and females live as equals though," she continued. "I've never actually visited one, so I have no idea if they really exist. They're probably just fanciful tales."

"Probably, but it would be wise to find out for certain," W'rath mused. "I expect if any Exile city had the audacity to attack First Home, the assault would originate from one in which the males had full use of their powers. They would have the freedom to experiment and stretch their abilities."

"Lovely," Lady Swiftbrook muttered. "Bad enough we have some enemy capable of opening portals from the Abyss and the Nine Hells, now I find out even the Veil isn't enough to keep out a truly determined army of Exiles."

"Best you learn that now rather than after they pop into the streets of First Home and start melting people's brains." If W'rath meant his smile to offer reassurance, he failed.

"You're determined to give me nightmares, aren't you?" Lady Swiftbrook said. Her stomach had started to clench, and she suspected she'd gone a bit green. "I don't suppose you have a solution to go along with your dire warning?"

"I leave the details of magic to you, madam," W'rath replied.

"I knew you'd say something like that. Fine, I'll just add it to my growing list of things to deal with when we reach First Home."

Raven suddenly gasped as the ship seemed to shift elsewhere. Even W'rath reflexively grabbed the side of the ship. Lady Swiftbrook grinned, pleased something had finally caught the male unawares. "It's an illusion of sorts. Like a rainbow it always appears someplace you can't quite reach. The disorientation you felt was us passing through it. Look—now it hangs behind us at quite a distance."

"And if we hadn't been elves?" W'rath asked.

"I'm told that most of the time they find themselves off the coast of the southern islands called the Chain of Dragons. Provided the dragons aren't active, they most likely come out of it fine."

W'rath chuckled. "I suppose that's preferable to cluttering up the ocean floor with ships and corpses."

"It's enough of a warning to keep nearly everyone but the most greedy or foolish from making the trip out here. Now, if you'll turn your attention away from our security measures, you can see the tallest spires of your new home."

ЖЖЖЖЖ

The glistening, iridescent structures of First Home rose from the mists. Raven's mouth formed an 'O' and a child-like wonder filled her face. W'rath stared more soberly, not sure what he'd expected, and not sure how he should feel.

"What is that?" Raven said, pointing. From out of the clouds appeared a floating citadel of black glass.

W'rath felt the world reel and he nearly toppled to the deck. Lady Swiftbrook caught him. "By the First, are you all right?" She said. "You've gone grey."

"Jolly fine, madam," he managed with a rueful twist to his lips. He restrained himself from staring at the horrifying structure. That it still existed after all these years, even though everything else had changed so much, was simply staggering.

"I knew you couldn't get by on just meditation," Raven chided, making light of his fainting spell. He noticed her taking surreptitious glances at the citadel, though. She wasn't an idiot. She knew the floating structure was the source of his distress.

"Perhaps you're right, my dear," he said, allowing Lady Swiftbrook to help steady him. A wave of emotion surprised him. He'd only just met the girl, and yet she chose to trust him and keep his secrets. Being so circumspect had to go against her nature. She would demand answers soon. What would he tell her?

"Are you done fainting?" Lady Swiftbrook asked.

"I shall be fine, madam. Just a brief bout of vertigo. These last few days have been... trying." He straightened and made an effort to show he had fully recovered. He gestured at the citadel. "I believe you were about to enlighten us as to the origins of this structure?"

Lady Swiftbrook nodded. "The black citadel," she said, "served as Umbral's prison for the eighty-five years he spent locked up prior to his banishment to the Abyss. The First himself created it from the same volcanic glass he used to form the first Shadow Elves."

"Traitor's Heart," Raven said. "I never knew it floated." She seemed nearly as awed by it as she had the Veil.

"That, and it's enchanted so psions cannot use their powers anywhere in or around its walls. There was concern those loyal to Umbral would attempt to rescue him, so the First ensured Umbral's people could not so much as mind speak with him."

"Does anyone occupy it now?" W'rath asked.

"No, of course not," Lady Swiftbrook said. "No one so villainous has walked among the elves since that time. It's said Umbral had gone raving mad by the time they finally pulled him out to face his banishment. No one wants to subject another elf to such a fate. Now it serves as a monument, a reminder of those dark times."

*Raving mad, eh?* W'rath worked to keep his face neutral. Well, perhaps he had lost his mind, but just a little. After all, they celebrated his one hundredth birthday by dragging him from his dark prison so his father could toss him through a one-way door into a living nightmare. A certain amount of hysteria had been called for. Still young, he'd yet to learn how to put on a stoic front. Leave it to the historians who came after to turn it into something more than a young elf's terror at being fed to monsters.

Dark times indeed. But based on the events these past few days, even darker times had found them. Ten thousand years ago, one angry youth lashed out at his father. When it came down to it, his tantrum should have doomed no one but himself. Whoever, or whatever, had chosen to attack Second Home had succeeded in delivering a devastating blow to the entire Elven Nation.

"We'll arrive soon," Lady Swiftbrook said, breaking into his introspection. This time it was she who looked ready to faint. W'rath understood her distress. In a short time, she would address thousands of her people, and watch as her news crushed their souls.

"How will the people react?" Raven asked.

The Sky Elf shook her head. "We've never faced anything like this before. I have no idea what to expect."

W'rath cocked his head. "How do you want them to react?"

Lady Swiftbrook raised a silver eyebrow. Raven frowned.

"You've discussed your homecoming with K'hul?" W'rath prodded.

"Some. In between arguing about you two."

W'rath chuckled. "Tell me, what would the Supreme Warlord like to see happen?"

"He feels we need to rebuild our army. He expects the attack will incense people enough, each and every one of them will take up arms and swell the ranks."

W'rath shook his head. "We already have proof that won't happen. Only about half the people Raven rescued chose to stand and fight."

"They were traumatized," Raven said. "I'm surprised they weren't driven insane by the ordeal." Her hands clenched on the ship's railing as she struggled with her own memories of the attack.

"Perhaps," W'rath mused. "But if you've faced the worst possible situation, and you're still unwilling to stand up for yourself, despite knowing the results will end in disaster, I fear there isn't much hope of you finding a warrior buried somewhere inside yourself. I believe K'hul shall meet with disappointment if he thinks any more than half the populace will care to join with him."

"Unless?"

"What makes you think there's an *unless*, madam?"

"I haven't known you long, but I've already learned you always have a scheme bubbling about in your brain. So what is it? Use your mind powers to shape the thoughts of the people?" She put on a look of intense concentration and waved her hands about, presumably her attempt to emulate a psion using his mind powers.

W'rath made a face. "I would never resort to something so crude, madam. No, I reserve such mind games for the manipulation of enemies, especially ones whom I plan to dispatch soon. To use such methods on your own people, aside from showing poor manners, does more harm than good. It's also completely unnecessary. It takes skill and timing, but a charismatic leader can reach into his people's souls and convince them they *want* to change."

"In truth, I don't know if I care for such a fundamental change to take place. Our people bring beauty to the world now. We're creators, not destroyers." Lady Swiftbrook saw the frustrated set to W'rath's features and relented somewhat. "It isn't that I'm blind to what you're saying. I see all too plainly the dangers we face. But I also know how hard our ancestors worked to evolve into more than just a massive army of death."

"If we don't fight, everything our ancestors worked for shall be wiped from the pages of history. All their art, writings and structures gone—stolen or destroyed by our enemies." An edge had crept into W'rath's voice. He reached up and pinched out the last embers of his spent cigarette, and Lady Swiftbrook flinched.

"I don't think you need to worry about everyone falling into barbarism," Raven added, worriedly looking from one to the other.

"I know," Lady Swiftbrook said, dragging her eyes from the dying wisps of smoke. "I'm overreacting, I'm sure. I just can't shake the feeling this would be a terrible thing for us. It's much easier to stand up to a known foe, but in this case, the demons were a sword wielded by the hand of an unknown enemy. If we put the fire of retribution into the heart's of our people, I fear we may lash out blindly, and bring the world down upon our heads."

"That foolishness again," K'hul rumbled, joining them. "One human is as wretched as the next. The world will hardly fall upon us if we happen to obliterate a few extra city-states full of the vermin."

"We call some of those 'wretched humans' allies," Lady Swiftbrook countered.

"Do not confuse trade agreements with military alliances. Two countries open their ports to us and nothing more. If you approached their leaders for military aid, they'd laugh you back to the ship you sailed in on."

ЖЖЖЖЖ

Lady Swiftbrook and K'hul moved off to continue their debate. Their animated gestures attested to the passion the two shared for the topic at hand.

W'rath settled next to Raven. "You look like you ate an extra putrid bug," Raven observed.

"I wasn't prepared for the great golden warrior to make any sense," W'rath replied.

"You can't be serious?" Raven hissed. "He just suggested wiping out whole populations of humans in our search for the attackers."

"Not exactly. He said the rest of the world wouldn't unite against us if we happened to wreak collateral damage on an innocent populace or two."

"And you're okay with that?" Raven said.

"Not at all. Proceeding in such an imprecise manner would be a terrible waste of elven lives and resources. However, I find myself trusting in his view of world politics. I also agree we mustn't confuse trade partners with allies. If it proves too dangerous to do business with us, they'll cut us off, fearful that our enemies will target them next. After the events at Second Home, others will see us as weak—vulnerable. No one will want to tie their fates to us."

"Gods," Raven murmured. As much as W'rath's callous disregard for non-elves troubled her, the picture he painted concerned her more. "We could find ourselves faced with even more enemies if people turn against us in the hopes of appeasing whatever power has set its sights on us."

"Now you're starting to understand the way of things," W'rath said, beaming, apparently pleased with her revelation. "I haven't had the chance to familiarize myself with the current state of the world, however it's clear we face a rare and powerful enemy, one whom most other populations will wish to avoid being noticed by. I can almost guarantee those two countries K'hul mentioned have already closed their ports to us."

"You think they already know what happened?" Raven leaned against the ships railing, taking comfort from its solid support.

"Of course they know."

"But how? We haven't told anyone, and the closest city to Second Home is over a week by road. Even if someone managed to survive and escape, they haven't reached a place where they can tell their story."

"Ah, but you forget our hidden enemies. It's in their best interest to make sure anyone friendly to us understands the consequences of maintaining relations with us. Isolate your enemy, drive them to despair and then wipe them from the memory of the world."

Raven gaped at W'rath in horror. "Wherever did you hear such a horrible thing?"

W'rath gave her a knowing wink. "That's a direct quote from your beloved *god* the First. You've obviously consumed the wrong history books if that tidbit escaped you. He's famous for those words."

"I've read a lot of history books and I've never run across such a quote. No one ever portrayed him as so brutal."

"How old were those books you read?"

"Fairly modern," Raven admitted. "I've never had access to anything truly old. It's the main reason for my visit to Second Home."

"And you went in search of these older books because...?"

"Because I suspected the newer books of bias—at least in matters concerning Umbral. I'd read so many supposed histories contradicting one another, I couldn't help but feel the writers had agendas they wanted to promote instead of presenting plain facts. I'd hoped to find something old enough it wasn't twisted by time and cultural changes."

W'rath nodded, just a hint of a smile playing across his face. "So, lass, if the historians altered the facts concerning one person, does it not make sense other historical figures suffered a similar fate?"

"Yes, but the First?" Raven said, radiating distress. "He's the father of us all. How could he have been such a heartless bastard?"

W'rath didn't answer right away. Instead, he watched the First Born and the Sky Elf as they continued to argue, their faces so close they could probably feel one another's words. W'rath must be amazed at the naiveté of the world he's wandered into, Raven thought. From his point of view, it was probably a wonder something like Second Home hadn't happened sooner.

W'rath finally tore his attention away from the argument and continued with his tuition. "You're making the same mistake as your modern history books, child. You're trying to apply your mores to an elf who lived before anything resembling a true civilization existed. People didn't negotiate then. They didn't have the option of relocating to a better place. There *weren't* any nicer places. Enemies swarmed everywhere. Volcanic activity constantly tore apart the world and remade it, making livable land the rarest of commodities. The goblinoids hated the elves. The giants raged, terrifying and maddeningly difficult to kill due to their extreme resistance to magic. If you wanted to defeat them you had to follow the First's mantra.

"And just so we're clear, the First was *not* the father of all elves. He created the first Shadow Elves. Period. He created the Shadow Elves for no other reason than he required a new weapon to use against the enemies of the elves. He needed spies. He needed assassins. He needed a small, quiet people who could disappear in the shadows and escape the notice of others. He bent his will against Mother Magic and forced her union with a jagged field of volcanic glass—beautiful but deadly sharp. *That* is our origin."

The familiar story Raven had once thought of with fondness, now chilled her. Despite her belief that historians had suppressed the full story of Umbral and his betrayal, she'd never stopped believing that the First had loved the Shadow Elves. But W'rath's retelling of their creation story rang with disturbing truth. The First had no reason to create a new race of elves for the sake of companionship. It only made sense he'd done it because he needed a tool to use against his enemies. "What about the female who he had Umbral by? Surely he cared for her?"

"Can you tell me her name?" W'rath asked.

"I... I don't know." Raven's shoulders sagged and the solidity of the railing alone kept her from sinking to the deck.

"Don't feel bad, lass. No one knows her name. I would stake my life that the First himself couldn't tell you a thing about her. She served as an outlet for his lusts, and died bringing a mewling brat into the world. It's a miracle the child survived. Umbral was the first child born to the elves. I'm surprised they didn't kill him, assuming him to be some parasitic attack by their enemies, sent to tear them apart from the inside out."

"They must have seen animals give birth," Raven reasoned. "They weren't stupid." Her voice had grown small and defeated. How could she find herself so unanchored? She wanted to completely discount W'rath's words. She knew from experience what sort of bitter denouncements her fellow Exiles made concerning the first elves. And yet, nothing he'd said had come across that way. When her mother had spoken of their ancestors her voice had always seethed with anger and loathing. Raven responded by rebelling against that hatred. She'd drawn great comfort from the idea of an all-loving creator who would forgive and one day bring his wayward children back to the fold, uniting them with the rest of their kin.

W'rath had delivered his lesson in such a matter-of-fact manner, with none of the venom usually accompanying such words, she found herself questioning the beautiful world she'd created for herself. If he spoke the truth, then she was truly alone—godless. She couldn't even turn to the ancestor worship the other elves embraced. How could she revere the First if he didn't have enough compassion to preserve the memory of his son's mother?

"Lass," W'rath called to her and Raven struggled out of her dark thoughts. He placed himself in front of her in an attempt to conceal her from the others. She stood head and shoulders taller than him, though, so he had no hope of hiding the tears running down her cheeks. Fortunately, everyone's attention seemed focused forward and not toward her.

"Child, how have I upset you so?"

Raven almost laughed, but managed to restrain herself. No need to come across as hysterical. Was he joking? How could he not understand? "I'm lost," she choked. She swiped at the tears on her face. "With one flick of that glib tongue of yours, I find myself without faith, completely alone."

"If I can dash all your beliefs in just a few breaths, child, your faith was a pale thing to begin with."

"So I've just realized," she said, not bothering to hide her disgust.

"As for you being alone—you've never been less alone. You have already won the love of all those whom you saved. Your young friend resides within you, bound to you flesh and soul. Both Lady Swiftbrook and I stand by you, even if one of us isn't particularly adept at sparing feelings."

Raven didn't trust herself to speak. Lady Swiftbrook had it right, he *was* a little imp, and a complete mystery. One moment he voiced frightening pronouncements, making it clear he understood battle and wholesale slaughter, and the next moment found him apologizing for making a silly girl cry. If a non-elf dropped at his feet in need of aid he would more than likely walk right across their back, and yet his attempts to reassure her showed he had at least some capacity for compassion. "I don't understand you," she said at a long last.

One corner of his mouth quirked up into a lopsided smile. "Of course you don't. You're much too sweet a lass to comprehend a wretch like myself.

"Now come," he said, offering an arm she had to reach down to grasp, "even our two fellow council members have stopped their squabbling and stand dry mouthed as we pull into port. They must find a way to tell their people why they've returned with only a handful of our folk in tow. They must break the news that a hidden enemy reduced Second Home to a smoking, demon-infested necropolis."

"And what do *we* do?"

"For now we stand by them and lend them our strength—even if one of them behaves like a self-aggrandizing prat."

"And then?"

"And then? And then, lass, we'll just have to see."

# CHAPTER 6

Lady Swiftbrook's stomach churned. Bile rose in her throat, and she fought to keep from retching, as the last of the survivors trudged down the gangplank, and thousands upon thousands of her people realized their loved ones would never return to them. Even now, some depraved horror might feed, or worse, upon the body of their son, daughter, parent, lover or friend.

Aside from the nausea, the rest of her had grown numb from grief and exhaustion. Her elation at surviving had turned to guilt. Why had she come through the devastation when so many others had been torn apart at the claws of the demons? Out of her entire battalion, only she survived. How would she face the families of those who had served with her? What could she tell them?

As a member of the High Council, her duty also included helping the populace cope with their loss, and to turn their thoughts to seeking retribution against those responsible for the attack. She had no idea how she would manage to do that.

As much as she hated combat, she had joined her people's army so others might live free of the horrors of war. What a foolish fancy. Over two thousand years old, and she'd never faced a conflict more severe than her ladies squabbling over the colors for the Spring Ball. Until now, she'd never truly understood what it meant to lead hundreds of souls into battle. *I only played soldier. Every one of their deaths is on me.*

And now all her silly dreams and higher moral ground meant nothing. A terrible sense of loss filled Lady Swiftbrook as she watched K'hul raise his powerful voice to her people. W'rath hadn't thought K'hul could count on more than half the elven people joining him in his quest for revenge, but the Shadow Elf hadn't realized that the loud, boastful First Born had the one element W'rath claimed a leader needed in order to sway so many to take up arms—the passion to change hearts through any means necessary.

As the survivors disembarked, K'hul, the eldest surviving member of the First's line, told their stories. First came Baeldyn, a silk weaver, who found himself unable to do a thing to save his lover and their child. If only he had trained and kept a weapon at his side. If only his mate could have done more than shield their child with her body. The boy had lived just long enough to see his mother consumed by dozens of tiny fiends.

Next came Aelatar. A gardener, and one of the fifty consumed by the devil Raven killed. All of his apprentices perished, and the devils reduced the elves' beautiful living art to a blackened memory. K'hul helped the sobbing elf down the gangplank as the devastated gardener cried over and over how he couldn't help his apprentices.

This went on for an agonizing age, and Lady Swiftbrook stood helplessly while her lover ignited the fire of their ancestor's in her people's hearts. Many tears were shed, but the outrage and cries for blood made the very air vibrate.

"He's good at this," W'rath said. The grudging admission darkened Lady Swiftbrook's mood further.

"Happy now?" The Sky Elf hated that she sounded petulant.

"Happy? No. You have to understand, lady, we need a balance. I have no desire for our people to turn into a mindless juggernaut sweeping the world in fiery death. We cannot, however, expect to keep all of the beautiful aspects of our culture without fighting for it. There will always —always exist those who wish to deny us our freedom, life, even how we choose to dress. We must stand up to them and thwart them at every turn.

"Negotiation..." she started to protest.

"Negotiation only works if you're dealing with someone who has values similar to your own. They must already possess the capacity to respect you. The enemy we face now has revealed they are neither reasonable nor forthright. They hold no value for the lives of even our children. They willingly slaughtered your precious non-elves simply for associating with us."

Lady Swiftbrook shuddered as anger and despair fought for supremacy within her. She wanted for W'rath to be wrong, but the horror of what they'd survived told her otherwise. "Damn you."

"Madam?"

"How can someone who claims to have lived alone in a cave, for ancestor's-knows-how-long, have such a fine grasp of our situation?"

"While I have lived on my own for quite some time, and the world has changed much in those years, people's motivations have not. Greed, jealousy, faith, power... as long as people roam the world, regardless of race, these factors will always come into play."

Lady Swiftbrook squeezed her eyes shut in a vain attempt to compose herself. Wiping away a tear she, gave a ragged laugh. "You know, you and K'hul should be fast friends. You certainly seem to agree on enough."

"We might agree, though I suspect for different reasons. I believe many of your fears concerning our people exist because you see in K'hul something that frightens you."

"Bah. Now you just sound spiteful."

"Never, madam."

W'rath's spoke lightly, but Lady Swiftbrook remembered when they'd first met. She had seen what simmered within his eyes. Spite, and much more, lay well within his capabilities. Yet something else he had in common with K'hul. *Ancestors preserve me—there's two of them now.*

Raven joined them. The young female's earlier excitement had disappeared, replaced by a pensive, nervous posture. No doubt she had grown apprehensive about their arrival at First Home. Her mouth pinched into a frown as if she wrestled with her feelings. Lady Swiftbrook reached out to squeeze the girl's arm. "We'll get through this," she said. "Let's see about introducing you to your new people."

When Lady Swiftbrook drew the two Shadow Elves to the top of the gangplank, the angry and unruly crowd fell into an eerie silence. Someone suppressed a sob. All eyes turned toward the newcomers, expressions as varied as the numbers of elves present.

W'rath studied the elves of First Home, trying to read them. He'd done his best to hone his skills in observation. He didn't believe in relying only on his psychic gifts. His time imprisoned in Traitor's Heart had taught him that. Eighty-five years trapped in the wretched place, with only Uverial Stormchaser's visits to keep him sane, had driven home that situations would always arise where it was either impossible to use his psionics, or their use would result in unwanted repercussions.

Right now, he had to forego any use of his powers because of the damage he'd caused himself at Second Home. Until he healed, and sadly the brain regenerated slower than any other body part, he had to rely on his ability to read faces and body language.

He simply listened as Lady Swiftbrook introduced Raven and him to the gathered elves. He bowed at just the right time, but never took his eyes off the crowd. Curiosity far outshone hostility. Here and there people whispered to one another, and as Raven stepped forward to perform an awkward half bow, half curtsy, more than one person pointed or gestured excitedly in her direction.

W'rath raised an eyebrow. *They already know*. Those she had saved had wasted no time in telling friends and family about the towering ebon goddess who had slain the devil lord with a single stroke of her sword. No doubt the amazing tale would grow with each retelling.

Despite his own part in things, people's eyes barely registered W'rath once their gazes fell upon Raven. It wasn't surprising. Raven was glorious. Her ill-fitting sailor's clothes did nothing to hide her powerful build, and her height nearly brought her on par with the Sky Elf at her side. A breeze caught up her ice white hair and sent it flowing out like great wings. W'rath smiled at the quiet gasps that floated up from the crowd. Raven apparently heard them too, as she drew back, uncomfortable with the attention.

W'rath's smile broadened as people began to murmur. The people weren't interpreting her mannerisms as insecurity, but rather graciousness and quiet strength. Raven hadn't even stepped foot on First Home and already she had won over the people.

W'rath didn't mind that the crowd barely noticed him. For now, he preferred to keep a low profile. It amazed him he had yet to meet an elf even half his age. While he suspected he had changed greatly over the years, he worried someone would notice something familiar about him. No, for now keeping to the background, unremarkable, nearly invisible, suited him fine. He thought of it as sleight-of-hand on a grand scale. While Raven's radiance diverted people's attention, he could quietly work in the shadows doing as he liked, keeping alert for anyone who could expose him.

His gaze shifted from the crowd to K'hul. The old boy did not share in the crowd's enthusiasm. The people might respect him for his prowess, or even simply for his bloodline, but he was just one of many soldiers who had fought the devils coming through the gateway. Raven had single-handedly slain a leader among the devils. Numerous individuals could point to her and claim she had saved their lives. K'hul couldn't hope to compete with that. The scowl on his face betrayed his displeasure at Raven's instant popularity. *Careful, lad, your face might freeze that way.*

"Quit grinning like a loon and wave to everyone," Lady Swiftbrook hissed in W'rath's ear. Obediently, he put on a more solemn expression and acknowledged the rising welcome from the people of First Home.

"There's not a single Shadow Elf out there," he whispered back.

"That's not surprising," the Sky Elf replied. She swept her arms forward, continuing to smile amiably, showing the people that one of their trusted councilors welcomed the strangers to disembark from the ship and step foot on the soil of First Home. She turned back as if chatting about the most inconsequential of things. "Ever since Lord T'sane and Lady Reaper took office, we've seen less and less of any Shadow Elves. They live underground—pretty much cut off from the rest of us. They may not even know what has transpired."

"That has an ominous sound to it," W'rath muttered. His thoughts turned once again to the dying Reaper. Fanatical and full of self-loathing, he doubted she and T'sane had seen properly to the welfare of those under their care. He worked to keep his misgivings from his face. Pretending to feel more honored than he felt, he bowed and accepted Councilor Swiftbrook's gracious invitation, and followed Raven down the gangplank.

"Once we get through the crowd, we can make our way down. I've never made the hike, so I have no idea what to expect," Lady Swiftbrook said.

"I don't think it's necessary to rush down immediately. I'd prefer to avoid meeting them dressed like a beggar, tolerated by the rest of the council out of charity. Raven and I earned our place on the council and we should look the part. If my growing fears prove true, Reaper and T'sane betrayed those we represent, and we must deal with the momentous task of restoring their faith."

They finished their descent and found themselves swept into the crowd, making further conversation impossible. Emotion reigned, and people surged forward seeking answers, making demands, or simply desperate for reassurance. Some wanted to touch Raven, murmuring their gratitude. They mobbed the three, and W'rath, much smaller than anyone else in the crowd, had trouble keeping Raven in sight. Someone trod on his hair and he only just managed to keep from reflexively lashing out and leaving them a broken heap. These were civilized, cultured people, he reminded himself, but the slaughter of their people had so devastated them, their normal restraint had broken down. W'rath understood well the animal fear gripping them.

W'rath silently thanked his nephew when K'hul intervened. He and about a hundred of the soldiers under his command moved into the crowd and began to restore order. Eventually, a path cleared and the Shadow Elves and Sky Elf made good their escape. "I cannot say I much enjoyed that," W'rath said once they gained their freedom.

"Sorry about stepping on your hair," Lady Swiftbrook said.

"That was you? Madam, you have no idea how close you came to having a shattered ribcage."

Raven laughed shakily. "Wouldn't that have started a scandal. Not five minutes on First Home soil and Exiles start running amok, assaulting people. They'd dust off Traitor's Heart, for sure."

W'rath grimaced.

"Before something else like that happens, you might do something radical like, oh, I don't know, trim off a foot or two? It seems preferable to you doing bodily harm to anyone unlucky enough to step on your precious locks."

"That is not unreasonable," W'rath conceded. "Perhaps we might take care of that at the same time as we find something more suitable for Raven and myself to wear."

Lady Swiftbrook nodded. "If you come with me to my home I can arrange for some tailors to come by."

"And an armore`r. Raven needs to give off the appropriate air of authority."

"Oh, surely not!" Raven protested.

"Something spiky and dangerous looking," W'rath continued, ignoring Raven's objection. "Blood red enamel would add a nice touch."

"Why not stick some skulls on there, while you're at it?" Raven said, her voice taking on a distinct growl.

"Excellent idea, my dear. Now you're getting into the spirit of things."

"That's cruel," Lady Swiftbrook chided.

W'rath grinned. "Perhaps just a little."

Raven's eyes widened as she realized W'rath had been winding her up. "So I don't have to slog about in full plate?"

"Of course you do," W'rath said to his dismayed companion. "Chin up, lass. You're more than strong enough to manage it, and as the new representative of the warrior branch of the Shadow Elves, you need to set an example for those who will look to you for leadership. Obviously, you won't have to wear the armor all of the time, but certainly we should look the part when we first meet our people. Among other things, you're a symbol. Awe should follow in your wake. Those whose eyes fall upon you, should want nothing more than to *be* you. However, we can forego the spikes and what not. We don't have a month to wait for that amount of customization anyway."

"I'm not at all comfortable with that," Raven said, refusing to be cheered by W'rath's enthusiasm.

"Of course you aren't, but you'll grow into it. You needn't worry. It seems overwhelming right now, but Lady Swiftbrook and I shall stay by your side the entire time. We won't let you stumble."

W'rath's hope that Lady Swiftbrook would step in and help allay Raven's fears went unanswered. The frozen smile on the Sky Elf's face couldn't have fooled one of the Exiles' lobotomized males. Obviously the dear lady's skills must lie elsewhere.

Raven glared at the both of them and then shook her head with a sigh. She started to trudge inland as if heading to her own execution. "Come on then," she said. "Let's get this debacle over with before I run the other way and try to swim back to the mainland."

✖✖✖✖✖

When the small party of Shadow Elves finally emerged from the tunnel, the sun hung low in the sky. Even with the tall gates surrounding the arena, the light blinded the youngsters. They cringed and covered their eyes.

"There's no one here," Ryld said.

"How can you tell? I'm as blind as those stupid fish we ate on the way up," Caeldan groused.

"I can kinda make out the arena through all the watering. Plus, it's stone quiet. At least a few people should be sparring."

"Seer!" Ryld called out. "Where is everyone?"

No one replied. Finally, a tentative voice piped up. "She gave up hours ago. She said it was wrong for us to greet the Exiles, anyway."

"Is that you, Seismis?"

"Uh... yes."

Caeldan chuckled. "Pay up, brother."

"Well bugger!" Ryld cursed. "I thought for sure he'd keel over a mile back and curl into a fetal position."

"I can hear you," came the petulant words.

Ryld ignored him. "I'm going to have to owe you. I didn't bring my bags of vast wealth with me."

"That's okay, I know where you live. Right now I'm just annoyed we're nearly blind and have no idea what's going on."

"I say we worry about that after we find some water," Ryld said. He staggered off to his left. When last they'd been topside, there had been an area for the soldiers and students to rest. A natural spring spilled into a deep basin, and the elves could use ladles to quench their thirst while they watched those still practicing in the arena.

Fortunately, things hadn't changed since they had last lived topside. The small group collapsed in the shade of the overhead trellis and drank their fill of the chilled spring water.

"Ancestors, I didn't realize how thirsty I was," Ryld said.

"Yeah, pretty stupid of us to not take more water with us," Caeldon replied.

"It wasn't even a league."

"In our condition it felt more like ten times that. The ones who didn't make it here have to be in a bad way. We need to get water to them soon."

"Right now, I can't even contemplate something so strenuous. In fact, I'm thinking I might just slip into a coma."

Caeldan snorted. "That's sure to impress our new leaders."

The mention of the mysterious Exiles, roused something in the others. "Where are they?" came a quavering voice.

"We need them," another chimed in, even more pitiful than the first speaker.

More cries and whimpers started up. Still hampered by the sun, Ryld couldn't see clearly, but he thought Seismis might have started wringing his hands again. "Now look what you've gone and done," he chastised his brother.

"Sorry, allow me to correct my earlier statement: Comas for everyone. Much better than all of this whining."

"What will a pair of Exiles think about all this bellyaching?" Ryld said. He wondered if they'd made a mistake in bringing the others topside.

"Oh they'll probably just kill us all and start over," Caeldan said, so deadpan that, for a moment, he fooled even Ryld into believing him. The others didn't understand Caeldan's dark sense of humor, and abruptly they fell silent.

Ryld and Caeldan chuckled, settling back into the blessed quiet to wait.

*****

Raven felt as if she wandered, trapped in a bizarre dream. Never in a million years could she have envisioned herself encased in blood red armor, marching forth to meet people her to lead them. She shook her thankfully helmet-free head as she pondered all that had brought her to this point.

She and W'rath traveled down a hallway leading back to the main hall to regroup with Lady Swiftbrook. She could still hear the fretful mutterings of the armorsmith who had equipped her. From the beginning, he'd apologized profusely, explaining he would have to make a custom suit to her exact measurements. For now he resorted to piecing together a full set from various suits young First Born had outgrown as they matured. To Raven's eye the pristine red enamel, with its gold edging, appeared exquisite. However, the armorsmith had an artist's heart, and fretted over hundreds of flaws only he noticed.

The armor wasn't nearly as heavy as she'd expected. She'd expected the armor's joints to impede her movement. Whether through skill, or magic, or a combination of the two, her fears proved unfounded. She moved almost as fluidly as if she wore regular clothing. She had no intention of admitting it to W'rath, but it felt almost natural. She suspected Linden's presence within her had a lot to do with that. Definitely surreal, and disturbing, she wasn't sure if she'd ever get used to this twin-souled nonsense.

Beside her, W'rath tripped along easily, appearing as comfortable in his new finery as he had in his malodorous kilt. No suffocating plate for him. His mostly black outfit consisted of a high necked long coat with numerous gold buttons.  Aside from the buttons, the only other sign of color, a deep purple, glowed from the oversized cuffs and the sash around his waist. The skirt of the coat split four ways and flowed out and behind him as he strode forward. Black pants and thigh high leather boots encased his lower body.

Of course, before all of the wardrobe work had come the hair stylist.

W'rath had reluctantly allowed a sour looking Sky Elf with a pair of shears to trim off a couple of feet of hair. It still touched his ankles at that point, and there followed a minor dustup between W'rath and the elf with the shears on what to do with it next. W'rath thought it fine just hanging straight down his back, but the other fellow argued it lacked style and grace and several other things which made Raven's eyes glaze over. They'd finally both agreed on a ponytail that stood out a good six inches from W'rath's head and then spilled down like a waterfall. Somehow, the two males determined the style to be fashionable yet practical. Raven had a suspicion W'rath just liked that it made him appear taller.

Then the elf with the shears turned his attention to her.

She'd thought to keep the fuss down to a minimum by getting her hair cut as she'd always worn it. She'd always kept it in a short bob, and the great curtain of hair she found herself burdened with now, felt completely alien. When she told them what she wanted the look of horror on W'rath's face caused her to relent and keep enough length so it fell just below her shoulder blades.

Now she fumed. Why had she caved in? It was her bloody hair! Bad enough her new role compelled her to project an image completely foreign to her, but to then let W'rath's personal preference dictate her hair length? A scowl settled on her face.

"Excellent. You're looking positively fierce. You're sure to impress anyone we meet."

Raven glowered at W'rath. "I'm not trying to impress anyone. I'm angry."

"Indeed? Everyone, aside from K'hul, has been shockingly cordial. What could you possibly find so upsetting?"

Raven imagined flames shooting out of her eyes to set the little male alight. While he didn't so much as blister, his expression did turn to puzzlement as he realized her ire was directed at him. "Me?"

"Of course you. Ever since we met you've directed my every move. I can't even get my hair cut the way I want anymore."

"I didn't say a word about your hair, lass."

"You didn't have to. You gave me a look."

W'rath had the good grace to try not to laugh, but failed miserably. "How delightful. It would seem I have no need of my psychic powers. I need only *look* at people and they'll bend to my will. If only I'd realized the extent of my talent years ago, I might have avoided a lifetime of unpleasant living conditions."

Raven's shoulders sagged. Her entire world had turned upside down. The last time she found herself this emotional her coming of age ritual had loomed before her. She'd grown so irrational she'd literally begged her father to help her, even though he shouldn't have had any ability to aid her. That he'd turned out to possess undreamed of resources, still staggered her.

W'rath too gave every indication he was much more than an average Shadow Elf male. He had skills and knowledge that he could have only gained through leadership and combat experience. Despite his gender, he gave orders as though he expected people to do exactly as he wanted without question. Gods only knew how many millennia he'd lived, and what kinds of things he'd dealt with in that time. Certainly, he had more understanding of the world than a girl of twenty-one trapped in an adult body.

"I'm sorry," she said at last.

W'rath's brow knitted, mystified by her words. They'd come to a pair of closed double doors, where he pulled ahead of her and stopped. He turned to face her, blocking the way. *What now?*

Despite her new conclusions, she felt her frustration levels begin to rise again. "That not enough for you? You need me to spell out just how right you are and how wrong I am?"

W'rath shook his head. "No, lass. You have no reason to apologize. You speak from your heart. I admire your plain honesty. You needn't hold back—at least with me.

"This," he continued, gesturing at the empty hall they stood in, "is the first time we've had any privacy since we met. Once we go through these doors we'll reunite with Lady Swiftbrook, her attendants and any number of other people. The coming days will be filled with council meetings, training, study and rebuilding. We have only these few minutes to come to an understanding, but we must do exactly that. Right now."

Raven swallowed hard and nodded. "All right." He wanted her to present all of her concerns right here and now, but she had no idea how to articulate so much pure emotion. She'd wanted to have her say, yet now that he'd offered to listen, she had no idea where to begin.

"You said that ever since we met I've been... choreographing every aspect of your life," W'rath prompted. "I'm pretty certain this isn't actually about your hair."

Raven gave a sad little laugh and shook her head. "I'm just so frustrated. It seems like everything I want or believe in you trample on. I know I'm young, but I'm used to thinking for myself. Suddenly, I find I have control of nothing. I'm some state hero, I've joined a council I'm not qualified to sit on, and I'm supposed to put down my books and pick up a sword. I'm about the last person who you should expect to wade into battle. The hair... I'm angry with myself about that. You're right, you didn't say a word, but I saw your expression and I found myself changing to suit your desires, not mine. I wish you had use of your psionics so I could at least pretend you forced me, but I don't have that for an excuse."

Raven realized she'd started pacing and came to a halt, self-consciously lowering the arms which started to punish the air as her agitation found voice. She fell silent, wondering if W'rath could even begin to understand what she was experiencing. She had no skill as an orator, and nothing she'd said seemed to adequately convey the helplessness she felt. Did he have capability to share empathy for someone so different from himself?

Leaning against the doors, W'rath had lost his usual sarcastic demeanor. Surprisingly, her words seemed to have affected him more than she'd expected. It was as if some long forgotten memory had resurfaced, triggered by her confession.

"In looking at you," he said at last, "it's easy, even for someone like me who knows the truth, to think of you as a seasoned leader. Until now, the concepts of duty and sacrifice, to a cause larger than yourself, have never had a place in your life. Circumstances have thrust a great deal upon you very quickly. Too much."

Raven ran her hands over her armor encased body and shook her head. "I did this to myself. I thought of myself as a pacifist, but when I saw Linden die trying to protect me, I lost control. I forced this change, and now I feel like I've lost something I can never get back. I know I'm acting childish—thousands of people died a handful of days ago and I'm feeling sorry for myself."

"It's easy to know something on an intellectual level," W'rath said. "It's much harder to act in a rational manner when we have a strong emotional bias. Over the years, with a lot of practice, one learns to control behavior, but that doesn't stop us from feeling. When you're young, passion can completely overwhelm all logic and restraint. You did lose something, and I am sorry that happened to you. You've already done more for the elves than they could demand of anyone—no less a child.

"However, that does leave you with a decision. Lady Swiftbrook appointed you to the High Council, but it didn't occur to her to ask if you desired to take on such a responsibility. You can walk away from this, but you need to decide now."

"I can't do that!" Raven protested.

W'rath silenced her with a sharp shake of his head, his sympathy for her dilemma locked behind a stony, uncompromising mask. "You cannot stand before the Shadow Elves of First Home as their leader and then later decide it's too hard and abandon them."

"Lady Swiftbrook is counting on me..."

"You must not worry about what Lady Swiftbrook wants. This isn't about embarrassing her. It's not about what you think I want you to do. You have this one chance to look deep within yourself and decide what *you* really want. Will you force your mind and spirit to match your body?"

Raven took a step back from him. She had dreamed that someday she would uncover some great hidden truth, something that would elevate and redeem the Shadow Elves. Now she had the opportunity to affect their lives in a much more direct manner. W'rath was right though, it would require even more sacrifice on her part, and the bookish little girl in her found that terribly unfair. She was bright and philosophical but inexperienced. She needed guidance, but resented authority.

"Let me ask you this," W'rath said as she struggled with her inner debate. "When we fought at the gate, and you had to take control of the refugees while I meditated, how did you feel?"

"Terrified."

"Yet those people depended on you. I depended on you. You took control of the situation and kept them fighting long enough to keep all of us alive. Then, you reached inside yourself and brought forth the power to save my life. In so doing, you saved every elf there. A frightened little girl did not accomplish all that. How did it feel to stand in defiance as *that* person?"

"You're only asking me because you already know the answer. You've felt all those same things, haven't you?"

W'rath allowed a smile to creep onto his face and nodded. "Spending one's life as shop keeper or a librarian has merit, but for every ten that pass from this world, twenty more wait in the wings to take their place. Leaders, though? True leaders who make a difference in the course of people's lives? They're more rare than the most precious of gems. You have the makings of one of those people, lass."

"The makings?"

"You're young and green. You will have more episodes like this of self-doubt. When I said earlier that Lady Swiftbrook and I will guide you, I wasn't talking about just today. We're here for you for as long as you need us."

Raven felt some of her calm return. She didn't like admitting it, but having W'rath and Lady Swiftbrook help her fit into this new world was a comfort. However, one thing still bothered her. "All right, I'll do this, but I need some things to change."

"I see," W'rath replied. Raven couldn't help but notice his self-satisfied smirk had slid back into place.

"First of all, yes, I'm new at this, but quit treating me like none of my opinions matter. I will continue to think for myself and I expect to actually get my way once in a while."

W'rath's smirk turned into a full blown grin. "And second?"

"And second..." she said, shaking a finger at the little male. "And second... I'll have to get back to you on that." Blood rushed to her face.

"As you wish, lady," W'rath managed, with only a hint of a chuckle. "Now prepare yourself. We are about to wade into the thick of it."

With a heave, he pulled both doors open and a very startled Lady Swiftbrook nearly fell upon him from the other side. "There you are! I thought you managed to get lost."

“Hardly, madam,” W’rath replied. “We merely wished to admire the exquisite portraits lining this hallway. The Swiftbrook family boasts its share of noble visages.”

Lady Swiftbrook gave him an exasperated look. “As if we have time for you waste sightseeing.”

“Has something happened?” Raven asked.

“Only the most surprising of things,” the Sky Elf said, turning on her heels and marching off in a hurry. Her entourage of ladies scurried to keep up with her. She only stopped again when she realized the two Shadow Elves hadn’t adopted her sense of urgency.

“Well? Are you coming? Aside from T’sane and Reaper, no one has seen a Shadow Elf for at least twenty years. They’ve come topside, and they’re asking for you.”

# CHAPTER 7

None of the youngsters who had journeyed to the surface knew what to expect of the two Exiles replacing T'sane and Reaper. Most of them had never laid eyes upon a healthy Shadow Elf, so when the entourage of councilors entered the arena, straight backed and glittering in their armor and finery, Raven and W'rath's race wasn't immediately evident.

Six councilors turned to face them. Of those six, Caeldan and Ryld recognized Lady Swiftbrook, though enough years had passed since they laid eyes on her, their memories didn't do her shining, ethereal beauty justice. The giant First Born male had to belong to the K'hul family. Every male of the family line looked so much alike, it was almost eerie. Beside him loomed a broad-shouldered female First Born neither of them recognized. Her close-cropped blond hair made her appear stern despite the simple beauty of her unpainted face. Next to Lady Swiftbrook, a male Sky Elf, completely unknown to them, pretended to fuss with his robes. Tall and willowy, like most Sky Elves, his hair fell down his back like a sheet of midnight. When he thought no one would notice, he peered at the young Shadow Elves with poorly hidden trepidation. Or perhaps, that was just his natural state of being, as his posture hinted at someone ill at ease with the world outside the quiet confines of his study.

That left just two elves. "Gods," Ryld breathed, "are we supposed to look like that? Maybe we're the normal ones and they're the freaks."

"*They* look like elves. We look like grey-skinned toads. I'm pretty sure they aren't the freaks," Caeldan whispered back. He had a sudden urge to flee back to the darkness of the caves. He hadn't missed the flicker of horror that passed across nearly every face of the delegation. Only the little male Shadow Elf maintained a completely neutral expression. Surreptitiously, he touched the female's hand and drew her gaze. He didn't say a word, but shook his head ever so slightly. The female quickly schooled her face into a more placid expression. Their eyes betrayed them, though. They burned with fury.

"I think I'm in love," Ryld said, going moony.

"Just a second ago you called them freaks," Caeldan said.

"He's still a freak. Look at him. Even in our condition, he's still a shrimp compared to us. But she's a goddess. Just look at her! She could snap my spine with her bare hands and I'd die a happy elf."

"You're such a romantic." Caeldan shook his head in amazement.

Ryld swatted at his twin. "Hush—something's happening."

Lady Swiftbrook stepped forward to address the pitiful little group. "By now you've no doubt heard about the devastating attack that befell us at Second Home. I'm sure you have many questions, only some of which we have answers to, and all of which will have to go unvoiced for a bit longer. For now, know that councilors T'sane and Reaper perished trying to fend off the demonic invaders who flooded our city. Their courage and dedication to the Elven Nation was beyond reproach."

Dubious, Ryld and Caeldan pursed their lips. Even living in isolation, they knew diplomacy when they heard it. "They may have dedicated their lives to the *Elven Nation*, but they sure as hells didn't give a toss about us," Caeldan muttered.

"Normally," Lady Swiftbrook continued, "we'd raise two of you to the vacant spots left by T'sane and Reaper. However, during the assault on our city, two strangers, former Exiles, distinguished themselves by saving a great number of us, myself included. They have agreed to honor us by serving on the High Council."

Even though the group already knew about the Exiles, and the fact they would replace T'sane and Reaper as their leaders, the official announcement brought forth murmurs and gasps. Raised since birth to think of Exiles as little more than demons in elf form, the idea of being handed over to a pair of them chilled the youngsters.

Ryld and Caeldan didn't join in the chatter. Instead they turned their gazes from Lady Swiftbrook to the strangers—and froze. The male stared directly at them. Before he broke eye contact, his eyes narrowed and just the slightest hint of a smile passed across his lips. Free of his hellfire gaze, the twins started to breathe again.

"Traitor's balls!" Ryld exclaimed. "What in the Nine Hells just happened?"

"Something about us caught his attention." Caeldan swallowed hard and wiped suddenly damp hands along his tunic.

"Not sure I'm altogether thrilled about that."

Lady Swiftbrook raised her hands and patted the air in an attempt to quiet the agitated youngsters. At last they calmed and she resumed her speech. "I realize this is a lot to take in. We're elves—dealing with sudden change does not come naturally to us. But someone else has seen fit to force this upon us. In the end, I believe all of us will benefit from the addition of new blood. Now please, welcome your new councilors, Lady Raven and Lord W'rath."

Lady Swiftbrook stepped back in line to stand next to the other Sky Elf councilor, and the two Shadow Elves stepped forward. Twenty-seven expectant pairs of eyes turned to them. The female shifted uncomfortably and cleared her throat. "You'll have to forgive me," she began, and her deep, smoky voice settled over them like a warm blanket. She started at the sudden widening of already too large eyes and the slight intakes of breath.

"Uh, right… As I started to say, I'm not used to giving speeches. But in seeing you here, I now find I need to address a few things. The elves as a whole have suffered a terrible tragedy these last few days. However, it's plain that one segment of our society has suffered greatly even before this. The treatment you've suffered these past years is monstrous."

The cluster of grey faces turned to the rest of the councilors and saw the discomfort filling their faces. All except W'rath seemed to wish they could sink into the stone beneath their feet. K'hul started to interject, but Lady Swiftbrook laid a hand on his arm, forestalling an angry outburst.

"There *will* be changes," Raven continued. "The first one will be the removal of those damnable collars from your necks."

Instantly an eruption of chatter, gasps and shouts filled the air. "Lady Reaper herself insisted upon them," someone protested.

"Shut up, Seismas," Ryld snarled.

"Interesting," Lord W'rath said, speaking for the first time. He moved toward the twins, and Ryld cursed himself for drawing the attention of the creepy little male. He had that mild look of amusement flitting across his face again, and he padded toward them in a disconcerting, predatory manner.

He stopped in front of Ryld and Caeldan, fixing them with an intelligent gaze. Despite their stooped posture, they still stood several inches taller than him, and yet, the aura of power he gave off made him seem to tower over them.

"What do you call yourselves?" he asked.

The din of the other young elves had completely subsided, leaving the twins feeling much too exposed. Ryld seemed to have lost his voice, so Caeldan finally answered, though not before glaring hard at his twin. "I'm Caeldan and the mute is my brother Ryld."

"We assume we're brothers," Ryld corrected, finding his voice.

"Well, we do look exactly alike. We're obviously twins."

"Except that I'm way better looking," Ryld countered, completely forgetting he wanted to avoid drawing attention to himself.

Lord W'rath cleared his throat and the two fell silent. "Now that we've established I made a terrible mistake in coming over here," he said, "let me continue with my questions before I completely forget what I meant to ask."

The brothers bit their lips, willing themselves into silence. After several seconds of quiet, Lord W'rath nodded, satisfied the two weren't about to start into another round of banter. "Did I understand correctly that Reaper..."

"Lady Reaper!" Seismis corrected from the back.

Lord W'rath leveled a glare at the unfortunate Seismis, who cringed and slinked behind one of his fellows. "Reaper," the councilor said deliberately, "is the individual who considered it a good idea to hinder her people's ability to use their powers? Are you certain?"

"Yes," Ryld and Caeldan said simultaneously. They looked at one another, and Ryld shrugged, letting Caeldan finish for both of them. "She felt we carried the taint of Umbral's sin. Only through dedicated servitude to the nation could we hope to redeem ourselves."

"I see..." Lord W'rath said. "How exactly did she expect you to accomplish this when she kept you isolated underground, unable to access your gifts because of your collars? It seems to me Reaper and T'sane set out to make certain you couldn't do much of anything, no less 'redeem' yourselves."

"Let me guess," Lady Raven said, joining them. "Reaper thought that, as males, you carried the same flaws as Umbral. She considered you unclean and prone to weakness. She didn't trust you to use your powers responsibly, and since she didn't have any psionic ability to help thwart any aberrant behavior, she insisted on the collars. How close am I?"

For a moment Caeldan could do nothing but stare at the beautiful creature towering over him. He gaped at her like a cave fish, and it wasn't until Lord W'rath snapped his fingers in front of his face, that the boy came back to himself. He felt his face burn with embarrassment. Ryld had the right of it, goddess indeed—a goddess in want of an answer. "How did you know?"

Lady Raven tossed her head in disgust. "I've seen it all before. That's how the females of my birth city view males. They tend to use more unpleasant means than collars to keep the males docile and powerless. A favorite method is to hammer a small magical spike into the front of the skull. It's jokingly referred to as the Third Eye."

"Very clever," Lord W'rath mused. "The magic in the spike negates the victim's regenerative abilities, so he stays lobotomized. If for some reason it's decided he needs all of his faculties back, they simply remove the spike and let him heal."

The murmurs and gasps of horror, which had started up because of Lady Raven's words, grew louder and angrier now. Lord W'rath cocked an eyebrow, seemingly surprised by the emotional display. His attention finally settled on Ryld and Caeldan's stricken faces. He shrugged. "I didn't say I considered it a civilized or proper way to treat one's people. However, it is a practical means of controlling a large population of potentially dangerous psions. Cheer up, lads, apparently you've gotten off easy all of these years."

"What's that old saying?" Ryld asked his brother.

"If you don't think things can get any worse, you lack imagination," Caeldan replied.

"Yeah, that's the one."

ЖЖЖЖЖ

W'rath turned to regard the other councilors. "While less barbaric than a spike in the brain, these collars still need to come off."

Raven's attention shifted to Lady Swiftbrook. "You told me two councilors have to do something to get the collars to come off?"

"Of course, K'hul, please assist me."

K'hul scowled. "I agree our cousins have suffered, but decent food and fresh air will heal them. I'm not at all comfortable releasing a pack of psions to spy on our thoughts. The collars should stay on."

Beside W'rath, Raven's fists clenched. The young First Born she'd merged with had a strong sense of honor, and his passion fueled Raven's anger, overcoming her youthful insecurities. Once she had more experience, that would come in handy. For now though, a heated outburst would just make her a target for K'hul. *He already sees me as a threat—let's keep his hostility focused on me.* "Either you view us as allies, or you do not," he said, making sure his deep voice projected and echoed throughout the arena. No one could mistake the challenge.

W'rath suspected few stood up to the councilors directly descended from the First. Based on his brief encounter with the dying Lady Reaper, a great many years had passed since a Shadow Elf opposed the will of a K'hul. *Oh, you're really going to come to loathe me, nephew.*

"Of course you're our allies!" Lady Swiftbrook said, moving quickly to insert herself into the discussion before it deteriorated further. "I'm sure Lord K'hul didn't mean to imply otherwise."

There was a snort of derision and the group turned as two new elves arrived. "Your pardon, Lady Swiftbrook, but the K'huls have a fine tradition of mistrusting any and all Shadow Elves, as if each one were perchance Umbral reborn," the male newcomer said.

"Wood Elves," Raven murmured, just loud enough for W'rath to hear.

"Really?" W'rath replied, surprised. They were nothing like he'd imagined. He had learned, while on the ship, that after his banishment, and the world had stabilized, a segment of the Sky Elf population had taken it into their heads that the wild places of the world required guardians; champions who would stand as a defense against the many enemies of the natural order. They had transformed themselves as a means of adapting to their new role.

The changes they'd wrought upon themselves were far more substantial than he'd expected. While the Sky Elves were very tall and willowy, the Wood Elves stood much shorter, on par with Shadow Elves. Though still slender, a wiry strength rippled through their taught muscles, replacing a Sky Elf's ethereal grace. The Sky Elves had skin so pale, ancient humans had thought them undead. The Wood Elves' skin shone a tawny brown. Even their hair color differed. The male Wood Elf had dark red hair and his companion had a strange combination of umber and forest green tresses. Both had brown eyes.

"You don't need him, councilor," the male continued. "Both Kela and I have our rings. We can assist in deactivating the collars."

"You don't have the authority to decide that on your own," K'hul said, brushing past Lady Swiftbrook. He encroached on smaller elf, trying to intimidate him. Either the Wood Elf hid his fear well, or he didn't care about having K'hul's massive frame tower over him.

"I suppose you want to put this to a vote?" the female, Kela, said. Her accent startled W'rath. Not only did it differ greatly from the rest of the elves, it bore no resemblence her companion's. W'rath frowned. He hated not knowing everything.

"Yes, we should put it to a vote," K'hul said. "We have a council for a reason. We debate the pros and cons of a situation and then proceed based on the will of the majority. The council instated the collars by that method. It stands to reason we should deal with their possible removal in the same manner."

Again there was a snort, and W'rath realized it came from the female, Kela. "Everyone except the Sea Elves are here, and since they vote whatever way the descendant of the First votes, it's pretty clear how things will fall out."

The male nodded. "We'll vote for the removal of the collars, as will the Sky Elves. You and the Sea Elves will vote to keep the collars. That's a tie until you figure in the votes of our two new recruits here, and it's pretty clear how they feel about the situation. So... the collars come off."

"Not that something like this should have come to a vote," Lady Swiftbrook said, ruefully. "When Reaper came to us with her plan, we should have removed her from office and replaced her with someone who didn't hate her own people. We all share in this shame. Let us not draw it out any further."

K'hul's mouth worked as though he might wish to argue further, but at long last the female First Born spoke up. "I'm new to this post," she said, "but I must admit I find it distasteful for us to argue in public, especially about something so blatantly wrong. I agree this collaring of fellow elves should never have been allowed to come about in the first place. Insisting on putting it to a vote just prolongs the injustice, and speaks ill of us as a people. Let us be done with it."

"The day continues to bring surprises," W'rath said under his breath. Apparently, not every First Born subscribed to K'hul's view of things.

From the look on K'hul's face, his counterpart's little speech had taken him by surprise as well.

"Bah, enough of this orc shit," Kela snarled, "Foxfire, let's put an end to this idiocy."

"Already done," the male Wood Elf grinned, holding up a black ring he'd pulled from his finger.

Kela pulled a similar ring from her hand and the two said, "Vaes'tyl si tylas."

"Ancient Elvish," W'rath said to Raven. "A phrase of unbinding."

"So... why aren't the collars *unbinding*?" she replied.

She was right. The collars remained intact, locked around the necks of their victims. The Wood Elves blinked and turned to Lady Swiftbrook in confusion. As baffled as her smaller cousins, she could only lift her shoulders in answer. Only K'hul seemed unsurprised. W'rath's eyes narrowed. "Something you'd care to share with the rest of us, K'hul?" The words barely came out through his tightly clenched teeth.

"My father did not trust that all of the councilors would stand by the results of the vote. He and Reaper agreed a First Born councilor should be required in order to release the collars. Since Councilor Culna'mo hasn't received a ring yet, that means you need me to do the unbinding, and until we have a proper majority vote I'm not doing it."

A stunned silence settled over the arena. W'rath continued to glare at K'hul. Either he enjoyed dragging things out as a means of forcing his connection to the First down everyone's throat, or he had a means of gaining more votes, and keeping the Shadow Elves collared. While that seemed impossible, given Foxfire and Kela's analysis of the votes, K'hul smug face led W'rath to conclude he had some way of adding more support to his side. Lady Culna'mo, the female First Born, opposed the collars, so that left the other new councilor, a male Sky Elf no one had bothered to introduce. All of them had assumed he'd feel the same way as Lady Swiftbrook, but W'rath now realized that was a naïve assumption. Lady Culna'mo had surprised them with her views, why couldn't the new Sky Elf possess an equally surprising outlook?

W'rath switched his attention to the Sky Elf. The fellow worked hard to remain inconspicuous. He kept his eyes cast down, refusing to insert himself into the volatile situation. So, he *was* in K'hul's pocket. He appeared ashamed of the association, but obviously wasn't strong enough to break free. Where in blazes had Lady Swiftbrook found this creature? *Ah, madam, later you and I shall have words.* But for now...

He waved for Foxfire to make space for him near K'hul. The Wood Elf complied, backing away, his face full of curiosity. For his part, K'hul appeared bemused as the small Shadow Elf stepped right up to him. "I would have a private word with you, K'hul," W'rath said, managing to sound almost conversational.

"I have nothing to discuss with you, Exile," K'hul replied.

Using a trick he'd learned when still just a child, W'rath ducked his head, as if intimidated, and spoke so quietly K'hul couldn't make out the words. The ploy worked and K'hul, confident in his superiority, bent down close to W'rath's head. "What did you say, runt?"

W'rath raised his head so his lips rested close to K'hul's ear. "I said, you will come and speak with me in private or I shall turn you over my knee and paddle your arrogant behind in front of everyone here."

K'hul's eyes widened and he straightened so abruptly he had to take a step back to keep his balance. "Impossible," he hissed.

"Are you absolutely certain? There isn't even the slightest bit of doubt in your mind? So much to risk over such a simple request."

"There's a private sparring room over there. We'll *talk* there," K'hul finally said in a voice loud enough for all to hear.

W'rath bowed and gestured for the First Born to lead the way. K'hul complied, but W'rath caught the flicker of apprehension that crossed his face. He didn't like turning his back to W'rath. *Oh, what fun.*

⋈⋈⋈⋈⋈

As W'rath and K'hul departed, Foxfire whistled in amazement. "Just like T'sane, eh?" he said to Kela. Once again her responded with a very unladylike snort—apparently her preferred method of stating an opinion.

Foxfire turned his attention to Raven. "We haven't been formerly introduced," he said. "I'm Foxfire, and this she-badger is Kela. You must be the famous Lady Raven." He thrust out his hand to her.

"Famous?" Raven said, staring at the hand, at a loss as to what he expected her to do.

"Stop that!" Kela said, coming to Raven's rescue. She pushed Foxfire's hand down. "You spend too much time away from your people. You're always behaving strangely."

"If more of us mingled with the rest of the world, maybe we wouldn't have gotten caught with our pants down at Second Home."

The conversation had the sound of an old and oft repeated argument. While Raven wasn't privy to the whole of their debate, it did shed some light on the reasons for the two Wood Elves being so different from one another.

Kela was much like the other Wood Elves Raven had met when she had first come to the surface. Dressed in leathers, decorated with feathers and beads, she looked the part of a wild forest dweller. Even her abrupt, aggressive means of speaking sounded much like what Raven had come to expect of a Wood Elf.

Foxfire had a much more worldly air about him. He wore a shirt made of fine cloth, with puffed and slashed sleeves. His tall boots, nothing like Kela's soft moccasins, looked like something made for one of the fine gentleman in her books. Or, Raven mused, spying the lute strapped to his back, something a bard, used to playing in front of a well-heeled audience, might wear. That also explained his more gregarious manner. Though how a Wood Elf had ever come to lead such a life struck her as quite the mystery in itself.

Her curiosity could wait for the moment, Raven decided. She turned back to the young Shadow Elves standing in a tight, nervous cluster, unsure of their fate. Only a couple dozen or so had gathered in the arena. The others must have stayed below. Then something dawned on her, and she examined them more carefully. They were so desiccated she had trouble determining their sex, but every single one of them wore a containment collar which implied...

"Are all of you male?" she asked.

A brief bout of shifting and twisting of heads commenced, but in the end they confirmed Raven's suspicions. The one called Caeldan responded for them all. "Seer started to come up, but she gave up early on. T'ara wouldn't even try. She's too strong a follower of Reaper's beliefs, so she didn't want to have anything to do with meeting you. She and Seer both took Reaper's death hard. They're less than thrilled to have an Exile stepping into her position."

"That's just two. Couldn't any of the others make it up? Are they too ill?"

Caeldan and Ryld shared a glance. "There aren't any others, Councilor," Ryld said. "Seer and T'ara are the last."

Raven's breath caught in her throat. Behind her, she heard the others make various noises of shock and disbelief. Rather than take comfort in knowing they hadn't been privy to the devastation of the Shadow Elves, she felt her anger burn hotter. She spun around and let her fury wash over each of the councilors. "We didn't know," Lady Swiftbrook said, her voice almost a whisper. Her hands fluttered at her sides like frightened birds trying to escape.

"That's not good enough!" Raven snapped. "You had to suspect something terrible was going on down there . You admitted you hadn't even seen any Shadow Elves besides T'sane and Reaper for years."

She swung back to the young males. As one they flinched, ready to bolt at what they saw in her face. She trembled violently, and felt like the only thing keeping her from flying apart was her armor. Losing herself to her fury wouldn't do the boys any good. For their sake she reined in her and Linden's rage. She still had one question, though. "How many total are you?"

"Including you and Lord W'rath?" Caeldan asked. He wouldn't raise his eyes from his nervously shuffling feet.

"Yes?"

"The last I counted... that would make us fifty-three in all."

Raven gaped. With only two females and forty-nine males left to them, the Shadow Elves of First Home were as good as extinct. They couldn't possibly recover from this without finding additional people elsewhere.

This much destruction to the population had to have been deliberate. Reaper must have planned it this way. She'd kept the Shadow Elves below ground, out of sight and easily dismissed by the others. T'sane's involvement was unclear. Had he willingly participated in the slow genocide of his people? Or, like so many of the males Raven had known in her home city, had he suffered so much abuse by the physically superior Reaper, he couldn't stand against her?

Raven shot a glance toward the small dojo W'rath and K'hul had entered, her face set in a terrible mask of pain and fury. If W'rath wasn't able to make the First Born see reason, she'd remove the damn ring from his hand herself—with a sword.

Now that they were away from the others, and any possibility of public humiliation, K'hul's confidence reasserted itself. He faced W'rath, arms crossed, his face hostile. "You have me here now, Exile. What do you plan to do? Chew on my ankles?"

"Really, lad, short jokes? Even among the Shadow Elf population, I'm shy several inches of average. I've heard every possible insult there in existence. You'll have to work much harder if you wish to provoke me. Oh, I know, threaten to keep my lads helpless and labeled as inherently evil. That will get my attention."

K'hul raised an eyebrow. "*You're* lads? Until a few days ago, you didn't even know they existed. Until a few minutes ago you'd never laid eyes upon them. How can you call them 'your lads' when you don't know a thing about them? Their own councilors wanted them collared. You just strut in and decide they should have full access to their psionics without first finding out why your predecessors thought it was a bad idea?"

"Interesting." W'rath cocked his head. "That actually came across as a coherent argument."

"So we're done with this, then?"

W'rath chuckled. *Ah, so young, so naïve.* "Of course not, lad. Those collars will come off. But since you went to the effort to put together a logical reason for your obstinacy, it's only fair I do the same."

"Or, since we both know nothing you say will change my mind, we could just skip that part and move on to where I pummel you into a jelly. A very small jelly."

"Charming. However, isn't that a bit archaic? Isn't the whole purpose of having a council to facilitate communication and the exchange of ideas? Or am I mistaken and it's really only an attempt to put a civilized face on our government while the First's descendant continues to bully the rest of the population?"

"I'm the bully? You've already made it clear you expect the collars to come off regardless of the outcome of any discussion. In fact, you used threatened violence to lure me here in the first place. So be it. It worked well enough for the First, I'm only too happy to continue the tradition."

W'rath had only a fraction of a second to chide himself for underestimating his nephew before the huge First Born smashed a granite-like fist into his jaw. He attempted to roll with the punch, but the lad's speed shocked him, and W'rath felt the bone shatter. Most people wouldn't expect someone of such size to also have the agility and quickness of a hunting cat, but W'rath, of all people, realized he should have known better.

The force of the blow sent him flying across the room. He landed and continued to tumble across the floor until a wall brought him to a bone rattling halt. He spat out blood and teeth, but already felt his body regenerating, knitting the bone back together. Another fifteen minutes and he'd completely heal. Of course, K'hul wouldn't allow him to regenerate in peace. His father hadn't either.

"I knew that without your psionics you'd lose miserably in a fight," K'hul gloated, "but really, Exile, I still expected better. What were you thinking? Is this how you go about turning me over your knee and giving out a good paddling?"

He swaggered over to W'rath, hands on hips. "Did you think because I'm younger than you, you can lord it over me? Or, maybe you think I'm just some big, dumb fighter you can tear apart with your self-imagined superior intellect? Lesson one, Exile, never underestimate your opponent."

*I agree entirely.* With the speed of a striking snake, W'rath lashed out with his legs, hooking onto K'hul's ankle with one of his feet and smashing the side of a knee with the other. An resounding crack echoed off the walls as the knee exploded. K'hul crashed to the floor, howling in pain and surprise. The entire dojo shook with the force of his massive body splitting the floorboards.

With reflexes honed from years of surviving in the Abyss, W'rath sprang up and forward, smashing K'hul's ruined knee, causing the First Born to nearly bite through his tongue in his efforts to keep from bellowing in agony. Even so he could not help but cry out as the Shadow Elf launched himself into the air using the shattered knee for leverage. The older elf fell back earthward, smashing the elbow of the hand that had seconds earlier broken his jaw. He tumbled forward and came to rest with his knee against K'hul's throat. He pressed just hard enough to make it clear how easily he could crush the huge elf's windpipe.

K'hul went to brush the Shadow Elf from his chest only to find his other arm pinned to the floor by a knife, humming with faint magic. Tendons neatly sliced, the embedded knife kept him from healing. For now the arm lay useless. He starred up into W'rath's furious face in horror.

"If you ever strike me again," W'rath said, struggling to enunciate through broken teeth, and a partially healed mandible, "your current injuries will seem but pleasant memories. I shall break every joint in your body, and then march up this puffed up chest of yours to smash every bone in your face. If your bloodline to the First survives as unsullied as you claim, you may regenerate perfectly, but odds are you won't present quite as handsome a visage as you're used to."

K'hul gaped at the Shadow Elf, confirming W'rath's suspicions that no one had ever dared speak to the young warleader in such a manner before. K'hul nearly choked on the blood from his partially severed tongue. W'rath grinned. "Oh, yes, the various races of elves may differ in a great many ways, but one thing you can always count on is our vanity. Lad, you may hate me with every fiber of your being, but by all the ancestors you hold dear, you *will* respect me.

"And now... if you don't mind, I do believe I have won our... debate."

ЖЖЖЖЖ

Outside there a collective gasp of wonder filled the air as the solid collars around the necks of the Shadow Elves sprang open, clattering to the white stone of the arena floor. The boys touched their throats. "I can sense your mind again," Ryld said to Caeldan, fighting back tears.

From across the way, two figures emerged from the dojo and approached. "I think K'hul's limping?" Foxfire asked.

"That's blood on his sleeve, too," added Kela. For first time since her arrival, she sounded cheerful.

Lord W'rath looked worse for wear himself, the twins noted. His fancy ponytail had come completely undone, attesting to a violent encounter. That and the way he gently tested his jaw suggested a very large First Born had thrown a few punches.

"A master of diplomacy," sighed Lady Swiftbrook.

"Sometimes violence is the only answer," Kela said.

Lady Swiftbrook frowned. "Not for us. We evolved. We rose above this sort of thing. Rolling about in the muck, scratching at each other like savages, is beneath us."

"Someone forgot to tell those two," Raven said.

The new First Born councilor, Lady Culna'mo, bent down and retrieved one of the fallen collars. Her shadow had more substance than the fragile youngsters before her, the tallest of whom came up to her waist. "Perhaps their fisticuffs are a good thing," she mused. "This elevated lifestyle you speak of, Councilor Swiftbrook, where all controversy finds resolution through rational conversation, can only work if the entire world thinks the same way. The events at Second Home make it clear we're dealing with someone who does not embrace your ideals.

If we wish to prevail against this enemy, we need individuals who retain the fighting spirit of our ancestors."

"Or we could acknowledge that establishing a city on the mainland was a poor idea, and stay here on First Home away from the rabble." This last remark issued from the new Sky Elf councilor. When the others turned their attention upon him, he shrank back from their scrutiny.

"Councilor Icewind," Lady Swiftbrook said, finally putting a name to the cringing fellow, "as much as I abhor violence, I refuse to believe we should allow others to drive us from the world."

The group fell silent as K'hul and W'rath rejoined them. K'hul went to join his female counterpart, more dour than ever. W'rath combed out his freed hair, inscrutable until he came to stand next to Raven, where Ryld and Caeldan caught sight of the sly wink he gave her. The brothers grinned. For the first time in over two decades they felt a tiny spark of respect for their leadership.

✱✱✱✱✱

With the young elves at his back and Raven at his side, W'rath addressed the rest of the council. "Lord K'hul and I discussed our differences. He had many valid arguments, but in the end we both agreed, it is in the best interest of First Home if none are denied access to their gifts."

K'hul, who had been growing redder by the second, on the verge of erupting, relaxed upon hearing W'rath's words. Lady Swiftbrook raised an eyebrow, surprised and impressed. She'd half expected W'rath to gloat. She didn't doubt he understood the value of sparing K'hul embarrassment, but found it amazing his ego hadn't won out over good sense.

✱✱✱✱✱

Lord W'rath fell silent, allowing Lord K'hul a chance to speak. The First Born nodded as if he and the Shadow Elf had indeed participated in a civil debate that ended in a solid agreement built upon respect. "As we go forward in our quest to name our enemy and bring them to bay, we will have need of the skills all our people wield. All of us will have a part to play in avenging our fallen and in rebuilding our nation."

The twins pursed identical mouths. "Has nothing to do with it being just plain wrong to collar a fellow elf," Caeldan muttered to Ryld.

He bit back a cry of surprise when an instant later an elbow connected with his ribs. It wasn't intended to hurt, just get his attention, but in his condition even the air chafed. He glared and found himself locking gazes with Lord W'rath. The councilor didn't say a word, but the steely gaze spoke volumes. *Your collars are off, you foolish magpies—use your gift to communicate your sarcasm.*

Caeldan swallowed, feeling blood creep into his face. "*Sorry boss,*" he sent.

Lord W'rath's angled brows rose in surprise, and for a moment Caeldan thought he'd blundered by acting too familiar, but then surprise turned to amusement. Caeldan sighed in relief, and Lord W'rath, now grinning, turned his attention back to his fellow councilors.

Lord K'hul continued on for a bit, warming to the idea that, despite his earlier misgivings, this was a magnificent opportunity for the elves to come together and remind the world of their greatness. Fortunately, he paused just a bit too long between refrains and Lady Swiftbrook took the opportunity to come to everyone's rescue. "Thank you very much, Councilor," she said, leading the group in a round of applause. "Now it's getting late and these boys look ready to collapse. It's not right they've had to stand all of this time. They should be recuperating after their long ordeal."

"Councilor," Caeldan interjected, "we're in better shape than most of the others who didn't make it to the surface."

"I already have someone taking care of that," Lady Swiftbrook assured him. "Lady Sera, the head of the House of Healing, has put together several teams of healers and casters to head down there. As soon as the healers can transport the others safely, they will join you. In the meantime, we must find you quarters and work on getting you properly fed."

"Better late than never," Ryld muttered under his breath.

"I have another elbow, lad," W'rath hissed over his shoulder, and the boy abruptly fell silent.

Just then a retinue of Sky Elves arrived carrying stretchers. Half of them headed toward the archway leading to into the caverns below the surface of First Home. The other half set about tending to the youngsters already topside. a flurry of activity followed, with the healers quickly checking over the young Shadow Elves. The healers loaded the weakest of the group onto the stretchers and whisked them away. The rest, including the twins, walked alongside with their Sky Elven guides, the healers either excitedly chattering at the boys, or shyly peering at them, curious about their strange appearance.

Raven started to follow the boys as they left the arena. Already she felt protective of the pitiful youngsters. Letting them out of her sight made her nervous. W'rath laid a hand on her arm to stop her. "Let the healers do their work," he said. "We have business elsewhere."

"Oh? Where?"

W'rath gestured with his chin toward the archway leading deep into the island's belly. The Sky Elves who had entered moments before already gone, swallowed up by the darkness. "We have more people below and a domain to inspect."

"You two ready?" Lady Swiftbrook asked. She walked up to them, popping globes of light out of a wand. They bobbed about her as if excited to explore the long hidden world of First Home's Shadow Elves.

Raven restrained herself from groaning out loud. When she'd fled her home to relocate to the surface world, she'd prayed she'd never have to traverse the paths of such a place again. Either W'rath was right, and there no gods existed to hear her prayers, or the rat bastards just didn't care. She sighed. "Very well. But I'm not going anywhere until I get out of this damn armor. I've had enough of impressing people for one day."

# CHAPTER 8

The journey down held none of the dangers inherent to the world Raven had called home. Aside from meeting up with small groups of Sky Elves, carting filled stretchers to the surface, they met no other living creatures. Peace and solitude held sway here. The silence was one of the few things Raven missed about her former home. She'd had no difficulty in finding secret spots to curl up and escape her life for a brief time. The surface world held too much life for it ever grow truly quiet. While she cherished this bright, vibrant world, at times she wished she could shut it all out—the pulsing stars, the insistent crickets, the constant caress of the breeze.

The faces of the healers, transporting their patients out of the tunnel, clearly said they saw absolutely nothing to love about this subterranean world. The mage globes lighting their way highlighted their expressions—from extreme discomfort to near panic.

Raven had seen those expressions before. The surface elf captives brought to her city had worn those same looks. Her father had explained to her, for those not born to it, most found the idea of having miles of stone above their head terrifying. He told her that they felt as though they'd been buried alive.

She found W'rath peering at her. "You've grown contemplative," he said.

She nodded. "Traveling underground again brings back a lot of memories. Most of them not good."

"I could see why you would find living in pitch blackness oppressive," Foxfire said. Aside from Foxfire and Lady Swiftbrook, no other councilor had joined them on their expedition.

Surprised, Raven asked him, "Is that what you think? The Exile cities are dark but lit with many different colored lights. They also have what we call sun stones. My mother taught me to take very good care of ours. She said without them, we couldn't survive. Apparently, while we can see perfectly well in total darkness, we were never intended to live that way for an extended time."

They passed a sconce carved out of a natural mineral formation, though no light emitting stone rested there. W'rath searched around the area and found some sparkling shards. "What's left of a sun stone?" he asked, showing Raven a few glittering fragments.

"Maybe. Someone destroyed it, though. There's no way of telling exactly what it was now."

"I don't think there is any doubt that it was. We can be pretty certain who destroyed it too," Foxfire said. "Reaper. Or T'sane at Reaper's behest." He spoke their names as if he were trying to get a bad taste out of his mouth.

Lady Swiftbrook had forged farther ahead, but returned now to find the little group examining the sconce and the shards. "There are more of these at regular intervals along the way. I'm not sure what the point of destroying them was. Shadow Elves don't need light to see by."

"But other elves do," Foxfire pointed out. "It's a means of helping isolate the Shadow Elves from the rest of us. Not all of us can conjure balls of light." The accusation hung in still air.

Lady Swiftbrook's normally perfectly straight posture wilted. She turned pained eyes to them. "I knew things weren't right down here, but I swear I had no idea Reaper and T'sane would stoop so low."

"You weren't meant to know," W'rath said, dusting the fragments from his hands. He started down the tunnel and the others followed.

"I should have made the effort to come down here and see for myself. Councilor Stormchaser told me my interference would do more harm than good. I shouldn't have listened to her." About her the mage lights fell into a chaotic jumble, reflecting her distress.

"Perhaps," W'rath mused. "Tell me, madam, what field of study did she specialize in?"

"Divination. She read the future through various means. It's one of the most difficult of the magical domains to master. It requires the caster learn how to interpret symbols and seemingly incoherent visions. Even what appears as a clear sign of future events, can mislead the diviner if taken out of context." Lady Swiftbrook's voice grew unsteady. "Like all of her family line, she had a gift."

"If she was so gifted then why didn't she know what went on below her feet?" Raven said, unable to hide her bitterness.

"I expect she did know what took place down here. She kept it to herself for the same reason she did nothing to stop the annihilation of Second Home," W'rath replied.

That stopped them all in their tracks. "What?" W'rath said, turning back to regard their shocked faces. "How is this not obvious? Raven, lass, back on the ship you told me she spoke to you right before walking directly into the explosion that killed her."

"Gods!" Raven gasped. "Linden and I discussed it later, but only in terms of her knowing our fates as individuals—not that she had known about the attack. Linden knew she'd seen his death. It just didn't sink in that she had foreseen the whole travesty."

"So we must ask ourselves, when exactly did she know about the attack?" Foxfire mused.

Lady Swiftbrook's eyes had grown large with realized horror. "Weeks," she said. "At least three weeks."

The others stared at her silently, willing her to enlighten them. "I noticed a change in her a few weeks back. Often when we met, she had swollen eyes, red as if I'd just interrupted some terrible bout of grief. I asked her several times what troubled her, but she waved off my concern. She'd claim she had fallen into a foolishly sentimental mood, and that I need not worry. Then, just a few days ago she came to me. She told me I would meet two strangers whom I would learn to trust with my life. And then she gave me a gift."

"Well, you don't have to train as a diviner to figure out who she meant," Foxfire said, rolling his eyes. "You're just now recalling this?"

Lady Swiftbrook blushed. "Really, there's been quite a lot going on. We were at Second Home a week prior to the attack. I hadn't seen much of any of the councilors. I completely put her words out of my mind. For all I knew, I wasn't to meet these strangers for another hundred years."

They'd started moving again, Lady Swiftbrook's floating light globes throwing strange shadows along the walls of the cave as they slunk along beside their mistress, seemingly as depressed as she.

"I would like to know what gift she gave you," W'rath said.

"She has... had the most beautiful garden. I always admired it—envied it to be honest. She gave me a sapling, the offspring of her most prized twilight pine, and a collection of seeds from all of the varieties of flowers that call home to the glade she created."

"I see." W'rath cocked his head toward Foxfire. "And what did she give you and Lady Kela?"

Foxfire blinked, startled. "How did you know she gave us anything?"

"I didn't. It occurred to me, that faced with her impending death, she might have felt compelled to get her affairs in order, perhaps even provide gifts to those she knew would survive."

Foxfire started to reply, but Lady Swiftbrook interrupted him. "I can't imagine how a sapling and some seeds could help us in our current situation," she said.

Raven frowned, fully expecting W'rath to repeat his question to Foxfire concerning Lady Stormchaser's gifts to him and Kela. Even Raven interpreted Lady Swiftbrook's interruption as a clumsy attempt to silence the Wood Elf. But W'rath seemed to content to let the Sky Elf steer the conversation away from whatever topic she wished to avoid. "I confess, I have no answers," he said, shrugging. "Just a random musing on my part, which may have nothing at all to do with reality. She may very well have given them to you simply because of your friendship."

"I think warning us, so we could save all those people, would have been a much better gift," Foxfire muttered, face set in a scowl Kela would approve of.

"Unless," Raven said, "she saw far enough into the future to know that if she prevented the disaster at Second Home, it would lead to something even worse. Or maybe we needed to go through this horror in order to achieve some necessary goal later on."

Foxfire grimaced. "That's a lovely thought. Hopefully, she left a note or something explaining herself."

"That's a nice thought," Raven said. W'rath, nodded in apparent agreement, no hint at all that she might possess the information they needed. He was so much better with secrets than she. It didn't seem right to keep the books from their new friends, but if W'rath was right, and they contained information that proved unpopular, it would make it much harder for them to implement change on behalf of the Shadow Elves.

"We'll have to visit her place tomorrow," Lady Swiftbrook said.

W'rath made a face. "We still have most of the night. We can take a quick tour of this hole in the ground, see where the Shadow Elves have been rotting away for these past years, and then we can do a thorough search of Lady Stormchaser's abode before someone else does."

"In case you've forgotten," Lady Swiftbrook said, throwing W'rath an exasperated look, "we've only just made it through a tiring, emotional day. Councilor Stormchaser's estate won't vanish overnight. I hardly think someone will ransack it in the meantime."

"She's right," Raven said, feeling the full depth of her own weariness. "I'm past tired—I'm exhausted. Seeing the condition of those boys just about did me in. Part of me wanted to punch something and part of me just wanted to cry." She felt the stirring of anger once again and her hands balled up into fists. She wasn't used to struggling with such anger. How much influence did Linden have over her? How much could she still claim as her own?

"Forgive me, ladies," W'rath's deep voice drew Raven out of her uncomfortable thoughts. "I'm used to pushing on without hope of respite. You're absolutely right. This isn't an Exile city. We have no reason to believe a pack of hoodlums will compromise the sanctity of Lady Stormchaser's residence while we rest."

"I wouldn't be so sure about that," Foxfire said. Lady Swiftbrook tried to cut him off again, but Foxfire ignored her and pressed on. "You wanted to know what Councilor Stormchaser gave Kela and me? She gave me the lute on my back. Traveling the world as a bard gives me access to almost all people of every part of society. There's hardly a place I can't enter and gather information. Everyone, especially after they've had a few drinks, likes to talk to the bard. I'm willing to bet there isn't another elf who knows more about humans than I."

Raven saw the flicker of disdain that crossed W'rath's face at the mention of humans, but for once he held his tongue. Something in Foxfire's tone, and Lady Swiftbrook's attempts to quiet him, piqued her curiosity. "What does that have to do with Lady Stormchaser's estate?"

Firefox turned, body taunt, to face Lady Swiftbrook. "Shouldn't our new councilors be privy to everything we're dealing with?"

"We've had other concerns, in case you've forgotten," Lady Swiftbrook snapped, her own frustration finally coming to a head.

"Right. You're right. Even so..." Foxfire sighed, and made an effort to compose himself. Once he regained control of his temper, Foxfire addressed Raven and W'rath. "Even before this latest disaster, the Wood Elves have been at war with a human kingdom that wants to drive us from the forest where we live. Lady Stormchaser was one of the few who supported us, not just by voting in council," he paused to focus his displeasure on Lady Swiftbrook, "but by acting on her convictions."

W'rath made an odd choking noise Raven felt expressed her own incredulity perfectly. *We're just now hearing about this?* For his part, Foxfire seemed encouraged by what he saw in her face and gave her a brief smile of gratitude before continuing.

"So, Lord W'rath, to further answer your question, because of the war with the humans, Lady Stormchaser gave Kela several hundred bows. We're fine crafters. We build strong, well-made bows. But we don't have much magic left to us, so our weapons tend toward the mundane. Councilor Stormchaser sent us highly magical weapons. They're almost impossible to destroy, have incredible range, and they conjure their own ammo through the act of drawing the bow.

"But the most stunning part? Not one other councilor has stepped in to provide us with any aid. So, no, I wouldn't put it past someone to search Lady Stormchaser's property for anything that might help their cause or hinder ours." He stopped abruptly, drawing himself as straight as possible, bristling with indignation, daring the much taller Sky Elf to try to deny his claims.

All eyes shifted to Lady Swiftbrook. She sagged against the cave wall, lips thin and pale. This day was proving decidedly uncomfortable for her. "Lord K'hul felt strongly about taking an isolationist view of the conflict. We voted. The First Born, Shadow Elves and Sea Elves voted as a block to deny any involvement. They had the majority vote, so even though Councilor Stormchaser and I supported sending aid to the Wood Elves, we had to abide by the results of the vote."

"In other words, you left us to swing in the wind. It's all fine for everyone living on a chain of islands protected by a great magical shield, but what about those of us on the mainland, surrounded by those who think of us as savages, unworthy of the slightest consideration?"

"I didn't say I agreed," Lady Swiftbrook said. "However, the vote was valid, so like it or not, we had to abide by the results."

"Councilor, I have always seen you as a good person, but the fact that you would withhold aid to us because of what *others* want makes me think being good just isn't enough."

Lady Swiftbrook flinched, as though struck, but she stood her ground. "What you're proposing would bring chaos. If we don't bow to the will of the majority, any faction with an agenda could wreak havoc among the populace."

The cords in Foxfire's neck tautened, and it seemed to Raven his spiky red hair was trying to puff up like the tail of angry squirrel.

"That's already going on," the Wood Elf said. "The Sea Elves don't make decisions based on any knowledge or understanding of the situations they're voting on. They look to the First Born and do whatever the current descendant of the First wants. We're expected to bow to their will regardless of the consequences facing us. They couldn't care less about the politics going on among people a thousand miles distant from them. Of course, if they manage to unearth the culprits behind the fall of Second Home, they'll expect us to drop everything and help wage war against them. And of course we'll do that, we want to help, you're our kin, but we expect the same in return. That currently isn't happening."

"I take it relocating to First Home isn't an option?" Raven asked.

"Our Sky Elf ancestors remade themselves to provide guardianship for that forest. We've called it home since the Great Settling." Foxfire's voice had grown so loud it echoed throughout the cave system. "I'm the most worldly Wood Elf you'll ever meet, and even I grow sick at the idea of abandoning the forest, over two million acres, that the Wood Elves have nurtured for seven thousand years. King Oblund will take that land so he can build siege weapons for the purpose of going to war with his neighbor King Luccan. The man is insatiable. It won't happen in his lifetime, or even his son or grandson's lifetimes, but eventually they will destroy the entire forest in their quest for lumber, game and new farm land. I will not just sit back and let that happen no matter what anyone on the council votes."

A long silence followed. Foxfire stalked ahead of them, hands clenching and unclenching, simmering with fury. Raven regretted opening her mouth, while Lady Swiftbrook appeared to be trying to merge in with the cave wall. W'rath eased past them, thoughtful. Preoccupied, none of them realized immediately that the narrow cave they'd traveled had suddenly opened up into a vast blackness. Lady Swiftbrook's floating lights sped away upon her command, soaring about the cavern, illuminating a treasure unseen by any but Shadow Elves for generations.

Gold lit up at the touch of the magic lights only to find itself outshone by the sparkle of deep purple crystals and amethyst. What wasn't tiled in gold or overlaid with gems, gleamed with black lacquer.

Despite their ability to see in pitch black, the two Shadow Elves had no way of seeing the colors and details of this world without the light provided by Lady Swiftbrook's mage lights. They stood gaping at the sight just like their companions.

The cavern, a bubble within the rock, spanned for miles. Enormous multi-colored fungus crowded together forming a vast forest of mushrooms and toadstools. Stalactites and stalagmites gleamed like dragon's teeth. Yet all was dwarfed by the massive structure towering above it all. A great castle of gleaming black wood so dominated the cavern, it fooled the eye into thinking everything surrounding it was tiny. But then the sudden appearance of the lights sent a half-dozen desiccated Shadow Elves staggering in distress for the shelter of the castle. The mushrooms rose like ancient redwoods around them.

"Fuck me," Firefox said, his anger swept away as he took in the immense underworld realm.

"Well said," replied Raven.

Supported by the gleaming walls, the roof was the true glory of the castle. Tiled in purple crystal, the edges swept up into golden sculptures of all manner of fantastic creatures. Whether intended as guardians, or simply as decoration, Raven had no idea, but seeing how much skill and magic had gone into the building of the structure, one thing became clear: "Those who built this had great love for the Shadow Elves," she murmured.

"I've never seen anything like it," Lady Swiftbrook murmured. "The air vibrates with the amount of enchantment imbued into it. You're right, Shadow Elves didn't build this—they don't have the ability to channel the magic used here. This took the combined strength of Sky Elves and First Born to create."

Raven continued to marvel at what lay before her, memories of her former home surfacing. T'odol mas os si Merdaesalael—*Midnight Star of the Subterranean.* Many considered it the most magnificent of the Exile cities. Even with its slave-created sculptures, and sparkling colored lights, it was a slum compared to this one wondrous structure. The fungus gardens surrounding it outshone anything she'd experienced.

Her brain finally shook itself free of the dazzling sight, and she found that tears trailed down her face. She brushed at them, but more escaped her eyes. What a joy to find that, after Umbral's exile, the Shadow Elves who stayed true to the First, had not been ostracized. That meant this underground palace couldn't have been built, no *created,* until three thousand years later when the Great Settling occurred. So, at what point had things gone awry? Had a second falling-out, no one outside of First Home knew of, occurred? Or had things deteriorated as the result of a few sick minds from the last hundred or so years?

It wasn't until Lady Swiftbrook answered that Raven realized she'd spoken out loud. "I truly do not know," the Sky Elf said. "To my knowledge, no other conflict arose that would have caused a schism among the resident Shadow Elves and anyone else. Admittedly, the Shadow Elves felt the need to prove their continued loyalty. Over the years it changed to something more akin to a celebration, a rite of passage for young elves when they reached adulthood. They'd receive a simple assignment involving the gathering of information or objects from somewhere on the mainland. More fun than anything—a scavenger hunt of sorts. We had an annual festival honoring all of those who underwent the trial each year." She stopped speaking, her brows knitting in puzzlement.

"What is it?" Raven asked.

"It's very strange. I cannot for the life of me remember when we last had one of those festivals. They were so important to everyone on the islands. Why can't I remember when or why they stopped?" A flash of fear flickered in her eyes.

W'rath came to her rescue. "I shouldn't worry over much about it, madam. I must confess, when I found you in Second Home, my concerns lay with your immediate sanity, and due to the danger surrounding us, I might have spent less time than I normally would sorting out the particulars of your memories. Either your mind will repair itself in the coming days, or once I can use my powers overtly again, without causing myself injury, I shall put things to right."

Lady Swiftbrook laughed shakily. "That's a relief. With all that's gone on, I feared someone had purposely erased my memories. You've got me seeing conspiracies everywhere."

W'rath shrugged. "Also an entirely plausible explanation."

"You really do enjoy being an ass," the Sky Elf muttered.

"Getting back to the topic at hand... I can't say that I remember any such festivals at all," Foxfire said, "Keep in mind though, I only just arrived at First Home to join the council about twenty years ago. The festivals must have already stopped by then. Kela joined the council then, too, so there's no point in asking her."

The grin that had formed on W'rath's face at Lady Swiftbrook's pronouncement of his character dropped as the significance of Foxfire's words sunk in. "You and Kela have only served on the council twenty years?"

"Yeah, we took office after the last two went missing."

"So... the collars were already in use when you came to First Home. It was the previous Wood Elf councilors who voted in opposition to their implementation?"

"That's right."

W'rath waited while the others thought through the implications Foxfire's statement.

"You're thinking their disappearance had to do with them opposing the collars?" Foxfire asked, his voice tinged with the beginnings of dread.

"Indeed."

Lady Swiftbrook's shook her head in denial, backing away as if the act of distancing herself from the terrible words, could make them untrue. "How can you even contemplate the idea of councilors murdering other councilors? Besides, it doesn't make sense. Councilor Stormchaser and I also opposed the collars, and no harm came to us."

"Ah, but did you go so far as to use your rings to unlock the collars?"

"Of course!" Raven said, seeing the connection W'rath had made. "All of you were surprised when you couldn't remove the collars with your rings. Why make that change if someone hadn't already defied the council and removed the collars themselves? The previous Wood Elf councilors must have done exactly that and then..."

"They vanished off the face of the known world," Foxfire finished. Even in the uncertain light, his skin had gone noticeably pale. Lady Swiftbrook covered her mouth with a trembling hand.

W'rath's gaze traveled across the cavern of seemingly endless fungus, mineral formations and the magically created castle. "I have a good idea where they vanished to," he said.

"We could search for months and still not find their bodies," Raven said.

"With the help of a blood mage we could speed the process up to perhaps a few hours," Lady Swiftbrook said. She appeared ill, almost faint.

"The question is, do we want to?" W'rath said, almost to himself. When the others protested, he shrugged and explained. "Say we find our missing Wood Elves. What then? It's fairly obvious T'sane and Reaper had a hand in it, but did they act on their own? We have no way of knowing. I don't relish a blanket of suspicion falling over every Shadow Elf because of what those two did. Frankly, it's highly doubtful they acted without the blessing of the recently deceased Lord K'hul. The way they did everything in their power to ingratiate themselves to the *Voice of the First* means they probably acted on his orders. Of course, we'd have to prove that, and I'm confident making such an accusation, even with the assistance of a blood mage, would do even more harm."

"So we do nothing?" Foxfire said, through clenched teeth.

"To what end? Both Shadow Elves perished, and I can testify to the fact they suffered. The First Born councilors also met their demise during the battle, so if one or both were involved, they're beyond our ability to punish them."

"I suppose," Foxfire said. He stared across the cavern's expanse as if he could will it to give up its secrets.

"Buck up, old boy, despite all of the horror we've discovered, you have reason for renewed hope."

"How's that?" Foxfire said, dubious.

"First of all, you'll no longer find yourselves thwarted at every turn during council votes. Raven and I have no intention of playing lackey to the First's descendant. That leads us to the second item—you have a human pest problem, and I am nothing if not a bane of human vermin."

"That will only work if the previous vote gets overturned," Lady Swiftbrook interjected. "The Sea Elves will continue to back whichever K'hul holds the seat of *Voice of the First*. K'hul may not have gotten on well with his father, but I doubt he's any more likely to view the Wood Elves' plight as a worthy endeavor. Considering our current situation... I don't think he'll have much difficulty in swaying our other new councilors to agree with him."

"Really, madam, do I strike you as a chap who will go meekly into the night because of a vote? I think I've already demonstrated I'll go to great lengths to do as I see fit."

"Yes," Lady Swiftbrook said, dryly. "How's that jaw doing?"

"Quite excellent, thank you. The last few molars grew back before we started down."

"So, what is your plan? Every time the vote goes against you, you'll assault the opposing councilors?"

"In my defense, your hulking beau chose to escalate our disagreement to the physical. I foolishly allowed him to take me by surprise. He, in turn, was reckless enough to believe he could finish me off so easily. We both learned much."

"That doesn't exactly answer my question. Despite your charming demeanor, even I may see fit to oppose you in council now and again."

They had continued their trek, descending the switchback trail, which lead into the cavern. Now, as W'rath considered his words, they found themselves traveling among the forest of mushrooms, along a soft, lichen covered path. The mushrooms glowed with a faint luminescence making the paler skinned elves appear ghostly, while the Shadow Elves' black skin shimmered with the purples and blues of the reflected light.

"Though I admit, I am keen to spar with you, madam, you make a valid point: We cannot simply take up arms every time we disagree with one another. However, I believe we must implement a policy that allows for a certain amount of autonomy among factions. If K'hul does not wish to commit troops to assist the Wood Elves, he should have the short-sighted right to stand by that decision. But his desires should not prevent the rest of us from aiding our cousins."

"He'll argue we need everyone in order to combat the evil that attacked us at Second Home." Lady Swiftbrook said. " I know his mind well. He won't agree to a proposal that splits our already weakened numbers."

"All the more reason to help the Wood Elves. If we free the them from their current predicament, we gain their aid in facing our mysterious foe," W'rath said.

Foxfire chuckled, but without mirth. "He won't consider that a worthwhile gain. Outside our forests, our magic is so severely limited, we're not considered of much use."

"If that's the case," W'rath countered, "then we Shadow Elves have even less value. You saw the condition of our lads. It will take quite a while, even with their ability to regenerate, before any of them can fight. I doubt those lads even know how to hold a weapon, and with those collars clasped about their necks, they certainly never learned out to properly use their psionics. Based on your argument, we should be free to throw in with you."

"Not to disparage your offer," Foxfire said, making way for a newly arrived group of healers, "but how can a handful of sickly children help us?"

W'rath dismissed Foxfire's words with a wave of an elegant hand. "The children have no part in solving your predicament. They'll stay here and concentrate on recuperating and relearning how to function as upright, walking, sentient beings. I am all you need to turn the tables on the rabble threatening your home." He gave Foxfire a winning smile and passed through the gateway leading to the inner sanctum of the castle.

Foxfire held back, and the two females paused, brows raised in curiosity. "I think maybe we've exchanged one form of insanity for another. Doesn't he strike you as just a *little* overconfident?"

"Well, let's see," Lady Swiftbrook said, "first he slaughtered several demons to get to me. Then he healed my mind after a psionic attack drove me insane. Next he teleported us blind to where we met Raven. He then teleported us, and fifty odd survivors, to the Eastern Gate—again sight unseen, with only my memories to guide him. Once there, he played an instrumental role in shutting down the gate to the Nine Hells. I'd say he's earned the right to his confidence."

"All right, I'll grant you he's an incredible psion, but he hurt himself, didn't he? Ancestors know how long until he's able to use his powers to any extent. Just how much help can he be without his powers?"

Raven cleared her throat. "Don't forget he beat the piss out of an elf who stands nearly three feet taller than him and outweighs him by a couple of hundred pounds of pure muscle?"

"Well there is that," Foxfire admitted.

W'rath's voice drifted back to them from the gateway. "Do you three wish to spend the entire evening gossiping about me, or shall we explore this place?"

The three started guiltily. "We just wanted to admire the view from here," Raven said.

"Of course you were, lass," W'rath chuckled. "You keep practicing; you'll get the hang of subterfuge eventually."

More glow balls, set loose by the healers who had entered earlier, flittered about the hallways of the Shadow Elf castle. More beautiful craftsmanship greeted them. Their footfalls echoed, attested to the abandoned nature of the structure. Less than a hundred elves had lived within its walls for years, yet its size attested to the fact it's builders had intended it to house thousands.

They skirted along an inner courtyard where a garden and meditation area had gone wild, overgrown with colorful fungi. The bamboo fountain no longer worked, it's water source choked off by subterranean plants. Even so, the elves could easily imagine the courtyard's former beauty. "Did anything like this exist where you came from?" W'rath asked Raven.

She shook her head. "It had a beauty of its own, but nothing like this. What about your former home?"

The memory of a volcanic landscape flashed across W'rath's mind. In many ways, the early days of this world had more in common with the Abyss than this current, cooler version with its brilliant blue oceans and skies. "No, I've never seen anything like this. Most of this structure is constructed out of wood. We never would have had access to so much timber."

"There's no way they dragged this much wood down here," Lady Swiftbrook observed. "They must have opened portals and transported it that way."

W'rath made a face. "I must say I've developed a healthy dislike of portals."

"Understandable, but we use them for a great many things. We travel to and from the islands of First Home via permanent portals. Even our sewer system makes use of them. You saw the faces of the healers from earlier. We're short on portal magi due the attack. Only the team we just followed into here has a pair assigned to them. Those other groups would have dearly loved to escape to the surface through a portal."

Angry voices drew them from their conversation. W'rath took out running and the other three raced to keep up. They arrived in yet another courtyard. This one held the Sky Elf healers, and presumably the last of the Shadow Elves. The largest of the Shadows Elves, probably one of the females, fended off the Sky Elves with a long, elegant sword. She wasn't in much better condition than the rest of the young elves, but the sword glinted nastily in the flickering glow of the mage lights.

One of the healers turned as the councilors arrived. "She won't let us get close enough to help anyone," he said.

Lady Swiftbrook rolled her eyes. "There's one of her and six of you. She may have a sword, but you have magic. On top of that, she's half dead and blinded by the light you brought with you."

The healer shrugged helplessly. "We didn't want anyone to accuse us of hurting her."

The sound of a fist hitting flesh brought them all back around. The sword bearing elfess sunk bonelessly to the ground, unconscious. Raven stood over her, shaking her hand. "That hurt more than I expected."

"You punched her?" Lady Swiftbrook gaped. She turned to W'rath. "Did you make her do that?"

"I am as surprised as you as you, madam. Pleased, but surprised all the same."

"Sorry," Raven said, ducking her head in embarrassment. "It's just everyone around here talks entirely too much and does very little. She glared at W'rath as if wondering if he really had healed enough to use his powers to manipulate her. W'rath simply winked at her, and she turned back with a sigh. "She'll be fine. We have a room full of healers and it just seemed like a better solution than giving her the chance to hurt someone. Not that she posed much of a threat—these mushrooms have faster reflexes."

The rest of the Shadow Elves had backed against the wall. Some of them crouched defensively and pointed at Raven, squinting at her through watering eyes. "The evil has come," hissed one, and others muttered their agreement.

Raven scowled at them. "I'm here to help you."

"Don't waste your breath, lass," W'rath said as Raven's words elicited a hostile chorus of "Exile!", "Traitor!" and other less than complimentary labels.

"Silence!" Lady Swiftbrook's voice rang out. The young elves might think of W'rath and Raven as enemies, but they had a hard time disregarding someone they'd grown up viewing as an authority figure. She might consort with the Exiles, but their upbringing made it difficult for them to work up the nerve to dismiss her, at least now that their leader lay in a heap on the floor. They fell silent and crouched expectantly.

"These people," Lady Swiftbrook said, gesturing at the healers, "have come down here to help you. You don't realize it, but those you trusted, twisted your entire perception of the world. Please cooperate. None of us want to hurt you, but if you resist, we'll protect ourselves and subdue you."

The youngsters glanced from Lady Swiftbrook to their unconscious female, and then to Lady Raven. Frowns and trembling lips shown from every face, and most of the boys tried to back away, eyes darting about, searching for a means of escape. Their legs could barely hold them, though, and they had nowhere to flee. Slowly, they lost their defensive stances and sank to the floor. They wouldn't go to the healers, but resigned to their fate, they put up no further resistance.

The healers prepared the sick elves for the journey to the surface. Four of them unpacked stretchers while the two portal magi began to summon their means of escape. The portal would save them two plus miles of hiking while burdened with their newly acquired patients.

Lady Swiftbrook turned back to her fellow councilors. "We should have this place searched for any others still in hiding."

"I'm certain we've found them all," W'rath said. "Caeldan and Ryld indicated there are fifty-one of them in all. With those we met on top, the others we saw carried out of the lava tube earlier, and these we've just dealt with, we have our fifty-one. Not to mention, they don't seem all that keen on breaking off on their own."

"Still..."

"Oh, I don't disagree, the entire compound requires a thorough search. I, however, would like to be the one doing the exploring. This place holds many secrets and I mean to discover them. I have no desire for some well-meaning scholar to run off with books he thinks could damage the fanciful history you've all managed to conjure up for yourselves."

Lady Swiftbrook glared at him. "Your sarcasm is duly noted."

"There's also the chance you might stumble across a few corpses during your search," Foxfire contributed.

"Excellent point," W'rath said, approvingly. He was starting to like this Wood Elf quite a lot.

Lady Swiftbrook twitched with agitation, torn between exasperation and genuine hurt. W'rath ignored her distress, not in the mood to spare her feelings. While he had learned a great many things this day, many of those revelations had proven unpleasant. Not for the first time, W'rath wondered how so profound a change could have come over the elves. Granted, ten thousand odd years had passed since he'd last mingled with them, but he still had difficulty imagining these indecisive, weak-willed folk as descendants of the warriors he had known as a child. Even the strongest among them, K'hul, retained more of the weaknesses, than the strengths, of the ancestor he so revered.

Well, that wasn't entirely fair. The Wood Elves appeared to have some grit left to them. Perhaps, living on the mainland without allies and powerful magic, provided enough challenges to keep them sharp.

Kela's bluntness and sharp-tongued, amused W'rath, but he suspected she'd spent her life too isolated in the forest to provide him with the knowledge he needed to eradicate the hostile forces he faced. Still, when the time came, he saw in her the strength needed to follow through with anything asked of her.

Foxfire, on the other hand, seemed a very likely source of intelligence. In his own way, he had stepped in and done the work normally expected of Shadow Elves. But a single elf, no matter how dedicated, couldn't hope to uncover every plot set up against the elves. While he focused on keeping the Wood Elves safe from the forest coveting king, someone else slipped in and brought disaster to Second Home.

So, they needed to deal with the wretch king quickly. Not only would defeating the humans free the Wood Elves to assist their cousins with any unpleasantness First Home might soon face, but in aiding them, W'rath felt he would gain steadfast allies. The other elves might dismiss the Wood Elves because of their more primitive lifestyle and weakened magic, but W'rath doubted they had managed to survive without having some valuable skills.

W'rath finally allowed himself to see his companion's weariness. Even Foxfire's passion had sputtered out, and Raven sagged as if she'd marched the entire day in her armor. He would never admit it, but the weight of the last several days had taken its toll on him as well. He needed a quiet place to meditate, to allow his mind a chance to repair itself. He regarded the hated portal. The healers trotted through it without concern, just happy to escape the cavern with their patients. With a last inward sigh, he came to a decision.

"As intriguing as I find this place, I see we're all about done in for today. Might I suggest we utilize the portal Lady Swiftbrook's people have so kindly provided, and get some rest?"

"The council meets tomorrow," Lady Swiftbrook said. W'rath wasn't sure if she intended her words to convey agreement or as a warning of more tiresome bickering to come. Perhaps both.

Foxfire groaned. "I can't wait for another chance to be ignored and ridiculed," he said.

"I assure you, I want to know every single morsel of knowledge you hold concerning the various human nations on the mainland," W'rath said. "Odds are, the enemy behind the attack on Second Home is human, so the council had best listen to anything you have to say concerning those who might have the capability of tearing open doorways to other planes."

Foxfire crooked his mouth in doubt. "Like I said, I know more about humans than any other elf I know, but I don't know that anything I can tell you will help pinpoint who attacked Second Home."

"You know more than you realize," W'rath assured him. "However, even if your knowledge does no more than allow us to whittle down our list of suspects, you'll have done us a great service."

Foxfire smiled and nodded, encouraged. "Shall we then?" he said, gesturing at the portal.

"With a song of joy upon my lips," W'rath said, and the four stepped through the portal and returned to the night above.

# CHAPTER 9

Raven was relieved to learn that Lady Swiftbrook had made rooms available at her estate for W'rath and her. As beautiful as she found the Shadow Elf castle, she had no desire to sleep there. It felt haunted. Its halls echoed with tragedy. She couldn't stop thinking about the two Wood Elf councilors, elves who had tried to do the honorable thing, rewarded for their efforts with death. She knew Lady Swiftbrook still harbored hope that a less horrific explanation existed for the disappearance of the two Wood Elves, but Raven felt certain the two had met their end somewhere in the mushroom forest surrounding the castle.

Now seated around an immense table, which dominated Lady Swiftbrook's dining hall, they settled in for a late dinner. Everyone else in the household had retired for the evening, but Lady Swiftbrook's cook had set out dinner for them in anticipation of their eventual arrival. Covered and kept warm via an enchantment, the food itself seemed out of place on the delicate, floral plates. The generous servings of venison, wild mushrooms and soft bread stood out as austere. "Lord Firemane is a First Born," Lady Swiftbrook said, seeming to read Raven's mind. "What he lacks in imagination, he makes up for in skill. You'll never taste better venison. Fortunately, he wanted his daughter to apprentice under me, and this is the arrangement we agreed upon."

Raven knew she should be famished, but everything they had witnessed that day weighed upon her, dulling her appetite, making it impossible for her to do more than nibble at her meal. To her right, W'rath busily polished off his venison, pausing only to mutter something appreciative of the absent cook's abilities. Raven had never seen anyone with such a scandalously huge appetite. Nor had she missed the covetous glances he'd been casting in the direction of her still laden plate. For all his cultured words, he definitely approached his meals like someone who had lived alone, unsure of when next he might hope to eat. He brightened when she offered him her mostly untouched meal. Without the slightest hint of embarrassment, he set to work on his second dinner.

Now that they had returned to the surface, Kela reappeared and joined them. She looked just as wild and disheveled as when they'd left her, all the more obvious now due to the luxurious surroundings. Across from Kela, Foxfire kept up a steady stream of conversation, attempting to recreate through words the wonder of the Shadow Elf castle and its environs for the other Wood Elf. It wasn't lost on Raven that he completely avoided any mention of the suspected fate of the previous Wood Elf councilors. In fact, his earlier outrage and horror were nowhere in evidence. Since she doubted Foxfire had shrugged off the experience, his behavior had to be an act for Kela's benefit.

"You've never seen anything like it," Foxfire concluded.

"And I never will," Kela replied, stabbing a piece of meat and shoveling it into her mouth. She chewed it to death and swallowed, pausing to wipe her mouth on her arm before attacking the next slice of meat. "We should have the sky overhead, not miles of stone."

"A lot of our enemies frequently make their homes underground," Foxfire pointed out.

"That's why we have them," Kela said, pointing her fork at W'rath and Raven. "By the way, I've decided I wish to have a child."

"Uh... what?" Foxfire said, baffled. "Whatever does that have to do with what we're discussing?"

"Nothing. I see no point in talking about something I'll never see, and I want to have a child, so I thought I'd tell you."

"Okay..."

"We can get started tonight."

"I wasn't aware you two had become mates," Lady Swiftbrook said.

"Me neither," Foxfire said, his face nearly as scarlet as his hair.

Kela looked up from her plate. "It makes sense. We're the leaders of the Wood Elves, we should reproduce. I can overlook your prissiness."

"That's generous of you. Not particularly romantic..."

Kela made one of her now familiar snorts. "Romance belongs in those silly songs you sing. I'm strong and I fight well, you should be pleased that I've chosen you."

Foxfire appeared anything but pleased. "Do we wait for bed, or do you prefer to simply rut right here on the table?"

Much to everyone but Foxfire's amusement, Kela seemed to give that some serious thought. Then she flashed a wicked grin, betraying her intent to have some fun at Foxfire's expense. "I guess it should wait until we're alone," she said.

"Thank the gods for that little bit of decency," Foxfire sighed. "I probably shouldn't ask this, but what if I don't want to have anything to do with this?"

Kela blinked, genuinely surprised. "I've already made it plain I'm a superior choice for providing our people with offspring. How could you not want to be a part of that?"

"Well, there's that bothersome romance thing you mentioned."

"I thought males liked to fornicate. Wait a minute... you don't prefer owl bears do you?"

"Owl bears?! Who the hell would screw an owl bear?!"

"I've heard rumors about my cousin G'odlin," Kela said. "He's definitely odd. Always goes about looking stunned and smelling funny."

"Yeah, that's suspicious all right. Gods... Can we discuss this tomorrow? I really need to take some time to wrap my head around the whole idea of doing my duty as opposed to giving a girl flowers and maybe reciting some poetry to her before jumping on top of her."

Kela shrugged. "Do what you must. There will be no jumping on top of me, though. I won't have your bones stabbing into me. We'll do this civilized, with me on top."

"Oh, of course! How thoughtless of me," Foxfire said, standing. "If you folks will excuse me, I've quite lost my appetite."

Without another word, Kela jumped up and followed after Foxfire, presumably to torture her male counterpart further with her views on elven reproduction. With them gone, the remaining three exchanged looks of amusement. "I'm fairly certain there isn't a single thing I can say this evening that will top what just went on here," W'rath chuckled.

Raven laughed as well, and suddenly realized she felt better. A thoughtful expression settled onto her face. Surely, Kela hadn't staged the whole exchange. Could she really be that perceptive? And that subtle?

"Has your appetite returned, lass?" W'rath suddenly asked.

"It has," Raven said, amazed. She looked sheepishly in Lady Swiftbrook's direction.

"I'll see what I can manage," the Sky Elf smiled.

*****

Once they escaped the scrutiny of the others, Kela grabbed Foxfire's arm and dragged him toward her room. "Kela, seriously, I'm not interested," Foxfire said, trying to pull free from her iron grip.

"Quit being an idiot and come with me," Kela snarled. All sign of her earlier lewd behavior had evaporated, and Foxfire realized her routine at the dinner table had been a ruse to get him to leave so she could speak with him in private. He stopped resisting and followed her into her bedroom.

Once inside, Kela proceeded to check all the windows and draw the blinds. She finished by moving about the room and whispering to each of the plants cluttering up the place. Greenery covered nearly every flat surface in the room, probably Lady Swiftbrook's attempt to make the Wood Elves feel more at home. Each plant Kela spoke to started to glow. Foxfire recognized the magic. The plants would create a sort of interference and confound anyone trying to eavesdrop on their conversation.

"You think someone is spying on us?" he asked as she finished with the final plant.

"I don't know what to think anymore," Kela replied. "I don't want to take any chances though. Little of what I saw today made me feel optimistic."

Foxfire nodded. Kela's speech patterns had changed now that she was confident of their privacy. When around non-Wood Elves she preferred to speak in the clipped, unsophisticated manner most outsiders expected of their people. She felt it gave her an advantage—that others would underestimate her. Foxfire wasn't sure he agreed, but he couldn't deny her skill as an actress. She'd fooled even him this evening and he knew about her dual persona.

"So what's so important you couldn't wait until after dinner to talk to me? You embarrassed the hells out of me," Foxfire said. While he admired her acting skills, he wasn't keen on being made a fool of.

"You tell me," Kela said. "You're the one who babbled non-stop about ebony castles and giant glowing fungus."

"You *were* listening," Foxfire said, unable to hide his surprise.

"Of course," Kela replied, "but more importantly I heard what you weren't saying. Something happened during your visit down there—something awful—and you skated all around it, trying to distract me with talk of shiny rocks. You may not share my bed, but remember, I'm the one who found you half dead all those years ago and brought you into my clan. -I taught you how to survive here. I know you too well—you can't distract me with pretty stories."

She was right, of course, Foxfire knew. When she'd found him he'd been more dead than alive. Knowing he suffered from hypothermia hadn't done him a bit of good. A fire, lots of furs and hot drink, all provided by a primitive of the forest, had been worth more than all his years of learning. He should have known she'd see right through his false cheerfulness during dinner.

"I planned to tell you after we said our good nights to our hostess," he said. Even to his ears he sounded petulant. He flopped into a velvet upholstered chair and regretted it immediately. The carpenter had built it for someone much taller than a Wood Elf, and his legs dangled above the floor in a less than dignified manner.

Kela smirked at his discomfort, but didn't let it distract her. "You know I have the patience of a human," she said. "I wasn't about to sit there for another two hours while you pretended nothing was bothering you."

Foxfire sighed, resigned to the fact that he couldn't postpone telling Kela about the probable fate of the previous Wood Elf councilors. There was no point in trying to work into it slowly. Kela wasn't exaggerating about her lack of patience. "Lord W'rath thinks someone murdered Felfahl and T'yone, and then stowed their bodies somewhere down in the Shadow Elf cavern."

Whatever Kela had been expecting, news about the disappearance of Felfahl and T'yone wasn't it. She dropped down onto her bed as if her legs had been cut out from under her. "How does he know this? Can he see the past?" All of the cockiness had left Kela's voice. She sounded much younger than her five hundred and sixty-three years.

Foxfire ran a hand through his spiky hair. He'd nearly been ill back in the cave. Between his anger and his sense of helplessness he'd been nearly overcome. "No," he said, watching the emotions flitting across Kela's stricken face. "He deduced it based on how the timing of the Council's decision to collar the Shadow Elves coincided with Felfahl and T'yone's disappearance, and because of our surprise when our Rings of Unbinding didn't work. He believes the change in the requirements for the ring's usage came about because our kin defied the council and removed the collars."

As much as he understood the emotions Kela felt, she still took him by surprise when she leapt from the bed and launched herself at him, dragging him from his chair by the front of his shirt. "Those bastards killed them for that?" She snarled into his face, shaking him as though she suspected his involvement.

"Their disappearance happened at the same time as the collars—it's just too much of a coincidence," he managed in between shakes. When Kela finally released him he collapsed onto the floor. He'd never been able to match Kela's fire, he tended to approach controversy ... well, how he had in the caves—lots of words and little action.

Kela turned away, shoulders, arms and fists tensed, ready for a fight. When she finally spoke again her voice had taken on almost an animal growl. "What are we going to do about it?"

Foxfire had to force himself to answer. W'rath's words came back to him and he dreaded Kela's reaction when she heard what the Shadow Elf had said. "Lord W'rath doesn't believe any good can come of pursuing the matter. Since Reaper, T'sane and Solorn K'hul died at Second Home, making accusations at this point would only harm the living. He's concerned the Shadow Elves would take the brunt of any conflict that erupts."

The expected flurry of outrage didn't manifest. Kela's shoulders slumped. She didn't say a word, but nodded, the only acknowledgement she gave that she'd heard and understood him. Slowly, her hands, no longer clenched, reached up to cover her face.

Foxfire came to his feet, more alarmed than he'd ever been when faced with Kela's fiery passion. He drew up to her, but didn't dare touch her. She sensed his closeness, though, and her entire body shuddered with her attempts to rein in her grief. "Kela," he said, not at all sure what she needed from him.

"What has happened to us?" she said.

Foxfire shook his head, as at a loss as she. She couldn't see the gesture, but his silence provided all the answer she needed. She sucked in a big snuffling breath and composed herself. "You're better at reading people than I," she said. "Do you think we can trust this Lord W'rath?"

The bard's mind tripped over the events of the past several hours. "Right now our agendas align, so for now I'd say, yes."

"Damned wishy-washy answer," Kela muttered, a trace of her normal self reemerging. "I guess that's as good as we can hope for right now."

"He says he'll help us with Oblund," Foxfire said. Kela stood a little straighter upon hearing this news. Foxfire still wasn't certain W'rath could provide them with the help they needed, but he needed to give Kela something positive to focus on.

Kela's breathing returned to normal. "Tomorrow during the council meeting we need to make sure we tell them about the magi Oblund has hired on. It may help convince the rest of them to throw in their lot with us."

"Only if they believe there's a connection between the magi and what happened at Second Home," Foxfire replied.

Kela turned back to face him. Damp streaks still stained her cheeks, but she had buried all other traces of the despair that had gripped her seconds ago and replaced it with determination. "You are the worst archer I've ever met," she said, "and every time you use a knife I half expect you to cut your own hand off. But when it comes to jabbering, no one can do a better job of persuading people to side with us. You'll make them see that aiding us will help the entire nation."

"That was almost a compliment," Foxfire said. As much as he wanted to protest Kela's assessment of his fighting prowess, in truth he had even less faith in his abilities than she did.

"It's the best you're likely to get from me," Kela replied. She had taken up his long-fingered hands in her root strong ones, and stood gazing intently at him with her chestnut brown eyes.

Foxfire realized he'd been too quick to assume Kela's had dismissed her grief. It still radiated out at him from those bottomless eyes. Her pride would never allow her to openly admit to being vulnerable. "I know I was pretty adamant earlier," he said, "but considering all we learned today, I don't think we should sleep alone."

Kela snorted and shoved him back into the uncomfortable chair. She turned away, but not before Foxfire caught a glimpse of the gratitude she tried so hard to hide.

ЖЖЖЖЖ

It took an act of will for Raven to force herself to undress before collapsing into the great cloud of a bed dominating the guest room she had been assigned. She needed to bathe again, but exhaustion chased away any serious thoughts on the matter. Raven didn't even have enough energy to admire the soft, feminine decor, so different from the rustic tree house she'd called home these past three years. Instead, she carefully tucked her precious books from Lady Stormchaser under her pillow, and burrowed into the bed, pulling the down filled covering over herself.

She still felt guilty about not telling the others about the books. But even the most recent entries in Lady Stormchaser's journal were written in the ancestor of the modern Elven language, and she couldn't divine its meaning. W'rath claimed he could read ancient Elvish, but until they found him some reading spectacles, that wasn't going to happen. She decided she would bring it up to him in the morning and see if they couldn't find out how to acquire a pair for him. She knew he'd insist on discretion, he couldn't help himself, but she doubted they could keep something like this from getting around. An elf old enough to have eyes which had adapted to seeing only distances clearly would cause gossip. Most likely, the jeweler would have to create the spectacles completely from scratch, and because of the specialized nature of the enchantment for the lenses, they would have to bring in an additional party to help out. Raven and W'rath couldn't hope to keep word from spreading.

The strangest part was that W'rath's advanced age had proven such a novelty. She knew why the Exiles didn't live for several thousand years. Treachery and danger filled the cities of the Exiles, and it took supreme skill and luck to live beyond four or five hundred years. But the people of First Home? Many elves as old as W'rath, if not older, should reside on the protected islands of First Home. She had fully expected to meet legends when she arrived, but instead it appeared there weren't more than a handful of elves over three thousand. Not one of the original elves seemed to exist any longer. Raven had gotten the impression K'hul was no more than five or six hundred years old, and yet he would step into the High Council as the oldest living descendant of the First. How could that be?

In all the reading she'd done over the years, she'd never run across any mention of the fall of the First. He'd had many children by many females over the years, and yet, aside from Umbral little information could be found on them.

What had happened to them?

✶✶✶✶✶

In his own room, W'rath sucked thoughtfully on one of the fragrant burning sticks Stench had given him, and pondered much the same thing as Raven. Cut off from the rest of the elves for thousands of years, he'd heard little about what took place after his exile. Until the moment he walked off the ship, and no one had said a word, W'rath had feared someone from his past would recognize him and reveal him to the masses. Instead, he found a people devoid of their past, their histories rewritten, their society completely changed, and none old enough to have marched with his father into battle.

From what he could gather, even information concerning him, the elves greatest pariah, stood completely at odds with reality. Not entirely surprising, of course. His father would have seen to it. But some of the things Raven had told him seemed very odd. His physical description, in many of the historical works she'd studied, painted him as a grotesque, twisted creature, barely recognizable as an elf. In all his days, W'rath had never seen such a thing among his people. Other races suffered from birth defects as little to no magic flowed in their veins, but elves were magic incarnate. They weren't born with club feet or cleft palates or any other flaw.

W'rath supposed that the descriptions of him could have originally been intended, not as a true depiction of his appearance, but rather as a metaphor for his inner self. The writer's meaning, lost over time, could have inspired those who had not known him personally to portray him as a physical monstrosity.

W'rath shook his head and inhaled the aromatic smoke into his aching lungs. If any one of them had truly known his father, they'd realize that the First would never have tolerated a defective child. While other cultures left their unwanted babes on a rock to die of exposure or animals, the First would have feared the child might somehow survive. He would have seen personally to the child's destruction. Even so, the First had looked with shame upon W'rath's small size and less than impressive strength. He'd wanted a child who could stand toe-to-toe with the massive orc and ogre clans they fought against; instead the fates had mocked him and given him a son who had to use trickery, guile and a powerful mind to subdue his opponents. It didn't matter how many times the First ran into a foe who simply could not be overwhelmed by physical or magical means, he still loathed the boy who made victory possible through other means.

*Hmmph, and now you're gone, and here I am left to deal with another one of your messes, Father.*

W'rath stretched out on the bed. In truth, he found it quite comfortable and he could understand how these young, soft elves had come to enjoy the embrace of sleep. He didn't think it likely he'd manage to wean them from such dangerous behavior, but he had far more important issues to concern himself with at the moment.

The mystery of what happened to his ancestors would have to wait as well. For now, he had to focus on the more immediate problem of the hidden enemy who had obliterated Second Home. Knowing so little about the modern world vexed him. He doubted Reaper's memories could have provided the answers he sought. She had led as isolated a life as most of the other elves of First Home.

Still, he berated himself for not delving deeper into Reaper's mind. W'rath had been in a hurry, though, and had mostly focused on learning the modern language and the basics of the elves' culture. Discovering exactly what atrocities she and T'sane had committed would have been useful. He wished he knew how much the previous *Voice of the First* had involved himself in the near genocide of the First Home Shadow Elves. And had he given the order that had doomed the previous Wood Elf councilors?

No point in fretting about such things now. While Reaper or T'sane might have foolishly kept a journal, something that would make plain the extent of the conspiracy, W'rath doubted it. For now, all his questions would have to simmer in the back of his mind until he had the opportunity to investigate further. He needed to focus on learning from Foxfire all he knew of the various existing cultures. He also needed to do whatever he could to free the Wood Elves from their conflict with the annoying King Oblund.

He pondered the possibility that King Oblund could have instigated the attack on Second Home. He quickly dismissed the idea. If the fellow had that sort of magical firepower at his command, he could have defeated the Wood Elves ages ago. For that matter, he wouldn't have need of siege weapons for his attack against his rival.

W'rath sat up, frustrated, wreathing his head in the curling smoke of his cigarette. All his life he'd primarily worked as a scout and a spy, acquiring knowledge and getting the jump on his enemies. Even after being cast into the Abyss, he'd eventually ended up performing the same sort of work for the demon lord, Ruaz'Daem. While free of that place now, W'rath found himself in the unpleasant position of having to play catch-up. He still knew too little in order to feel effective. Foxfire had been dubious about his grand boast of cleaning up the human problem. *Sadly, lad, I'm beginning to realize you were right to be skeptical.*

*And sitting here grousing about it isn't going to help one bit.*

Fortunately, he *could* control his own physical and mental needs. W'rath escaped the seduction of the soft bed and pinched out the remainder of his cigarette. He placed it in the bowl of the incense burner he'd found waiting on the dresser when he entered; no use in annoying Lady Swiftbrook any more than necessary with his annoying new habit. He settled himself on the floor, slowly willing himself into a state of deep meditation. Someone less skilled would have had a hard time blocking out the many questions and problems facing him. W'rath had practiced meditation since before he could wield a knife, or will an orc's brain to explode. Uruvial Stormchaser had taught him. She had always been there for him.

And so, using Uruvial, the one bright star of his childhood, as a focal point, W'rath settled into a trance and soothed his mind and body.

ЖЖЖЖЖ

Lady Swiftbrook stood on her balcony, gazing up at the night sky. The distant stars looked chill and full of secrets. Foxfire had told her they were actually suns, but so far away they were visible only at night. That seemed farfetched, but Foxfire knew odd things. Of course, his trade required a fanciful imagination, so perhaps he'd made it up. If so, it seemed a less than romantic explanation. She would have thought he could come up with a tale that didn't sound like he'd pulled from a book written by gnomes.

Behind, she heard someone enter her room. She'd hoped for privacy this night so she could contemplate the stars and her own shortcomings. She'd seen the disappointment and anger in the eyes of W'rath, Raven, and Foxfire. Even worse, the sight of the pitiful Shadow Elf youths as they'd stood, wavering in the fading sunlight, had punished her with shame. How could she have let this go on? *In some ways, I carry even more blame than those who committed these atrocities.*

When she didn't leave the balcony, the visitor came seeking her. "Kiara," K'hul said. "Didn't you hear me come in?"

"I sought solitude," she said, ignoring his implied chastisement for not running to him as soon as he entered the room. Right now, despite their intimate relationship, she found even his use of her given name annoying.

K'hul in turn ignored her desire to be alone and joined her on the balcony. He came up behind her and wrapped his arms around her. "We face evil times," he said, "none of us should isolate ourselves."

"I have much to contemplate, and my thoughts concerning you are not particularly kind right now." She remained stiff, refusing to submit to the lure of his solid warmth.

"You have invited a viper into our home and already he poisons us." He kept his voice soft, but his embrace grew noticeably tighter.

"It wasn't W'rath who stood there today and argued against freeing those children from the terrible wrong done to them. When your father sat on the council, you spoke constantly to me of how you would do things differently. Yet the moment you joined the High Council, you transformed into him. Explain to me how you can rationalize treating children in such a cruel manner?"

"Umbral was a child."

"So that's what it comes down to? The actions of a single person? You can't condemn an entire race because of the failings of one individual."

"While a great leader, the First made a mistake in creating the Shadow Elves. He allowed their beauty to seduce him, and he fathered a monster. He gave Umbral everything and the creature tried to murder him."

By now K'hul's embrace had tightened to the point that Lady Swiftbrook felt her ribs creak protest. "You conveniently forget one thing," she said, resisting the urge to struggle.

"My lady?"

"Umbral wasn't created. He claimed both a Shadow Elfess *and* the First as his parents. He was half First Born."

K'hul sprang away as though he suddenly found himself entwined with a serpent. Lady Swiftbrook spun and stared into his furious eyes. "It's the First Born, not the Shadow Elves, who are known for their explosive tempers. It seems to me, the boy who lashed out at his father that day, may have looked like a Shadow Elf, but it was his First Born half that lead him to attempt patricide!"

For a moment she thought he would strike her. She narrowed her eyes and raised her chin, daring him to prove her point. At last he lowered his trembling arm, but his fist remained clenched. "I am not my father," he said, his voice breaking with his barely contained rage.

"Then stop standing in the way of righting the wrongs he committed. Help the Shadow Elves. Help the Wood Elves."

"The Wood Elves?"

“Their ongoing war with the Kingdom of Teresland. You’re father didn’t want us getting involved in the affairs of the mainland,” Lady Swiftbrook explained.

“So much for that. We’re deeply involved in the affairs of the mainland now. Whoever attacked Second Home saw to that. We should have never built a city there. Why my father supported such a project, I’ll never understand.”

“Normally he wouldn’t have, but your father had a weakness for books, and when the Consortium of Knowledge approached us with the idea of housing collections of writings from all over the known world, he finally agreed. With him voting for the city, we gained the votes of the Sea Elves as well as the Shadow Elves.”

“I’ve never heard of the Consortium of Knowledge.”

Lady Swiftbrook bit her lip to suppress the sarcastic quip that popped to the front of her mind. Perhaps W’rath *had* poisoned her just a bit. “They’re a group of scholars, represented by all of the sentient races of our world. I’ve heard, though never confirmed, that they even have goblinoid races among their numbers.”

K’hul’s lip curled in derision. “Sounds like something gnomes would come up with. You can’t trust gnomes.”

“Gnomes did start the consortium.” She smiled. “Sadly, I share that particular prejudice with you. I had a cousin who had to regrow an entire arm when some ridiculous gnomish invention blew up. He was lucky he didn’t bleed to death before the vessels repaired themselves.”

“Bloody gnomes.”

They both laughed, and the tension between them dissipated. K’hul shook his head ruefully. “All right. We’ll revisit the Wood Elf issue tomorrow. We’ll see about putting an end to their troubles with the fool who wants their forest.”

“And you’ll be nice to W’rath?”

“Not likely.”

“Well, that’s a start at least,” Lady Swiftbrook sighed.

"You awake?" Caeldan asked his brother.

"You know I'm awake, you git," Ryld replied. "Ever since those collars came off, we've been completely aware of each other. Why are we even talking? We can send to each other."

"We're out of practice," Caeldan sighed. "Before the collars, we were one person in two bodies. Now I feel like an interloper in your head."

"You're an interloper in my ears," came a voice. "Would you two shut your traps? Some of us would like to sleep."

"Is that you, Seismis?"

"I'm not saying."

"It's Seismis all right."

"Since when did he get so bossy?"

"Since he got a good meal. Still just as whiny, though."

"I really don't think it's bossy *or* whiny to want a decent night's sleep. Between you two and the bugs, I'll never get any rest."

"The bugs?" Ryld wondered.

"Can't you hear them? Gods, they're horrifying! I swear they're plotting something. I think they're coming to get me."

Ryld and Caeldan exchanged looks. Seismis had always been an odd one. Among their small family of outcasts, Seismis wasn't just the youngest of them, but the strangest as well. Well, unless you counted psychotic females hell bent on killing everyone off slowly.

"Sorry, Seismis. We'll leave you and the bugs in peace. We should practice our sending anyway."

The two fell silent and grinned at one another. *Wait for it*, Ryld sent.

*Three. Two. One.*

"Oh, gods, the bugs! The bugs!"

*There it is.*

The two brothers tried to stifle their laughter, but completely lost it when they heard multiple pillows slam into Seismis, accompanied by various threats and curses. He yelped. "Okay, for you," he pouted. "Just so you know, when they're done with me, they'll come for you. Just you wait."

That prompted a chorus of disparaging remarks and finally everyone settled in again. Ryld and Caeldan lay back on their pillows, but couldn't stop smiling.

*I do believe we're on the mend*, Ryld sent.

*Indubitably,* Caeldan replied and shut his eyes to sleep.

# CHAPTER 10

Like everything else W'rath had seen so far, the council chamber for the elves of First Home proved both functional and elegant. The furniture, finely crafted, gleamed, the wood shimmering like moonlight. The upholstered cushions followed a theme, depicting the settling of First Home and the raising of the protective wall of light. Each showed a unique scene, yet the weaver had taken great care to ensure the entire set went well together by using a common color pallet and a flowing design that drew the eye through the story.

Enormous paintings adorned the walls, detailing important historical events. The artists had rendered each figure exquisitely, and assuming they had taken pains to ensure the accuracy of the likenesses, viewers could easily recognize individuals, even those not the main focus of the scene. W'rath found the poses overly dramatic and the expressions a bit too exaggerated, but he forgave the artists their excesses since the stories portrayed in the paintings were intended to fill the viewer with a grand perspective of their past. A certain amount of overindulgence was to be expected.

The cavernous hall echoed with the click of W'rath's boot heels as he crossed the glass-like floor, it's cloudy translucence reminiscent of snow opals. He stopped in front of one of the paintings where another had already paused to admire it. "What have we here?" he asked the Sky Elf councilor, Kiat Icewind.

I've always loved this one," the fellow replied. The previous day he'd spoken hardly a word, but now he seemed more in his element. "It tells the story of the First's historic defeat of the Frost Giant army. Just look at the detail! Here the First battles the giants' leader, Jarfang Frostbeard. You can even see the steam from their breath. See the expressions on all the other people's faces—such intensity. Even the magic and the falling snow appear swept up in a dance."

"Magic?" W'rath said. "That's very odd."

"How so? The First manipulated fire with unsurpassed skill. Of course he would use magic in battle."

"Not against giants, he wouldn't. They were notoriously magic resistant—almost immune. Even fire magic barely affected the Frost Giants. Not to mention the concussive force of many spells increased the likelihood of avalanches, which proved much more damaging to the elves than the giants. The elves quickly learned not to waste their strength tossing powerful spells at the giants. They switched to using personal enhancement magic. They bolstered their strength, put up magical shielding and heightened their reflexes."

Raven, the Wood Elves and Lady Swiftbrook joined them. "Well, I expect the artist merely wanted to make the scene more dramatic. The fire magic also helps break up the predominantly blue and white of a winter scene," Kiat said.

W'rath let that go. He'd already said more than he should, so he refrained from commenting further concerning the accuracy of the painting. Raven had no such qualms. "That doesn't explain why the painter chose to show the First facing off against King Frostbeard." She cocked her head and tapped her lip as she studied the painting, puzzling over its flagrant inaccuracies.

"Well obviously," Kiat said, trying to sound authoritative, but managing only thin-lipped petulance, "because of all the battles against the giants, this one decided everything. Every last one of Frostbeard's thanes met their end that day."

"But that's not how it happened at all. I assume by your robes you're a scholar—you should know that."

Kiat's cheeks grew pink, but Raven didn't seem to notice, her interest focused on the painting. "Lord W'rath is right, magic was useless against the giants. Their immense size and strength also put them at a distinct advantage over the much smaller elves. The elves, in order to have any chance against the giants, had to swarm them. Their massive losses forced the First called a retreat."

"That's outrageous! The First would never back down from such rabble. I've never once seen any of the things you claim in a history book."

"Then you're reading the wrong history books," Raven replied.

"We don't read books written by Exiles," K'hul said, his huge frame casting a shadow over the rest of them as he approached.

"How about books written by the respected scholar, Prentice Steamcaller?" Raven challenged.

"Sounds like a gnome name. They're all mad, you know."

W'rath chuckled. The others looked at him. "I apologize," he said, "but he has a point—they *are* all mad."

Raven scowled at W'rath, and he smiled back, all innocence, before turning his attention to K'hul and Kiat. "That being said, the lady is correct in pointing out that others seem to have a more accurate grasp of our own history. Did your ancestors form a committee and go through every written word, rewriting anything that made the First appear fallible? While a great *War Leader*, the First didn't single-handedly march across the world slaughtering all comers. He sometimes had to do what all leaders do—delegate."

K'hul snorted in derision. "Our ancestors lived in simpler times. They had no need of complex strategies."

W'rath silently scolded himself for opening his mouth again. No point in falling silent at this juncture, though, he'd merely give his nephew the impression he'd won. *And we can't have that now, can we?* "For the most part you're right, but when going up against an enemy like the Frost Giants, he found his usual tactics didn't work. He didn't have any choice but to seek out new ideas. Like you, old boy, he had an enormous ego. Even so, he managed to master it once in a while and utilize the strengths of others."

"Next you'll claim the First asked Umbral for help in defeating the giants?"

"I don't think *ask* is the right word," Raven said. "According to Professor Steamcaller, the First *demanded* his son attend him, and then tasked the boy with the seemingly impossible job of defeating the giants. Umbral, who had grown tired of his father's poor treatment, demanded in turn that if he took this challenge and succeeded, his father would publicly acknowledge his deed, and elevate him to the same status as Lady Stormchaser. The First agreed, and while no one can know his mind for certain, the professor believed the First expected Umbral to not only fail, but to perish in the endeavor."

"Ridiculous!" Kiat said, K'hul's presence bolstering his confidence. "Where did this professor gain his information?"

"He cites many sources," Raven said. "He even claims to have interviewed an ancient blue dragon who watched as these events unfolded. The dragons hold no love for Umbral, so there's no reason to believe any of them would lie for the purpose of making him look good."

"Assuming he interviewed a dragon at all, and this gnome scholar of yours didn't just make it up to give his tale the ring of truth," Kiat scoffed.

"First it's Exile propaganda, and now it's lying gnomes, falsifying their sources," Foxfire said, matching Kiat's skepticism with an equal measure of disgust. "Frankly, this corroborates a story I heard while up north in Clan Craig's lands. I'd like to hear the rest."

"Dwarves know this story?" Raven said, eyes widening in surprise.

"You bet," Foxfire said, ignoring the curious glances his phrase drew. "The world knows all kinds of things about us. Mostly, it's the older races who retain knowledge of the old days. The dwarves, the gnomes and the dragons have long memories, and enough interest to write things down. For the most part, they don't have reason to alter the facts like we apparently do. But come on—finish telling the story."

W'rath caught the pleased smile Foxfire's words brought to Raven's face. *She's enjoying this.* He didn't blame her. She'd spent a good part of her short life researching, and probably had few opportunities to share what she had learned.

"So," Raven said, "Umbral had his task and he took it back to the Shadow Elves under his command. Since most of them, aside from Umbral, couldn't channel magic, and weren't large enough or strong enough to trade blows with an enemy, they'd long since taken to looking at problems differently than their larger, magically adept cousins. After a time, they hammered out a plan.

"Umbral put together a small team. Only his very strongest psions would participate as the plan they'd developed required mental strength, discipline and endurance. In the dead of night they set out for the Frost Giant camp. There were only a few hundred Shadow Elves and thousands of giants. Using their skills at stealth and their ability to hide in shadows, they entered the camp and sought out candidates for their task. They teleported onto their targets and hid within their hair, psychically burrowing into their minds. The elves sifted through the Frost Giants' brains, learning about their fears, hatreds and desires. Using that information, they planted false memories, stirred their passions and suppressed their inhibitions.

"The Frost Giants awoke to find themselves embroiled in battle, not with the elves, but with their own kind. Real and imagined wrongs consumed them, sending them into a blind rage. Elf against giant in a fight didn't generally end well for the elf, but giant against giant served the elves much better.

"The violence spread. Once a giant fell to the weapons of his kin, or found himself so committed to a fight he couldn't hope to escape, the Shadow Elves teleported to new victims. As more giants entered the fray, it became easier to urge them into killing their fellows. The carnage was terrible."

Raven threw her shoulders back and brandished an imaginary sword. "Umbral sought out King Frostbeard and perched boldly on his shoulder, burying his sword into the giant's muscle and using it to anchor himself. He wanted his father to see him as he obliterated the giant army. He completely subjugated the giant king's mind and sent him into battle against his people. King Frostbeard waded through his thanes, slaughtering any who got in his way. Those still free of the influence of the Shadow Elves banded together to try to stop their maddened king, all the while oblivious to the tiny elf on his shoulder.

"King Frostbeard stumbled up to the First, nearly bled dry, one of his arms chopped off at the elbow, his body nothing but a mass of wounds. Spears protruding from his chest and back, he collapsed to his knees before the Supreme Warlord of the elves and breathed his last.

Face grave, Raven gazed past her audience as if the deeds of that terrible day played out somewhere in the distance. "Beyond the dead king the last of his people lay dead or dying in the snow. Not a single Shadow Elf had fallen during the entire battle. Umbral had succeeded in the task given him by his father."

"Nicely told!" Foxfire said, clapping appreciatively.

Raven made a half bow and then waved off the applause, suddenly bashful. "I really love those old stories."

Kela stepped closer to the painting and made a show of examining it. "You're painting needs touching up," she said. "The giant king needs to lose an arm and have a few dozen spears sticking out of him. And someone needs to paint a tiny Shadow Elf up there on his shoulder."

"Oh, very amusing," Kiat said, arms crossed defensively across his chest, lips turned down in a sulk.

"No more comments on the veracity of the story, K'hul?" W'rath prompted, deliberately dropping the use of 'Lord'. He tried to keep his grin under control, but he hadn't had so much fun in quite a long time and his efforts proved futile.

Surprisingly, K'hul appeared completely unperturbed, either by the story or W'rath's overly familiar manner. "In truth, I've heard this version of the story too. My father told it to me. The K'hul line makes a point of passing on important family history to each generation. The story doesn't end there, though. Perhaps Lady Raven would like to elaborate on the complete story?"

Raven shook her head. "I don't understand your meaning."

"Really, lady? Your gnomish scholar and his dragon didn't expound upon the events that came right after the Frost Giant defeat? Allow me then. The arrogant upstart, Umbral, jumped down from the dead king's shoulder and demanded of the First his promised reward. The First, enraged that Umbral had treated the battlefield as an opportunity to show off, thereby trivializing all of the elven lives lost in the war against the giants, refused him. At which point the wretch, drunk from his success over the savages, thought himself better than the First and attacked him with the full force of his mind and his coarse magic. Though gravely wounded, the First responded to this knavish attack with might of his summoned elemental companion, and crushed Umbral like an insect. I don't think I need go on. Even the least informed of us know how the rest of the tale goes."

"No one likes a show off," Kiat said. He wilted under W'rath's baleful gaze, and quietly slipped behind K'hul's protective mass.

"I guess I've learned something," Raven said, voice thoughtful. "I've read dozens of accounts about various historical events, but none actually tied a specific incident with the fall of Umbral." She smiled at K'hul. "Thank you, Lord K'hul—that explains so much and fills in some gaps for me."

W'rath barely managed to suppress his laughter. The stunned expression on K'hul's face was priceless. Raven seemed genuinely grateful for the information, completely ruining any hopes K'hul had harbored to embarrass her. *How very disappointing for you, old boy.*

"Wait," Kela said. She looked at those gathered in disbelief. "You're saying all of this hate and discontent between Shadow Elves and the rest of us is because the First broke his promise and his incredibly powerful son threw a tantrum?"

"I expect the resentment the two felt toward each other had built up for some time before that incident," Raven said. "This final insult simply triggered Umbral's rage."

"He had his father's temper," Lady Swiftbrook said. Her eyes met K'hul's and his lips twitched in disgust.

W'rath caught the look and recognized a sore point when presented so nicely for him. "K'hul, old chap," he said, enjoying the dismay the sound of his voice brought to his nephew's face, "are you of the crowd that likes to conveniently forget Umbral was half First Born?"

"He may have had father's temper," K'hul said, "but he inherited little else from his father. I expect even Lady Raven's famed gnomish scholar didn't describe Umbral as bearing any physical resemblance to the First."

"Not if you mean general things like build, height, and skin color," she said. "He did mention that Umbral supposedly bore a strong resemblance to his father, facially. Unlike the elven texts I've read, Professor Steamcaller's works describe Umbral as a handsome youth, small but well-built due to the exertions of the life he lead."

Nearly forgotten, Kiat peered out from behind K'hul's back. "That's a ludicrous claim. Why should we take an outsider's word for any of this? We have multiple works concerning Umbral, and a great many of them portray him as a monstrous being who none could look upon without feeling pity or disgust. He's the reason we don't allow Shadow Elves to reproduce with any other elven race—the twisted, hideous results are just too much to bear."

W'rath's eyes widened. He'd had no idea the elves restricted mated pairs by race. What a truly ridiculous notion. Raven's clenched teeth and balled fists told him she agreed. W'rath hated to remain silent, but Raven's gnome scholar mentioning his strong resemblance to his father, made him cautious. Raven could handle this argument. He'd hold his tongue and do his best to look as dissimilar to the First and his overly angry nephew as possible.

"How can you even say that and not feel a total fool?" Raven said, her anger with Kiat getting the better of her. "Do you truly believe no other children came about from mixed unions? Umbral was simply the first of many such children. Once the First took a Shadow Elf as a lover, it's not surprising others would seek companions from among them as well—if for no other reason than to mimic their leader."

Raven's aggression took even Kiat by surprise. He retreated several steps and seemed on the verge of fleeing. With a toss of her head, Raven dismissed him and switched her focus to K'hul. W'rath tensed, ready to intervene. The young First Born soul sharing Raven's body seemed to be firing Raven's passions, leaving her with little sense of restraint. Verbally abusing Kiat held few dangers, but tearing into K'hul held more risk.

Much to W'rath's relief, when Raven spoke again, she addressed K'hul in a more moderate tone. "It's more logical to assume that when Umbral attacked the First, he also used magic. It wasn't his psychic powers alone that so gravely wounded the First, but the combined might of mind and magic that frightened people.

"When the First created the Shadow Elves, he didn't need a people with magical talent. He needed spies and assassins, so he molded their essence so they could hide almost in plain sight. Suddenly the elves found themselves with a population of mixed blood elves, who looked like Shadow Elves, possessed their ability to hide and use psionics, but who may have inherited the ability to wield magic."

"Pure speculation," K'hul said, refusing to acknowledge the logic of Raven's argument.

"But speculation based on much more solid evidence than the so-called facts found in so many of your books," Raven countered, her voice growing sharp once gain.

"Our ancestors lived in savage times," Lady Swiftbrook interjected. She interposed herself between K'hul and Raven, and placed a placating hand on her lover's chest.

That Lady Swiftbrook had managed to keep quiet so long, amazed W'rath. He appreciated her intervention, though. He had no desire for Raven to make a target of herself for K'hul's ire. And if things had continued in the same vein, they'd waste the day clawing one another's eyes out over events thousands of years dead.

Now that she had their attention, Lady Swiftbrook, swept her arms toward the table dominating the hall, urging them away from the painting which had started the entire ordeal. "We mustn't do our enemy's work for them," she said. "Everyone put your personal grievances away, sit down, and let us speak of current events. We can rehash old wrongs when we face less dire circumstances."

"Damn, I was hoping for a fist fight," Kela said, cracking her knuckles.

They turned from the painting that had triggered this latest squabble, to find themselves facing an out of breath Lady Culnámo. "I'm sorry I'm late," she said. "I got lost—never actually been here before. Did I miss anything?"

ЖЖЖЖЖ

The large conference table shimmered like an oasis, radiating with imbued magic. Like most elven works, time and weather had no effect on it. It would require heavily enchanted weapons or powerful spells to do so much as blemish its finish. At the moment, though, the elves made use of one of its more showy enchantments. It projected a three-dimensional representation of the world. At one end, a sphere floated above the table, accurately showing the shape and location of all known continents, islands and bodies of water. On the other end of the table, a smaller area displayed a more traditional map layout with the exception that the terrain, trees and miniaturized cities had shape and form. The mountains' elevations rose, accurately represented in relation to everything else. Lakes, seas and oceans shimmered, appearing to move either from the tide or unseen weather. All in all, a most impressive piece of work.

Lady Swiftbrook raised an eyebrow as W'rath poked a finger into a lake. It reacted to his touch, sending out ripples, eventually reaching the shore as gentle waves. "Fascinating," he said, making no attempt to hide his delight.

"Don't get too excited. Nothing you do to the map affects the real world."

"Now *that* would be something." He squinted, trying to read the names hovering above various locals. He bent over the table, his face hovering above the human city of Scarin. "Be afraid, you slow-witted apes. I'm coming for you." He finished with a deep throated chuckle.

"*That* wasn't creepy at all," Foxfire said. He motioned for those gathered to give him some space near an area which depicted a heavily forested area. He'd nearly fainted when K'hul had told Kela and him he'd decided to reconsider his father's decision to withhold assistance in the Wood Elves' fight against the invading forces of King Oblund. Kela harbored a multitude of suspicions, but Foxfire wasn't about to over analyze the unforeseen change of heart. He would do his best to present the situation and make sure K'hul decided to fully support their cause.

"This," he said, waving a hand over the forested area, "depicts the southernmost edge of our forest. King Oblund currently has his forces encamped on this huge grass plain. We estimate his numbers at around thirty thousand."

"What are your numbers?" Lady Culnámo asked.

"In this part of the forest, we have about twelve hundred elves. If we manage to drag all of the clans from the northern territory, we might get our numbers up as high as six thousand. In addition, other woodland residents will fight—dryads and nymphs primarily, but they're entirely bound to the forest. They can only help if the humans enter the forest proper."

"With thirty thousand men, you'd think they'd do exactly that," Raven said.

"Early on they sent in a sizable force. When his army first arrived at our doorstep, the king thought he'd crush us in a single afternoon, and begin cutting down trees before supper. I wish I could have seen his face when not a single one of his men made it back out of the forest. He lost a quarter of his army that day."

Foxfire kept his face unreadable, but Kela grinned at the sudden sharp intakes of breath from the others. W'rath finally spoke up. "Lad, do you mean to say, your troublesome king started out with forty thousand troops, and in one afternoon, you killed off ten thousand of those fellows with only twelve hundred elves?"

Foxfire stood a little straighter. "We may not have the most powerful magic to draw upon, but within our element we're extremely capable."

"I'm not easily impressed," W'rath said, "but that definitely impresses me. You hardly seem to need outside help." He gazed upon Foxfire and Kela as if seeing them for the first time, and gave them a nod, a warrior acknowledging their accomplishment.

"We thought he'd slither off after getting his ass kicked like that," Foxfire said. "Unfortunately, he decided he'd rather set up his army just out of bow shot. Not even the magic bows Lady Stormchaser gave us can reach them."

"So you're at a stalemate," Lady Culnámo said. "He won't send more troops into the forest, and you're not able to stand up to his forces outside your home. What does he expect to gain? It's not like he's laying siege to a castle where the residents have limited resources. Meanwhile he's feeding an enormous number of troops. Either his men will starve soon, or he's spending an outrageous amount on a supply train."

"While annoying, we could tolerate it if he wanted to camp outside the forest for all eternity," Foxfire replied. "Unfortunately, he's added another element to the original setup. He's hired four mercenary magi from the city state of Tassilia. They've kept us busy with summoned creatures—minor demons, mostly. They only send in one or two at a time, but they cause plenty of havoc."

The intensity of the others heightened at the mention of demons. Even Kiat leaned in closer, drawn to Foxfire's announcement. "Seems a common theme these days," K'hul stated. His angled brows dipped to meet in a V on his scowling face.

"They haven't actually ripped open a gateway like they did at Second Home. They're summoning individual creatures," Foxfire said.

Kiat nodded. "Of course they'd want to do that. With only four of them, they don't have the strength to cast as powerful a spell as a planar tear. It would kill them for certain. Summoning individual creatures allows them more control, and they can specify the sort of demon they get—ensure that they don't leave a mess for the king once the fighting ends."

"We think the demons are just to keep us busy," Kela broke in.

"Ah, now this I want to hear," W'rath said, eyebrows rising along with his heightened interest.

Foxfire picked the story back up. "Ultimately, King Oblund's hopes to get his hands on our land. It won't do for the magi to burn us out because there goes the trees he wants. He can't have them send in poisonous gas because that would also kill all the game he wants to hunt. While nasty, strong, and hard to kill, the demons they've sent against us don't have any special traits and they don't cast magic. Plus, they only send in one or two at a time. He wants to keep us busy, but doesn't want to have a forest full of demons once he wins."

"His army just squats there, stinking up the land ... waiting," Kela added.

"Any idea why?" Kiat asked.

"We've done some scouting," Foxfire said. "We sent some birds from the forest to check their camp. The information didn't help as much as we'd hoped, but we did learn the mercenaries are working on a ritual. Three of them work on it while one sits out, presumably to summon a few demons and then rest. The ritual has gone on for some time, over a week, day and night. We expect something ugly to happen when they finally finish."

"Since he still seems intent on using his men," Lady Swiftbrook said, "they could be working on a mass protection ritual. Depending on the numbers and types of protections they've chosen to weave into the ritual, it could take several days to complete, but no more than three or four."

"They may not limit it to protection," Kiat said. "That sort of ritual works well if you add in enhancements like speed, strength and density. It would also account for the additional time they've spent working the spell."

"Interesting," K'hul muttered. Despite his earlier reluctance to get involved with the happenings on the mainland, the mention of the demons, and the apparent strength of the magi involved, had piqued his interest.

"So let's start laying out our options," Lady Swiftbrook said.

"Well, W'rath told us he could take care of the problem by himself," Kela said despite Foxfire's attempts to shush her.

"Presumably he made that claim before he knew about the four magi," Kiat said.

"While true," W'rath admitted, "it wouldn't change my original plan should you decide to move forward with it. However, considering other things we've learned this day, I'm thinking we have more to gain by a massive show of force on the part of the entire Elven Nation."

"You originally planned to slip into the camp and assassinate the king, didn't you?" Foxfire asked. He feared his original assessment of W'rath's sanity, or lack thereof, might be true. Who blithely walked into a an enemy encampment and expected to stick a knife in the back of a king without having an entire army rip him limb from limb?

W'rath shrugged, unfazed by the incredulous tone of Foxfire's voice. "Provided someone could get me to the general area, there isn't a camp, castle, or dragon-protected stronghold I can't enter."

"That's quite a claim," K'hul said. He narrowed his eyes, scrutinizing the Shadow Elf as though he could discover all of W'rath's secrets through conscious effort. Foxfire didn't think even the stolid will of a K'hul could figure out the enigmatic Shadow Elf.

"There's nothing exotic about it," W'rath said with a lazy shrug. "I've worked my entire life as an assassin and spy."

"I thought you were a psion," Kela said.

"Of course, my dear, I most certainly am. However, psionics are merely a tool, like your bow, or this enchanting table. You don't rely entirely on your bow, right? You also have a large knife on your hip, I see. The same goes for me. I have developed many skills over the years. I've had the good fortune of surviving enough unpleasant situations that I've learned to diversify my knowledge. Rely on only one tool, and someday that tool will fail you. That day you die."

Kela grunted, and Foxfire knew W'rath had won her over with his straight forward explanation. Foxfire couldn't help notice, though, W'rath hadn't mentioned what diverse skills he possessed. Perhaps Kela could see something Foxfire could not. He hoped so.

"That's all very interesting," K'hul said, his tone making it clear he found it anything but, "however let's get back to the matter at hand.

You seem to think your assassination plan isn't such a good idea any longer."

"While I meditated last night it occurred to me, after the events at Second Home, the elves as a whole need to make a statement. Already, word has spread that the elven people suffered a humbling, devastating defeat. With each retelling the stories will grow more exaggerated. We can ill afford to have the world see us as weak."

"We allow that and every greedy upstart will harass us thinking us easy targets," K'hul said, slapping his hand upon the table with each word.

Lady Swiftbrook nodded. "Already our trading partners have sent their regrets. For the time being, they no longer desire our presence in their harbors. They're frightened that merely associating with us will draw the wrath of whomever attacked us."

"Cowards," Kela spat.

"Don't judge them too harshly," Foxfire said, spreading his hands, calling upon them to understand the world's fear of the unknown. "Who wouldn't find the idea of an enemy, powerful enough to rip the fabric between two worlds apart and flood your city with death, terrifying?"

"So we hunt down the bastards who did this and make new boots from their hides," Kela snarled.

"Charming," W'rath said, and Foxfire suspected he meant it. "But we get ahead of ourselves. First, we must remind the world what a terrible force we are when roused to anger. Your arrogant king has inadvertently provided the perfect opportunity for our demonstration."

Lady Culnámo nodded and touched several spots in the area surrounding the enemy encampment. "We set up several miles from the camp. With nature all around us we won't find ourselves cut off from our elemental powers, and we'll have plenty of time to call on our elementals—we won't have a repeat of Second Home. We go in heavy, don't give the humans a chance to react. The First Born should summon earth elementals and rain fire down on the enemy's head. The Sky Elves can call down lightning and break up their camp with tornadoes and air elementals. Wood Elf sharpshooters will pick off any who try to escape."

Foxfire had never had any dealings with Lady Culnámo before. Her no-nonsense tactics style came across as typical for a First Born. That she stepped in without consulting K'hul, though, spoke of a confidence most wouldn't possess. This trait alone explained why Lady Swiftbrook had chosen her to fill a seat on the council. Still, he doubted she'd had any experience with humans. Too often elves, even First Born, moved at a casual pace compared to humans. "Just so long as you mean hours and not weeks or years," he warned. "Remember, we're not fighting other long-lived beings. If we set this up in our usual methodical manner, they'll have finished their ritual, taken the forest, died, and left a new generation to annoy us."

"So we need to decide on a final course of action right now," K'hul said, "and implement it swiftly."

"A lot of how fast we act depends on how long we have until they finish their ritual," Raven said.

"We can't possibly know the answer to that," Lady Swiftbrook said. "They could finish in a month or an hour."

"We'll have to assume the worst," K'hul said. "We don't have the luxury of taking our time to put together a huge campaign, but I believe with a small, powerful force, we could prevail against them." He paused, his icy eyes spearing each of them with his fury. "We go tonight."

"Tonight?" Lady Swiftbrook gasped. "We need more time than that. A week at least—longer even."

"Normally, I would agree, madam," W'rath said, "but if we give them time to finish their great casting, we could find ourselves up against an army impervious to much of our magic. Even the physical superiority of the First Born could be neutralized if their spell enhances the strength and speed of their soldiers. Therefore, we're in a position where we'll have to keep our strategy simple and overwhelm them with devastating force. "

Lady Swiftbrook frowned fiercely at K'hul and W'rath. "I don't believe this. You two agree on something? On this?"

The two grimaced but nodded. Lady Culnámo added her perspective. "I agree, it's rash, but it's the right course of action. If these magi are of the same caliber as those who attacked Second Home, we could doom ourselves by giving them more time while we prepare the perfect battlefield."

"You told us over a week has passed since they started their ritual—that alone bodes ill. Is there anything else you can tell us that would help determine what they're up to?" Lord Icewind asked Foxfire and Kela.

The two Wood Elves conferred together for a few moments before Foxfire answered. "When we didn't get the kind of detail we wanted from the birds, we risked sending a group of scouts to infiltrate the camp. They set off a magical ward, and alarms alerted the humans to their presence. Of the five, only one made it back. When the alarms went off, four of them tried to make a run for the forest, but the humans have light cavalry, and our people couldn't outrun them. The one who survived continued to head into the camp, and used the confusion to help him hide.  He spied on the camp for some time, and clarified some things for us. He's the one who determined only three of the magi perform the ritual while the fourth summons a few creatures and then rests. He knows where the mercenaries have set up their tent."

"All useful information, but it does nothing to tell us when we can expect for them to finish their task," Lady Swiftbrook said.

"It does give us some idea of the sort of men we face," Lord Icewind said. "They're well trained and disciplined. Humans don't normally possess the stamina needed to perform such a long ritual—even with one of them resting. Also, it takes a great deal of skill to rotate individuals in and out of an ongoing casting. I don't think I'm jumping to conclusions by suggesting a direct connection exists between these men and those who attacked Second Home. Regardless, I have to agree with Lord K'hul and Lord W'rath, and suggest we launch our assault as soon as possible; we do not want them to finish whatever they have started." His piece done, the slender mage jumped as if remembering where he was and who he faced. He shrank down within his robes, trying to appear inconspicuous.

"I see how this is shaping up," Lady Swiftbrook said. She turned to Raven. "I suppose you support them in this as well?"

Raven nodded. "I completely understand your concerns. After all, we're still in shock from what happened at Second Home. It's only been a few days since the attack and only one since we docked here."

"Precisely," Lady Swiftbrook said.

"However, we have one advantage, and we shouldn't waste it," Raven continued. "Word has spread quickly about our defeat at Second Home. If Lord Icewind is right, and the magi working for the king came from the same place that launched the attack against us, they have to think we're in no shape to come to the aid of the Wood Elves—even if we wanted to. Up until now, we've shown no interest in wanting to help."

"That's because no one did," Kela grumbled.

"The point being," Raven said, ignoring Kela, "they're not expecting us—period. When we pop onto the battlefield, ready to dump spells on them, we'll take them by surprise. They won't have a chance to mount a defense or retaliate. Their fancy magi, stuck in the middle of their ritual, won't be able to help."

"Depending on the actual context of the ritual," Kiat said, seeming to unfold like a flower, as his magical knowledge gave him a brief burst of confidence, "it might even prove dangerous for them to break it off before it's complete."

"Very true," Lady Swiftbrook admitted. She dropped down into one of the ornate chairs and tugged at the high-necked collar of her gown, perhaps wishing for more substantial armor. She glared at her fellow councilors as if they somehow shared fault for the poor behavior of human magi and kings.

"Does that mean you've come around to our side of things, madam?" W'rath gently jibed.

Lady Swiftbrook rolled her eyes, and gave up her attempts at defiance. "I suppose it does."

"I have to write a song about this," Foxfire said. "I don't think I've ever heard of an elven council coming to an agreement so quickly."

"Assuming the Sea Elves don't have some arguments to present," Kela said, a devious gleam in her eye.

"I don't understand," Raven said. "If they're not involved why would they even have any input?"

"She's making a joke," Foxfire said. "You see, the Sea Elves have so dedicated themselves to the K'hul family line, they generally don't bother attending any of our sessions. They always accede to whatever choice the *Voice of the First* makes."

Foxfire saw W'rath's right eye twitch. Given the Shadow Elf's barely controlled temper, he didn't think it would take much more to send W'rath over the table to kick K'hul in the teeth.

"They're not much better than T'sane and Reaper," W'rath muttered.

"What's that?" K'hul said. True to form, W'rath's words elicited a flare of hostility from the First Born.

"Nothing at all, old boy," W'rath said, his tall ponytail giving him the appearance of a combative little rooster. "It simply explains why so many asinine rules exist around here. Nothing gets done without the express approval of a K'hul. You come to the table with two votes already in your pocket. How lovely for you."

The two locked gazes, and it seemed Kela's hoped for fist fight might erupt. Ever the peacekeeper, Lady Swiftbrook once again intervened. "Before this dissolves into another pissing match between you two, can we decide on our course of action?"

Lady Culnámo jumped on the suggestion right away. "First, what is our ultimate goal? Do we intend to wipe them out to a man? Do we take prisoners? What about the magi? Do we take any of them for questioning? What about Lord W'rath's initial assassination idea? Do we go through with that?"

"Interrogating one or more of the magi could be helpful," Foxfire said. "Tassilia, where they hail from, specializes in magic for hire. If their people attacked Second Home, it's unlikely they did it for personal reasons. Someone with a grudge against us hired them."

"What a fascinating people," W'rath observed. "Completely apolitical, without any moral standing, or sense of loyalty to anyone other than the highest bidder, and apparently completely unconcerned with any of the consequences associated with their mercenary work. I can't believe they've been allowed to continue to exist for any period of time. I would very much enjoy the opportunity to question one of them." He rubbed his hands together, anticipating the chance to get one of the magi alone. All the while, though, his eyes never left K'hul.

"So, we've decided to capture one of the magi and attempt to gain information from him?" Foxfire asked. A chorus of agreement answered him. "Now... what about prisoners?"

"No prisoners," Kela said. "We only need the mage for putting him to the question. We don't care about ransom, and we don't use slaves, so they'd just get in the way."

"So... kill everyone?" Kiat said, shocked. His hands clutched at his robes in his distress over the imagined slaughter. Kela's proclamation surprised Foxfire as well. He knew she didn't care for humans, but he hadn't realized how deep her feelings ran.

"Those foolish enough to stand and fight, certainly," Lady Culnámo said. "If we take them by surprise, utterly overwhelming them with a show of force, they should break quickly."

"What if we allow any who flee to escape the battlefield?" Foxfire asked, relieved Kela didn't respond with one of her derisive snorts.

"Only the regular soldiers," K'hul suggested. "Anyone who appears to have any command standing should be finished off. We don't want those with authority to rally the troops once they get a safe distance from us. You mentioned they have cavalry. That puts us at a disadvantage once we settle into one spot on the battlefield. We can't allow them to circle around behind us and hit us with lances or spears."

He looked around to see if everyone agreed with him and saw W'rath's confused face. "You have a question?"

Foxfire guessed the proud psion disliked admitting he didn't know everything. Satisfying his curiosity won out over his embarrassment though. "I am not familiar with the term *Cavalry.*"

K'hul snorted in amusement. "You really have been living in a cave."

"Humans keep animals as slaves and force them to serve as mounts," Kela said. They mostly use horses. When the humans ride them, they can move much faster than those of us on foot."

"Here," Kiat offered. He recited a simple spell and with a few graceful motions of his hands, brought forth a shimmering image that hovered above the table. The image clearly showed a lightly armored human seated on the back of a powerful animal. The creature raced around in the air above the table, displaying its ability to make quick changes in direction. All the while, the human sat, elevated above his fellows on foot.

"They've made themselves into centaurs," W'rath said, intrigued.

"Actually, it's believed they came up with the idea from observing centaurs," Kiat said. He waved his hands, and the image dispersed into wisps of pastel smoke.

"We have nothing to counter this?"

"Large explosions should work," Lady Culnámo said with a grin.

Kela scowled at her. "It's not the beasts' fault. And no, we don't have anything like it because it's a vile practice." This last she directed at W'rath, who made placating gestures with his gloved hands.

"Peace, lass," he said. "I only ask because surely intelligent fae creatures exist who would agree to assist us in battle, serving in place of these horses."

"Most of the truly fae have left this world with the sprites and the faeries. They didn't like the changes the rise of the humans brought about, and they left to form their own pocket universe," Lady Swiftbrook said.

Lady Swiftbrook's statement left W'rath blinking, stunned. Foxfire supposed, as an Exile, stuck underground for most of his life, W'rath might have reason to be ignorant about the exodus of the fae. His apparent dismay surprised Foxfire, though. Why miss what you had never known?

"No wonder the world feels so mundane," W'rath said. The perpetual fire in his eyes dampened.

"There are still a few left," Kela said. "The nymphs and the dryads live in our forests. A few Unicorns still walk the woods."

Foxfire tried to draw upon the persuasiveness Kela claimed he possessed. "We fight for them as much as for ourselves. When the Sky Elves, our ancestors, chose to make themselves into the first Wood Elves, they did it because they felt an obligation to the wild things that couldn't speak for themselves. We still take that commitment very seriously."

"All the more reason to make sure King Oblund, and anyone associated with him, learns that rising against us is a very bad idea," Raven said. "Since the main force of our attack will probably fall on the heart of the enemy camp, what if we have the Wood Elves use the chaos as cover to get close in and make sure the cavalry can't form up. That way we can spare the horses. If anyone actually manages to get on a horse, you shoot the rider and the horse can escape. With luck, the horses will panic and add to the confusion."

Foxfire found himself nodding in agreement. A quick glance at Kela ensured she approved as well. They would have a large number of responsibilities, but with some twelve hundred Wood Elves they could easily split their people into teams accordingly. "We can pick off any we see trying to make a break for it. Most of the commanders will have horses, so we can pinpoint them easily while the rest of you make things explode."

K'hul's gaze settled back on W'rath and Raven. "That leaves you," he said. "Obviously your minions cannot assist us. The two of you could infiltrate the camp in order to capture one of the magi and the king."

"That seems a bit much," Lady Swiftbrook protested. "Lord W'rath hasn't recovered the use of his psionics yet."

"You needn't worry yourself, madam," W'rath said. "As I stated before, even without my psionics, I am quite capable, and all Shadow Elves can blend into the shadows, making us nearly undetectable. Thanks to the quick thinking of the Wood Elf scout, we know where the magi keep their sleeping quarters. The king's tent should be easy enough to spot. Someone that arrogant isn't going to hide in a rough tent in order to blend in.

"In addition, we know the humans have a security perimeter set up that can tell friend from foe. It's possible it's keyed to detect race, but not likely. A much simpler spell requires only that a person carry a small token. Usually, a caster sets a charm on a mass of small stones or chits, and then hands them out to the perimeter guards. Take down a handful of those guards and we'll have easy access to their camp. Do you concur, Lord Icewind?"

Kiat reflexively glanced at K'hul before answering. K'hul merely made an impatient gesture. "Uh, yes, you're well informed concerning the forms such spells can take. Specifying within the spell who to allow in and who to react to provides much better security, however such detail makes the spell quite a bit more difficult to cast and maintain. I don't doubt these men have the capability of performing such a spell, but with them deeply involved in ritual magic, it's likely they went with a more simple version as you suggest."

"You couldn't just say 'yes'?" Kela muttered.

"Assuming that's true, then our scouts could take out a few of the guards and relieve them of their tokens," Foxfire said. "We've kept an eye on them and we know when the guards have their shift changes. We can take them down just after a new shift starts. That will give you plenty of time to get into the camp without them realizing they have intruders."

"Very good," W'rath said. "So, we have a means into the camp, locations marked out, and targets established. I will have need of Lady Raven's strength. She and I shall enter the camp, and converge on the tent where the resting mage sleeps, and capture him. We shall next visit the king. My question to you—once we confront the king—what do you wish done with him? Shall we kill him? Take him prisoner? Or... something else?"

"If I may," Lady Swiftbrook said before K'hul could take control, "This plan of ours shall result in enough killing. Sparing the king, because we can, will benefit us in the long run. If we kill him, his people may feel honor-bound to seek revenge. If we leave the king alive, but obliterate his army, he will return home and spread word of our power. Once he recovers from the blow we've dealt him, he can find himself someone less fearsome to make war with."

"Like that other king he wants to fight, using siege weapons, made from our trees," Kela said.

"Precisely," Lady Swiftbrook agreed.

"Very well," W'rath said. "While it goes against my nature to leave the fellow alive, and I honestly doubt he'll behave in the rational manner you've described, I shall abide by your wishes. That will leave Raven and me with two captives. I assume, at that point, you'll have fully engaged with the enemy, making it much more difficult for us to leave the way we came in. We shall require a means of escape."

Once again, the Shadow Elf focused on Kiat Icewind. "Yes, well, that is certainly possible. We can use sympathetic divination to locate you and then open a portal at your location."

K'hul had enlarged the representation of the battlefield. "We'll break the area into sections and have contingents made up of Sky Elves and First Born assigned to each. Lord Icewind will stay with me to aid in coordinating the battle. We'll place one of his people with each of the contingents to help, both in communicating with us at the command post, and to facilitate troop movement. Once Lord Icewind locates you, we'll send in people to assist you and get you out of the human camp."

Kiat had gone pale while K'hul spoke. W'rath eyes regained their inner light and a mischievous smile curled his lips. "Is there a problem, Lord Icewind? Had you not planned to join our little adventure?"

"No, of course not! My skills lie in scrying. I excel in the subtle arts. I have neither the constitution nor the unrefined nature needed to engage in the sort of savagery we've outlined today."

The cold stare K'hul leveled at Kiat positively wilted the slender, black-haired mage. "No insult intended, Lord K'hul," he whispered. "And of course, in light of the strategy you've outlined, I yield to your wisdom as *War Leader* and will be more than happy to make myself available to you in the running of the battle."

W'rath chuckled and K'hul's scowl switched to him. "Don't look at me, old boy, he's *your* toady."

"First Father preserve me," K'hul snarled. "Everyone out of my sight. We have our tasks—let's get to it."

# Chapter 11

K'hul watched as the others to left while Kiat made a show of examining the map for the best place to have his team of casters open portals. Kiat muttered under his breath and the area in question magnified and took over the table.

That the inquisitive Lord W'rath hadn't decided to stay and watch Kiat's work, surprised K'hul. W'rath had paused just long enough to present a long strand of hair to the diviner so he could use it to locate the Shadow Elves during the battle, and send aid and their means of evacuation. Then, without another word, W'rath headed out the council room door, as though he had another pressing engagement, Lady Raven close on his heels. No doubt W'rath had some mischief to attend to.

K'hul scowled at the thought and started to voice his suspicions to Kiat when he looked up to find Lady Swiftbrook still standing at the table. She wore much the same expression of suspicion as he, only hers was directed at him, and not the wretched psion.

"Don't you have troops to rally as well?" she asked.

She knew perfectly well he did, but obviously she didn't like leaving him alone to consult with Kiat. *His toady.* K'hul's teeth ground. *How dare that runt say such a thing in front of the entire High Council!*

"Lord Icewind may specialize in the subtle arts, but *you* do not," she continued when the only answer she received was the sound of his grinding molars.

"You asked me to reconsider helping the Wood Elves, and now, not only have I done so, but I've decided to provide them assistance. Can I not spend time with Kiat, arranging for the best possible battlefield, without having my motives questioned?"

The flash of the Sky Elf's eyes said she didn't believe a word he said. Her lips thinned. "I'll need to know how you want me to break up my people into teams, and which warriors I can expect from the First Born so I can assign them accordingly."

"You'll have that in a few hours."

"Right. I'll leave you to it then. Your strategizing."

She strode from the hall her back even straighter than usual. From his left K'hul heard Kiat take a deep breath of relief. *Bloody coward.*

"She knows," Kiat whispered.

K'hul peered at the slender elf shivering in his robes. "What exactly do you think she knows?"

"That we're plotting against Lord W'rath, of course!"

K'hul rolled his eyes. "You're acting overly dramatic. I'm just after the truth."

"Then why do you keep things from her?"

"Because she is completely beguiled by the creature," K'hul said. "She says he cured her madness during the attack on the city, but I'm more inclined to believe he did something to her to make her trust him far more than she should." He forced himself to remain calm and not cross over to loom over the diviner. Fanning himself with a long hand, Kiat already looked ready to faint. K'hul hadn't spoken to anyone about his suspicions until now. Kiat might have the backbone of a jellyfish, but he commanded respect among a large portion of the casters. Keeping him as an informed ally could ensure needed support in the future.

"Mind control," Kiat gulped. "Ancestors, preserve us."

"If you're done pissing yourself, maybe you could tell me what you found out during the council meeting." K'hul ignored Kiat's pout. He might need allies, but his patience with Kiat's constant state of terror had grown thin.

After a time the finger wiggler seemed to realize waiting for an apology for K'hul's coarse words was futile. "I don't know what you expected to find out in this sort of setting, but I put up the spell as you asked."

"And what sorts of untruths did you uncover?"

"Not a thing," Kiat said, spreading his hands, as empty as his information. "Why you would expect differently, I don't know. If you want to find out if Lord W'rath truly stands with First Home, you'll need to ask him a direct question while I have a truth knowing spell up. However, nothing suspicious came up during our meeting. He didn't even fake his lack of knowledge about the human's use of cavalry." He shook his head in wonder over the Shadow Elf's ignorance.

K'hul snarled and paced around the room. "I don't understand. I can smell the lies coming out of him. What about his claim that he's a superior assassin?"

Kiat's lips thinned, K'hul's suggestion that he'd missed something finally bringing forth a reaction not seated in fear. "He wasn't lying. It's possible it's not true, but he honestly believes he's an one elf army."

"Ridiculous! Someone that competent, living like a hermit, for who knows how long, and he just happens to wander into Second Home during a demon attack?! I don't believe it for a second." He spun back on his heels and marched over to glare down at Kiat, no longer concerned if he sent the smaller elf into a faint.

The Sky Elf cringed in the shadow of the huge First Born, but doggedly continued to try reasoning with him. "I don't know what to tell you, Lord K'hul. Unless you make those accusations to his face, and force a response from him, I cannot tell you one way or the other."

"And his accent—have you noticed it?" K'hul said, not at all interested in Kiat's attempt at logic.

“I didn’t notice any accent, just some strange mannerisms,” Kiat said. His shoulders slumped in defeat.

“Precisely! He has no foreign accent. He sounds like any elf from First Home—well, except for all of the irritating ‘old boys’ and such. Raven has an accent. She’s obviously not from here.”

“I sensed no deceit from her either,” Kiat said. He stepped back, putting a chair between himself and K’hul, as if he expected another tirade.

K’hul waved Kiat’s words away. “My concerns do not lie with her. She’s just an overgrown sword maiden. If anything, she’s in over her head. But W’rath ... he’s tricky and sneaky. You don’t live away from people as long as he claims and suddenly pop out of a cave with a civilized tongue and foppish manners. He makes me want to punch something.”

Kiat gave up on trying to calm Lord K’hul, and decided staying silent was his best strategy. He wasn’t exactly sure what he’d let himself in for now. He’d been surprised and honored when the *Voice of the First* had approached him to fill the Sky Elf vacancy on the High Council. It was unusual, since each elven race nominated their own councilors, but apparently, in this case, Lord K’hul and Lady Swiftbrook had exchanged roles, and she appointed the First Born councilor.

Kiat hadn’t realized Lord K’hul even knew he existed. Now he recognized he’d been chosen because Lord K’hul felt he could control him. Moodily, he dragged his hand through the projection of the Wood Elves’ forest, causing the trees to bend and wave crazily as if caught in a hurricane. If only he had *that* kind of strength, but sadly, Kiat reflected, Lord K’hul was right about him. He couldn’t even drum up enough ire to take exception to Lord W’rath referring to him as Lord K’hul’s toady.

Only a few minutes had passed, but Kiat sagged from exhaustion, as if he’d been trapped with Lord K’hul for hours. The First Born had finally wound down. “Very well, Kiat, focus on getting us well-positioned against the humans. We'll revisit the problem of *Lord* W'rath once we finish with this situation."

Kiat inwardly flinched at the overly familiar use of his given name, something Lord K'hul had done throughout the meeting, showing his complete disregard for propriety. If anything, it was more insulting than Lord W'rath's 'toady' comment. He didn't have it in him to protest the lack of honorific, though. "Perhaps his over confidence will get him killed tonight," he offered.

"Heh," K'hul snorted, turning to leave, "we should be so lucky."

ЖЖЖЖЖ

Lady Swiftbrook caught up to Raven and W'rath as they exited the council hall and stepped into the sunlit garden surrounding the domed structure. W'rath had just lit one of his offensive clove cigarettes. He raised an amused eyebrow as she arrived, skirts hitched up so she could run. "Perhaps more practical garments are in order, madam?"

"I hoped to give off an air of dignity and appear less warlike during the meeting," she said, flushing.

"Odd that," W'rath replied. "I was under the impression we had you to thank for K'hul's willingness to reconsider fighting on behalf of the Wood Elves. Was I mistaken?"

The Sky Elf's blush grew even greater. "You're not mistaken."

"So, in point of fact, we're going into battle because of you," W'rath said, obviously enjoying the lady's discomfort.

"Yes, all right, get your jollies at my expense. I wanted to help the Wood Elves, not slaughter thousands of people."

"Then you've succeeded, madam," W'rath said with a chuckle.

Lady Swiftbrook scowled in confusion, but Raven caught on to the implication behind W'rath's words. She pursed her lips. "Humans *are* people."

"Really? Since when? Are orcs and goblins people now too? No one informed me."

Lady Swiftbrook glared daggers at the small male. "We took a vote while you sat mumbling in your cave. For your information the civilized peoples include: humans, gnomes..."

"Gnomes?! Oh, surely not!" W'rath clutched at his heart and staggered several steps. Raven turned away in a futile attempt to hide her laughter.

"Gnomes," Lady Swiftbrook plowed on doggedly, "halflings, dwarves and barbarians."

"You would think the fact they're called barbarians would indicate they do not qualify as civilized," W'rath observed.

"He has you on that one," Raven said, no longer bothering to hide her mirth.

"I'll concede the point, but despite the seeming contradiction, all of those named, *including* barbarians, are universally accepted as people."

"I'm assuming elves of all stripes appear on that list?" W'rath asked.

"Of course, that goes without saying."

"I suppose I'll need to discuss that with King Oblund then," W'rath mused. "He doesn't sound inclined to acknowledge Wood Elves as people."

"From the description Kela and Foxfire gave of him, I don't think it would matter," Raven said. "He's perfectly willing to make siege weapons to use against a fellow human."

"Good point, lass," W'rath said. "He's the sort of chap who believes he has to the right to possess anything that catches his fancy. We'll have to see if we can't break him of the habit."

Lady Swiftbrook continued to frown through the exchange. At the mention of the human king, she finally remembered her initial purpose in chasing down the Shadow Elves. "Do you really want to enter the camp alone, and go after both a mage and the king?"

"Stealth will be our ally," W'rath explained. "We're referred to as Shadow Elves for a reason. Give us any subdued light and I dare you to notice us. Obviously, we won't traipse about the camp in heavy armor, but dark leathers will ensure our natural abilities aren't compromised."

Lady Swiftbrook raised a dubious eyebrow. "And I suppose you're going to have Raven throw the mage over her shoulder?"

"Actually, yes, you've divined my plan exactly." W'rath beamed at the frustrated Sky Elf.

"I thought you needed me as a body guard, not a pack mule," Raven muttered.

"Your size and strength make you suitable for many roles. I mean no insult, but felt it important to keep you off of the front lines. You and I should face far fewer threats than those engaging angry and frightened soldiers."

"I slew a devil..." She didn't bother to finish. The situation had been completely different. Fueled by her fury, she had smote the foul creature with the full brunt of her psionics. She had lost her psionics, and didn't even have her rage now. How would she fare on a battlefield with just the skills she'd absorbed from Linden, fighting desperate, frightened men who just wanted to survive?

"Once this nastiness is behind us, you'll have plenty of opportunities to hone your skills, lass," W'rath said, giving her a knowing smile. "Besides, I shouldn't expect a self-professed scholar to relish the idea of rushing into a likely blood bath."

"That's true," Raven admitted. Her stomach twisted in disgust as she realized she'd actually felt disappointed to miss out on the combat. As sweet as Linden had been, he had possessed a warrior's heart. Now that fire belonged to her, and it threatened to overwhelm her. In her new role as co-leader of First Home's Shadow Elves, Raven knew she'd have need of Linden's strength and energy, but she couldn't allow it to dominate every aspect of her personality. She and Linden would have to learn to accommodate one another. This twin-souled business was proving to be a bloody nuisance.

"All right, does that settle things?" W'rath wanted to know.

Raven nodded, but Lady Swiftbrook shook her head, unsatisfied. "Can either of you speak Terish? Or even the common trade language?"

"Of course not," W'rath said. He looked to Raven, but she shook her head.

"Before going to Second Home I'd never even seen a human," Raven said. "I've yet to speak to one."

"So, you two plan to march up to King Oblund and do what, exactly?" Lady Swiftbrook grinned wolfishly.

"Rude gestures come to mind," Raven said. She demonstrated, directing an especially elaborate and crude hand sign at an imaginary king. She cocked her head and grinned. "Of course, if that fails, holding a sword to his throat should encourage him to cooperate."

Lady Swiftbrook chuckled. "I doubt a human, who knows little about elves, would understand our gestures. The sword may help subdue him, but it won't allow you to communicate with him."

"Very well, madam, you have made a valid point," W'rath said. "Since the council decided to allow the wretch to live, we will require a means by which to communicate with him. Perhaps you have some sort of magic rings we might utilize for such a purpose? Or perhaps you wish to volunteer yourself as translator?"

Lady Swiftbrook made a face. "Ancestors forbid! I don't speak a word of any human language. Depending on the language, it's either like trying to speak with a mouth full of pebbles, or rocks. The only thing worse is Orcish." She fluttered a hand in front of her face as if dispersing W'rath's suggestion as she would an annoying fly. "No, what I had in mind, is for you to take Foxfire along with you. He's fluent in dozens of languages and since he's a Wood Elf, he's nearly as stealthy as a Shadow Elf."

"Not to mention he'll make sure the king doesn't accidentally fall on your sword three or four times," Raven added.

W'rath glared at the young warrior, insulted. "I'm more efficient than that. He need only impale himself once."

"So you *had* planned on murdering him!" Lady Swiftbrook said.

"Not at all, madam. I agreed not to kill him, and I shall abide by that decision. I found the concerns expressed at the meeting valid, and given my lack of current knowledge of human culture, I bow to the collective wisdom of the rest of you. I merely wish to make clear, in the event he did die by my hand, I would finish the task in a clean and efficient manner. Well ... perhaps not so clean. Slicing people open usually results in spraying blood and tumbling entrails."

Lady Swiftbrook rolled her eyes. "Thank you so much for that image."

Raven empathized with Lady Swiftbrook's plight. Trying to have a serious conversation with W'rath was like finding oneself trapped in a labyrinth. Every time it seemed obvious what he would do, W'rath set off in a completely different direction, and his victim fell into yet another pit trap.

"Don't look so exasperated, madam. I won't fight you on using Lord Foxfire as an interpreter. If he agrees to it, he's welcome to come along with us on our little adventure."

"Fine," Lady Swiftbrook replied, though her tone suggested she still suspected W'rath of plotting some unsavory end for the king. "I'll also see about getting the two of you a couple of translation rings. That way you can at least understand the conversation even if they cannot understand you."

"Splendid," W'rath said, blowing out a thin stream of smoke, and daintily tapping a bit of ash off of his cigarette. He smiled innocently until the Sky Elf turned on her heel and stormed off. "She needs to learn to be more trusting."

"What are you up to?" Raven asked, as perplexed as Lady Swiftbrook.

"Why, absolutely nothing, lass. I've never met people so easy to toy with."

"You're an ass."

"On occasion, people have described me as such."

"So, aside from annoying one of our few friends, what did you just accomplish?"

"Ah, look at this," W'rath said, waving his arms, emphasizing the empty space around them. "We seem completely on our own."

"And?"

"*And* we may now pay a visit to Lady Stormchaser's estate, and ascertain if she had any information pertinent to hunting down those who masterminded the attack on Second Home."

As they started to walk, Raven tried to wrap her head around the W'rath's thinking. "If you had mentioned it to Lady Swiftbrook she would have wanted us to wait until she could join us—is that it?"

W'rath nodded. "This way, if our tour of the estate upsets her after the fact, we need only apologize for our thoughtlessness. The other would have put us in the position to either go against her wishes or to deny ourselves the opportunity to explore."

Raven shook her head in disbelief. "We're going into battle tonight and all you can think about is pawing through Lady Stormchaser's belongings? Shouldn't we ... I don't know—work on our attack plan?"

"Planning with whom exactly? You and I make up the entire Shadow Elf strike force. Our plan consists of sneaking into the camp, finding the resting mage, subduing him, and paying the king a visit. Foxfire shall aid us in communication, and one of his kin will point us in the right direction. All we have to do is avoid discovery. If a human exists who can see us when we merge with the shadows, I'm an incredibly attractive gnome."

"You make it sound quite simple."

"It really is, lass. Provided the king doesn't start running about, trying to assist in the battle, we should have no trouble capturing him. As long as we get to him before the First Born and Sky Elves launch their attack, that shouldn't happen."

Raven scowled. She could think of dozens of things that could go wrong. "What if the mage fights back? How do we conceal him once we *do* capture him? What if the king has a lot of people with him? What if..."

"Lass! Please!" W'rath protested. "First of all, the mage in question will be resting from his very exhausting ritual. He may have a few tricks up his sleeve, but his fatigue will keep him from doing much. On top of that, unless he's set up an elaborate magic alarm, he isn't going to know we're around until we pop out of the shadows and knock him senseless. You will then sling him over one shoulder, and once you merge with the shadows again, he'll be just as well hidden as you."

"Hmmph. Maybe. What about the king's guards? Based on the knowledge I've gained from Linden, the king will have at least four. There's a good chance he'll also have some advisors present."

W'rath took the information in stride. "There will be three of us, and we will have the element of surprise. If hostilities erupt, drop the mage and lay about yourself. You have more than enough skill to deal with a handful of rabble. You possess at least a portion of a First Born's strength, which means you're much stronger than a human. Even if one of them manages to injure you, you'll quickly regenerate—they won't. If anything more threatening than a common soldier threatens us, I'll finish them off quickly and move on the king. You and Foxfire can clean up the rest, and then join me for a short and sweet conversation with King Oblund. We'll take him captive and escape through the portal provided by Lord Icewind's subordinate."

"Just as simple as that?"

"Just as simple as that."

"When this blows up in our faces I'll remind you of this conversation."

"I would expect nothing less of you, lass."

Appearing much too smug, W'rath came to a halt and grew quiet. It took Raven a moment to realize they had arrived at their destination.

Before them, a pure white structure blossomed from amid the acres of pristine forest surrounding it. Myriad graceful curves, stretched into the sky, impossibly high. Perhaps a trick of the eye gave it the appearance it moved, as though alive, at once organic, and yet, completely beyond any worldly description.

"Supposedly, Lady Uverial Stormchaser herself, designed this place," W'rath said. "I managed to corner Lady Swiftbrook's cook this morning, on the pretext of learning her recipe for scones. I had little trouble learning interesting tidbits about this place."

"I suddenly feel very insignificant," Raven said. She couldn't imagine the power and skill required to create such a structure. Then she remembered the sprawling Shadow Elf palace from the day before. While vastly different, she could still see the same power at work here.

They stepped from the dappled shade of the glade's silver oaks, and slipped reverently up the expanse of steps leading to the gracefully carved doors. More enchantment was at work here, protecting the polished stone, silver wood and subtle washes of color from filth and exposure.

At the doors W'rath hesitated, and Raven suspected he felt the same air of anticipation about the place she sensed. She wondered where the feeling came from, and then it struck her that the surrounding forest had grown silent. No birds chirped. No cicadas buzzed. Even the gentle breeze that had accompanied them here had died away.

"The place seems deserted," she said. She knew she stated the obvious, but felt the need to insert herself into the stillness, disrupt it.

"It's possible she lived here alone," W'rath said, though he didn't sound convinced. While casters of her caliber often had retreats where they could study their craft in peace, this place was much too vast. Even from the outside, the many balconies, windows and floating bridges, made it obvious it housed many smaller rooms suitable as bedrooms or private studies.

"Hundreds of people could have lived here and only occasionally met another soul in passing," Raven said, her voice dropping to a whisper. "Where did they all go? Surely, Lady Stormchaser didn't take them all to Second Home with her to be killed?"

"That's a disconcerting thought," W'rath murmured. "I think it more likely they merely relocated in deference to this place's new owners."

"What do you mean? What new owners?"

"Why us, of course," W'rath replied, giving Raven a mischievous wink. "You've obviously felt the strange atmosphere surrounding this place. It's been waiting for us."

Without another word, W'rath placed his hands on the silver doors and the air round them burst into sound. Rather than the peal of an alarm, which Raven had feared, a sweet chime of welcoming washed over them, spreading out in a wave, awakening the birds, the insects, and even the recently stifled breeze. Raven turned, seeing the trees shiver, their leaves quaking at the sound's passing. Magic carried that sound and continued on, spreading across the island.

She turned back to W'rath. "All of First Home will know of our inheritance," he said.

"But we already have a home built for us."

"While beautiful, we don't belong there," W'rath said. "It's isolated. K'hul, and those like him, will assume we're down there cooking up some evil scheme. Up here, we remain seen and included. We stop being *them* and become *us*."

Raven thought about all the many tragedies that had gone on, sight unseen, for so many years, and had to agree. The damage T'sane and Reaper had done to the Shadow Elf population might well prove beyond repair. That only the Wood Elf councilors had tried to do anything for the youngsters, sickened Raven. Probably murdered, the two lay dead somewhere, as forgotten as the young Shadow Elves. How could such a thing happen?

She voiced her puzzlement to W'rath, but he didn't reply. Hands pressed against the silver doors, he appeared in the midst of communing with them. Satisfied with whatever the door conferred to him, he pushed it open and strode inside. "Oh!" Raven gasped as she followed him into the huge front gallery.

The structure's creator had used light to great advantage. Not only did windows dominate every wall, but mirrors, gems and exotic crystals gleamed from strategically placed ledges and niches, capturing rays, bending them and sending them on, transformed into a rainbow of colors. Outside, the walls shown white, but the interior glowed with a dazzling assortment of reflected light.

As incredible as Raven found the light show, the sculptures flanking the grand staircase left her breathless. The statues towered above them, easily twice as tall as any First Born. On the left a slim, elegant Sky Elf stood, so perfect she gave the impression she could break from her pedestal and stride into battle. Her hair fell in a straight sheet down her back, down to her ankles. Clad in chain armor, she carried a slim sword in one hand. In the other hand she held a tome. Uverial Stormchaser had been a fierce warrior, but she had also brought the written word to the elves, and supposedly had recorded all of the history from those early days. W'rath and Raven moved into the gallery and stared up at her. "The First lead us into battle," W'rath said, "but if not for this lady, we would have remained savages. All the beautiful things the elves love today would have never come to pass without her."

Raven had never heard such a tone of reverence come from W'rath's lips. She peered at him, startled to see his eyes glittered with moisture. "I thought you didn't believe in gods," she said.

"Ah, lass," he said, turning to her with eyes that suddenly gone deep, fathomless, "not viewing them as gods takes nothing away from them. If anything, it makes them more heroic. Flawed, they knew fear, and pain, and loss. By calling them gods, we belittle their accomplishments and excuse ourselves from not achieving more."

"Admire them, but don't worship them?"

"Perhaps a bit of an oversimplification," W'rath said, turning toward the second statue, and blinking owlishly at it. Puzzlement flitted across his face. "They're important figures in our history, but more than that, our culture is built upon the foundations they lay. Selectively ignoring their good and bad aspects paints an inaccurate picture of our history. We make saints and villains out of people who most likely a embodied a mixture of many traits—heroism and altruism, certainly, but also ambition and cruelty. Without taking into account all of these things, important moments in our past lose all sense."

"Like that painting of the First and the giant king?"

"That's an excellent example of how history gets altered because the individuals involved have grown into something mythic instead of historic. It's not enough for history to present the First as the most powerful of us, he must also has to have possessed flawless honor, intellect and compassion. I won't deny his status as a great *War Leader*, however his greatness didn't stem from perfection, but from having the foresight to surround himself with people who excelled in areas where he fell short."

"One of those being his son Umbral," Raven said. In wonder, she strode up to the second statue, and let her fingers trace the words etched into the plaque on its base.

W'rath joined Raven at the base of the second statue. His eyes widened in surprise. His gaze traveled back and forth from the plaque to the statue proper. A brief thrill of terror ran up his spine until he truly focused on the features of the sculpted face. The subject of the piece had the gangly build of a youth, probably intended to represent him just before his imprisonment in Traitor's Heart. That would have put him at about fourteen. He had never seen his reflection until after spending quite some time in the Abyss. Either the sculpture was highly inaccurate, or he had changed quite a bit over the years. He looked again at the sculpture of Lady Stormchaser. She appeared exactly as he remembered her. So, as a boy, he probably had resembled this pensive little creature with the silly stub of a ponytail poking out the back of head.

"I'm not imagining this, right? You see it too?" Raven asked.

"I admit to some surprise," W'rath agreed.

"Surprise? More like bloody amazing! Don't you see?" Raven continued to trace the etched words on the base plate as if certain the moment she pulled her hand back, Umbral's name would blink out like a mirage.

"Apparently not, lass."

"One of the most controversial topics in the history books involves the truth about Umbral's appearance. You heard Kiat and K'hul earlier. There are people who believe any child born of a Shadow Elf and another sort of elf will come into this world as a monster. This single statue completely invalidates that argument."

"Assuming it isn't simply a romanticized depiction of the boy. He and Lady Stormchaser were friends, after all."

"Do you believe that's the case?" Raven challenged.

"No, I do not," W'rath said, studying the much younger version of himself. "It does beg the question though: if this statue has stood here all this time, why does any question remain concerning the boy's appearance?"

"Yes!" Raven cried triumphantly. "Finally, someone else sees the discrepancies that have bothered me since I started my research." She grabbed W'rath by the arm and dragged him back over to the statue of Lady Stormchaser, pointing at the tome held by the great lady. "She wrote down our history, right? Where did it go? Why have dozens of elven scholars written and rewritten what they think happened back then? We should simply be able to turn to the source."

"Obviously it's gone missing and any copies of it as well." He studied both statues, his brow pinched in confusion. "And not just the books, but their authors as well. We know Umbral's fate, but what of the others? What of Lady Stormchaser herself? For that matter, what of the First? Can you tell me what happened to them? Of anyone from that time? We don't age. We're immune to disease. We regenerate from wounds. Even given the violence of the time, and the expanse of years, at least a few people from then should call these islands home."

Raven's searched the room as if the answer would magically present itself, or one of the ancient elves would pop out from behind the statues. "You know, when I spoke to Linden about my research, I thought his lack of knowledge stemmed from a lack of interest, but now..."

"But now you suspect something else?"

"I do. You're right, at least a few ancient elves should live on First Home, but even in the short time since we arrived, we've seen no sign of anyone that old. Aside from you, I get the impression Lady Swiftbrook is the eldest member on the High Council. She told us K'hul is the eldest male of the First's descendents, and he's only a little over five hundred. And not a one of them seems aware of the strangeness of it all."

W'rath nodded. "You recall Lady Swiftbrook's concern yesterday over her inability to recall when they stopped the Shadow Elf coming of age festival?"

"I thought you did it when you healed her insanity," Raven said.

W'rath pursed his lips. "I admit to acting with all haste, but I *am* very good at what I do. I in no way damaged her mind. Yesterday, when she mentioned her gaps in memory, I suggested she suffered some side effects from the healing as a means of easing her fears. I had no answers then, and I still don't."

"Sorry, my mistake," she said, and gave him an insincere smile.

"Excellent. Now that we've cleared that up—what I'm suggesting ... well, I'm not entirely sure what I'm suggesting."

"Do you think something is making people forget? Some kind of spell?"

W'rath didn't answer immediately. Instead he started up the grand staircase, his face thoughtful. Raven followed him up and they found themselves in a confusion of hallways and stairs. W'rath chose a hall at random and glided down it.

"It's no simple spell," he said at last, as they walked down the hall. "Something this powerful, long lasting, and subtle would require a ritual casting. It would have taken days, if not weeks, to perform, and involved dozens of casters. I expect the ritual the magi King Oblund has employed is a cantrip compared to what we're dealing with here."

"But why?" Raven said. The hallway, while wide, seemed to crowd in upon them as painting after painting, depicting important personages of the Stormchaser line, hovered over them. Their faces, severe or placid, stoic or mischievous, held no answers.

"I can't imagine," W'rath admitted. "We've seen the result—written histories mixed with fact and fantasy, conflicting and completely unreliable, and yet used to indoctrinate our young. We have more prejudice and suspicion than ever. Whoever did this had an agenda, but he wasn't alone. He had help, and quite a lot of it."

W'rath slipped down the hallway, paying little attention to the portraits, allowing instinct to pull him along. Or perhaps the will of the structure guided his feet. Regardless, their travels brought them to a lone door set at the end of the hallway. Raven pressed up against him, and he knew if he turned now he would catch her peering over her shoulder, as if she suspected the paintings had somehow herded them to this place. Perhaps they had.

"Something must have happened," he said, "something significant, but due to the elves' isolation here on First Home, the rest of the world moved on, completely unaware of event. There was a ... disagreement." W'rath took the last few steps needed to bring him to the door and stopped, turning before Raven could crowd up to him again. He gave her a penetrating look.

"You mean a civil war?" she said.

"Yes."

"And the winners wanted to change history, but couldn't, so they did the next best thing—made everyone forget the truth. That's a frightening suggestion."

W'rath nodded and let her think further on what his theory meant. From their talks on the ship, he knew she had fantasized about the beautiful elven culture denied her as a child of the Exiles. Her dream had come true, but now she faced the possibility that something ugly and insidious had its grasp on the place and its people, as surely as hate and depravity had consumed her former home.

Raven swallowed and at last found her voice. "Gods, it will happen to us too. How long do you think we have before we don't remember and don't care?"

*Oh, bravo, lass.* "That will *not* happen," W'rath said, and turned back to grasp the handle of the hallway door. For the second time that day, the magical peal sounded. The two staggered as the force of it washed over them. With its passage W'rath's vow turned into something far greater than the words of a determined soul. The magic bound those words to them, and ripped the claws of the ancient curse from their minds, leaving them gasping, not just from the force of the spell, but the realization that the creeping forgetfulness had already started to worm its way into them.

Raven and W'rath's eyes met. "What in the Hells was that?" Raven said, voice gone to little more than a whisper.

"It would seem Lady Stormchaser planned this all very carefully. As a seer, she arranged for this very thing. She's freed us, perhaps even this whole property, from the curse."

"Maybe all of First Home?" Raven dared hope.

"As powerful a spell as we just experienced, I doubt it was strong enough to free all of the islands of the curse. If I'm correct, it's held dominance here for thousands of years. The best we can expect, is a bubble free from the curse. We now stand in an oasis—a place where the truth can survive."

"House of Memories," Raven said.

"Very appropriate, lass. We have a name for our new home. Now let us see why Lady Stormchaser lead us here." He opened the door.

Their initial view revealed a study bright with light and white marble walls. Upon their entering, it started to transform around them. Magic shimmered, and the walls shifted to a deep, rich mahogany. Stone transformed to carved wood. The clear glass of the two-story windows became awash with deep colors of purple and emerald, the pattern of an upright, wingless reptile emerged, its clawed legs posed as if in the midst of springing upon a victim. It reminded W'rath a great deal of the hunting lizards he had seen as a child. The reptiles were small, but hunted in packs, using intelligence and cooperation to bring down larger prey. He had admired them and often likened them to his small band of psions. The dear lady had known even this about him.

As the last of the items altered, the silver desk by the windows turned to a deep, hand polished brown. Raven gazed about, ruby eyes sparkling in amusement. "Obviously, this is your study," she said. "I'd prefer something a bit less imposing."

"My refuge in a tower of blinding light. Surely you can allow me this one tiny sanctuary?" He gave her a bow, beseeching her to grant him this boon.

"I suppose," Raven said with a grin.

The room finished settling into its new appearance, and W'rath, hands on hips, nodded his approval. Above him, regarding the pair, hung a pair of portraits, two of the few things that remained unaltered by the magical transformation.

"Lady Uverial Stormchaser and Lord Umbral K'hul," Raven said, pointing at the paintings. "Somehow she kept all of this protected from whatever horror befell First Home. I'm starting to think, despite its size and the number of rooms, only one person at a time ever lived here."

W'rath considered her words, nodding slowly. "That makes a certain amount of sense. The current resident would choose an heir, presumably someone in the line gifted in divination and the interpretation of visions. Only someone supremely talented in those areas would have the ability to free themselves of the lies, and accept the guardianship of this place, knowing one day it would come to us."

"And all the rooms housed here," Raven said, dawning wonder touching her voice, "are meant to house a new generation of Shadow Elves!"

W'rath dropped into the chair rising throne-like behind the desk. As many amazing things as he'd seen in his life, he had difficulty trying to fathom the Stormchaser's ability to foresee so many events thousands of years before they happened. He found it easier to accept that only pieces of the puzzle had presented themselves to each successor. Why else would they have made no attempt to stop the terrible things which had come to pass? He had never been one to simply sit back and accept something as fated. If they were slaves to a predefined destiny, why bother acting upon anything, for any reason? He couldn't accept that.

Like most things, reality probably fell somewhere in the middle. Perhaps the only thing clear to each successor was the need to protect and prepare the structure for the future. Raven's spoken musings had the ring of truth to them, though. Certainly the child had intuition. Backed by the fire of youth, those instincts encouraged her to act rather than idly let the world move around her.

He contemplated the painting of his childhood self and saw the same fire there. Ah, but that child had had much less self control than Lady Raven. His had been a passion that turned to murderous rage. Had something similar caused a large number of elves to throw a shroud over the hearts and minds of the people of First Home? Surely, he didn't have to shoulder the responsibility of that as well? Bad enough his actions had resulted in the schism that made possible the dark and depraved society of the Exiles. He didn't think he could stand to find a second civil war had erupted in his name.

He blinked, realizing he had been staring for some time at the desk before him without really seeing anything. His eyes struggled to focus on what lay before him—a sealed envelope with his name on it—written in letters large enough, even someone as blind as he could read it. His real name.

Raven heard his gasp and came over from the bookshelf she perused. "What did you find?"

Before she could notice, he slid the letter beneath a pile of papers and quickly checked the rest of the items on the desk, hoping to find something to explain his shocked exclamation. What he saw nearly made him betray himself a second time. Instead, he recovered and grasped the sheathed sword lying upon an ebony stand on the desk. "This," he said in unfeigned wonder.

He held it up for Raven to see, and then grasped it just behind the guard and pulled. With a soft click, it released, and W'rath drew the blade free a few inches, enough for Raven to see the shimmering wave pattern playing down the blade's edge.

"Is *that* Umbral's sword?" Raven gaped at the weapon, body practically vibrating in awe.

W'rath gave her a sharp look. "What did the books you studied say about his weapon?"

"There's a certain amount of controversy about that, as you've probably guessed. The most popular hypothesis states it was more a toy than anything because his twisted legs and spine made it impossible for him to fight properly. Of course, after what we've seen today, it's safe to say Umbral wouldn't have had any trouble wielding a true sword. Of the stories stating Umbral had a proper weapon, and not a toy, the most common belief is the finest smith at the time, Amryth Earthfire, designed it especially for Umbral. He's said to have taken into account the individual for every weapon he made. He wasn't one to mass produce weapons. He would have custom made the sword to suit Umbral's size, strength, fighting style, and even his use of psionics.

"Most First Born and Sky Elf blades have a slight curve. They take advantage of the fact those elves need a blade that disperses impact shock. The curved blade works well with their graceful, but powerful, sweeping strokes. Being small, and young, and in need of a quick kill, a straight blade, which he could quickly pull from its sheath, would have suited Umbral more."

W'rath nodded, impressed, not so much with the scattered histories, as with Raven's reasoning behind the type of sword the young Umbral would have used. He supposed he had to give at least some credit to Linden. As a First Born, he would have studied weapons. Despite his general ignorance of history, his life as a soldier would have required he know something about the tools of his profession.

He finished drawing the blade from the sheath, and as Raven had predicted, it gleamed between them, nearly straight, and definitely meant more for stabbing and quick slashes as compared to the blades of the larger elves.

"Amryth named the blade Shadow's Edge. Some of the histories, the ones I'm starting to think of as more reliable, said that it's so finely balanced, and so light, it allowed Umbral to wield it with precision and speed that, when combined with his fighting style, made it possible for him to fell foes much larger and stronger than he. Supposedly, the edge is so keen, even magically imbued plate armor will part before it."

She gasped, impressed as W'rath balanced the weapon on one finger. It seemed to float there light as a feather. "This last bit I hope isn't true. The tale goes that Amryth considered Shadow's Edge his single finest work. He killed himself after completing it, as he felt he had nothing left to aspire to."

"That does sound like a bit of romanticized rubbish," W'rath muttered. Much of what Raven had learned, while true, competed with so much fanciful fabrication, and out and out contradiction, it was no wonder no one could decide if Umbral had prowled the world as a talented assassin and spy, or skulked in his father's shadow, a crippled, and angry demigod. Certainly, the tale about Amryth offing himself after creating Shadow's Edge didn't have any basis in fact. When W'rath still lived among his father's people, Amryth had still breathed. As one of the few First Born to stand by him during those dark days, W'rath remembered him well. If something unpleasant had befallen the smith, W'rath suspected it had more to do with his father culling dissenters than some dramatic display on the part of a tortured artist.

W'rath rose and put the sword through a few quick slashes and smiled as Raven jumped at the keening sound it made. Amryth may have named it Shadow's Edge, but the enemy in the field had often referred to it as Weeping Death. It still felt good in his hands. Despite the passage of time, the bond between he and the sword remained strong.

Raven touched the sword dragging from her hip and frowned. "Perhaps I should carry something more like Shadow's Edge," she said.

W'rath presented the straight sword to her, and with reverence she accepted it. Her eyes positively lit up at the chance to touch such a piece of history. She backed up and put herself through a set of practice moves. Frowning, she tried again. At last she handed the precious weapon back to W'rath, shaking her head. "It's beautifully made, but it doesn't feel at all right in my hands."

W'rath slipped the blade back into its ebony sheath. "Amryth made it for someone much smaller than you, someone who fought much differently than a First Born. Linden was a First Born, so the part of you that is him knows no other way of fighting. Shadow's Edge doesn't suit you. In truth, Linden's sword isn't perfect for you either. We'll need to see about having something custom made for you. For tonight, using the weapon your other half is most accustomed to will do."

W'rath stuffed the sheathed Shadow's Edge through his belt. "It's like Amryth made it for you," Raven said.

W'rath chuckled to hide his discomfort at her observation. "I would appreciate it if you would refrain from saying such things around the others. K'hul already hopes to find a good reason to have me dumped in the ocean."

Raven laughed. "I doubt even he would claim to believe in reincarnation just to get rid of you."

"If it suited his agenda he might choose to open his mind to such a possibility," W'rath said, playing along. The turn in the conversation left him decidedly uncomfortable, though, so he was only too happy to find something by which to change the subject. "I say, what have we here?"

On the desk he reached for a small case and flipped it open. Something sparkled from within and he pulled it out, where it revealed itself as a delicate contraption made from shaped gold wire. Garnet red glass glittered in oval frames made from the wire. He eying it curiously, and showed the object to Raven, who clapped her hands in recognition. "Those are what I told you about on the ship—spectacles! Flip those little arms out. They go behind your ears and that little piece there sits on your nose."

W'rath slid the glasses on per Raven's instructions. The bridge felt best perched near the tip of his aquiline nose. He peered over the top of them at Raven. "Now what?"

"Here," Raven said, excitedly. She dug into the bag she'd taken to carrying everywhere and fished out one of the books Lady Stormchaser had given her. "See if you can read this now."

W'rath flipped it open and scanned the first page. Looking over the top of the spectacles the page still looked blank, but when he switched to peering through the deep red lenses, words suddenly jumped out at him. "Fascinating!" he said, truly impressed. He scanned down the page and flipped to another and another.

"So, can you read it?" Raven asked, impatiently. She practically hopped from foot to foot.

W'rath grinned at her youthful enthusiasm. "You have in your possession the original journal of Lady Uverial Stormchaser, my dear. True, unblemished history.

"Oh, my gods!" Raven practically squealed, in strange contrast to her muscular physique. She began pulling the other books from her satchel. "Look at these too."

W'rath obliged her, cracking open the thicker of the two. Its red binding smelled of new leather, but he had no doubt that its origins stretched back thousands of years. "*From Then to Now: The First 3,000 Years*," he read. "This would seem to be the original copy of Lady Stormchaser's history of our people. I hold in my hands the very thing we discussed earlier—that which has been lost all this time allowing for the proliferation of false histories."

"So not lost after all," Raven said, "but hidden to keep it safe from those who would destroy it. It's so thin, though."

"W'rath laughed at Raven's disappointment. "It contains more pages than are apparent. I expect you'll find the same enchantment on the journal."

"Oh, right," Raven said, pinching the bridge of her nose, disgusted with herself.

"And last but not least," W'rath said, opening the final book. He froze as he realized what he held. So many years had passed since he'd laid eyes on it, he'd all but forgotten it even existed.

"What is it?"

"Lady Stormchaser gave you quite a gift, lass," he said at last. He looked up at the girl and saw she had already guessed what she'd carried with her these past several days. No wonder she had refused to let it and the other books out of her sight.

"It's his, isn't it? Umbral's journal?"

W'rath nodded. He flipped to the front of the book and grinned at the childish scrawls he found there. "Lady Stormchaser taught him the written language she developed. She was the closest thing he ever had to a mother. I expect the first few years of entries will prove of little historical value, but they may provide some amusement."

He lifted the book toward Raven to show her the drawing on the page. Next to the drawing, in Lady Stormchaser's elegant hand, the words *Troll Orc* flowed across the page.

"I saw that earlier," Raven said. "What is it?"

W'rath feigned shock. "What? You cannot tell this fine piece of art depicts the rare and deadly troll orc?"

"I've never heard of a troll orc."

"Of course not, we're fortunate that such a creature has never existed. It would seem young Umbral, unsatisfied with the regular array of creatures the elves faced, made up some disturbing hybrids"

"An orc that could regenerate would be pretty awful," Raven said. "I can think of something worse, though. A troll dragon!" Raven raised her hands up, curling her fingers into claws. She bared her teeth in a fearsome display.

W'rath winced in imagined horror. "I don't wish to think too hard on how such a thing might come about. It would be interesting, though. Imagine, a fire breathing troll dragon. Invincible against all but it's own sneezes."

Raven's laugh rang out like music, deep and comforting like a precious memory. W'rath found himself simply staring at her over his new spectacles, every bit as smitten as the boys had been the previous day. Raven gave him a curious look, and he shook himself out of his stupor. *Behave, you old git.*

He shut the journal and turned serious once again. "I know you're not comfortable leaving these behind, but I think it unwise to take them with us tonight."

Raven studied the room, brow furrowed in worry. "Do you think the magic of this place will protect them?"

"If a safe place exists, this is it," he replied. "House of Memories won't admit anyone who intends us ill. If I had realized that earlier, I wouldn't have insisted on rushing over here."

"Oh, yes, you would have. You make a gnome seem incurious."

"You have me there, lass," he said, accepting the satchel and placing the three books inside. He carefully stored them in one of the desk drawers. Under his breath he muttered a protection spell to help hide the books. Though confident the magic of their new home would keep the precious books safe from intruders, it never hurt to add in some extra security.

"What did you say?"

"Just wondering what secrets these lovelies will reveal to us," he said. Add one more thing to the list of her amazing gifts, the hearing of a dragon.

Raven drooped a bit. "Stupid king. I'd much rather study these than clean up his mess."

W'rath rose from the desk and ushered his companion from the room and back toward the exit. "That definitely is not Linden speaking," he said. "You might wish to let him out to play this evening. I doubt the good king will desire to discuss philosophy. A good old fashioned shield bash might be much more appropriate."

They trotted down the grand staircase, Raven reluctant to leave her books, and W'rath itching to explore the rest of the many rooms. The mysterious letter he'd hidden for later perusal pricked at him as well. They did have a king to quash though, so they must all endure some sacrifices. They glided past the two statues and out the front doors where they both came to an abrupt stop.

At the bottom of the steps leading to the doors, Lady Swiftbrook stood, arms crossed, foot tapping.

# CHAPTER 12

W'rath smiled and pressed a hand over his heart as he bowed. "Madam, you've come to welcome us to our new home. How gracious."

The gracious lady made a rude gesture. Two girls in matching green gowns, presumably apprentices, flanked her. They fell into childish giggles at the sight of their instructor's crude behavior. "Your antics have caused quite an uproar. The ancestral home of the Stormchasers has given itself over to you and not everyone applauds the change in ownership."

"I can't imagine why," W'rath said, trotting down the stairs. Raven followed, trying to mirror his confidence. "Do any Stormchasers remain who feel entitled to this place?"

Lady Swiftbrook shook her head. "At least none who carry the Stormchaser name. Extended family exist who feel slighted they weren't considered."

"Lady Stormchaser felt otherwise. The magic laid upon this place wouldn't have welcomed us otherwise."

"I'm not arguing that, however, it doesn't stop people from protesting."

"They're more than welcome to visit," Raven said. "I think once they see the main gallery, they'll understand better."

Lady Swiftbrook's brow furrowed in puzzlement, and W'rath made a sweeping gesture, inviting her to see for herself. She traipsed up the stairs, trailed by her still tittering ladies. They stepped into the entryway and Lady Swiftbrook's jaw dropped at the sight of the towering statues. "Where in the Nine Bottomless Hells did that come from?" She swept into the room, ignoring the statue of Uverial Stormchaser, coming to a halt before the sculpture of Umbral. She read the plaque and turned to W'rath and Raven. Her young companions pushed past her to read the plaque for themselves. They exchanged excited squeals.

"He's adorable!" the redhead exclaimed, and the two dissolved into another round of girlish mirth. Lady Swiftbrook cringed, mistaking W'rath's sudden embarrassment for discomfort over her ladies' foolish behavior.

"I'm guessing you've never seen this before?" Raven asked, ignoring the entire exchange. W'rath had known the lass just long enough to understand that she had an immense passion for history, particularly when she discovered something that filled in some of the gaps in her knowledge. Becoming giddy over a boy, though, especially one who had, no doubt, perished some ten thousand years prior? No, that would belittle the memory of one she'd viewed as a god for most of her short life.

"I've visited this place hundreds of times over the years," Lady Swiftbrook answered. "The statue of Uverial Stormchaser has always been here, but I've never seen this one of Umbral." She spun back to face the statue as if expecting it to have vanished in the few moments she'd had her back to it. She shook her head in disbelief. "Ancestors! I even commented once on how the empty space looked strange, and that she should commission an artist to do a companion piece. She just smiled at me. All this time it stood here? Why did she keep it hidden?"

The blond maid rolled her eyes. "Isn't it obvious? Uverial Stormchaser was in love with Umbral K'hul."

Lady Swiftbrook gawked at the girl. "Ooh! What a delicious scandal," the redhead said, clapping her hands. Lady Swiftbrook's gaze switched to her for a moment before settling back on the statue. And then, as the girls continued to chatter, she at last turned back to W'rath and Raven.

W'rath found he could do little more than stare straight ahead, but he had no trouble imagining the mixture of surprise and amusement on Raven's face. He knew *his* expression radiated complete shock. He found the entire situation outrageous. "That can't be," he said. "He was just a boy."

"Well, technically, only a year, three at the most, separated them in age," Raven said. "She wasn't born, but sprang fully grown from the mating of Mother Magic and the wind. Umbral was the first elf born of an elf, and if we can believe anything written, his conception occurred soon after the First forced Mother Magic to bring forth the first Shadow Elves. Umbral was fourteen or fifteen when he turned on the First. That would have made her no older than seventeen or eighteen. Regardless of her years alive, she had the body of an adult. She would have had an adult's desires. Umbral was one of the few at the time who appreciated her intellectual gifts. It's possible their closeness caused her to want something additional from him."

W'rath shook his head. "At that age, he would have been oblivious to any such feelings."

The young ladies by the statue clasped their hands and looked starry-eyed. "Unrequited love. How tragic!" they cried in unison. Each brought the back of a hand to their to their brow as if they might swoon.

Lady Swiftbrook rolled her eyes. "I'm regretting bringing you two."

"If you hadn't you wouldn't know the truth of this heartbreaking tragedy," the blond protested.

"Nothing but foolishness," Lady Swiftbrook retorted. "Everyone knows Uverial Stormchaser served as the First's mistress for centuries. He had three children by her. Two girls, who went on to carry the Stormchaser name, and a boy who took on the mantle of the First.

Trust me, I've heard in tiresome detail the origins of the family line from K'hul."

"That wouldn't have happened until after Umbral's banishment," Raven said, head cocked in thought. "So it's very possible her true feelings lay with Umbral."

W'rath remained transfixed in horror. They spoke of history, without understanding the personalities of the people they discussed. Assuming this wasn't another grossly inaccurate distortion of history, brought on by the curse infecting First Home, Uverial had suffered terribly after his banishment.

The First had always taken his role as *War Leader* to mean he reigned supreme. True, he'd gathered those around him to provide council and sound strategy, but he never once let anyone forget he was the biggest, the strongest, the most powerful, and the most terrible of all of them. That meant any female who caught his fancy, he claimed, regardless of how anyone else felt about the matter. Most went with him willingly, attracted by his power, and happy to share in it in any capacity. Those who resisted, though, once he finished with them, even their regenerative powers weren't always enough to save them.

"W'rath, you look like you're going to be ill," said Lady Swiftbrook. "It's not like you to refrain from inserting an opinion."

W'rath fixed the Sky Elf with such a glare she took a step back, his seeming queasiness quickly replaced by fury. "That," he said, pointing at the statue of Umbral, "is not a representation of the First. *That* is a memory of the boy Lady Uverial Stormchaser raised, a boy who shared her passion for learning and the written word. The First had no interest in those things and only tolerated such *nonsense* because Lady Stormchaser worked as his chief strategist. She, in turn, only tolerated him because the majority of the elves accepted him as their leader, and she had no desire to bring about a schism that would leave thousands dead. She loathed him, as he represented everything she wanted to change in the elves. Once he discarded his son, her closest friend, she would have hated him with a passion not one of us can comprehend. If she acted as his mistress, as you claim, and had his children, it wasn't by choice. The elves lived like savages back then, and the First was the most savage of all."

Trembling, W'rath turned on his heel and stormed from the building.

ЖЖЖЖЖ

Lady Swiftbrook and Raven shared shocked looks. One of the girls started to make a strange, high-pitched keen. "If you two start crying, so help me..." Lady Swiftbrook admonished. The noise abruptly cut off. "What was that about?" she asked Raven.

"W'rath really admires Lady Stormchaser. I'm guessing he didn't know about her and the First." She gazed after W'rath, brow creased with worry.

"How very odd. He seems to know just about everything about her. I wonder why that tidbit got by him?"

"I never knew those things until I came to the surface and read quite a lot. Everyone in my city knew various versions of elven history from before Umbral's banishment, but anything after that time would be unusual for an Exile to know."

"Thank goodness K'hul wasn't here," Lady Swiftbrook said with a grimace. "They would have been at each other's throats."

Raven shuddered. "Do you think he's right? Did the First..." she couldn't bring herself to finish the sentence.

Lady Swiftbrook gazed around the gallery. W'rath had the right of it, she saw nothing devoted to the memory of the First. At no time, could she recall noticing anything in this place—a painting, a fresco, not even a tapestry detailing anything about the elven *War Leader*. Yet here stood a larger than life sculpture of Umbral, standing on equal terms with the Great Lady herself. Whether she had viewed Umbral as a son, best friend, or potential lover, on some level Uverial *had* loved him. And the elf who had banished him to certain death in the Abyss would have earned her hatred. There was no way she would have forgiven the focus of that hate. No way she would have gone willingly to his bed. "Yes," she said at last, "that bastard raped, repeatedly, his greatest adviser. Ancestors preserve us if this gets out."

"We cannot let people know what we've discovered here," Raven said. "It would tear First Home apart. We'd finish ourselves what the demons started."

Lady Swiftbrook regarded her apprentices. No longer giddy young girls, they cringed in fright, distressed witnesses to an ugly truth. Fear wouldn't keep them from telling what they had learned, though. "Are you going to kill us?" they whispered.

*If only,* Lady Swiftbrook thought uncharitably. *Was I ever so brainless?* "I can cast a geas on you to keep you from gossiping about what you've seen and heard here. Assuming you can live with that, it shouldn't prove fatal."

The girls nodded enthusiastically to show their acceptance of Lady Swiftbrook's terms. "Very well," she said, "we'll return to my residence and perform the spell there."

She shooed the girls outside, and the group started down the steps. Lady Swiftbrook paused, taking in the surrounding grounds. "However, first let us see if we can't find our very angry Lord W'rath. We don't need him punching squirrels... or unicorns?"

The four females gawked at the impossible tableau before them. In a small clearing, surrounded by silver oak, and littered with every possible hue of wildflower, W'rath stood in apparent conversation with a unicorn.

"I thought," the redhead started to say.

"You're right," Lady Swiftbrook interrupted.

"Oh! It's beautiful," Raven said, completely oblivious to the half comments of the others. Then she grew sober. "I wish I could approach it."

Lady Swiftbrook turned incredulous eyes on Raven who shrugged. "Back when I first found out about the coming of age ceremony, I got this crazy idea that maybe I had to be a virgin for it, so I went to a brothel and hired a boy for the night. The only thing I accomplished was annoying my mother because I wasted money on a whore when we had plenty of males around the household. Among other things, my mother was very cheap."

"Great Lady, preserve me from any more revelations this day," the Sky Elf said, her gaze returning to W'rath and the unicorn.

For the first time, the significance of the situation wormed its way into Raven's consciousness. "Oh! Oh, my!" she said. She put a hand to her mouth to stifle the laughter threatening to escape.

"How old do you mark him at?" Lady Swiftbrook said.

"He's incredibly near blind, so he's at least five thousand," Raven said.

"That old?" Lady Swiftbrook said, startled. She'd placed his age at a bit over a thousand, which in itself made it remarkable he was still a virgin. Raven was right, though, if he suffered from near blindness, he hadn't seen his thousandth birthday in a great great while. "How...? And to think I... Oh, bother!" She made a face, disgusted with herself. She'd assumed the worst of the male and warned him off of pursuing Raven. He'd agreed to her demands without blinking an eye. Now she had to deal with the fact that, of the two, Raven had more experience in the bedroom. Perhaps, for all his flirting he did not care for the companionship of ladies? Did unicorns make such distinctions? *Ancestors, I wish alcohol affected elves.*

From the moment he stormed out of House of Memories, W'rath regretted his angry outburst. For someone who prided himself on his control, he'd done a remarkably poor job of maintaining his composure. The thought of his monstrous father brutalizing Uverial had hit him hard.

Another thought had occurred to him, and in some ways it struck him as an even worse scenario. He knew his father had initially spared his life because of Uverial's pleas, and then had postponed his banishment, again because of her intervention. What if the First had demanded something in return for those boons? And what if, for the love of a foolish and overly prideful boy, she had agreed to accept the First's advances? Agreed to bear his children? W'rath squeezed his eyes shut, trying to purge the thought from his mind, but unable to do so. Now that the possibility had presented itself to him, he had no way to cleanse himself of it.

When he again opened his eyes, he found he'd wandered blindly into a small clearing. Of more concern, a horned creature confronted him, proud head raised arrogantly, regarding him with seeming disdain. A unicorn, Reaper's memories supplied. One of the fae who had fought alongside the elves ages ago. As a child he'd known of their existence, but he'd never seen one as they were private, elusive creatures.

"Greetings, Umbral K'hul," the creature said in ancient Elvish.

W'rath took a shocked step back, horrified to hear his true name spoken by another being. He quickly looked around, but no one but he could hear the creature's words. The ladies had only just now exited House of Memories. He didn't think even Raven's remarkable ears could hear the unicorn's words, much less understand them.

"I've shed that name." he said, falling into the same language. Several millennia had passed since he'd last spoken his native tongue, but it came back to him in all of its strange, primal beauty.

"Really? What do you call yourself now?" The unicorn cocked its head, its eyes a swirl of color.

"I've taken the name W'rath."

The unicorn wrinkled its nose. "Ridiculous name. I refuse to call you that. Since you're so sensitive about your true name I shall simply refer to you as First Son. And since you couldn't possibly pronounce *my* name properly, you may call me Stone."

*Stone? Arrogant prat—thinks I'm an idiot.* Even humans could pronounce such a simple word without fear of stumbling over the complexities of Elven intonation. W'rath swallowed his quickly growing annoyance and instead asked, "How do you know me?"

"Long ago I accepted the tiresome duty of awaiting your return. The Great Lady told me that one day, you would gain your freedom. I sensed when the house welcomed you, and though dubious, I came as I'd been bid. Despite my doubts, your presence here proves the accuracy of the Great Lady's vision." The creature shook its mane as if incredulous that any elf, even one it referred to as *Great Lady*, could impress it.

"Lady Stormchaser?"

"Yes, though not the one you refer to. *She* had already passed from this world some time before. Her blood flowed true in her offspring, though. One of her daughters told me of your eventual return."

Inwardly, W'rath flinched upon hearing the unicorn's words. He'd thought he'd come to terms with the idea of Uverial's death. The emptiness suddenly filling him cold regret said otherwise. He'd still hoped ... *Foolish!* He forced his feelings aside, and returned to the matter at hand, sneaking a glance at the females to see if they'd drawn near. Surprisingly, they clustered together, astonishment on their faces, making no attempt to come closer. Perhaps Lady Swiftbrook and her young charges had seen a unicorn, but he doubted Raven had.

"Have no fear, First Son," the unicorn said. "They know to keep their distance. Our conversation shall stay private."

The fae creature must have had an easier time reading elven faces than the other way around. "You remain free of carnal taint," it said in response to W'rath's bafflement. "I must admit to a certain amount of surprise."

That explained the shock on the ladies' faces. The sound of muffled laughter reached his ears. He sighed. He would never live this down. "Pleasant female company is sadly lacking in the Abyss," he said.

The unicorn seemed to accept this without the slightest hint of amusement, and it expressed no further curiosity concerning the subject. Instead, when next it spoke it's words served only to fulfill the obligation given it so many years past. "You're familiar with the Great Settling?"

"I've heard people speak of it. Apparently, it refers to when the world started to calm and grow more hospitable."

"Yes, it started about five thousand years after your banishment. The popular explanation goes that once Mother Magic finished giving birth to the world's creatures, and the pain and struggle of creation released its grip on her, she set about nurturing her offspring."

W'rath rolled his eyes at the personification of the element of magic. Such a fanciful story had to have come from the imagination of a Sky Elf. The ever practical First Born would never dream up such a thing.

His father's people would have simply accepted the truth as it presented itself, and determined how best to utilize it. "Why do I care about this?" he asked.

The unicorn stamped a hoof and flared its nostrils, the first sign of true emotion it had shown. "For such a long lived individual, you show a remarkable lack of patience. You should care because as the world calmed, so did all the fighting. Food, land, clean water—all those things went from scarce to abundant, and the need to continually fight ended. The People changed, grew less warlike, and the desire to create beautiful things filled them. This new peace made possible this house you've inherited."

W'rath gestured to everything around them, the pristine gardens, the soaring spires of House of Memories, as pure white as the unicorn's horn. "So what happened to everyone? Aside from you, I've met no others old enough to have known anyone from that time. No one else remembers the events you speak of."

The unicorn twitched its tufted tail. It's strangely hued eyes took on the color of storm clouds, and hints of lightning flickered in their depths. "Much of what you need to know, you'll find in your new home. There were books..."

"The last Lady Stormchaser left two journals and a history book to Lady Raven. We have yet to read through them." He suddenly recalled the letter he'd hidden from Raven, still up in his new study unread, and ground his teeth in frustration. Raven's earlier dismay at having to leave her books for later perusal came back to him, and he felt a stronger sense of empathy now. "Will you at least tell me what happened to everyone?"

The unicorn snorted. Was that supposed to be amusement?

"I'm not here to give you a history lesson, First Son. But I will tell you this: The First had other sons by other females, and most proved far less pure of heart than Lady Stormchaser's offspring. They dealt with your father in a far less direct manner than you did."

*Direct? Well, I suppose attempting to will the old boy's head to explode qualified as direct.* "So someone else managed to succeed where I failed?"

"In a way," the unicorn said, and didn't react to the scowl of exasperation that flashed across W'rath's face.

When it was plain that the creature had no intention to elaborate further, W'rath attempted to prod it. "You'll need to explain."

"I need do nothing aside from fulfill my promise to the only one of you I ever much cared for," the unicorn said. "I've already left my forest unattended for longer than is my want. I wish to quickly finish with this tiresome conversation and return to my solitude. So, listen carefully, and take what you will from my words. Do not interrupted me further."

The unicorn seemed to take W'rath's silent fuming as cooperation and finally continued. "Lady Stormchaser wanted you to know, while it took a great many years, your father eventually matured to the point where he regretted his treatment of you, First Son."

The unicorn gazed at W'rath for a long moment, perhaps trying to gauge the reaction its words had on the lone survivor from that ancient time. W'rath's secretive nature assured that he kept much of what he felt buried, but even so his ice white brows met in a prefect V on his dark forehead. He couldn't entirely hide every frown and twitch that Stone's words sent flitting across his face. The unicorn waited, as if memorizing every tiny movement of muscle on W'rath's face for future contemplation. Once satisfied that W'rath grasped the import of its words, the fae continued. "In the end, his decision to rescue you led to his, as well as, a great many others' demise."

W'rath fought to compose himself. Even if they couldn't understand the conversation, surely the ladies understood more than a casual conversation played out before them. He could almost feel Lady Swiftbrook's penetrating gaze burning into him. He needed time to determine how much of this tale he could safely share. Despite the unicorn's earlier words, W'rath couldn't keep silent any longer. "That's not possible. If my father had launched an invasion to rescue me, I would have sensed his presence. No one came to the Abyss to aid me."

His eyes narrowed as he recalled the unicorn insinuating a son of the First might have subtly arranged for his demise. It would have required a great many elves to open a one-way door large enough for an army to march into the Abyss. Exhausting work, those marching wouldn't have participated in the ritual casting. Someone who wanted the invasion to fail could have altered the spell's intention. A son, or sons, of the First, wishing to oust the relic from their past, and put themselves in power, could have managed to convince others that a dangerous element like Umbral should not be allowed to walk among them again, and that the time had come for younger, more forward thinking individuals to take charge.

So *this* was the schism he and Raven had discussed earlier. It explained why the curse of memory had been unleashed on First Home. "Where did they end up?"

"I'm not certain," the unicorn admitted. "I suspect the Nine Hells, as it would take little effort to alter the spell to reflect a change of locale from one plane of horror to another."

W'rath's hands clenched in impotent rage. "War broke out once they left?"

"Yes, most of the fae, myself included, abandoned this place then. The savagery, which had lain dormant, erupted with renewed vigor. Only a few places, like this protected area, escaped the ravages of what the fae call the *Descendant's War*. Whatever came after, you'll need to learn from the writings of the Stormchasers. My promise to seek you out, when you returned, has provided my only link to this place since that time. Having done that, I have fulfilled my obligation to the Great Lady."

The unicorn turned, and all around it the air started to shimmer. Another forest, more wild and full of primitive magic, appeared as a hazy halo around the creature. The scent of damp earth drifted into the glade and the temperature dropped noticeably.

"Stone, wait!" W'rath instantly regretted using the unicorn's made up name. He saw it's withers shake with silent laughter. Too late to take the name back, he continued. "What do you expect me to do with this information?" he asked.

"Isn't it obvious, First Son?" The unicorn peered back over its shoulder. It's eyes had transformed into green pools as unknowable as the ocean. "Fix what has been done here. Raise the elves up. Restore. Heal. Redeem. Do that and perhaps my people and the rest of the fae will return to this place." It gave a final toss of its head and gracefully stepped through into its forest home, and with a flick of its leonine tail closed the way.

✱✱✱✱✱

W'rath stared at the spot where the unicorn had lectured him. "Lovely," he muttered. His feminine audience would want to know what had just happened. Certainly, he could trust Raven with the truth. The two of them had already pieced a great deal of the story together, and no doubt the books Lady Stormchaser had left to her would provide even greater revelations. But he didn't think Lady Swiftbrook would take the unicorn's story well. Beyond that, how *did* one go about introducing an entire population to the idea that most of what they accepted as fact was false, that their ancestors had betrayed them, and set the People on a course of slow decline and eventual extinction?

He would need to give it a great deal of thought, and the day of a major assault against King Oblund did not leave time for such contemplations. But he did have to tell the ladies something...

"Unicorns," he said, coming up to the little group, "unfortunately, are not the answer to our cavalry issue."

"Is that what the two of you discussed?" Lady Swiftbrook couldn't hide the amusement from her voice.

W'rath shrugged, and moved past them on a course leading away from the Stormchaser property. The ladies fell in step with him. W'rath fastidiously ignored the knowing titters from the apprentices. "Our discussion earlier, concerning horses and human cavalry, made me think we could benefit from the same arrangement. It's plain the Wood Elves would never give their blessing to anything involving the use of creatures who have no say in the matter. When I spied the unicorn, I decided to see if it were sentient, and if so, if its people would deign to serve as steeds for us. Sadly, as I drew close to the creature I realized my first mistake."

"They're quite small," Lady Swiftbrook said.

"Certainly too small for a Sky Elf to ride, which I had imagined serving as our cavalry," W'rath said. "I changed my expectations at that point—I thought, perhaps Wood Elves would agree to work with the creatures if they acted as equal partners, and not master and beast."

"I take it the unicorn didn't care for that idea?" Raven asked.

"As it turns out, assuming this particular individual is typical of the population, they are every bit as arrogant as we, and would never allow us to ride upon them. Very few of them still live among the People, finding us petty and tedious. They prefer their solitude and their forests. This one appeared only because it sensed the change in ownership of the Stormchaser estate."

"Hmmph!" Lady Swiftbrook exclaimed. "Perhaps you misunderstood and it meant just you."

"I didn't see it bolt from my company to come lay sweetly at your feet, madam," W'rath replied.

"Yes, well, there is a very simple explanation for that," Lady Swiftbrook said.

"Ah, yes, of course," W'rath said, a wicked glint appearing in his eyes. "Apparently, among all of us, only I maintain high standards."

He skipped ahead of a wave of outrage. He grinned at them over his shoulder, relieved he'd managed to divert their attention from the mostly one-sided conversation with the unicorn. No doubt, once they had more time to think about it, Raven and Lady Swiftbrook would start to wonder what had really gone on during his encounter with Stone. At least for now, his denigration of their honor concerned them more. Soon they would have their hands full with the attack on the human king. With luck, by the time it occurred to them to question him further, it would seem of so little import, they would dismiss any lingering concerns as unimportant.

Perhaps by then he would manage to devise a plan for tackling the much greater concern facing them all.

# CHAPTER 13

Foxfire fidgeted nervously in the dark, wondering how he had gotten roped into sneaking into an enemy camp to provide assistance for Raven and W'rath. Of course, there really was no mystery involved. Lady Swiftbrook had asked, and not wanting to look like a coward, he'd told her he'd love to help. No place he'd rather be during the battle than at the side of an overconfident psion with brain damage.

While very good at talking, and even arguing for the Wood Elves, Foxfire had spent most of his life trying to get along with people. Since he had found himself marooned on this primitive planet, he'd spent his time gathering stories, and providing a spot of entertainment for a world populated by people who had little to look forward to besides bringing in the next season's crop.

"I'm really not much of a fighter," he said, for the third time.

"We intend to avoid trouble," Raven said with a look of sympathy that surprised the Wood Elf. The huge First Born sword she carried and her muscular frame promised a violent end for anyone foolish enough to get between them and their goal. That she could have any empathy for him seemed completely at odds with her appearance.

They'd arrived via magic gateway about a mile from the human camp, a vast plain spilling out in all directions, the yellowing autumn grass coming to Foxfire's thighs. A copse of trees blocked any view of the gateway's cyan flare. Additional thickets and numerous large shrubs broke up the landscape, providing much needed cover for their approach to the camp. Sien, one of their scouts, met them at the gateway and went over the layout of the camp with them. They'd already studied a map made earlier, but some changes had occurred since then. Sien guided them toward the camp, quietly explaining the situation. "A couple of the nobles had a falling out. They've resettled their tents on opposite sides of the King's pavilion. At first I didn't realize what they were up to, but it turned out they were spending a ridiculous amount of time ensuring neither tent stood closer than the other to the king." He rolled his eyes, presumably at the incomprehensible nature of humans.

Once they got closer, Sien fell silent, and they made their way without further discussion. They hunched down to creep through the tall grass, taking advantage of bushes to mask their approach. A few hundred paces out from the camp, slouched shadows resolved themselves into the forms of bored guards.

Foxfire checked the sky and reassured himself clouds still blocked out the sky. No moon would illuminate the night, helping the humans see. With all the dry grass, no one had provided the guards with torches. Since the earlier debacle that had cost several Wood Elf lives, the king and his minions probably had the utmost confidence in their magical warning system. They had posted guards as little more than an afterthought. Foxfire hoped that boded well for the rest of the evening's events.

Sien motioned for everyone to hide themselves in a particularly dense area of growth. As they hunkered down, the scout let out a brief but convincing bird cry. Instantly, shadows rose from the grass behind the sentries, and the men crumpled, disappearing into the grass as if the ground had swallowed them up. A moment later, a trio of Wood

Elves arrived at the party's hiding spot and handed over three small chits to Sien. "Kela told us these are probably what you need to cross the magic wall safely," Sien said, passing the chits out to Foxfire, W'rath and Raven. "I took one from a guard yesterday and tested it. They don't look like much, but they work."

Foxfire had to agree, the chit he held didn't look impressive at all—little more than a small, smooth stone. He pushed it inside one of his gloves for safe keeping, trying to look indifferent, and confident in front of his kin.

W'rath nodded. "This is precisely what I expected." He slipped the chit into his belt pouch and Raven followed suit. "We'd best get moving. Any further delays and the fireworks will start before we're ready."

The three newcomers whispered well wishes and then dispersed to regroup with the rest of the Wood Elves. Sien lead Foxfire and the two Shadow Elves further in, to the very edge of the encampment. His assignment complete, he nodded to them and melted into the night.

Foxfire swallowed. Everyone expected him to share the same talent as his kin when it came to creeping about, but in truth, he was quite miserable at such things. Raven must have seen his look of dismay and came to his rescue. "Grab hold of my belt," she offered. "Once I blend into the shadows, you'll stay just as hidden."

"From here on we need to stay as quiet as possible," W'rath said. "We'll capture the mage first, but try to refrain from any chatter until we get our hands on the king. You *can* speak the local language, correct?"

Foxfire nodded, very much aware W'rath found his lack of martial skills... distasteful. Well, he guessed he couldn't blame him. No point in dragging his ass through the camp, adding risk to their travels, if he couldn't at least help them communicate with the humans.

Satisfied they were ready, W'rath moved into the flickering, shadow-ridden camp. Foxfire's eyes widened as the Shadow Elf simply disappeared. He grabbed onto Raven's belt and moved into the camp with her. He didn't feel any different, but as they shifted from tent to tent even those soldiers looking straight at them didn't react. After several such encounters, he finally allowed himself to breathe again. He still couldn't make out W'rath, but Raven moved with confidence. His own remarkable memory told him they traveled the exact route they had studied on the map. They quickly drew closer to the mage's tent.

One tent away from their goal, a slim hand shot out from the entry flap to tug on Raven's sleeve. Much to her credit, she did little more than flinch in surprise. Wordlessly, they stepped into the tent. Foxfire's eyes widened as he had to quick step to avoid tripping over the cooling bodies on the ground. All four men had a clean slash across their throats, and lay sprawled in a gruesome circle. W'rath must have appeared within their midst and made a deadly pirouette, taking all four by surprise. They had died in complete silence and couldn't have met their ends more than a few seconds prior to his and Raven's arrival. Foxfire tried to look away from the corpses, but the arterial spray decorating the tent walls proved just as disturbing.

"How..." Raven began, but W'rath cut her off with a sharp shake of his head. Foxfire realized the gruesome tableau stunned her just as much as it did him. W'rath, completely ignoring the carnage, waved impatiently for them to follow him further into the tent. As far as the psion was concerned, Foxfire mused, the humans were dead and therefore no longer worthy of attention.

The three huddled together and W'rath spoke to them in the softest of whispers. "We have ourselves a bit of a problem."

Foxfire started to point out the corpses sharing the tent with them, but thought better of it. The Shadow Elf couldn't possibly mean the dead humans, and suggesting as much would only serve to lower his opinion of Foxfire even further.

"Are the two of you familiar with the term *Rider*?" W'rath asked.

"You mean like traveling on an animal?" Raven ventured.

W'rath shook his head. "Very carefully peak out the tent flap and examine the guards by the mage's tent. Don't rely on your shadow walking ability—it won't do you any good."

Foxfire shared an alarmed look with Raven. Together they crept to the tent flap. At first, the men Foxfire spied appeared no different from any other human, but then he caught the flicker of fire in their eyes. It wasn't reflected light. It came from within. He withdrew back to where W'rath waited. Raven joined them, her expression troubled.

"What in the Nine Hells is going on?" Foxfire hissed.

"Fortunately, those creatures did not come from the hells," W'rath whispered. "However, denizens from the Abyss will still prove troublesome. Our lovely king plays a very dangerous game."

"Does this have something to do with the mage's ritual?" Raven asked.

"It does," W'rath said. "We wondered what they're working on, and we now have our answer. You create a *Rider* by binding a demon to a host. King Oblund has chosen to use his own men as the hosts, sacrificing them in the hope of defeating the Wood Elves with a very short-lived, but very dangerous demonic army."

"Short-lived?" Foxfire asked.

"Indeed. The *Rider* feeds on the host's life force. The human begins to age rapidly. As they have extremely short life spans, they can't hope to survive more than a few days. Once dead, the link to this plane breaks and the demon's spirit returns to the Abyss. In the meantime, though, they are quite formidable."

"Bloody hell!" Foxfire said, nearly forgetting to keep his voice low.

"A truly wretched way to treat one's own people," W'rath said, "but hardly what concerns us at the moment. The two chaps stationed at the mage's tent can see through our Shadow Walking ability."

"We can try around back—cut open the tent and slip in," Raven suggested.

"And hope there aren't any more of those *things* back there to see us," Foxfire said. "Or inside with the mage."

"If we don't do that, we'll have to wait for the others to begin their attack, and hope these two abandon their posts to join the fight. The mage will probably wake up, though, and we'll lose our chance to capture him without a fight," Raven replied.

At the mention of the coming attack W'rath grew still. "What?" asked Raven.

"One of the first things our people plan to do is disrupt the ritual," W'rath said.

"Isn't that a good thing? We don't need them making even more of those creatures," Foxfire said.

"It's also how they're maintaining control over the ones they've already created," W'rath explained. "Once the ritual halts, nothing will contain them—they'll run amok. Overall, that may benefit us, as the demons won't hesitate to turn on the humans. Since they're in amongst the camp they could very well do most of our work for us. The humans will have no choice but to focus their attention on the *Riders*, and the two sides will destroy one another. We simply need to finish off the survivors."

"The demons will massacre them," Raven said, horrified.

"Most likely," W'rath agreed, though the tone of his voice indicated his concerns lay entirely with the threat level the elves faced, and not the terrible fate awaiting the humans.

Foxfire tried to bend his own thinking along the same lines. The elves expected to face mundane humans, not demons masquerading as humans. Would the chaos caused by the uncontrolled riders prove more damaging to the king's people, or would the elves' magic attract the demons? Foxfire wished Sien had continued in with them. He considered his two companions. W'rath needed Raven. She could fight, and her strength would allow her to cart at least one, perhaps even two, adult humans if necessary. Foxfire had only his language skills to offer. The Shadow Elves had two of Lady Swiftbrook's translation rings, one of which they could force on the king so they could communicate. *I've just become redundant.*

W'rath's next words to him confirmed Foxfire's fears. "I need you to leave here and warn our forces of what they're about to face. Let them decide how they wish to handle the ritual—whether to disrupt it as planned, or to let the magi maintain control of the *Riders* and hope the wretches keep them from going completely berserk. Make sure Lord Icewind is ready for us; Raven and I have no desire to find ourselves trapped in the middle of a demon fight."

Foxfire wanted to protest, but his voice seemed to have failed him. "Focus, lad," W'rath said, reaching out to grasp Foxfire's shoulder with a hand that felt like it had been forged from iron. "You remember our path here, correct?"

Foxfire forced down his panic. He knew the way back. Along that path plenty of flickering shadows and difficult lighting would aid him. Most humans had poor night vision to begin with, and the small cook fires the soldiers used would blind them further, making it harder for them to notice a small camouflaged elf creeping from tent, to weapons rack, to supply crates.

"I'm sure you can manage," Raven said. "You can't have spent time with Kela without picking up a little something about stealth."

If Kela had been present Foxfire knew she would have laughed, or at the very least made one of her derisive snorts. But now wasn't the time to point that out. Before meeting Kela he'd never even set foot in a forest. The rest of his kin had chosen him for the council by default more than anything else. None of the other Wood Elves had the patience or social skills to get along with their fancier cousins. But now something more was needed of him. It terrified him, but if he didn't warn the others, something akin to the slaughter at Second Home could result. His lips set in a determined line, he nodded.

"Excellent," W'rath said. "We'll get you as far as that grey tent we passed. You exit the camp as quickly as you can, and we'll circle around have a go at the mage from the other side of his quarters." They double-checked that he still had his enchanted chit so he could cross the border of the camp without setting off the alarm. "Good luck, lad."

Foxfire safely on his way, W'rath and Raven examined the mage's tent from the back. So far, they had seen five additional *Riders*. The wholly human soldiers didn't recognize what walked among them. Though aware of a wrongness about certain individuals, their confused faces said the chill running along their spines didn't have an obvious source.

"Do you think there are any inside the tent guarding the mage?" Raven whispered.

She saw W'rath's jaw clench and worried for a moment she had somehow annoyed him. Then she realized it wasn't her but the necessity to speak out loud which grated on his nerves. If overtly using his psionics wouldn't debilitate him, he could converse with her in complete silence. For that matter, he could have communicated with the rest of the council members without having to send Foxfire off on his own. A broken arm could regenerate in a few minutes, but a brain took days, sometimes weeks to recover from a psionic overload.

"We haven't much choice, I'm afraid," he said at last. "I think it's safe to assume, though, even as skillful as these fellows seem, they'd still find it uncomfortable with a demon in the room, staring at them while they sleep."

Raven nodded, accepting his reasoning, and scanned the area to see if the path to the mage's tent was clear of *Riders*. With unspoken agreement the two took to the shadows and met up at the back of the tent. Without pause, W'rath slit the fabric and made an opening for them to slip through. Raven entered first, her sword drawn, alert for any attack. W'rath entered next and immediately pounced on the snoring mage. Finally! Raven had started to think the entire expedition cursed. No guardians and the mage asleep. *Thank you, Ancestors.*

Raven's relief was short-lived, though, as a small fanged creature launched itself from its perch and tried to eat her face. Purely on reflex, she snapped her hand up, snatching it out of the air by its slavering little head. She squeezed and a soft crunch met her ears. The thing went limp, bat-like wings drooping, tiny clawed hands falling to its sides. She dropped it in disgust and attempted to shake its brain goo from her hand. An imp, a common enough sight in her home city. It wasn't surprising that a mage who used demon magic would keep such a creature as a familiar.

She turned to see how W'rath faired with the mage and found her companion grinning at her futile attempts to fling the imp's grey matter from her hand. He gestured with his chin toward an elegant silk shirt draped carelessly over a chest. Gratefully, Raven used it to clean away the last bits of imp. When she finished, W'rath hefted the unconscious mage to a sitting position. She grabbed the fellow up and slung him over one broad shoulder.

The ease at which W'rath had subdued the man surprised Raven. Surely, the human had had some form of magical protection, but he hadn't even stirred. She gave one last glance at the dead imp, and wondered if the shock of his familiar's death could have contributed to the mage's lack of fight. Or did humans sleep so deeply they were helpless? W'rath had expressed disbelief that elves slept at all, but what she called sleep bore little resemblance to the exhausted unconsciousness of a human.

Their first goal achieved, the two quickly exited the tent the same way they'd entered. They flitted from shadow to shadow, keeping an eye out for *Riders*. Raven had to admit, without the nervous Foxfire clutching at her belt, they made better time. It almost turned into a game, quietly moving past the oblivious humans and ducking hastily behind crates, tents and wagons to keep the *Riders* from spotting them.

They had no difficulty locating their next destination. The king kept a large pavilion with fluttering pennants directly in the center of the camp. Unfortunately, as they drew closer the number of *Riders* grew, making the going more perilous. They studied the space between them and the entry of the royal pavilion. The two wholly human men at the doorway appeared quite nervous, touching the pommels of their swords as if to reassure themselves. A group of *Riders* moved by them, muttering in low, unwholesome tones. The men's eyes followed them, unable to focus on anything else. The elves saw their chance, and walked the shadows to appear before the startled guards. "No need to announce us," W'rath said with a wicked grin.

* * * * *

King Oblund III raised his goblet, and a boy, whose name he'd already forgotten, rushed to refill it. The boy poured Southern Red into the goblet, leaving enough space for the crimson nectar to breathe.

The king flicked a finger at the boy, who bowed, and slipped into the background.

Oblund sampled the wine, savoring it, allowing the woody scent of it to permeate his senses. He settled back in his chair, and studied the two guards standing on either side of the inner doorway of the pavilion. As sons of nobles, he had spared them the *enhancement* process the mercenary magi had been subjecting the common soldiers to. While he trusted no one, these two had proven they understood politics well enough to feign deafness during every conversation held within the confines of the war room. If they continued to prove worthy, he would arrange property and marriages for them. If not... well, anything could happen during times of war. Elven assassins lurked everywhere and the savages couldn't tell, or appreciate, the differences between a civilized man and a pig farmer.

However, the relative usefulness of noblemen's sons hardly concerned him at the moment. No, the man giving him indigestion just now was His Golden Eminence, Holy Purveyor of the Word, and Humble Servant of the Duality, Chalice Ungren Renour. A cancerous pain in the ass more like. Not to mention, a bottomless well of sanctimonious platitudes. Damned arrogant, too.

The king's black eyes glittered from beneath black brows, studying the human vessel of the will of the Duality. No frail and bookish priest, Ungren dominated any room with his commanding presence. His face boasted strong features and a lion-like mane of hair that fell in perfectly with his beard. It was as if a golden halo surrounded his face.

Even his single flaw branded him a hero. A savage scar marred his face, starting from his scalp, skirting his right eye, and ending just below his strong cheekbone. He'd fought his way across a battlefield to stand protectively by his king, sustaining the infuriatingly dashing wound in the process. Oblund loathed him.

And now the bastard had the audacity to lecture him. Apparently, there existed rules, even in warfare. Lines that men of honor should not cross. *Gods! Would he* ever *shut up?*

"Your Majesty, I implore you, dismiss the magi. The evil they do shall stain our people for generations. Even as we speak, the demons feed upon your men's souls. And for what? A bit of wilderness?"

"As usual, Chalice, you oversimplify the situation. Ours is a wood poor land, sharing a border with a hostile country which, even now, works to exploit that weakness. In order to protect ourselves we need to fortify our borders, repair our forts and build weapons. For that," he pointed a finger at the priest, "we need this forest. Unfortunately, the savages laying claim to it seem capable of making entire armies disappear. We need a powerful weapon, and only magic can provide that."

"Enlisting those who use demonic magic will doom us all," the Chalice countered. "Sire," he added belatedly. King Oblund did not miss the purposeful slight. This was intolerable. Even the discrete young nobles by the door could not ignore the fact that the wretchedly popular battle priest treated his king like a child in need of chastising.

The rustle of fabric from the back of the pavilion announced the queen's arrival. Slim hands gripped the king's shoulders and attempted to ease the tenseness they found there. She said nothing, but Oblund knew her eyes focused not on him but on the priest who, even now, bowed to her: His lover. Oh, he had no proof, but he had seen how they glanced at one another. Eventually, he would find a witness to their treason and both would lose their heads. His own fault for marrying a woman who thought herself entitled to an opinion. That Ungren encouraged her deviant behavior, despite holding a position which made it his job to uphold the doctrines of the church, betrayed his true nature. *I am beset by schemers.*

"Pardon us for disturbing your rest, Your Majesty," the priest said, bowing again. "It pains me you have so long suffered these ill conditions, and yet, I cannot help but rejoice in your presence. The men draw strength at the sight of you, knowing you share in their plight."

The queen laughed. "Chalice, I hardly think I suffer unduly. I consider it no more than my duty to stand by His Majesty and offer my support."

*Is that what you call it?* Ever since she'd arrived she'd argued with him as insistently as Ungren against hiring the magi from the mercenary city state of Tassilia. She had tried a different tact, claiming that, by laying siege to the Wood Elves forest, he left their kingdom open to attack from King Luccan. Admittedly, he hadn't expected things to play out so long. When ten thousand men had marched into the forest that first day, only to disappear without a trace, he'd realized he was up against something far worse than a pack of child-like primitives. They obviously possessed some unholy power.

His first instinct had been to contact the church. He'd even tolerated their decision to send Ungren to render his opinion. But, of course, the contrary bastard had insisted he could discern no unnatural communion going on between the elves and any of the planes of evil. He'd actually suggested they try to parlay with the elves, even volunteered to do so in the king's name. Apparently, the sun blessed priest spoke fluent Elvish, and felt certain he could reach some accommodation with the creatures.

Perhaps he should have allowed Ungren to make the attempt. The Chalice could have entered the wood to join the previous ten thousand lost, and Oblund would now be free of him. But no, the thrice-damned priest would have succeeded and come marching out of the forest, glowing in triumph, hand in hand with his new elf friends, a signed treaty in his messenger's pouch, and tiny bluebirds fluttering around his glorious head. *Fuck.*

So, instead, Oblund had decided to do something nearly as noxious. He'd turned to his wife, the queen, to provide war funds so he could hire four magi from Tassilia. Curse the church and their damned Duality for putting women in charge of the purse strings. She'd only agreed to give him the coin if he allowed her to stay with him at the encampment. Now Oblund found himself trapped between his shrewish wife and the priest.

Once the magi arrived, Oblund had expected the priest to start quoting from the pages of the Duality. Ungren had frowned, but surprisingly refrained from voicing any objections—at least at first. Oblund vetoed the magi's suggestions of fire and poison, and they in turn told him earth and plant magic would be useless against a people so in tune with nature. Eventually, the magi had shrugged and told him that defeating the elves would require the use of darker arts.

Rather than dismissing the men and sending them back where they came from, he'd found himself intrigued. Despite the priest's claims, Oblund felt certain the elves, if not demons themselves, had summoned Abyssal power against their betters. He would only be using their own weapon against them. And it was for the greater good.

He made one stipulation though. He had no desire for an army of demons to run rampant through his new forest. To this the magi provided an elegant answer. Men and boys, pulled from the peasantry, made up the bulk of Oblund's army. Unfortunately, the elves had shown a serious disdain for open combat and remained stubbornly hidden in the forest. Since the ten thousand had disappeared, without so much as a strangled death cry, the sodding peasants cringed at the mere sight of a tree. By binding a "*Rider*" to them, they grew fearless and much more formidable. Once they'd served their purpose, the host would perish as payment for the demon's assistance, and in turn the demon's summoned spirit would return to its home to trouble Oblund no more. If only all of his subjects behaved so well.

And as an added bonus? The entire plan horrified Ungren.

The hands kneading his shoulders had started to feel more like harpy claws, and Oblund realized, while he'd been reminiscing, the queen and priest had chatted on without him. *Of course they had!*

"What do you mean the men won't survive?" the queen asked.

"It hardly concerns you," the king interjected, vainly hoping to keep the Chalice from launching into another sermon. The harpy's claws paused in mid clench. Would she ever learn she had no business in the affairs of war?

"Anything involving the welfare of our people concerns me," she said. "Please, Chalice, continue. Though possessed of a woman's limited understanding in these matters, I pray you'll suffer me to understand the nature of the magicks involved."

"You do yourself injustice, Your Majesty," Ungren said, once again bowing. Oblund's eye began to twitch. "The magi have purposely allowed demons to possess our soldiers. Only through the force of their continued ritual, can they maintain control over them. Come midnight, they intend to send them en masse into the forest to eradicate the elves. Regardless of the outcome, those men carrying the spirits of the damned will die as a result of the possession."

The queen gasped and the claws withdrew. She took a step back from Oblund. "No wonder you've kept this from me! What a monstrous thing to do to our people! Surely your advisors did not approve this?"

Oblund launched himself to his feet and turned on her. "This is why women should not insert themselves into a war council," he snarled. "You haven't the stomach for the hard choices. Those peasants live to serve the crown. Even in death they shall fulfill their duty."

"And the council?" she insisted, not backing down despite his upraised fists.

"Old men who tremble and hide amid outdated laws."

"But laws all the same. Laws which you have no right to change on your own!"

He did strike her then. Pain shot through the bones of his fist, but he welcomed it. The feel of her face breaking as he struck her made any discomfort worthwhile. She spun, crashing into the curtains leading to her sleeping area. The servant boy cried out as she landed on him.

Oblund pivoted, anticipating Ungren's interference. The priest stood, shocked, hands reaching for the heavy mace on his hip. The boys at the doorway had gone rigid, wide-eyed and ready to flee. Technically, he had done nothing wrong. Surely, even Ungren couldn't find fault with his actions. According to the Duality, men and women both had their roles within society, and should not stray within one another's purview.

"By the twins, man! Have those magi possessed you as well?" Ungren roared. He only just managed to keep himself under control, trembling with the effort. Behind Oblund, came the cup bearer's panicked voice as he tried to assist the injured queen. She didn't reply. With luck he'd broken her jaw. "The Brother says men should protect women, not incite their terror!"

Gods, so he *could* find fault, even with this. "The crown I wear marks *me* as king!" he snapped back. "You would do well to remember that and obey instead of question."

"Majesty, you need the support of the nobles in order to retain your rule," Ungren returned, taking a step forward, his control starting to fray. "They, in turn, cannot function without the support of the commoners. You lose the confidence of the people, you lose everything. The elves will be the least of your worries."

An evil chuckle interrupted the priest's tirade. Even without the ability to understand the words, the menace behind them chilled the blood. *Ah, but we are very much the greatest of his worries.* Oblund felt his mouth go dry.

⁂

From the flickering shadows, materialized a small, dark being. The young nobles guarding the door jumped. They grabbed for their swords, but something snatched them from behind. Their heads crashed together and they collapsed on the carpeted ground. A much larger being stepped through the doorway. Ungren caught a glimpse of the other two guards from the outer entry—also lying in a heap.

"Demons!" Oblund roared, apparently immune to the irony of his outburst.

"No, Shadow Elves," Ungren said. He edged toward the king to protect him from this new threat. And enormous sword flicked to his throat, freezing him in place.

The smaller of the two elves raised a hand where a plain gold ring glittered. "I must give Lady Swiftbrook my compliments. I can understand their bestial tongue perfectly."

"What is it saying?" Oblund asked.

"They can understand us," Ungren said, choosing to leave off the more insulting aspects of the comment.

Perfect white teeth flashed in a smile from the elf's ebony skin. Crimson eyes caught the candlelight to gleam like embers, and shifted to the priest. "Excellent, you're more learned than expected. We need not share our rings with you. Whom do I have the pleasure of addressing?"

Ungren swallowed. He'd never seen Shadow Elves before, but everyone grew up hearing stories about them. His old nurse had terrified him as a child with tales of their cruelty. As an adult he'd come to view the stories as nothing but myth and nonsense. The gleaming blade held to his throat, by a much too steady hand, made him think he might wish to reassess those earlier conclusions. "I am Chalice Ungren Renour, Holy Purveyor of the Word of the Duality."

"What is going on?" the king demanded.

"We're just introducing ourselves," Ungren said.

The small elf moved into the light and Ungren blinked. He'd seen several Wood Elves, and all of them had appeared so androgynous and pretty, they seemed childlike. This fellow, though, had angular features, a chiseled chin and an aquiline nose. His voice, though musical, held a deep, and very male timber to it. Despite the almond eyes, the beardless face, and his small stature, no one would mistake this elf for a child.

For his part, the elf seemed just as intrigued by the priest's appearance. "A great deal of time has passed since I last laid eyes on your kind. Walking much more upright these days, I see. Just as horrifically hairy as I remember, though. I don't know how you can stand to procreate."

Ungren didn't know if the elf hoped to goad him into a rash act, or if he merely stated what he saw as facts, without any insult actually intended. Better to ignore the words and try to move things in a more productive direction. "I've introduced myself, perhaps you would return the favor?" he asked.

"How abominably rude of me," the Shadow Elf said, sounding quite sincere. "This winsome lass, with the sword to your throat, is Lady Raven. I am known as Lord W'rath. We serve as the Shadow Elf representatives of the Elven High Council. We've taken offense to your treatment of our cousins and have come to lodge a complaint."

"What is it saying, dammit?" the king snarled.

"Your Majesty, please meet Lady Raven and Lord W'rath of the Elven High Council. They're not happy with your campaign against the Wood Elves."

"*That's* a woman?" the king blurted, completely ignoring the more salient points of Ungren's words.

Ungren's gaze shifted to Lady Raven. She'd drifted slightly so that the candle light brought out her face more clearly. He'd expected anger, but much to his surprise saw hurt there. When he looked back at Lord W'rath though, the elf simmered with enough anger for both of them.

Oblund saw it too. "Even if it means your life, priest, your duty demands you protect me."

"I shouldn't bother if I were you," Lord W'rath said. "I assume, as leader of your people, he has a responsibility for their welfare. His actions make it clear another would serve better."

"W'rath!" the female said. "You promised the council you wouldn't kill him."

"A promise made before we knew he'd infected his men with *Riders*," came the curt reply.

"What about avoiding a war of revenge for killing their sovereign?"

"She has a point," Ungren ventured, and immediately regretted his words as the angry little elf turned his hellish gaze upon him.

"Who exactly will shoulder the blame when all of your lads start withering and dying in agony from the demons hosted within them? Surely, you don't expect me to believe your goodly king will admit he traded thousands of his men's lives in return for a brief tactical advantage?"

All of their eyes moved back to Oblund. "What?" he fumed.

"Lord W'rath believes you'll tell our people the elves are to blame for the agonizing deaths awaiting those possessed by the *Riders*."

The king shrugged. "We're at war. Of course I'm going to shift any blame to them. I need to use all available resources in the fight, and you cannot expect peasants to understand the necessity of my actions."

"Is that all our people represent to you, resources? Like a chair? If you break a leg, you simply replace it?"

The king nearly leapt out of his skin. His wife, forgotten, had come up behind him. She wavered, unsteady, supported by the servant boy. The whole right side of her face had swelled and bruised from the blow, to the point she couldn't see out of one eye. Her nose twisted oddly to the left side of her face.

Ungren cast a nervous glance at their captors, concerned the queen's sudden appearance might startle them to violence. Neither seemed surprised, though. So, they'd known of her presence all along. While he and the king hadn't heard a thing, the elves had completely dismissed her as a threat. The rumors of heightened elven senses were true, then. "Her Majesty, Queen Cherish," he said.

Lord W'rath frowned in disgust. "Your queen appears to have seen more battle than either of you."

"Talk to *me*, damn it!" the king erupted.

"Sire, Lord W'rath merely expressed concern over Her Majesty's injuries."

"It's none of its damned business," he said. His normally baritone voice had climbed several octaves.

The small elf leaped over the table before Oblund finished speaking. He bore the man down like a hunting cat. Perching on the king's chest, he leaned in close, nose to nose with the horrified king.

Ungren started by instinct to go to his liege's aid, but Lady Raven's sword block his way. "Please," she said, "you seem like a decent man. Don't make me hurt you."

Ungren nodded. He flicked his eyes over to Queen Chalice, worried for her. She'd grown pale beneath her bruises, and taken a few steps back, but for now she seemed well enough. The boy, on the other hand, looked as though he might faint. That's what happened when childhood nightmares came to life.

"Lass," Lord W'rath interrupted, "may I borrow your ring, please? I weary of this indirect communication."

"I think he's pretty clear on your meaning at the moment." She tilted her head at Ungren, silently warning him not to try anything, and took a step back. Only then did Ungren realize she had a body slung over one of her shoulders. She dropped it, and one of the mercenary magi landed in a heap at Ungren's feet. He breathed, unconscious but alive. When Ungren looked back up, the she-elf removed her ring, and then brought her sword back up close to his throat. It didn't seem someone so big should be able to move so fast, but as she tossed the gold ring to her companion, Ungren knew underestimating this lady would be a very foolish thing to do. Doubly so, as far as her male counterpart went. He didn't look when she tossed the ring to him. He simply reached out, and it landed in his hand, as if by its own volition. He patted the blade shoved through his belt as if to warn Oblund the fate awaiting him if he tried anything, and then with barely concealed disdain, the elf shoved the magic ring onto the king's hand.

"That's better," Lord W'rath said. "Now we can insult one another directly."

"I'm sure His Majesty didn't mean anything by the use of the word 'it'," Ungren said, once again attempting diplomacy.

"Of course he did," Lord W'rath replied. "I try not to be overly sensitive. Your people have always had trouble determining the gender of elves. So, in the name of peaceful negotiations, I'm willing to overlook the 'it' reference. I'm feeling generous and shall, this one time, forgive the rude outburst concerning Lady Raven. But the rest of it—plotting to send demons against the Wood Elves, and then laying the blame for the subsequent deaths of your people at our feet—I cannot abide. So, what *shall* I do with you, old boy?" His intense gaze drifted from the tongue-tied king to the queen. "What would your battered lady say, I wonder?"

Much to everyone's surprise the queen answered for herself. Though heavily accented, her Elvish was understandable as she forced the words through swollen lips. "What do you suggest? I wish to avoid as much bloodshed as possible."

In answer, the ground shook with a concussive force. Ungren frowned. The king had insisted the magi put a spell on the tent to keep people from eavesdropping on them. Not only had that backfired and allowed the elves to completely take them by surprise, but now something significant transpired outside and they could hear none of it. The elves noticed the unnatural silence too and an unspoken communion passed between them. For some reason the magic concerned them.

A messenger burst through the tent doorway, only to trip over the unconscious bodies of the guards. Raven snatched him up by his collar before he could hit the ground. He squeaked when he saw the Shadow Elf warrior holding him aloft.

Another explosion shook the ground, still eerily silent. "Report, son," the priest ordered the panicked young man.

The boy's eyes stayed fixed on Raven, but he managed to find his voice. "The elves, sir. They're raining fire and lightning down on us. They came out of nowhere. The magi, sir, they're dead!"

ЖЖЖЖЖ

W'rath rose from the king, leaving the toe of one boot pressed against the man's throat. Raven's brow furrowed in concern. "Either Foxfire didn't make it..."

"Or K'hul decided to press the attack with us still here amid all the *Riders*," W'rath finished.

"What does that mean?" the queen asked.

"It means, madam, that your liege's demonic horde is completely free to do as it pleases. Human and elf now find themselves equally at risk."

"We need to join forces," Raven said.

W'rath sniffed in disgust, but didn't disagree. The king, however, vigorously protested via grunts and animal noises. W'rath shifted his foot until Oblund's voice choked off. "You no longer have a say in what happens here."

The Shadow Elf regarded the priest and the queen. "This is our offer. Come with us now. Priest, rally your people, those still human, and join us in putting down the demons. Queen Cherish, we shall do our best to escort you and this wretch to safety. In exchange, he abdicates, and you renounce his actions."

"I don't have the power to make that kind of promise," the queen said. "Such things are not considered appropriate for women to decide. Even if the majority of the nobles agree to your terms, civil war could still erupt if enough choose to stand by my husband. Others may decide that they wish to take the throne by force, and each banner that rises will bring more violence until one man finally manages to take the crown and crush the rest." She nearly fell as another explosion shook the earth. The trembling boy at her side barely managed to steady her.

W'rath's scowl deepened. When he'd last seen humans, their primitive society, if it could even qualify as such, had been exceedingly male-dominated. He had assumed they had outgrown such things once they took to walking upright, but that was apparently naïve on his part. Playing nice with the enemy had never been one of his strengths, and his ignorance of their culture made things worse.

Raven attempted another course. "What about you?" she asked the priest.

"I can't usurp the throne," he said. "As Her Majesty stated, we have a council of nobles who would need to convene and consider whether His Majesty's crimes warrant his removal, and if so then put forth possible candidates as his replacement. The church would provide input as well. The nobles won't move against the king if the church upholds his divine sanction. We have scholars who can attest to the various merits of an individual's lineage. We adhere to a strict set of protocols."

"Surely, no one would continue to follow someone so clearly unbalanced?" Raven sounded as vexed as W'rath felt.

Ungren started to object, but W'rath interrupted him. "Before you reply with some stupidly misplaced declaration of loyalty to this... man, remember he bears the responsibility for turning at least half your army into a demonic horde."

"Only the peasants!" The King had managed to wriggle his head free enough so he could speak again.

"Peasants...?" W'rath tried the word, but even the magic ring wasn't able to find an exact translation that made sense to the elf. From the king's tone, he intended it as an insult, an indication he viewed said peasants as a lower life form. That did W'rath little good, since in his opinion, all humans qualified as such.

The Queen seemed to realize his dilemma. "The peasants are the common folk who serve on a lord's land, growing our crops and raising our livestock. In addition, the men and boys must come to their lord's aid when he requires additional military service in response to the demands made by the crown."

"Is demonic possession, followed by a gruesome death part of that pact as well?" Raven asked, drawing herself up to glower at the woman.

"No, of course not," the Queen said, going pink with shame. A trickle of blood escaped her nose and she wiped at it without thinking, and a flare of pain pulled a gasp from her.

Another thought occurred to W'rath. "If these peasants of yours keep your population fed, what will happen now that several thousand of them will not survive to return to their hovels?"

The queen dropped her eyes in shame. "We may struggle some this winter," Ungren finally said. That seemed as close to a criticism of the king as he would commit to—at least in front of elves.

Another seeming earthquake nearly knocked them all to the ground. The royal pavilion groaned and started to tilt. K'hul and company's attention grabbing attack had kept the demon's attention focused away from the tent, but eventually a demon or three would tear through, assuming it didn't collapse first. Regardless, they needed to leave now. Despite the uproar outside, none of the commotion reached their ears. The magi had cast a powerful divination spell upon the tent. It would play havoc with Kiat's attempts to locate them. They couldn't afford to wait while the humans continued to make excuses for not ousting their king.

Foxfire burst into the pavilion, artfully dancing over the fallen guards and skirting around the lad still dangling from Raven's hand. "Bloody hells, what are you people doing?" He said. "The world is ending out there, and you're having tea?"

The Wood Elf chattered in the human's native tongue as if it were his first language and not his second, third or even hundredth. Even without psionics, the fellow had a talent for languages and accents W'rath had to admire.

"We've been attempting a bit of negotiation, but I fear I haven't the talent for such things," W'rath said. "What seems logical and prudent to Raven and me, the humans find completely unworkable."

"Shocking," Foxfire managed. He couldn't stand still, his desire to flee reflected in every twitch of his muscles . "In case you haven't noticed, K'hul decided to follow through on the attack, so getting out of here comes before whatever passes for negotiations in your world."

W'rath purposely gave Foxfire a blank stare, and was rewarded with a magnificent view of scarlet racing up the Wood Elf's skin as he moved to a state of apoplexy. "Seriously? I have to explain why standard negotiations don't usually include holding a sword to the head cleric's throat, and crushing the sovereign's windpipe?"

With a small pang of regret, W'rath removed his foot from Oblund's throat. He hauled the human to his feet and shoved him in Foxfire's direction. Oblund massaged his bruised throat, glaring murder at the Shadow Elf . "Don't forget he's still the enemy, lad," W'rath said to Foxfire. "We're here because he brought an army to your forest to claim it for his own. If I had my way, we wouldn't negotiate at all. We'd kill him and anyone foolish enough to protest." He hesitated to make his point clear. "This is me playing nice."

"Yeah, I know," Foxfire said. With shaking hands he pulled a slender cord from his pack. When the king proved belligerent toward the idea of having his arms trussed behind his back, W'rath stepped in and quickly brought the man to his knees.

The psion watched as Foxfire fumbled with the cord and nearly dropped it. The lad had no business returning to hostile territory. Clearly, their current situation terrified him, and yet, he had left the safety of the elven camp and come back to aid his new allies. The boy had more honor in one pointed ear than K'hul had in his entire hulking body. W'rath slipped in close to Foxfire so he could whisper to him. "Are you all right, lad?"

"No, I'm not. I'm scared shitless. I came back because I was worried about you two. Kiat hasn't managed to locate you. I assume it has something to do with this tent, there's some magic on it deflecting his powers. So I get here, and you're just standing around acting like you have all day. I have no idea how you can stay so calm."

A memory of demonic armies closing in on one another in the Abyss came unbidden to W'rath's mind. An entire mountain range had turned to rubble when the two met and clashed. He gave Foxfire a reassuring pat on the arm and nodded his approval at the Wood Elf's work on the king's tether. "As long as it stands, the magic on this tent shields us from the noise and the magic firestorm. I expect we'll be suitably shaken once we leave this place."

He turned back toward the front of the tent. The queen and the boy had joined Ungren. Raven released the messenger and he knelt, attempting to revive the young guards lying insensate upon the ground. W'rath doubted the two would make it. Raven had yet to learn the extent of her strength. She'd probably given the chaps matching skull fractures. In his experience, humans didn't recover readily from such things. Perhaps this more evolved version of human had sturdier heads. *Not likely*.

"Very well," W'rath said. "We shall leave this place. Once free of the tent's enchantments, our colleague should provide us a means of escape. It may take a few minutes for him to locate us, so in the meantime protect your queen and yourselves, but raise no weapon against an elf. We shall endeavor to keep you alive, but if you do anything foolish, we will leave you to the mercies of your king's horde, and worry about the political backlash later. Agreed?"

For the first time no one protested or argued. Even Oblund had finally quieted down. The guards had come to, though they swayed, unsteady. W'rath still doubted they would survive without a healer. The messenger tried to explain the situation to them. Their unfocused eyes darted about in fear, but at last they nodded. At least they weren't so far gone they couldn't understand.

Raven pulled her sword from Ungren's neck and allowed him to take up his war sledge. They sized one another up for a time and came to a silent agreement. Only then did Ungren's eyes move to one of the young, unsteady nobles. "Lord Castle," he said, "make yourself useful and carry the mage for Lady Raven. She'll need to fight, and I think she'll do better without a man's dead weight dragging on her."

"Hypocrite," Oblund said.

"Sire, they don't follow our beliefs," he said, sounding weary. W'rath noted he didn't bother to point out that Raven was bigger and stronger than any of them. From what the queen had said, their doctrines didn't take that into account. But, despite his religious beliefs, Ungren had a soldier's practical view of survival. He used what tools he had available.

If the battered young man had any inclination to argue, years of instilled respect for one's superiors won out, and he began to pull at the limp mage. "Of course, Your Eminence." With some help from the messenger, he got the unconscious man slung across his back. The messenger and other guards clustered around him for protection.

A flaming missile tore through the pavilion, taking one of the unfortunate young men with it. The queen screamed as the tent came apart, disintegrating in a concussion of wind and fire. As the magic of the pavilion came undone, the roar of the outside world crashed in upon them.

# CHAPTER 14

The last remnants of the royal pavilion whirled away into the maelstrom. "So much for the tent's magic," W'rath said. "Lord Icewind should have a much easier time finding us now."

"Now do you see what I mean?" Foxfire said. Even his bard's trained voice could barely carry over the cacophony.

"Gods!" Raven gasped, her instinct to duck and hide nearly overwhelming. Then she saw the boy cowering against his queen, she remembered how she had clung to Linden during the attack on Second Home. He'd probably felt then like she did now, but he had dug deep and found his courage for her sake. Now she had to do the same for everyone here. Linden's soul rumbled his approval inside her. His fire and combat instincts sung through her veins. She turned with a snarl, searching for the enemy.

The demons obliged, rushing forward when they sensed her and the others. Raven spun and cut one down as it hurled itself at them. "Chalice, have your men protect the queen and the child!" she said, and tore into her next victim, body checking the demon and beheading it as it crashed to the ground.

ЖЖЖЖЖ

Ungren ordered the guards into position. They dumped the mage onto the ground near the queen and the servant boy. The Wood Elf prodded King Oblund into the protective ring of fighters. Four swords and one mace faced outwards, hoping for the promised means of escape, but not expecting it to come in time. In all his days, Ungren had never witnessed anything like the maelstrom of death surrounding them. He'd fought in battles against fellow humans numerous times. *The Ten Day War* pitted them against the orcs of Dire Mountain. What a terrible, bloody time that had been. The orc shamans killed with poisonous insect swarms and a horror the men called blood rain. He almost missed the orcs now. If he didn't know better, he'd swear the Abyss itself had opened its maw and swallowed them.

Fire and lightning fell all around them. Flaming meteors screamed from the sky, and arcing bolts of lightning consumed all they touched. Great chunks of earth exploded around them, lava shooting out of the fissures. *Riders* and humans alike turned to ash, ignited by the superheated death. Shrapnel tore through flesh, leaving torn bodies scattered upon the ground, filling the air with the stench of spilled blood and entrails. Bowel loosening bellows and roars echoed across the field. A choking bank of smoke cut off visibility, but a breeze cleared the distance enough that, for a brief moment, Ungren glimpsed an enormous stone and lava creature, nearly two hundred feet high, eclipsing the battlefield. It took a slow, ponderous step and more tremors shook the ground, rippling it like water. Bodies went tumbling, and the screams of the terrified and dying added to the discordance whirling around the priest and his group.

It was almost too much, even for a brave man. Only the priest's sense of duty to those who needed his protection gave him the courage to stand firm in the maelstrom. "My Queen, stay close," he said. His voice sounded small to his ears. Brother and Sister, what had they awoken by angering the elves?

ЖЖЖЖЖ

As a huddled group, they awaited the inevitable. King Oblund staggered up alongside Chalice Ungren. His eyes huge with horror, mouth gaping like a carp, the king didn't seem to notice his arms were still trussed tightly. Foxfire clung tightly to the thong attached to the King's bindings. "How can this be?" Oblund said. "The magi swore First Home would never commit to a conflict on the mainland."

No one answered him. Foxfire certainly had no interest in enlightening the bastard. If someone hadn't attacked Second Home using demons, and then also used them against the Wood Elves, Foxfire doubted K'hul would have agreed to come to their aid. K'hul wanted someone to pay for Second Home, and getting his hands on one of the mercenary magi from Tassilia offered the best chance he had of gaining the information he needed.

The breeze died and the smoke closed back in around them, leaving them isolated, unable to keep track of Raven and W'rath. Without direction, they continue to huddle in a circle, senses stretched, trying to glimpse death before it came for them.

A pack of *Riders* burst in upon them. Foxfire heard them a moment before they sprang, and barked out a warning. Ungren swung around to sweep them with his sledge. The weapon smashed into the torso of the first possessed man. Ribs shattered, and blood gushed from the man's mouth as bone fragments pierced the lungs, and the heart ripped from its anchors. Even so, the demon inhabiting the body shrugged off the pain, and forced its dying host to close with the priest. His companions spread out to surround and overwhelm the party.

Ungren cursed himself loudly, the enormity of his mistake all too obvious. You couldn't fight *Riders* as if they were still men. Anything that didn't outright kill them wouldn't stop them. The priest threw his free hand up and called upon his faith. "Begone!" he roared. A bright golden light shot out from his gesturing hand to hit the dying *Rider* and two of its companions. Immediately, the demons were banished from their hosts and the bodies collapsed, lifeless. Even the two unharmed by the sledge perished. Too long under the influence of the demons, the men's bodies shriveled into fetal positions, nothing more than spent husks.

The four surviving demons let loose hideous, slobbering screams. Their jaws appeared to unhinge, the bones groaning and snapping, their faces contorting. One of the young men shrieked like a child and broke from the party. The *Riders* pounced, preferring easy prey over the chance of banishment from the priest.

Chalice Ungren leapt to the soldier's defense, but came to a halt as one of the boy's arms landed at his feet. Grimacing, he backtracked, rejoining the group. Foxfire swallowed, nerves fraying further. He took stock of those who still lived. Much to his surprise, the queen still stood, shielding the youngster clinging to her. The rest of the guards weren't in much better shape than the child. Oblund had been straining at his thong, trying to flee, but the sight of the *Riders* tearing the soldier to pieces, brought a halt to his escape attempts. Now he leaned against his captor, shuddering and panting in fear.

"We have to hold firm," Foxfire called. "It won't take long for those bastards to finish their meal, and then they'll come for us. They'll forget they're afraid of your magic, or they'll find some friends to help them out. Even demons will cooperate if they have enough incentive. The minute one of us lets our guard down, or breaks, we're all doomed." He wondered at the firmness of his voice. His legs certainly weren't steady. They trembled so violently, it was a wonder he could stand. He drew his knife, for all the good it would do him. The demons would probably laugh when they saw it.

A dark shadow bounded out of the smoke, and Foxfire nearly fell trying to backpedal. The shadow resolved itself into W'rath. Even Oblund blew out a relieved sigh upon seeing the Shadow Elf. "We've lost track of Raven in the smoke. And one of the guards panicked..." Foxfire gestured at the feeding *Riders*.

"Lovely," W'rath said in disgust. He pointed in the direction he'd exited the smoke. "Head in that direction. I have serious doubts Lord Icewind will open a portal for us. While we're moving, I'll teach you how to fight these beasties." His words sounded neutral enough, but Foxfire knew a scolding when he heard one. Only because of his determination to see the mission succeed, did the Shadow Elf tolerate their immense stupidity.

They retrieved the unconscious mage, and forced their reluctant muscles to drag them forward, only to come to a startled halt as Raven materialized before them. They cringed at the sight of her. Her battles had left her ice white hair dyed scarlet with blood, and her leathers gore-encrusted. She'd found a tower shield, and from its battered condition, Foxfire surmised she'd used it to smash down the enemy before finishing them off with her sword. Though only separated from her for a few minutes, she'd been busy sending numerous *Riders* back to the Abyss. Her shoulders sagged though, and the sword dragged at her arm. Her chest heaved as she drank down the foul air. Acting the part of a one-elf army took its toll.

W'rath laid a concerned hand on her trembling sword arm. "Easy lass, you need to pace yourself. We're still on the wrong side of the lines, and I fear we may be on our own in making our escape."

"Right," she said, voice rough. "Tell that to the demons."

Something not human screamed in the distance and explosions shook the area. Time to go. The Shadow Elves led the way, Raven keeping a straight, steady pace, while W'rath popped in and out of the smoke, his own blade gleaming crimson.

As he skipped in and out of their presence, W'rath dropped tidbits of information. "Because they're now demon-possessed, pain has little affect on them. They use their hosts without regard for their well-being, so they'll think nothing of employing the bodies themselves as weapons. They're stronger now, burning bright with power as they feed on the life force of their host. Those demons able to cast magic in their normal form can do so as humans, also."

Foxfire saw the young guards and messenger exchange frightened glances. They couldn't understand a word the Shadow Elf spoke. He translated for them in the hopes of making them feel better. If anything their expressions grew more hopeless. "Surely, the human bodies make them somewhat vulnerable?" he prompted, hoping to raise their spirits.

W'rath appeared again, spinning through the smoke. Two *Riders* collapsed before them, hamstrings neatly severed. W'rath quickly slit their throats. "Most certainly," he said, pointing at the corpses. "Pain or no, they can't walk if they're hamstrung. Hit a major vessel and they'll bleed out. Taking off the head works too. *That* is how you fight them."

More smoke poured over them, wrapping them in a suffocating cocoon. Everyone except Raven and W'rath began to choke and cough. Like the First Born, they had a much higher tolerance of anything involving fire, heat and smoke. "I think the fire may kill us before the demons do," Raven said.

"The entire field must be ablaze," W'rath said. The smoke felt good in his lungs, but he knew the others couldn't survive for long. "You and I can survive this, but we'll never get the rest through the fire. Lord Icewind has failed miserably at his job. By now he should have easily divined our location and sent in a mage or two with a portal spell."

"Drop to the ground," Foxfire choked. "Air... a little cleaner." He followed his own advice, and the others soon followed. The queen and the boy collapsed, utterly overcome. Ungren knelt, eyes shut, lips moving as he prayed, appealing to his god and goddess for aid.

"He actually thinks he's calling upon higher beings?" W'rath muttered, amazed. "Foxfire!" He raced to the Wood Elf, as he too, completely succumbed to the smoke.

Raven searched, desperately, for some escape, and then turned to the praying cleric. "We'd better hope they answer," she said. "I don't think help is coming from anywhere else."

From his vantage point on the erupted plateau he and three others had raised, K'hul watched the battle unfold. Kiat stood at his side, raising magical shields as necessary. Most of the combat took place below, but occasionally, one of the more observant and ambitious of the demons sent a spell their way.

"Incoming," Kiat said. All around them the air sizzled with a kaleidoscope of colors as the caster's shield absorbed the magical attack.

The strength of Kiat's shield, while impressive, did not surprise K'hul. When K'hul had sought a new member for the council, he hadn't chosen Kiat simply to gain a pliable ally. He'd assured himself of the elf's competence as well. What *was* surprising, the Sky Elf, a cringing coward in most social situations, seemed perfectly at home on the battle field, shrugging off demon magic as if enjoying a spring drizzle. Once the magical assault ended, K'hul resumed his scan of the field below.

The elves' initial attack had focused on the three chanting enemy mercenaries. The combined might of a hundred spells ripped away the magi's shielding. The horrified wizards attempted to escape, but with their ritual interrupted, they staggered about dazed and helpless. The elves hadn't bothered with a second barrage, as the unleashed demons set upon those who had enslaved them, tearing them limb from shrieking limb. Then they did what demons do best—scattered in a hundred directions, destroying and murdering everything in their path. They had no cohesive leadership, but for the humans sharing the camp with them, it mattered little.

The suddenness of having more than half one's allies turn into howling, slavering, horrors sent the camp into chaos. Men died without drawing their weapons. Others panicked and ran from the camp only to come face to face with the elven army. In the dark, the night blind humans didn't realize what they faced until the elementals began to rip themselves out of the earth.

K'hul's elemental companion, a massive two hundred foot behemoth, glowed with the heat of an active volcano. Lava spilled from its maw, setting the field on fire. Others called upon their elemental companions, and the night turned to day from their fiery might. As the tall, dry grass caught fire, Sky Elves sent a great wind to push the flames toward the human camp.

K'hul's satisfaction at the sight soured as he recalled how none of them could bring such power to bear at Second Home. The bloody city itself, raised from magic, cut them off from the earth and sky, limiting their access to their powers. No elementals, no lightning storms, no flaming meteor showers.

K'hul forced his attention back on the drama unfolding upon the field. Terror gripped the humans, and they scattered, trying to escape demons, fire, and elementals. They bolted, only a few retaining enough sense to gather their fellows in an attempt to fight through the demons to freedom.

A few pockets of organized combat slowly formed up. Grossly outnumbered, though, the grass fire would soon cut off any chance of escape. K'hul's gaze lingered on the struggling humans. "I suppose we shouldn't let the poor bastards die," he said, at last. Like most elves, he had little love for humans, but even he couldn't see letting them die in so horrendous a manner. Besides, if he didn't make some effort to save them, a certain lady would be infuriated.

Kiat gestured to two of his fellow magi standing nearby. "Get a message to Lady Skúshil and Lord Baó. Sectors eight and thirteen have humans in need of assistance."

"Yes, Lord Icewind!" they said simultaneously. Via magic, they started relaying the *War Leader*'s will. Off to the east, the luminous blue of portal magic lit up the area. The beleaguered humans would soon find their numbers bolstered by a combination of heavy fighters and powerful casters.

"What about Lord W'rath and Lady Raven?" Kiat asked.

"I haven't spotted them yet," K'hul admitted. "You'll have to try scrying for them, again. We need that wizard they went to capture. They may have the human king, as well. I want to meet the wretch who thinks nothing of destroying the lives of thousands of his own people because he can't stand to be outwitted by our scruffy cousins."

Kiat tried briefly to find their Shadow Elf kin through mundane means, but gave up almost immediately. The fires burned bright enough to hinder his normally keen night vision, and worse, the smoke was becoming a real issue on the field below. He paused long enough to reinforce the threads of his shielding magic, then began casting a divination spell intended to pinpoint the location of Lord W'rath and Lady Raven. He used the strand of hair W'rath had given him as a focus for his spell. His earlier attempts to divine the location of the two councilors had failed. This time he felt a tug and knew his spell had succeeded.

No matter how many times he used the spell, it always startled him when it activated. Even though he didn't physically move from his perch with K'hul, it felt as if he suddenly rushed toward a spot far to the south. The scenery flashed by as the magic zipped toward its targets. When the magic reached its destination, the sense of flying ended so abruptly, Kiat staggered, his mind fooled by the illusion of movement.

He gasped as a slavering, demon-possessed human tore by through the smoke. A second later, a massive sword cut the demon down. Kiat recognized the sword as the standard issue weapon young First Born recruits carry. A now familiar black-skinned vision wielded the blade. Lady Raven—he had found them.

His quarry located, Kiat murmured words to adjust his view. The field of view widened, allowing him a greater sense of what their people faced. The smoke churned like something alive, making it difficult to see even with the spell. K'hul's voice floated ghostly in his ears. "Have you found them?"

"Yes," Kiat said, though his voice wavered as if he doubted himself.

"Show me," K'hul said, placing a hand on the slim diviner's shoulder. Touching Kiat allowed him to take advantage of the caster's magical vision and see the same area. In an Instant, he gazed upon the burning plain, watching Raven as she hurled herself at enemy after enemy. Her strength and skill stunned K'hul. The sword, intended for someone a good foot taller, didn't suit her, yet she wielded it as well as any First Born he had ever seen. His brow furrowed in thought.

"Do you see the way she fights?" K'hul asked of his companion.

"Yes," Kiat said, sounding not the least bit interested. "I'm trying to see through this blasted smoke. Lord W'rath should be here somewhere, too. Not to mention, you wanted to know about the wizard and the king."

"Of course," K'hul replied. "Keep searching. It's just very strange. She fights exactly like a First Born. It's as if she trained at First Home."

"Yes, very interesting," Kiat said, absently. "Perhaps her people kept First Born slaves to train their young fighters."

Both elves took a startled step back as W'rath burst out of the smoke to assist his tiring companion. In his wake, they saw two men, presumably *Riders*, collapse, spouting blood from nearly severed heads. Using Raven's current opponent for leverage, the small elf flipped around in a half circle to come up behind yet another foe, slicing through its tendons, sending the demon crashing to the ground.

Before the *Rider* finished falling, W'rath twirled, a deadly dancer, evading the blades of three more *Riders*, hamstringing them, and leaving them helpless on the ground for Raven to finish off.

W'rath yelled something at Raven, but Kiat's spell only provided a visual of the scene and no sound. They could only guess at his words, but K'hul suspected he berated Raven for not pacing herself. She breathed like a bellows. Her hair hung in sodden strands, soaked with sweat and the blood of her victims. The magic coursing through an elf's veins could be relied on for amazing stamina and recovery, but the warrior had managed to push herself beyond what her elven gifts could provide. K'hul had a sudden vision of a swath of death left by Raven's oversized sword and battered shield. In spite of himself, he was impressed.

The smoke finally cleared enough for Kiat and K'hul to get a view of the area behind the Shadow Elves. A cluster of humans and one elf staggered through the poisonous air. Even as they regrouped with the Shadow Elves, they began to collapse. W'rath shouted something and caught the elf as the smoke overcame him. "Foxfire," Kiat said, recognizing the Wood Elf. "He must have gone back to help them."

"Fool," K'hul muttered. Several humans accompanied the elves. The First Born had seen very few of them in the past, but in his mind the largest must surely be the king. The one with the gold hair and beard fit the part. Even as he succumbed to the smoke, he did his best to protect the smaller males, and the female traveling with him.

"Shouldn't we send people to help them?" Kiat asked.

K'hul made a face. As much as he would love to get rid of W'rath, it would be in poor form to lose three more councilors so soon. Not to mention the fact, they really did need the mage alive in order to interrogate him.

Before he could answer, though, a third voice enter the conversation. A very angry, female voice. "It's a simple question, *War Leader*. How long do you plan to deliberate the pros and cons of saving our people?"

Kiat dropped the seeking spell so abruptly both males nearly fell over from vertigo. Lady Swiftbrook stood next to them, her silver and blue armor coated in soot and blood. Her pale skin had gone scarlet with rage. "Which sector?" she snarled through clenched teeth.

"Two," Kiat squeaked. His battlefield courage evaporated. He tried to disappear behind K'hul's broad back.

Lady Swiftbrook gave them both a withering gaze before storming off to the edge of the rocky finger where her two apprentices waited. She stepped onto the wind walk spell they maintained, a nearly invisible disk of air, and the reason for her silent arrival. The three females stepped upon it and glided back toward the soldiers under Lady Swiftbrook's command.

"I was just about to send you in," K'hul called. Even as the words left his tongue, he knew how bloody foolish he sounded.

Lady Swiftbrook didn't bother to turn around. The gesture she threw back over her shoulder was clear enough.

⋈⋈⋈⋈⋈

"They're dying!" Raven cried. For the first time since they'd begun their bloody work, W'rath could hear fear in her voice. "I can cut down an enemy, but this fire, this smoke, I can't stop it. I can't save them!"

W'rath struggled to throw Foxfire's dead weight over his shoulders. Despite the Wood Elf's small size, he still stood a good half a foot taller than the Shadow Elf. "Yes, I forgot how difficult it is for most people to breathe smoke," W'rath grunted, finally settling Foxfire into a position conducive for travel.

"How will we help all of them?" Raven continued. She shifted from foot to foot, desperate to act, but unable to decide what exactly she should do. W'rath wondered if it was possible for someone holding a shield and sword to wring their hands.

He made himself pause before answering, reminding himself she was still a child. He would not act like his father and bellow at a youngster for finding themselves out of their depth. He had insisted she accompany him. She was *his* responsibility. "Lass, we can't save them all. We save our own and the wretch we need for questioning. If it comes down to it, you drop him as well. We do not abandon Foxfire."

Bleak despair fought with denial on her face. "You're thinking with your heart, lass." W'rath expected angry words, but they didn't come. Instead, she swallowed heavily and walked forward to pull the unconscious mage from the pile of humans, tossing him over her shoulder like a doll. Her eyes lingered on the queen, curled protectively around the young boy. She squeezed her eyes shut, turned on her heel, and marched past W'rath.

Raven paused for a moment. "Have you had to make choices like this before?"

"Yes," he replied.

"How do you live with that?"

"The same way you're going to. You put one foot in front of the other, lass."

W'rath watched her back, silently willing her to start moving. They'd been given a reprieve from the demons. That wouldn't last. It couldn't.

A sudden realization came to him. The smoke should have the same affect on the demons, housed as they were in human bodies. Most of what they'd run into were obviously the dregs of the Abyss, demons too stupid to do more than hurl themselves at the enemy and tear them apart.

It made sense that the magi would want to work with such easily dominated demons, creatures they could control and summon without putting out much effort. A handful of magi would go for quantity over quality in a case like this—the creation of a disposable army. But that meant the demons lacked the intellect to cast spells, and so they couldn't protect themselves from the deadly smoke.

But in fact, none of the *Riders* they'd run into had seemed the least bit affected by the smoke. So, sprinkled about the battlefield, at least a few more powerful, intelligent specimens lurked, assisting their lesser brethren, if not out of the goodness of their hearts, then because they needed them to serve as shock troops to help whittle down the humans and elves. They wouldn't enter the fray until their foes tired and their numbers dwindled. They would wait for just the right moment to attack.

W'rath's eyes went wide. "Raven!"

Startled, Raven paused in mid step. It saved her life, but the wall of emerald flame that erupted still engulfed her right leg up to the hip. She screamed in agony, and fell heavily, the unnatural flames already eating away at her leg. She rolled, and beat at the flames with her hands, trying to put them out. The fire rushed up her leg to her hands and arms, nearly reaching her shoulders. The flames licked at the mage's feet, as he lay sprawled and forgotten.

W'rath dropped the unconscious Foxfire and rushed to Raven's aid, pulling her further from the roaring fire wall. The flames clung tenaciously, attempting to spread as she continued to struggle to put them out. W'rath rattled out a counterspell, and the flames winked out. He kept dragging Raven back, her panic inhibiting him more than anything else. He dropped her next to Foxfire and started for the mage, but a deep-throated chuckle brought him up short.

"I thought I recognized you, Umbral," a voice rasped in Abyssal.

W'rath hissed and backed away from the flame wall as a figure stepped through it. "I wasn't sure at first. It's been so long since you murdered our glorious leader, and then fled like a craven worm."

W'rath watched the *Rider* warily. He had no way to recognize the demon, clothed as he was in human skin. His knowledge and skill marked him as what passed for nobility in the Abyss, though. The regular riff-raff couldn't cast the way this fellow could, and even fewer would have known Umbral, or served under the same demon lord.

"Presumably, you speak of Ruaz'Daem," he replied in Abyssal, stopping so he could keep himself between the *Rider* and his fallen comrades.

A vicious snarl ravaged the demon's face, tearing both sides of its host's mouth. The bottom lip flopped down like a grotesque tongue, just a long, useless piece of flesh now. "You are not worthy to speak his name!"

"You don't find it the least bit ironic you're outraged by murder?"

"Lord Ruaz'Daem was the finest leader we ever had. Because of him no one could stand against us. We had riches, power, and endless victory. He took you in and you repaid him with betrayal!" He flexed his hands as if used to wielding scythe-like claws. The flames around him danced in agitation.

"By 'take me in' I assume you refer to the fact he sent a pack of his minions to forcibly drag me before him so he could offer me the choice of either serving him or enduring a slow, torturous death for all eternity. Yes, absolutely charming fellow."

The demon spat out a spell and W'rath countered it. With Foxfire and Raven unconscious he felt safe displaying his magical ability. Not that he had much choice at the moment. Either he cast spells or he died. Keeping secret his mixed ancestry paled when faced with extinction.

"He taught you that!" the demon bellowed. "When you came to us you were little better than a slavering cur. A savage."

W'rath studied the *Rider* as if he could pierce the disguise the human's body afforded the demon. For the fellow to know so much about Umbral's stay with the demon lord, he had to have held a position within the upper echelon of Ruaz'Daem's command. Or perhaps, and W'rath kicked himself for not considering it earlier, the demon hadn't served in the army at all, but instead worked as a member of Ruaz'Daem's household. *Oh ho!*

"I didn't recognize you without your ruffle collar, Baez," W'rath said, fairly certain of his guess. "I'm shocked a demon of your stature would get caught up in a binding like this."

The words enraged the demon. He ripped bloody gashes across his host's body, and bellowed so fierce, the smoke cleared away from the area. W'rath thought his eardrums would burst, but ignored the pain and used the time to think. Baez had run the household. W'rath had ignored him as much as possible. Baez had presented himself as such a fussy, prissy little toad, W'rath had considered him mostly harmless. *Yet another spectacularly poor judgment call to add to the list.*

Baez regained control and took a menacing step toward the Shadow Elf. "You have Him to thank for your foppish manners, your education, and your skill with magic. He gave you everything, and then you destroyed him. When you did that, you brought me down too, reduced to what you see here—a pathetic shadow."

"Do stop, you'll make me weep. If I hadn't actually known the fellow, I would be aghast at my terrible betrayal," W'rath said, wiping away a nonexistent tear. "Despite his fine table manners, I have never known a more vile, loathsome being. I only tolerated him as long as I did, because I had to learn from him in order to kill him. I've had a very long life, riddled with regrets and poor choices, but slaughtering Ruaz'Daem is one thing I look back on with pride."

Predictably, Baez went berserk, and hurled himself at W'rath. W'rath smirked. One thing Baez had right, Ruaz'Daem *had* taught him how to harness his magical affinity, well beyond the parlor tricks he'd managed while still among the elves. At the time, he'd stung with disappointment when he'd learned his strengths lay in defensive casting rather than fire like his father. But now he was glad of it as he rattled off a series of syllables, and a shield flared up, ending Baez's charge in a painful crunch. W'rath dropped the shield and launched himself at the demon, tumbling over its prone body, his blade seeking a vital organ so he could end things quickly.

Baez proved to have a few tricks of his own. Sacrificing one of his host's arms, he spoiled W'rath's killing blow. He rolled toward W'rath, his severed arm flopping away. When the elf spun to face him the demon blinded him with arterial spray.

W'rath gasped and staggered back, his weapon coming up in a defensive position while dragged a sleeve across his eyes. The attack didn't come from Baez, though, but from behind. Too late, W'rath tried to spin free, but two pairs of arms wrapped around him and held him fast. One attacker pinned his arms to his sides and lifted from the ground, while the other grappled his legs. Both demons crushed with all of their might, and W'rath felt his bones would shatter into dust. He tried desperately to break free, but he had neither the strength nor the leverage to do more than squirm.

Blinking through the stinging blood, W'rath glared murder at Baez. "You're host is dying, you fool," he snarled. "You'll bleed to death in a minute, and your friends here shall be lost without your dubious leadership."

"Doesn't matter," Baez said. His bloody smile made all the more obscene by the flopping lower lip. "I have enough time to get revenge on you, and that alone will sustain me for a millennia in the Abyss. You see, while I watched you fight earlier, I thought, how strange, a Shadow Elf male fighting without using psionics. Once I recognized your fighting style, I knew I had found you. Such a curiosity, though, the most powerful psion I'd ever known relying entirely on his swordsmanship.

"I'm thinking all those years in the Abyss did something to you, and you can't use your mind magic on this plane. You're just a runt with a sharp stick now. No teleporting free of my minions, or making our heads explode. So, now you can watch while I kill something you love, and I can leave this place knowing I've done to you what you did to me."

*Love*? What did a demon know of such things? For that matter, what did *he* understand about a concept foreign to the place he'd called home for the majority of his life? "I'm fairly certain I'm not capable of that emotion," he told the demon.

Baez snorted his skepticism and turned toward Raven, Foxfire and the cluster of fallen humans. He staggered, blood still pumping from his terrible wound. With a word, fire danced along his fingertips and Baez scorched the stump of his arm to stop the bleeding. "You're right, this body won't last much longer. Humans are more fragile than I'd realized, so we'd best get this over with. Shall I simply drop acid fire on the whole lot of them? Or should I give some special attention to one in particular?"

W'rath didn't say a word. He'd hoped K'hul and Kiat would finally get reinforcements sent to them. While he wasn't a caster of Kiat's level, he felt certain the mage could divine their whereabouts now that the royal tent no longer blocked his spell. K'hul might rejoice at his death, but surely the great lout wouldn't sacrifice Raven and Foxfire, as well? And while W'rath didn't think K'hul cared for humans any more than he did, he didn't think the First Born would throw away the opportunity to interrogate the mercenary mage.

The fact remained, no one had arrived to help them. The reasons didn't matter. They had to survive on their own, and he was the only of one still in any condition to fight back. Baez was right. Ten thousand years spent in the Abyss had attuned him to that plane. His mind burned far stronger there than here, in the world of his birth. However, the demon's hypothesis that W'rath could no longer use his powers at all, was wrong. Despite the injury he had given himself, he hadn't burnt himself out like Raven. The power still coiled there, he could feel it. But he could also feel the sharp claws of pain, warning him of the price he would pay if he exerted himself before he fully recovered.

As Baez bent over to drag a filthy finger along Raven's jaw, W'rath knew he could not heed those warnings. He might not have the capacity for love, but he understood loyalty to one's comrades. Not once had he ever left one of his people behind during a mission. He would not start now.

❧❧❧❧❧

The Shadow Elf's two captors stared in confusion at their empty arms. They started to bellow a warning, but stopped, gawking. Baez still crouched over the female Shadow Elf, but instead of leering in anticipation, he gaped in horror at the small, dark figure who had appeared out of thin air in front of him. The Shadow Elf made a flicking gesture with his fingers and the demon's head vaporized. He then turned back to his former captors and gave them a tight smile. "When next you see Baez, tell him I find his gloating in poor taste."

That was all the warning W'rath gave them before their brains erupted, sending skull and gray matter into the filthy air. Their empty bodies collapsed, the evil spirits which had inhabited them, sent screaming back to the Abyss.

⋈⋈⋈⋈⋈

W'rath stood over Raven, barely able to think, pain tearing at his mind. Blood ran from ears and nose. The world reeled. He fell to his knees, his legs no longer able to hold him. Instead, he focused on the renewed fury of the wildfire, eating up the plains. Baez must have held back the fire so he could toy with his prey. With the demon gone, and fresh fuel to feed them, the flames came at them with deadly speed. If the lack of air didn't kill them, the flames certainly would. Even with his father's First Born blood running through him, W'rath didn't think he could survive the sustained fury of the flames for long. Could nothing go right this day?

*K'hul, wherever you are, I hope some demon rams a fist right up your tightly clenched ass.*

He collapsed on top of Raven, and with the last of his strength, reached out to lay a hand on Foxfire. His mind burning as if the wildfire already had a grip on him, he pushed himself on last time, and they vanished from the field.

⋈⋈⋈⋈⋈

An explosion of displaced air and a vibrant cerulean light announced the opening of a portal. Through it poured fifty pure casters and chain-clad sword magi. "Get this damned fire out!" Lady Swiftbrook ordered, and a localized deluge of rain poured from the skies, drowning the fire for a half mile around.

Bodies littered the ground. “Find our people! Quickly!” she yelled over the roar of the rain. Her stomach twisted in dread. It had taken too long to get here.

“We have the mage!” someone called.

The Sky Elf councilor marched over to the voice. Sera, one of their finest healers, knelt next to the human mage, the man writhing in agony, nothing left of his legs from the knees down. “Acid fire,” Sera said by way of explaining the horrific injury. “Should I heal him?” Her tone implied she really had no desire to assist the man who had helped bring demons to the field.

“We still need to question him,” Lady Swiftbrook replied. “He’s the main reason Raven, W’rath and Foxfire,” she couldn’t finish. The healer grimaced but nodded.

Lady Swiftbrook turned away to continue searching for other survivors. Already the ground was turning into a quagmire. A large group of bodies lay up ahead and more healers worked, trying to revive them. She slogged in that direction, hoping for good news and nearly fell when she tripped over a mud-covered corpse.

Decapitated. Her lip curled in revulsion even as the more analytical part of her brain noted there didn’t appear to be a head to go with the body. Nearby, sprawled two more corpses in the same condition. Damned peculiar, but they weren’t elves, so the mystery of their deaths would have to wait.

As she got close to the laboring healers, a smaller figure detached from them and approached Lady Swiftbrook. Kela.

“They’re not here,” she said.

“That’s impossible. The fire would have prevented any escape. They have to be here somewhere.”

Kela cocked a thumb toward the group of rescuers and rescued. “Those are all humans. The thrice-damned king is one of them. There’s a woman, a child, and four other men. That’s it.”

“Will they live?”

Kela made an unhappy grunt in reply. Lady Swiftbrook took that to mean ‘unfortunately’ in Wood Elf.

Lady Swiftbrook started toward the humans. "Only the yellow-haired man and the woman speak our tongue," Kela called. "I already asked. They have no idea what happened to our people."

*Damn it!* Lady Swiftbrook's hands clenched. She was glad of the rain, certain she was about to weep from frustration and guilt.

"Councilor!" She turned toward the voice, and out of the gloom one of her sword magi rushed up to her. She couldn't even recognize him, the mud coated him so thoroughly. "We've found them, ma'am."

"Where?" She looked over his shoulder, expecting to see another cluster of Sky Elves dragging their smaller cousins from the mud.

"Lady," the soldier said, touching her arm.

She gazed at him, suddenly full of dread, but found his muddy face full of wonder instead of despair. "Lady," he said, "they're safe. They found them back at First Home."

# CHAPTER 15

Standing in the dark, dank confines of Oblund's throne room, Lady Swiftbrook contemplated her soldier's earlier words to her on the sodden battlefield. Safe was a relative term, she told herself. Instead of dealing with the situation in front of her, her mind kept returning to W'rath and Raven. Foxfire had recovered quickly, thank the ancestors. Actually, thanks to W'rath. Certainly *not* thanks to K'hul. She'd run out of curse words for that one. She ground her teeth and fought the urge to have someone open a portal for home. She settled for pacing the grey stone room with its crude wall hangings—a caged and anxious animal.

The remnants of King Oblund's court had aged beyond their years. They gathered at a long oaken table, surrounded by rough hewn chairs, huddled together like starlings on a winter's day. The combination of the demon's single-minded ferocity and the elves' devastating magic had left them so broken, the majority did little more than weep or stare blankly at their conquerors. Unfortunately, a handful dealt with their defeat by pretending it hadn't happened. Obnoxiously aggressive, they refused to make decisions regarding the welfare of their people.

She tried to feel empathy. The elves, too, had just survived a terrible defeat. The humans had lost family, friends, and nearly all of their subjects. Not only had an enemy, supposedly beneath them, risen up to crush them, they now faced the realization their king was both fallible and heinous enough to betray them without the slightest pang of conscience. Yes, she tried to take pity upon them, but after hours of their idiocy, all she had left in her was disgust.

And boredom. Lady Swiftbrook let her mind wander back to when they had marched into Teresland's capital city. The citizens had lined the streets, bewildered and frightened, some clutching rocks or vegetables, intending to hurl them at the invaders. But the missiles remained in hands, or were quietly dropped to the ground. Perhaps the people of Teresland had expected an army of small, disheveled Wood Elves. Instead, hundreds of towering, armor-clad Sky Elves and First born marched into their city, many surrounded by flaming auras.

Foxfire had suggested the auras. He felt a simple act of showmanship would intimidate the average citizen, preventing them from committing any foolish acts. While Lady Swiftbrook found it hard to comprehend that a people could spend their lives bereft of even the smallest of cantrips, Foxfire's prediction proved accurate. The elves passed through the city unmolested. Even the small contingent of soldiers left to keep an eye on things during the king's absence, gave them no trouble. They took one look at the magical host and either fled or surrendered. The fortified castle fell to the elves without a single arrow fired.

*We have it—now what do we do with it?*

Kela strode up to her and made one of her small, angry animal noises. "We wouldn't have to deal with this mess if we had stuck to our original plan," she groused.

"A great deal changed when we learned we faced *Riders* instead of mundane humans," Lady Swiftbrook said. She didn't know why she bothered trying to explain. Kela seethed, full of anger since the battle. She was understandably furious at K'hul and Kiat for failing to evacuate their people, but her ire did not stop there. The wildfire itself had sent her on a verbal rampage. When Lady Swiftbrook pointed out nearly every spell cast by a First Born or a Sky Elf in combat involved fire, lava, wind or lightning, Kela's face went purple with rage. Reminding her that the Wood Elves had asked for the help of their fiery cousins only added to her anger.

For a moment, Lady Swiftbrook had thought Kela would savage her like a wolverine. In the end, she spun herself up into a foaming fury and punched one of the unfortunate human nobles blocking the path she chose for her exit.

"Yes, I know," Kela grunted, more civilly this time around. She tracked Foxfire as he approached the priest, Ungren, and Oblund's queen, and started a conversation with them. "Too much jabber."

"On that we can both agree," Lady Swiftbrook sighed. Originally, she'd thought to step in and handle negotiations with the humans. A few breaths into the conversation she'd realized she was ill-equipped to do anything constructive with them. She didn't understand them in the least. Kiat's language spell made their words understandable, but still, as a people, she found them utterly incomprehensible.

"I heard a strange rumor about you and one of theirs. Some form of alliance?"

Lady Swiftbrook made some sputtering sounds of her own. "As best I could understand, he expected me to cleave myself to one of their nobles for the sake of a political treaty. He seemed under the impression I came here to present myself as chattel for one of these alliances."

"He thought you wanted to enslave yourself to one of them?" Kela gaped. Her eyes, normally large anyway, grew to the size of robin's eggs.

"I don't think what I wanted interested him. He directed all of his words to K'hul. When I had the audacity to insert myself into the conversation, he sputtered like a broken gnome clockwork."

"Did you kill him?"

"What? No! Of course not. I did realize we don't have enough in common for me to work with them on restructuring their kingdom. I didn't want to give K'hul a chance to make progress with them, but his angry bellowing means more to them than anything I've tried."

"If you'd killed the human, those who still lived would have seen things your way," Kela said, thrusting her chin out.

"Yes, probably," the Sky Elf conceded. "As angry as it made me, though, I didn't feel it warranted murder."

"If it had moved things along, it would have been worth it."

That brought a small smile to Lady Swiftbrook's lips. She watched the animated conversation between Foxfire and the two humans. For the life of her, she couldn't understand how Foxfire could stand to deal with them. Perhaps, after the events on the battlefield, he had good reason to seek out the humans. His own people had certainly let him down.

Unfortunately, that reminder dredged up the grisly imagery Foxfire had described. The thought of Raven's terrible wounds made it difficult for Lady Swiftbrook to draw breath. Foxfire said he'd woken to find Raven's right leg completely skeletonized, the flesh from her right hip and hands mostly dissolved as well. Nothing but bone and a few tendons remained. The same acid fire that had eaten away the mage's legs was to blame, and while it no longer actively consumed Raven's flesh, it interfered with her ability to heal. It took a team of healers to remove remnants of the foul stuff so she could begin to regenerate.

Despite the appalling extent of Raven's wounds, no major internal organs had suffered damage. As an elf, she could regenerate all she'd lost. Of far greater concern was W'rath's condition. When Foxfire had left the infirmary, to return to the mainland, the psion still lay unconscious, bleeding from his nose, ears, and eyes. Of all the injuries an elf could sustain, those to the brain or heart had the greatest chance of proving fatal.

Once Lady Sera, First Home's finest healer, had done what she could for the captured mercenary's injuries, she left him in the care of two subordinates and returned home to tend to W'rath. As much as they hoped to get information from the mage concerning the attack on Second Home, they had to face the possibility he possessed no such knowledge. W'rath's welfare came first, and Lady Sera understood the delicate nature of the brain. Lady Swiftbrook prayed it would be enough.

Once again she found herself wishing she could simply flee Teresland, go back home, and somehow will W'rath to come back to them.

✱✱✱✱✱

A great many years had passed since Foxfire walked the streets of Teresland. The king at that time, King Oschell, had reigned much more moderately, and desired open, friendly dealings with non-humans. Foxfire had enjoyed acceptance at court as an exotic representative of a mysterious people. King Oschell, a man who possessed an endless enthusiasm for life, treated Foxfire with respect, and constantly quizzed the Wood Elf in his quest to learn about the wonders of the world.

Sadly, his great-great-grandson possessed none of those qualities. Worse, the nobles who had survived the battle behaved with the collective sense of a single goblin.

Despite Foxfire's anger toward K'hul, he had to admit the *Voice of the First's* heavy-handed approach to negotiations worked better than patient reasoning. In fact, Foxfire felt bad about chewing W'rath and Raven out for their rough handling of their captives during the battle. After a couple of days spent conversing with the court of Teresland, he now realized his naivety in expecting them to behave like their ancestors from four generations past. He had nearly reached the point of wanting to step on someone's throat, too. Gone were the people he'd known, replaced by a folk much more close-minded and superstitious.

He'd hoped Lady Swiftbrook could manage to smooth things over. Instead, the befuddled nobles assumed she wished to offer herself as part of a political marriage. While elves often paired off, sometimes for hundreds of years, the concept of marriage struck them as something akin to slavery. She had reacted precisely as most elves would at the suggestion that a single person possess them for all time. She'd blown up in a fury and left the men staring after her, mouths agape, completely baffled as to how they had offended her.

Even though his initial attempts had failed, Foxfire still felt his language skills and worldliness made him the best person to see them through their current difficulties. Right now K'hul and Kiat focused on a group of men who had served as King Oblund's advisors. K'hul tried to force them to put forth a candidate for the throne, and the lot of them dithered in turn, most likely stalling in the hope the problem would magically resolve itself. As advisors, the king must have found them maddeningly inept. If Oblund hadn't proven himself such an ass, Foxfire would feel sorry for him.

With the council worthless, Foxfire went through his other options. He looked toward Kela and Lady Swiftbrook , both of them glaring daggers at everyone involved in the proceedings. Definitely no help there.

Foxfire sighed. He'd dragged his feet long enough. He'd spent the majority of the last two days trying to research the changes since his last visit to Teresland. Time to put his newly acquired knowledge to the test. He'd toyed with an idea ever since the unfortunate marriage misunderstanding between Lady Swiftbrook and the nobles. He didn't know how his suggestion would go over. Things had simply changed too much over the last one two hundred years.

He approached the scarred priest, Chalice Ungren, and Queen Cherish. The two were being largely ignored, much the same as he, but he thought they offered his best chance for finding minds open enough to hear him out. Of course, it almost all depended on the queen. She might have little power in the making of war, but she should have a greater hand in determining the course of the kingdom as a whole. If not, her people would starve this winter.

"Your Majesty, Chalice," he said politely, bowing to the two. The queen gave him a tired smile in reply. At her side the servant boy from before continued to cling to her. The queen kept a protective arm around him. Foxfire felt fairly traumatized himself by the events out on the battlefield. He couldn't imagine what such a thing would do to a child.

Ungren's expectant gaze forced Foxfire back on track. "I don't think I have to tell you we're getting nowhere with the noble council."

The priest shook his head and gave a small laugh. "You're as unfamiliar with conquering a people as we are at being conquered," he said. "I didn't approve of His Majesty ignoring his advisors, but he's largely right in his belief they are old and ineffectual. Your people won, Councilor—you can force the issue and appoint whomever you wish. If you wait for them to present a new king, you'll grow old even by your standards."

"This isn't what we wanted. We just wanted to be left alone."

"Unfortunate for both of us. Aside from the Wood Elves, your people exist as hardly more than myths to us. I've traveled some, but until two days ago I never laid eyes upon a First Born, Sky Elf or Shadow Elf. It was eye-opening."

"That's an understatement, Chalice," Queen Cherish said, her words only slightly slurred from the teeth she'd lost from Oblund's brutality. Healers had tended to her bruises and her broken nose, but they could do nothing to help her grow new teeth. "It seemed as if the world had come to an end. We woke something in you with our invasion. I fear the rest of the world will not thank us. Please tell me, you didn't come over just to commiserate, Councilor, that you have some thoughts on how to resolve our woes?"

Foxfire smiled at the Queen's bluntness. From what he'd learned of her these past two days, she must hate living under the constraints of Teresland's twin gods. She'd held the title of Baroness before her uncle arranged her marriage to King Oblund. She'd put aside her own religion and adopted that of her new husband.

At the time, it had seemed an ideal arrangement for both countries as Erin's country, Scoffula, had a strong navy and access to numerous trade goods. Teresland, though wood-poor, had access to a great deal of prime mining fields. They produced large quantities of high quality iron, silver and gold. They also had a river, making access to and from Scoffula relatively convenient.

Unfortunately, Queen Cherish had failed to fulfill one of the major obligations of a king's wife: She failed to get pregnant. Even the poorest peasant snickered and called her the *Barrenness* behind her back. It was the sort of word play Foxfire would have enjoyed working into one of his songs. He didn't think this lady deserved such scorn, though, and felt bad his plans involved using her as a pawn yet again.

"As I understand it, women work directly in all aspects of government in Scoffula, Your Majesty. Both women and men have occupied the throne since your earliest days, and your god, a single entity, embodies both sexes. How could you stand to give that up, and live in the shadow of King Oblund?"

The queen stiffened. His choice of topic took her by surprise, and most likely, stung, an unwelcome subject, especially in front of her friend, a priest of the Duality. "I did it for the sake of my country," she said diplomatically. "In truth, I am not the best wife. I don't conform well. It wasn't my place to join His Majesty during his campaign. I forced the issue by threatening to withhold funds and supplies if he did not allow me into his camp."

"Your concern lay with the welfare of your people, Your Majesty. No one can fault you for that," Ungren replied, just as diplomatically.

"And yet we now approach winter, short on food because I couldn't keep the most vulnerable of my subjects safe."

"The rules limited Your Majesty's options," Foxfire interjected. "You're expected to see to the everyday maintenance of the kingdom, but the king made that impossible by running off with a huge chunk of the country's work force."

The queen grimaced, making a helpless gesture with her hands. "In the end it matters not. People will starve this winter regardless of where the fault lies."

"Your Majesty's uncle?" Ungren asked.

"Can send some aid, but Scoffula has always relied on trade rather than agriculture. They mostly trade across the seas for what they need. They fish, of course. He has his hands full right now with a northern invasion of pirates. He'll do what he can, but he can't provide enough to feed a whole country."

That was the opening Foxfire had been hoping for. "What if I offered you a way to lead your people to a new beginning?"

"I already told your Lord W'rath the people will not accept me as head of their army. And in truth, mine is not a military mind."

"Your Majesty, I think perhaps the Councilor means something else entirely," Ungren said.

“Then do continue, Councilor,” the queen said.

“It’s still pretty radical,” Foxfire admitted. He grimaced at the odd looks his phrasing garnered, but after a moment pressed on. “What if you merged Teresland with your neighbor, Renlin?”

For the longest time, Queen Cherish just gaped at him, eyebrows raised so high they seemed about to disappear into her hairline. For his part, Ungren kept his face neutral. Perhaps he had already suspected what Foxfire would say. “That is unconventional,” he murmured. “Majesty?”

The Queen clapped a hand over her mouth. Foxfire thought she would burst into tears, but instead she started to laugh. She slapped her thigh and continued on in a very unladylike fashion until she grew breathless and tears ran down her face. Even the boy lifted his head, perhaps afraid the one stable refuge in his life had lost her mind.

At last she got control of herself and wiped her eyes, waving away the concerned retainers who converged on them. “Oh, that’s rich,” she chuckled. “All these years, His Majesty feared Renlin would swoop in and gobble us up, and now I’m actually considering handing Teresland over on a platter.”

“You’ve done some fast learning, Councilor,” Ungren said. “Whatever made you think of such a thing?”

Foxfire hesitated. He had no desire to embarrass the Queen. He decided to attempt to be circumspect. “I learned King Luccan’s wife died giving birth to their third son. It occurred to me he might have need of a new queen.”

“You mean a queen who won’t muddy the waters with her own sons,” the queen said, nodding her understanding.

Foxfire winced, but the queen merely gave him a sad smile. “I know what people say about me. Everyone knows His Majesty sent a request to the church asking that they find a surrogate who could provide him an heir. I’ve lived with the shame and now I see, as the good Chalice here has told me numerous times, all things happen for a reason. An unexpected path has opened up for me. Chalice, will the church support this move and aid in its fulfillment?”

"I will personally present the case to them, Your Majesty. For quite some time they have felt Renlin hasn't supported the church with a proper tithing. Renlin's queen was so tight with their gold, my superiors referred to her as the Dragoness. I think if you eased the church's mind—make it clear they can expect a more generous tithing as part of the merger—they will more than support a union between King Luccan and Your Majesty's respective countries."

"Very good. Now we just have to hope King Luccan agrees to the idea."

"Majesty, have you ever known a king to turn down more land and wealth?" Foxfire said.

"No, I have not," she said, smiling, this time with more sincerity than she'd shown earlier. She gently pried the boy from her side. "You sit right here for a minute. I need to do something... queenly."

Cherish stood, adjusted her gown, and squared her shoulders. "I must thank you, Councilor Foxfire. You've helped me clear my head and see my way to leading my people again."

She turned and glided toward the dais where the noble council argued, and K'hul grew angrier and more frustrated by the minute. Foxfire knew K'hul would soon lose all patience and do something none of them would enjoy. Or he might simply turn and leave—let the dithering nobles starve with the rest of their people this winter. What the queen was about to do would require her to deal with men who weren't used to doing more than paying lip service to her. He understood the courage it took to purposely draw the attention of every soul in a crowd. That sort of thing could make a man's legs quake as badly as Foxfire's had during the battle.

Foxfire continued to watch, curiously, as the Queen entered the area dominated by her husband's depleted council and the handful of elves attempting to negotiate with them. He hadn't expected her to take to his idea so readily. But he supposed, when born into a family of royals, a person grew up expecting to make such sacrifices.

Currently, King Oblund stewed in his own dungeon. However, until the higher ups from the church arrived and provided their determination of his guilt, he technically retained his crown. While Foxfire didn't think much of the institution of marriage, he understood it better than most elves, and knew the majority of humans took it very seriously. Regardless of the situation, Oblund remained Queen Cherish's husband, and turning her back on him couldn't be easy. But the danger facing her people meant more than the fate of one man. She had an entire populace to feed, and in this area, she had every right by their rules to speak with authority and guide their future. Even the squabbling old men who had advised Oblund should defer to her.

As the Queen took the dais, she stood in front of both thrones. The room grew quiet. Even K'hul stopped bullying one of the old nobles and waited expectantly for the queen to address them. Once every eye focused on her she spoke. "Gentlemen, have you reached a decision?"

When no one answered immediately, K'hul scowled and addressed the queen, his voice full of disgust. "We have attempted to urge haste in resolving the situation, but these relics cannot decide what to eat for breakfast, much less choose one among you to replace Oblund."

"It's complicated," wheezed one of the old men. Foxfire thought he might be Lord Duncraft. He'd lost two sons and one daughter in the battle. The boys had served as soldiers and the girl had worked as one of the field healers. All three perished when the demons went berserk. He couldn't possibly have any love for Oblund, though Foxfire suspected he wasn't feeling particularly fond of the elves either.

Other advisors chimed in with their agreement, citing the need for a proper study concerning lineage and the requirement of church approval. It seemed as though things would deteriorate into another round of arguments when the queen broke in. "Gentlemen!" she shouted, instantly bringing the babble to a halt. "I understand the difficulties involved in determining succession."

"Majesty, we have yet to even convict King Oblund of any wrong doing," another voice piped, his tone indicating he felt the queen trod territory not suited to her.

"Lord Basil," the queen said, "let me make this simple for you. King Oblund *is* guilty of conspiring with demonologists to use our people as vessels for possession. Even now, a delegation from the Church of the Duality travels here to excommunicate him. They will arrive within the week. We already look foolish, let us not make things worse by giving the impression we condone his behavior.

"The man who should have guided us to glory allowed greed to corrupt him. The Duality granted him the crown and he squandered it. The sooner all of you accept that he is dead, dead and lost to us, the better."

"Outrageous!" a fellow with an enormous ruff protested. "Your Majesty speaks out of turn!"

Casually, K'hul grabbed the man by his ruff and gave him a good shake before dropping him. He yelped, and he and his chair clattered to the floor. Silence reigned unto Queen Cherish spoke again.

"Gentlemen, let me reiterate: I *will* make this simple for you," the queen continued as though nothing had just happened. "The war has ended. We lost. The church will excommunicate King Oblund, relieve him of his crown *and* his head."

"Fuck me," Foxfire murmured. It had taken some doing to get the queen to stand up to her husband's men, but now that she'd committed herself to a course of action, she played the part of imperious ruler to the hilt.

"With no king to lead us, and a royal council unable to make a decision, the general welfare of our citizens is threatened. We face a shortage of manpower and a shortage of food, both items which fall well into my purview. As such, I will send an emissary to King Luccan in Renlin."

The old men muttered, confused. "That's very nice, Majesty," Lord Basil said, keeping a wary eye on K'hul. "However, Renlin holds no love for us. Luccan will simply laugh at our emissary and send him back to starve with the rest of us. Our coffers lay mostly empty, thanks to the war, so we cannot even offer him payment."

"You misunderstand my intent, Lord Basil," Queen Cherish said. "I'm not a beggar at King Luccan's door. I am a queen, who will soon find herself widowed, and in need of a king. I shall offer myself to him, and all that goes with that. I shall offer him a kingdom."

The room erupted into a frenzy almost as chaotic as the battlefield had been. Elves moved in to protect the queen and subdue the angry nobles. "I've never seen this side of her," Ungren said. He reached for his mace before remembering the elves had taken it from him days ago.

"Will the church approve?" Foxfire asked.

"As long as they have a suitable subject to blame for this debacle, and they gain access to a greater piece of Renlin's wealth, they'll gladly support the union. The mercenaries from Tassilia will make excellent scapegoats, and Her Majesty already gives most generously to the church."

That's not the sort of thing I would expect a loyal member of the clergy to say."

"I am loyal to my calling. I believe in the words of our Brother and Sister. But that doesn't change reality, Councilor. Men run the church and as such the weaknesses of our kind—greed, hunger for power, lust, and any number of other shortcomings—creep into the running of an institution intended to guide and nurture the masses. The church can only stay as pure as the people running it. As such, the church concerns itself with what is best for the church. Everything else falls somewhere lower on the list of priorities."

"Does anyone else realize you're this cynical?"

Ungren's laugh sounded weary. "Only my wife. If you should ever speak of this to anyone I shall soundly deny it."

"A liar too?"

"I too am just a man, Councilor. Only kings are infallible, and apparently some less so than others."

On the dais, the queen quietly regarded those around her with the serene confidence of one who knows she had done the right thing. She seemed to glow. Of course, the Sky Elves flanking her were the more likely source of the luminous aura. The two had raised magical shields in order to keep the hysterical nobility from rushing the dais. "So, what's next, Chalice?"

"Well, let's see, Councilor... have you ever attended a wedding?"

# EPILOGUE

Raven sat, rigid, alert for any signs of distress from the small figure stretched out before her. The regeneration of her body burned almost as painfully as the fire acid had, yet she barely noticed it. It was just an annoying itch compared to the pain she felt looking upon W'rath's comatose body.

Light streamed in from tall, narrow windows, illuminating the sky blue wallpaper and the white decorative molding. Living flowers filled the hall with color and a subtle scent. Even the occasional bird flitted by, adding its song to the overall serenity of the scene. The House of Healing. Designed to fill all who entered with calm and a sense of well-being. None of it reached Raven.

"You really should get some rest," someone said. Raven ignored the voice. Just one of the healers again. Lady Snowdancer, her distracted mind supplied.

Lady Snowdancer had flitted in and out throughout the day to check on Raven and W'rath, and she always said the same thing. This time, the healer sighed, but didn't go away. She bent over W'rath's bed and gently adjusted the quilted blue comforter draped over him. She pulled it down a little lower, just below his shoulders, so it would look less like a decapitated head perched upon the plump pillow. She settled down on the cushioned bench next to Raven, and gently shifted the robe the Shadow Elf wore, so she could examine Raven's leg.

"Very impressive." The healer ran her hands over the newly-formed flesh. "You heal as quickly as a First Born. With your size, I have to wonder if you have a First Born parent."

"No," Raven said, speaking for the first time since she'd heard about W'rath. "My parents are both Shadow Elves."

"It's okay if one of them was; I'm not one of those who fears the second coming of Umbral will smite me."

Raven leveled her gaze at Lady Snowdancer. "My mother is a middle class merchant, specializing in slaves captured from raids made upon rival cities. She acquired my father during one of those raids. I can't vouch for the purity of my father's ancestry, but I can tell you my mother comes from a long line of very average Shadow Elf stock."

The healer's eyes went wide. "I'm sorry," she squeaked. "I didn't mean anything. I was just curious."

Seeing the girl's face, Raven felt a wave of shame come over her. "Gods!" she groaned, dragging a newly healed hand down her face. "I'm the one who should apologize. I've acted like an ass since I woke up. You've been nothing but kind."

"Easy there," Lady Snowdancer said, capturing Raven's hand. "It wasn't too many hours ago this hand was nothing more than bare bone. I've never seen such horrific wounds before. I'd heard of acid fire, but I'd never seen what it does to a person. You're lucky it mostly landed on your leg and hands. If it had gotten on your head or torso..." She shuddered.

Raven knew exactly what would have happened. An ability to regenerate would have done her no good if the acid fire had gotten to vital organs like the brain or heart. She'd be dead, and perhaps someone else would gaze despondently at her body, eaten up with guilt and fear.

The healer seemed to have a sense of where Raven's thoughts traveled. "I know it's easy to want to take blame for what happened, but you mustn't. Word spreads quickly, and by every account I've heard, you left a field covered in enemy corpses. Without magic, you had no way to fend off the fire acid."

The ordeal came back to Raven in flashes of light and pain. She remembered W'rath calling her name. It had struck her as so odd, him using her name, instead of calling her *lass.* She had paused more because of that than the sense of urgency in his voice. Then her world had turned into a blur of terror and agony.

She had no idea what had happened to the human mage she'd carried, and at the moment didn't much care. She should, of course. He, more than the conflict between Oblund and the Wood Elves, had brought them to the battlefield. The mage might provide the key they needed to solve the mystery of who stood behind the attack on Second Home. However, the immediacy of what lay in front of her made it difficult to focus on that aspect.

Presumably, W'rath had pulled her from the acid fire. Her memories provided no answers, but by then everyone else had succumbed to the smoke, so she assumed W'rath had come to her aid. She couldn't explain how he had neutralized the acid eating away her flesh, though. It just didn't seem like the sort of thing a psion could manage.

Seeing that Raven wasn't going to reply, Lady Snowdancer decided to try taking Raven's mind off her troubles with some good old fashioned gossip. "Lord K'hul is taking a lot of heat for failing to get help to you in time."

"He's a First Born, he can handle heat," Raven said.

The girl chuckled at Raven's poor joke, and leaned in conspiratorially. "There's a rumor that Councilors Foxfire, Kela and Swiftbrook plan to put forth a request for a vote of no confidence against him. They're furious," the healer whispered.

That brought some focus back to Raven's eyes. It hadn't occurred to her anyone would actually stand up to a direct descendant of the First. "How does that work, exactly?"

"Well, if the vote goes against Lord K'hul, he's supposed to step down from the High Council. Over the years, others have lost their seats, but none belonged to the K'hul family. It's hard to imagine them following through with such a severe sanction. But maybe it won't matter. The worst has already happened to the *Voice of the First*."

"Really? What could be worse than the shame of losing his family's seat on the High Council?"

The healer got an evil glint in her eye, and made a show of scanning the room as to ensure no one eavesdropped. "Supposedly, Lady Swiftbrook banned him from her bed, and told him to never darken the door of her estate again."

Raven's eyes widened. She hadn't known the two for all that long, even so it seemed obvious they had been together for quite some time. Reflexively, she turned to W'rath expecting a sarcastic observation, couched in an overly polite phrase. The sight of his still form brought reality crashing back on her. How trivial the split between two lovers, in light of W'rath's condition.

Raven's face filled with worry and Lady Snowdancer sagged in defeat. "Right then," she said, rising. "I'm going to go have something made up for you to eat." Raven didn't respond. The healer shook her head and made her way from the room.

Once again Raven relived those terrible moments on the battlefield. Flashes of possible memories teased her. A voice she didn't know, spoke a terrible language, so foul it threatened to drive her mad. She couldn't understand a word of it, and yet the very sound of it had burned her as much as the terrible magic eating her body.

She tried to force herself to remember more, but everything grew so vague and disjointed, she wondered if any of it was real, or simply a fabrication of her pain-addled mind. Frustrated, she turned her attention back to W'rath. Until now, she hadn't realized how animated and alive his face normally was. He lay quiet and placid, devoid of any expression. No slight quirk pulled at his lips. No amused, cocked eyebrow danced along his forehead.

His hair fell loose about him. That combined with his relaxed face made him appear, well, young, she decided. No elf ever looked old, but something about W'rath spoke of a long life—a very eventful life. In his current condition, all those years and experiences held no sway over his face. She gazed upon a shell without the force of personality that made him a person.

She squeezed her eyes shut as a wave of despair took her. She had tried to send her life force into him as she had done at Second Home, but couldn't get the magic to cooperate. Perhaps her injuries prevented her from molding the flow of magic, or maybe she lacked the discipline to focus. Regardless, she had failed him.

When she opened her eyes again, her vision blurred with tears. There above the bed hung an impressive painting of the First. She wiped her face angrily, ashamed of her weakness, even if her only witness was an effigy.

The First continued to gaze off to some unknowable future, paying no heed to Raven's tears. Strong features made up his stern face. It wasn't a typically beautiful lven face. The cleft chin and the aquiline nose made him distinctive. The strong, high cheekbones added more angles to an already complex face. It made her wonder if his looks were yet another lie, like so much of what the elves had come to believe.

Her gaze dropped from the painting back to W'rath, and she felt her heart stutter in her chest. Mouth gaping, she stared at one and then the other.

Raven clamped a hand over her mouth, certain a strangled cry would escape her throat, and bring someone running. She had to get control of herself. But the crazy thought that had blossomed in her mind wouldn't go away. *Don't be an idiot. Think this through.*

She went back over everything that had occurred up until now. Their enemies had attacked Second Home by using remotely opened doorways to the Abyss and the Nine Hells. W'rath had conveniently shown up at the same time. He could have stepped through the doorway from the Abyss just as easily as the demons had.

She recalled his appearance from then; matted hair and nothing more than a leather kilt and crude boots for clothing. He'd lived rough for some time, far rougher than a cave near Second Home explained.

And he was old—certainly older than any other elf she'd ever met. His shockingly poor near sight attested to a good many years spent looking afar rather than at books.

He also knew things beyond the norm for an average elf. He could read ancient Elvish, a language only the most dedicated scholars and practitioners of magic studied. His grasp of the past didn't mesh exactly with any book she'd read. His clarity of events, like the battle against the ice giants, spoke of a closer tie to them than the mere reciting of things learned. It seemed unlikely an Exile city would teach the stories in such a manner. While the Exiles were originally made up of Umbral supporters, after thousands of years of endured misery, love had turned to hate, leading to the deplorable treatment of all males among the Exiles.

And then, there was his personality. She'd never met a male Shadow Elf even remotely as aggressive and sure of himself as W'rath. Even her father, an elf working against the established female dominated society of the Exile world, had conducted himself in a quiet, soft spoken manner. She couldn't remember him ever meeting her gaze directly. Perhaps it had been an act to sell his role, but she doubted it. He'd obviously wanted for her to join his little group of revolutionaries, but when it came down to it, his people had bowed to her wishes and escorted her to the surface world. She couldn't for a second imagine W'rath giving in to the demands of a little girl.

The image of W'rath standing in front of the statue of Lady Stormchaser came unbidden to her mind. She remembered the glitter of tears in his eyes. At the time, it had seemed out of character, but in light of this revelation...

She stood so abruptly, the heavy marble bench toppled over. It hit the floor with a solid thunk, and sent the seat cushions tumbling across the room. Lady Stormchaser had known! No wonder House of Memories had welcomed them. It explained why she'd left Shadow's Edge in the office for W'rath to find, and why he recognized it instantly. Linden's knowledge of weaponry helped her now. Amryth Earthfire forged it for a small elf. W'rath was unusually short, even for one of their race. The weapon suited him perfectly, as if made especial for him.

"Oh, my gods," she whispered, and wished with all her heart the curse of First Home would take this knowledge from her. She couldn't banish her realizations, though. She had no idea how she would live with this secret. Umbral K'hul, the greatest hero and the most reviled villain in elven history, lay dying three feet away from her, and there wasn't a damn thing she could do about it.

# THANK YOU!

I cannot tell you how much I appreciate you spending time reading the first installment of the **Chronicles of Shadow** series. There are more adventures to be had in next volume, **Exile's Gamble**. Before you dive into that, if you could take just a minute to pop over to Amazon and leave a review, I would greatly appreciate it. The number of reviews a book receives can make or break a writer's ability to find an audience. As an indy author, I am greatly dependent upon the kindness of my readers. You don't have to write your own novel, just a couple of lines about your favorite character, the plot, dialogue, or any other aspect of the story stood out for you, will do.

Again, thank you so very much for picking up **Exile's Redemption**. Raven, W'rath and the others await you in **Exile's Gamble**.

# Also by Lee Dunning

## Exile's Gamble

### The Chronicles of Shadow: Book Two

The demon possessed army of King Oblund has been crushed but at great cost. The people of Teresland, betrayed by their king, face a winter without leadership, manpower or food. The elves, unwilling regents of this devastated human kingdom, struggle with understanding a people foreign and hostile toward them.

Now, the demons that destroyed Second Home have scented the vulnerability of Teresland and set out to draw the elves into more conflict. Conflict which they cannot ignore but are ill-prepared to face.

With Lord W'rath trapped within his own mind, comatose, the elves must prepare for battle without his strength.

Raven, restless to prove herself, decides on a reckless plan, one that could either provide the elves with a new weapon, or doom her and W'rath both.

Available in paperback at Amazon and B&N
Available in Kindle edition at Amazon

# DRAMATIS PERSONÆ

## First Born

**The First:** First elf believed to rise out of the lava of the newborn world of Alassea. The largest and the strongest of the elves of his day and the first in a long line of war leaders going by the K'hul family name.

**Lord K'hul:** The most recent First Born of the K'hul family to take the High Council seat set aside for the eldest of the line, along with the title, "The Voice of the First".

**Lady Arien Culna'mo:** Councilor chosen by Lady Swiftbrook because of her willingness to make her own decisions rather than follow the will of the "Voice of the First".

**Linden:** Young First born soldier. Under the age of one hundred, he has not taken on a surname.

**Amryth Earthfire:** Famous weaponsmith who lived during the time of the First. Is purported to have made Umbral's sword, Shadow's Edge.

## Sky Elves

**Lady Uruviel Stormchaser:** First in the Stormchaser line, friend of

Umbral and creator of the first written language of the elves.

**Lady Miriel Stormchaser:** Member of the High Council, accomplished diviner, and most recent occupant of the property known as "House of Memories".

**Lady Swiftbrook:** Member of the High Council. Adept in the use of lightning-based magic.

**Lady Sera:** A healer.

**Lord Kiat Icewind:** Powerful diviner chosen by Lord K'hul to fill a vacancy on the High Council.

## Wood Elves

**Foxfire:** City raised Wood Elf with a mysterious past. Bard and reluctant member of the High Council.

**Kela:** Curt and generally ill-tempered. Member of the High Council.

## Shadow Elves

**Umbral:** Half First Born son of the First. Powerful psion and mediocre magic user. Banished for attempting to kill his father.

**Lord W'rath:** Older and wiser Umbral K'hul, recently returned from the Abyss to make his way in modern elven society under an assumed name. Member of the High Council.

**Lady Raven:** Former resident of an Exile city, who relocated to the surface world. Newly made member of the High Council.

**Ryld:** Young Shadow Elf male from First Home.

**Caeldan:** Young Shadow Elf male from First Home. Ryld's twin brother.

**Seismis:** Young Shadow Elf male from First Home. Jumpy and in constant agitation.

**Seer:** Young Shadow Elf female from First Home. Can see distant current events with her single psionic ability.

**Reaper:** Female Shadow Elf warrior. Former member of the High Council.

**T'sane:** Male Shadow Elf psion. Former member of the High Council.

## Humans

**King Oblund III:** Ruler of Teresland.

**Chalice Ungren Renoir:** Priest of the Duality.

**Queen Cherish:** Wife of Oblund III.

**King Luccan:** Ruler of Renlin. Cousin to Oblund III

## People, Places and Other Things of Consequence

**Ruaz'Daem:** Demon lord of the Abyss killed by Umbral.

**Baez:** Demon and former major domo to Ruaz'Daem.

**Tassilia:** City State of mercenary mages.

**House of Memories:** Ancestral home to the Stormchaser family.
**Allasea:** The elven name for the world.

**Shadow's Edge:** Name of Umbral's personal weapon.

# ACKNOWLEDGEMENTS

A great number of folks helped me put this book together. If you think it sucks, please don't blame them, they did what they could with the material presented to them. S.J. Smith worked very hard to slap me and my manuscript into shape. Jakiblue, Daniel White, Robert Dunning, Lisa Douglas, and Roger Johnson all did me the kindness of beta reading my story and pointing out numerous issues. Jaki deserves an extra round of applause for putting me in touch with S.J. and convincing her to make time in her schedule to edit my work. In addition to reading my book, Daniel put up with my many many questions about formatting ebooks, and provided me with the information I needed to work with fonts. I'd also like to thank Dr. Lois Roma-Deeley and her class for working with me to improve some especially awkward sections. She is the reason the unicorn is named Stone, and I think it suits him perfectly.

# ABOUT THE AUTHOR

Lee Dunning has written stories in one form or another since grade school. Lured into the realm of fantasy by her mother who read "The Last Unicorn" to her, Lee has never escaped the pull of magical worlds and mystic creatures. Her sixth grade teacher, Dixie Gaisford, introduced her to the works of J.R.R. Tolkien, and from this came Lee's obsession with elves. Introduction to Dungeons and Dragons in high school ended any hope that Lee would escape and live a normal, boring life spent in the pursuit of a six-digit pay check and an early grave. Today she lives in the hellish desert with four siamese and one horrified orange tabby. The Pacific Northwest is calling and she hopes to relocate there soon.

If you enjoyed this book, please stop by Amazon and post a review so others might benefit from your experience. And for more information, book reviews and a smattering of art, please visit Lee at: **wildhuntreviews.com**

Made in the USA
Las Vegas, NV
04 October 2022

56511737R00184